BILLY GOGAN

AMERICAN

A NOVEL BY
ROGER HIGGINS

June 25, 2016

Enjoy the adventure!

Roger

SOLAS
HOUSE

SOLAS HOUSE FICTION
PALO ALTO

Copyright © 2016 by American Memoir LLC

Travelers' Tales and Solas House are trademarks of Solas House, Inc.
2320 Bowdoin Street, Palo Alto, California 94306.
www.travelerstales.com

Cover Design: Creative Communications and Graphics, Inc.
Page Layout: Howie Severson, using the fonts Goudy and California Titling
Production Director: Susan Brady

Library of Congress Cataloging-in-Publication Data

Names: Higgins, Roger J. (Roger James), author.
Title: Billy Gogan, American : a novel / by Roger Higgins.
Description: First edition. | Palo Alto : Solas House Fiction, [2016]
Identifiers: LCCN 2016002194 (print) | LCCN 2016012335 (ebook) | ISBN
   9781609521158 (pbk. : alk. paper) | ISBN 9781609521165 (ebook)
Subjects: LCSH: Generals--United States--Fiction. | United States--Social
   life and customs--19th century--Fiction. | GSAFD: Historical fiction.
Classification: LCC PS3608.I36655 B55 2016 (print) | LCC PS3608.I36655
   (ebook) | DDC 813/.6--dc23
LC record available at http://lccn.loc.gov/2016002194

First Edition
10 9 8 7 6 5 4 3 2 1
Printed in the United States of America

During the last few years fiction—although its popularity is by no means on the wane—has had a new and unexpected rival in the shape of the Memoir; under which heading may be classed Biographies, Autobiographies, and Reminiscences . . .

Statesmen, Bishops, Judges, Generals, Actors, Artists, all have taken to pen and ink as naturally as ducks to water . . .

At the present time there seems to be no reason why any man over fifty, whose name has been before the public in any capacity whatever, should not publish his memoirs; and should not, if he proceed upon the principles laid down by those who have already obtained popularity in the same path, find a ready sale for them, during one season at least.

—Memoir Mania, ALL YEAR ROUND *A Weekly Journal* conducted by Charles Dickens (July 27, 1889)

I have to conclude that fiction is better at "the truth" than the factual record. Why that should be so is a very large subject and one I don't begin to understand.

—Doris Lessing, *The Golden Notebook* (2007)

Table of Contents

Foreword

June 2015

SOME YEARS AGO, SHORTLY BEFORE HE DIED, my father gave me four packets, each containing a separate manuscript. A short note was appended to the first manuscript:

> *September 15, 1915*
>
> *My name is Billy Gogan. This is my story of how I became an American.*

The note was unsigned.

My father did not say much about the manuscripts other than to tell me that his great-grandfather, Brevet Major General William P. Gogan, USA (ret.), had "written his reminiscences" shortly before he died, and apparently had "never shown them to anyone." The manuscripts were subsequently passed down in the family to my father, and when he gave them to me, he suggested that I "should read them sometime." That "sometime" did not come until many months after my father's death.

Once I had read the manuscripts, I immediately regretted neither having read them nor spoken about them with my father before he died—particularly as he, William Patrick Gogan IV, the last member of our family to bear that name, had been a professor of military history for some thirty-five years, ever since he had resigned his commission as a U.S. Army captain at the height of the Vietnam War. Not the least of my questions was why my father did not publish the manuscripts. I'll never know the answer to that question, although I have my theories.

I wondered also why the manuscripts had not been published a century ago, when they were first written. A partial answer may lie in the fact that they were neither typewritten nor written in General Gogan's hand. Indeed, the manuscripts were drafted in a fair and obviously feminine hand that was not his wife's, because the handwriting did not match that of several letters from the General's wife to him, written over the course of their marriage.

This book contains the first of the General's four manuscripts, which relates his adventures from the fall of 1844 through the summer of 1845. The remaining manuscripts recount young Billy Gogan's story from then through the closing stages of the American occupation of Mexico City in early 1848. I have not edited this first manuscript—or at least, I have done no more than cure the odd misspelling or grammatical solecism. The General wrote in a very colloquial manner, quite unlike his contemporaries, whose language was far more formal. I have preserved this informality almost in its entirety. I also have used modern spellings for place names, and I have also added a short glossary of some of the more unfamiliar terms that the General used.

A word about the slang that the General uses. As long ago as 1865, R.W. McAlpine lamented that such a "corruption of our language … is fast becoming the characteristic of ordinary conversation." He also reminded the readers of his generation (he and the General were contemporaries) that:

> [t]he existence of a slang element in the Army can-
> not, of course, be prevented. It came from home,
> where the fault lies. But to what is due its increase?
> We have considered some of the influences bearing

*upon all alike. There is another, which is confined to
the service. The too common use of by-words, words
of argot, … gives a stamp of genuineness to this false
coin …, not because its intrinsic worth is greater,
but because there is a glitter about it which the legal
tender lacks, and because it passes current with the
titled ones. It may be that to the illiterate man slang
is a dialect more readily mastered and more easily
handled than the* linguapura …

McAlpine went on to remark, after giving the reader some
interesting examples of military *argot* from the late Civil War:

*Now that literature has given a permanence to our
language, no other tongue will ever be spoken on
this continent. How important is it that it should
be kept free from those influences which tend to
debase; that it should be passed down from our
generation to the next pure and undefiled; that
every new element of its strength should be drawn
from a pure source, and applied religiously to the
development of a perfect language! …*

*Let the soldier drop the disgusting obscenities, the
useless by-words, the irrational slang, which army
life makes so familiar. Let the officer to whom men
look for example discourage impure language, bearing in mind that every member of his military family, on returning home, will influence, in a greater
or less degree, for good or for evil, the community
to which he belongs. It is a duty all these owe to
society, to humanity, not to abuse that which is the
property of all. Language, like water, is a common*

necessity. Impure, it causes disease; fresh and spar-
kling, as it flows from the pure fountain, it adds
vigor to life, and in a thousand ways is an instru-
ment of happiness and comfort.

Apparently, the General was not of a similar mind as R.W. McAlpine. I should also mention that the General also used what, today, we refer to as ethnic slurs. I did not remove them from the text, for to do so would change the meaning of what he wrote. So I ask you to remember that such words were commonly used during his day, and as you read, please observe who uses them and why.

I hope you enjoy this reminiscence written by an old man a hundred years ago about events that occurred almost 170 years ago.

—NIALL GOGAN

Glossary

Term	Definition
A good swim	"Good luck to you." Irish slang.
Absquatulate	To disappear in the sense of Snagglepuss's famed, "exit stage left." By comparison, "skedaddle" was widely used in the U.S. Civil War to mean "rush off," as in fleeing a battlefield. American slang.
Accommodation house	A brothel. New York slang.
Agrá	A term of endearment used by an older person to a younger person of either sex, often seen as, "mo ghrá," which in English is roughly, "my dear." Irish.
Anti-fogmatic	Hard liquor, usually whiskey or gin. American slang.
Apron up	Pregnant. American slang.
Autum	A church. An autum bawler is a preacher. An autum cove is a husband. English, then New York slang.
Bastún dall	A "bastún" is an uncultured person or lout. "Dall" means ignorant. Used thusly. Irish slang.
Beached	Unemployed. American slang.
Bible banger	A preacher. English, then New York slang.

Term	Definition
Bit of mutton	Sexual intercourse or a woman, particularly a prostitute. English, then New York slang.
Bog	An outdoor lavatory. 19th century public school slang.
Boiled brains	A hothead. American slang.
Bottom	A boxer's term for endurance or heart. 19th-century New York slang.
Brown salve	An exclamation of surprise at what is heard. At the same time it means, "I understand you." A 19th-century English public school slang.
Buttock broker	A madam. American slang.
Cadet	A tout specializing in finding fresh "cherry-ripes from the boats," as Black Muireann so delicately put it. American slang.
Cap'n Hackum	One who uses a Bowie knife. American slang.
Catamaran	An ugly woman or a harridan. Also, a run-down horse. English, then American slang.
Catamite	Used since the 16th century, it literally means, one who dresses as a woman. More usually, a young boy kept by a pederast. English, then American slang.
Cherry-ripe	A virgin, usually a temporary virgin. Note that a "cherry pipe" was a grown woman. "Cherry" did not gain its current American connotation until about 1900. English, then American slang.
Chuideen	"My little dear." Pronounced "kideen." Irish.
Clart	A dirty woman. Irish slang.
Cloven	A young prostitute who pretends to be a virgin for her cully. English, then New York slang.

Term	Definition
Corinthian	A bad woman who moves in respectable society. English, then New York slang.
Crinkleneck	"The sort of fish that swims by an overboard discharge, waiting to feed from the effluvia." Reputedly 20th Royal Navy and U.S. Navy slang. But clearly used here in a much earlier era.
Cully	A prostitute's customer. Comes from the Irish, *cuallaidhe*, meaning companion. Cully originally meant "pal," and then only later evolved in meaning. A "bene cull" is a "good fellow," a "bene cove" a good man and a "benen cove" a better man. Irish, then New York slang.
Dallachán	A blind or stupid person. Irish slang.
Dead ráibéad	A big lug. Pronounced very much like "dead rabbit." Irish.
Dange	A sexy young African-American woman. American slang.
Dell	A prostitute. "*Une belle petite*" is "a young and pretty prostitute of the superior class." English, then American slang.
Dhia	God. *Dia Uas* means, "oh Noble God." Roughly pronounced as, "gee whiz." Irish.
Doodle	A fool or dullard. American slang.
Dutchy	An immigrant, typically German, who had yet to assimilate and still retained his old-country crudities. In the 18th century, the term was unambiguously a nickname for Germans. American slang.
Exflunctication	An utter whipping or beating. American slang.

Term	Definition
Faggot	In the mid-19th century, "faggot" was a general term of abuse aimed at women and children. It could also refer to a prostitute. Its present meaning as an offensive term referring to gay men did not become current until 1910 and later. American slang.
Fear buile	A madman. Irish.
Fice	A "silent breaking of the wind, 'more obvious to the nose than to the ears'." English slang.
Flah	To engage in sexual intercourse. Irish slang.
Four-in-hand	A coach harnessed to four horses. English and American slang.
Free-jack	A freed slave. American slang.
Fuadh bocht	A wretched man. Irish.
Gabbey	A weak and foolish fellow. New York slang.
Gammon and pickles	Stuff and nonsense. To "blether" is to talk nonsense. English slang.
Gawnicus	A dolt, the word being analogous to the English gawk, meaning a fool or a simpleton. American slang.
Get	"Get" is "a bastard child," and thus a term of abuse. In Ireland, the expression is often, "a whore's get." Irish slang.
Giobstaire	A saucy little hussy. Irish colloquialism.
Grind	As a verb, it denotes sexual intercourse. American slang.
Knight (or brother) of the Gusset	A pimp. English, then New York slang.

Term	Definition
Hair about the heels	Socially inferior. American slang.
Her Mope-Eyed Ladyship	Lady Luck. "Mope-eyed" means blind. American slang.
Homeboy	Used since the 19th century to denote a denizen of a particular neighborhood or gang. American slang.
Honeyfuggle	To swindle or trick, to "sweet talk" or to cuddle up to. It could also mean having sex with an underage girl. American slang.
Huckleberry above the persimmon	Although it meant no more than "a cut above," the expression was capable of infinite variety in meaning and form. "Huckleberry," by itself, meant a fellow or a boy. Thanks to Mark Twain's *Adventures of Huckleberry Finn*, it eventually came to mean a person of little importance. American slang.
Jonathan	An American. Originally a Yankee as in someone from New England. Often referred to as "Brother Jonathan." American slang.
Ken	A house. A "stepping-ken" was a dancehall. A "boosing-ken" was a saloon. A "snoozing-ken" was a bawdy house, as was a "coupling ken." A "panel-ken" was a brothel with false panels in a room's wall through which a thief could enter while a cully was with his blowen. English, then American slang.
Kid leather	A very young, child prostitute. A "kid stretcher" is a pedophile. English and American slang.

Term	Definition
Knight and barrow pig	A knight and barrow pig is, as Grose says, "more hog than gentleman. A saying of any low pretender to precedency." "Knight of the barrow pigs" is a term of the General's invention. English, public school slang.
Leanbh bocht	Poor child. Irish.
Limbo	Jail or prison. New York slang.
Limes Americanus	The American frontier. The term is a play on "*limes Romanus*," or the frontier of the Roman Empire. One such *limes Romanus* with which the General would have been familiar as a young man was "*limes Britannicus*," which was Hadrian's Wall.
Mo chomhbrathair	"My bosom companion." Irish.
Mab	A harlot. English, then New York slang.
Moll	A woman. American slang.
Molley	A young woman or an effeminate young man. American slang.
Mort	A woman. A "dimber mort" is a pretty, young woman. A "bleak mort" is a beautiful woman. English, then American slang.

Term	Definition
Morton's Fork	A classic dilemma of two unpleasant alternatives. So named for John Morton, an opportunistic turncoat who chose the right king just before the Battle of Bosworth in 1484. The newly-crowned Henry VII rewarded Morton by making him a cardinal. He thereafter was noted for his tax collection efforts, in which it was said he told the gentry from whom he was collecting, "If you are living modestly, it must be that you are rich and can afford to give something to the King. If you are living well, then you certainly are rich enough to give something to the King."
Paddy Murphy's pig	The "ne plus ultra of Hibernicism."
Pegtantrum	Dead. Originally, "gone to Peg Trantrum's." English, then American slang.
Penny toff	A working class person who can only ape the manners of his social betters. English slang.
Pigeon	A mark. American slang.
Póg mo thóin	"Kiss my posterior." Allegedly immortalized in the name of an Irish bar in Cleveland, named Pug Mahone's. See www.pugmahones.com. Irish slang.
Poteen	Often illegal, small-still Irish whiskey, clear, with a smoky taste. Produces a fine case of the jim-jims if over-used. Irish slang.
Prim	A proper, handsome woman. English, then New York slang.
Public building inspector	An unemployed man. American slang.
Reathai	A wild man. A runner, a stroller. Irish.

Term	Definition
Reps	A woman who has a good reputation. American slang.
Rhino	Engraved (as opposed to paper) money. To be "rhino fat" is to have plenty of cash on hand.
Riding academy	A brothel. An academician, in this context, is a prostitute. Not surprisingly, "academy" could also mean a prison. Mainly English slang.
Ruais	A clown or a stupid fellow. Irish.
Sassenagh	A "Sassenagh" (or "Sassenach") is an Englishman or Protestant, and use of the term in Ireland is today (and was then) a quite derogatory term. The term derives from the English, "Saxon," and is usually dated to the early 18th century as a Scottish Gaelic term later coopted by the Irish.
Settled	Murdered. English, then American slang.
Shandrydan	A "shandrydan" is a light carriage with a hood (notwithstanding the General's memory). The Oxford English Dictionary notes the term "in jocular use for any kind of rickety vehicle." Irish colloquialism.
Shaver	A cheat. Compare to a "sharper," who is one who obtains goods or money by any kind of false pretense or representation. English, then American slang.
Shut (one's) pan	A now-obsolete variant of "shut up." American slang.
Simkin	A fool. English, then American slang.
Slantendicular	Slanting, or at a slant. English, then American slang.

Glossary

Term	Definition
Spalpeen	An itinerant agricultural worker. Now considered to be a pejorative. Irish.
Spice	To steal. Verb. English, then New York slang.
Square	Honest. English, then American slang.
Stachaile	A loose woman. Irish colloquialism.
Teas	Heat, passion, excitement or the highest temperature, and it is pronounced, "chazz" or "jazz." Some have attributed the origin of the term, "jazz," to "*teas*." "Jazz" was used during the 19th century "as a common vulgarity among Negroes in the South" as both a verb and a noun to describe sexual intercourse. It was only in the 1920s that "jazz" came to denote the "latest thing in music." Irish.
Tout	A thief's lookout or a man offering betting advice, depending upon who's defining the term. English, then New York slang.
Upper customer	A member of the upper tendom who is a boxing fan. New York boxing slang.
Upper tendom	A member of the social elite. New York slang.
Wain	A small child. Irish.
Waking snakes	To get into trouble, or alternatively, to run away. American slang.

PART ONE

Tá Éire Tar Éis Thréig Mé
(Ireland Has Forsaken Me)

DUBLIN AND COUNTY CORK, IRELAND
SEPTEMBER 1844

CHAPTER 1

Cricket

⌒

"YOUR FATHER'S A TRAITOR, GOGAN," the disembodied voice hissed in the night.

I looked up, startled, only to see that it was Phillip Murray, a fellow fifth-former at St. Patrick's College for Young Men. His father and mine had been close, once, but no longer, and Phillip had occasionally bullied me for it. I stared at him for a moment, his face outlined by the weak moonlight filtering through the clouds. "I beg your pardon, Murray?"

"You heard me, Gogan. Your father has betrayed all true Irishmen."

"Do you really want to have it out here? Now? How utterly tiresome, Murray." I affected an indifference I did not feel, gesturing at the bog, which I had just left. The heavy night smell belied the new building, reputedly built as part of a campaign by the Board of Governors to show how modern an Irish public school could be. It already bore the signs of heavy use by a hundred boys.

"You are such a superior shit, Gogan. Utterly frightful, you are."

I ignored the dig, and instead asked in a patient tone, "Why do you think my father a traitor, Murray? He's worked with O'Connell for Repeal since before either of us were born. Your father has, too, in his own way, such as it is."

"It's obvious, Gogan," Phillip sneered. "Your old man talked O'Connell into surrendering to our high and mighty *Sassenagh* overlords." Phillip glared at me in the moonlight as I reflected on eight centuries of English rule over the Irish. "And d'you know, it was worse than that. Your old man talked the Liberator," Phillip practically spat the word, "into licking the Lord Lieutenant's Saxon boots after the bastard proscribed the Clontarf monster meeting. This—after what the great man, himself, said just three months earlier? His great Mallow Defiance? Those words will be engraved on the heart of every true Irishman for a hundred years: 'The time is come … gentlemen, you may soon have the alternative to live as slaves or to die as free men.' To a man, they cheered the Liberator, Gogan, and d'you know what they replied back to him as if they were but a single voice? Do you?" Phillip grimaced at me, and snorted, "'We'll die free men.' Your father ended that by what he did, and he has condemned us to live as *Sassenagh* slaves. He cost Ireland its best chance at freedom in two generations."

The Mallow Defiance had been but one of O'Connell's triumphs during what he had proclaimed as the Repeal Year, 1843, when he promised an end to the hated Acts of Union between England and Ireland. Those many months had been marked by a series of monster meetings, as they came to be called, at Mullaghmast, Mallow and Tara, and at half a dozen other gathering places all over Ireland. Each meeting had been bigger than the last, with the crowds cheering O'Connell as he spoke of an independent Ireland, free of the heavy boot of the Saxon for the first time in centuries. Clontarf was to have been the last of them before winter—and the biggest. A million Irish men and women from all walks of life were to gather at the famous meadow where Brian Boru had won Irish independence from another invader eight hundred years ago. But the Lord Lieutenant couldn't abide the thought of that many Irishmen in one place at one time. Not with just a few thousand redcoats in the country, he couldn't, what with most of them being poor *spalpeen* who had flown to take the Queen's shilling just to avoid starvation.

"It's true, Gogan," Phillip said. "All O'Connell had to do was to have the courage to hold the meeting. Ireland would have been ours. And your old man talked him out of it."

I thought of what Father had said at the time, that O'Connell had sworn that there'd never be open rebellion. And going ahead with the Clontarf meeting after the Lord Lieutenant proscribed it would have been just that.

I clenched my fists with agitation and then opened them again, trying to control my anger. "O'Connell, himself, has always said that armed rebellion didn't succeed with Wolfe Tone in '98, and it won't succeed now with the Liberator. And he knew that. And you know that because every Irishman knows what the Liberator also said." I glared hard at Phillip. "He asked us all, what if we'd resisted at Clontarf? With only a gaggle of solicitors with cockades in their hats to protect us, armed with wands and riding horses hired for the day? The lobsterbacks would have ridden us down like vermin and had our guts for garters. And then the *Sassenagh* would have descended upon all of Ireland just like Cromwell did—slaughtering and pillaging as they went. Ireland needs to win its independence peacefully."

"The *Sassenagh* would never have had the bottom for that," Phillip snapped. "Not in this modern day."

"Well, that's not what Father told me," I replied doubtfully. "Anyway, what does it matter? My father—unlike yours—stood by O'Connell when they came for him, and he went to Richmond Gaol for his beliefs." Just a few miles from school, Richmond Gaol was, they both being in nearby suburbs of Dublin. But I'd never gone to see him. Not permitted, so I was told. Dismissing this from my mind, I defiantly asked, "What's your old man doing now, Phillip? Publishing a newspaper? Where's the courage in that? He's never sacrificed a day of comfort in his life."

"The *Nation* is the voice of Young Ireland. Most popular broadsheet in Dublin, don't you know," Phillip said loftily. "Focusing the

Saxon mind on the prospect of real rebellion—not on those 'on one side and then the other' ways of O'Connell and your father. Standing up to the *Sassenagh* is the only way to rid ourselves of the bastards."

"As long as someone else does the actual fighting, I suppose. Like my father."

"No," Phillip snapped. "Your father was a coward to surrender, and he was a traitor to Ireland to talk O'Connell into surrendering. O'Connell should have gone into hiding. Forced the English to be beastly—or to go home, their tails between their legs."

"Burning farms and homes and killing unarmed men, like they did in '98, more like."

"That was fifty years ago. A different time. They were afraid of the French using Ireland to conquer England. The French Directorate, Napoleon, guillotines and all that nonsense. We're at peace now. The Saxon oppressors wouldn't dare repeat their bloody ways."

I almost laughed at Phillip unconsciously mimicking the over-wrought language of the *Nation*.

Phillip continued, "Not today. They wouldn't dare. Not with the eyes of the world looking on them. And if they did, the whole of Ireland would erupt, and cast the heathen Saxon into the Irish Sea, once and for all."

"Well," I said, "my father thinks you're wrong, and that's good enough for me."

"What a patsy you are, Gogan. You really are pathetic. Worse than your old man. *Anfoltach* that he is." Phillip laughed.

Phillip had called my father an evil and bankrupt man. The last time some bastard had said that to me, I'd blackened his eye for his trouble. So the words erupted from me before I was even conscious of them. "That, you son of a bitch, is utter bosh."

Phillip stopped laughing. "Don't you—"

"Call you a son of a bitch?" I was now just inches from him, my rage flaring and his face looking down at me from half-a-head taller. I swallowed hard and said to him, "You fucking son of a bitch."

Phillip's fist crashed into the side of my head, and I sank to my knees.

"Pathetic." And then he was gone into the gloom.

The gall of it burned me for days afterwards, and it had hardly begun to subside when Phillip confronted me once more, this time in front of twenty others, at the top of the stone stairs leading down to the school's great hall. He took care not to mock my father—or Daniel O'Connell for that matter—for that would have led to a general donnybrook, as half the school felt as I and my father did, while the other half were of the same mind as Phillip and his father. He instead proclaimed loudly to me, "Gogan, you chicken, I'm going to bat for a century against you tomorrow."

I swallowed a sudden surge of panic at being so publicly confronted, and said as nonchalantly as I could, "Not a chance, you old catamite. One bowl and put out, more like."

Then, to the great pleasure of the howling mob, I hurled myself at Murray, and we fell to blows, tripping and rolling down the stairs, landing at the feet of a very upset Father O'Muirhily, our Latin and Greek master. We hadn't done each other much damage, and within the hour the headmaster had caned us both for our sins.

I was feeling pretty liverish the next day as I made my way to the cricket grounds, another recent—and extraordinarily expensive—improvement by the school's Board of Governors. I was put out for having been caned merely for defending myself, my backside little better than raw meat from the caning, and my left eye swollen half shut from that last punch from Phillip, delivered just as Father O'Muirhily tore us apart, swearing in Latin under his breath. I could only hope that Phillip was feeling worse.

"Gogan, you look frightful," Mac, our resident professional, exclaimed when I hove into the clubhouse. "You all right to bowl today?"

I raised my hand in general assent. Mac was a regular brick, and I appreciated him, even if some of my fellow fifth-formers sneered about him having been sent down from Marylebone, the very mecca of English cricket, for being a peloothered paddy-whack. He shook his head and handed me a silver flask produced from within his long coat. I swigged from it and damn near choked.

He smiled tolerantly. "This, me cove, is naught but a little pick-me-up for a man beset with a proper injury. 'T'ain't no mere hair o' the dog." Mac grabbed me by the scruff of my neck and appraised my face. "Hmmph. Get your arse onto the ground and start warming up."

I fielded and batted to no great distinction in the first innings. I bowled in the second, finding my mark more often than not, and otherwise generally avoiding making a boggle-de-botch of it. That is, until Phillip came to bat. He opened his account with four runs off a vicious hit that whizzed past my ear before I could even react. His pleased laugh echoed in my ears. On the next pitch, I tried to put the ball at his feet, hoping to strike the wicket on a hard hop, but he swatted it away harmlessly and ran for yet another pair of runs.

I could hear a bit of sledging directed at me from Phillip's side. The umpire moved restively, but gave no indication that he was ready to silence them. I strove to ignore the eggsuckers, and gave Phillip another hard rounder. He returned the favor by smashing it into the hedge bordering the far side of the field from the clubhouse. Good for another four runs. I stood motionless, trying to ignore the jeers, which were even louder now. Phillip then ripped a slow underhander for still another pair of runs. He hovered next to me for an instant on his last run, just as the ball was being fielded and thrown my way, and whispered none-too-softly, "Told you, Gogan. A century. You ready for it?" I ignored him, imploring the ball to come so that we could run him out. Phillip then muttered, "*Póg mo thóin*, boyo," and was gone, safe to the other wicket, leaving me to fume.

With Mac glaring at me, I gathered up the ball and stared at Phillip as he set his bat and crowded the front of the wicket in a most unsportsmanlike way. I gave him my very best fast bowl, and watched in dumb fascination as the red ball caromed off the grass a yard or so in front of him, spun over his bat and struck him in the head. There was a collective gasp of horror as Phillip fell like a sack of potatoes. Everyone, Mac, both sides' players and spectators alike, rushed to him. Everyone, that is, except me. I stood watching, feet rooted where I'd planted them, conscious that underneath my horror at the result, I was feeling an unsettling sense of satisfaction at my tough bowl having settled my score with Phillip.

I remember little of the game after he was carried senseless to the clubhouse.

Nobody said a word to me afterwards. Not even Mac, who seemed to be on the other side of the clubhouse, his gaze studiously averted, whenever I saw him that afternoon. Father O'Muirhily, the only other person whom I could have confided in, had been nowhere to be seen since he'd dragged Phillip and me to the headmaster for our caning, even to the point of having missed lecture that day. To a soul, my fellow fifth-formers gave me a wide berth that night and all the next day, ceasing to whisper among themselves whenever I hove into view. The juniors merely quailed in my presence. Perhaps they were terrified that they too would be felled and rendered senseless by a red cricket ball.

Finally, just as the midday bell struck, the head boy summoned me. He refused to meet my eye and didn't reply when I asked him what was going on. He just deposited me wordlessly in the headmaster's outer office, where I cooled my heels for what seemed to be an eternity. I was interrupted from my reverie when a short man dressed head-to-toe in a quite funereal black emerged from the headmaster's sanctum sanctorum. Our eyes met. I had half expected it to be Phillip's father. I was dreading that encounter. But this was someone I'd never seen before. Neither old nor young, he was at first glance quite unprepossessing. But this air quickly struck me as a mere façade of dissemblance. Indeed, his face was that of a zealot, thin lips and a fixed mouth surmounted by a beak nose, flat, coal-black eyes and equally coal-black hair that descended into the type of magnificent whiskers that General Burnside was to make so famous a generation later. Worse, the man's manner induced me to inwardly shudder. He gave me a cold, appraising glance. Then he was gone.

I thought nothing more of the man that day, for in the next minute the headmaster's private secretary was ushering me in, and the headmaster was asking me to sit in the elegant Hepplewhite side chair catercornered from the one he was sitting in, opposite from the magnificent raised dais of a mahogany desk from which he normally greeted scuts fresh from their mothers' tears and dispensed justice to deserving miscreants—a place I'd been hardly twenty-four hours before. I'd never even been conscious of the chairs before, and I sat quietly, reflecting upon the unexpected honor as the headmaster worried his pipe with one of those new-fangled lucifer matches.

After a few moments, Headmaster said, not unkindly, "Well, Gogan, you have had quite the last few days, haven't you?"

"Yes sir."

"You know, Murray is still unconscious. The damned doctors fear for him." Headmaster shook his head tiredly. "His mother is distraught, of course, and his father has taken quite ill over it all. His heart, they fear. So I am told."

I numbly stared at him.

"I know, son. A ghastly incident. MacKinnon said he'd never seen anything like it in all his playing days. Not even at Marylebone. You bowled a perfect pitch, he said. With an unaccountable hop." Headmaster looked at me. "And so here we are, aren't we?"

Words failed me once again.

"But that's not why I sent for you. Well, not entirely. Although, we do need to talk further of Murray and you and what is to be done with you over it all."

"Sir?" I croaked.

"We've had news from Dublin Castle." Headmaster paused and fiddled with his pipe once more until a wreath of smoke issued. "Yes," he mumbled. "News from Dublin Castle. O'Connell is to go free today. The crowds are gathering now, so I am told. They're going to greet the 'Great Liberator' as the conquering hero. Ireland's greatest man in generations."

"And my father? I haven't heard from him for weeks, and as you and Father O'Muirhily have told me, I could not visit him. Is he to be released as well?"

Headmaster seemed not to hear me nor even see me, for he murmured, "They say it was gaol fever." Headmaster looked at me unhappily.

"Gaol fever?"

"Yes."

"Is he all right? Can I go and see him now?"

Words failed Headmaster, and I damned near vomited at the implication.

"He's …"

Headmaster started from his reverie, as if I had poked him. "Yes, my poor boy. Your father passed away from his illness."

I thought later that I should have cried at the news. But I did not. I merely stared at Headmaster.

He looked at me queerly, and mumbled, "Your cousin, Mr. O'Creagh, has sent for you."

"But …"

"He will explain it all to you."

"Sir?"

"Then we shall see what lies ahead, son." There was a bleakness behind the surface kindness of his eyes. "Then we shall see."

⌒

Not an hour later I had been deposited into as mean and disreputable a pony trap as I'd seen in a very long time. As it lurched forward to leave St. Patrick's College, my school these past five years—not a soul to see me off—I heard Father O'Muirhily cry from behind me, "Stop."

The trap, driven by a surly *spalpeen*, didn't stop.

"Stop, damn your black Irish hide. Stop!" It didn't occur to me until much, much later to be shocked by Father O'Muirhily's language.

The trap stopped. "Beggin' yer pardon, Father. I didn't hear yers the first time."

Father O'Muirhily ignored the supplicant and grabbed my arm. "I am so sorry, my son. I had no idea. Your being sent down like this. An utter outrage. I shall give Headmaster an earful, and then the Bishop. This is an utter outrage."

If I'd uttered a word to the man, I would've bawled.

"I will come to you." Father O'Muirhily grasped my arm and searched my face. "All shall be well. You may count upon it, my poor, poor boy."

⌒

CHAPTER 2

Be Gone … and Damn Yer Hide

THREE DAYS LATER, I WAS AT MY COUSIN Séamas O'Creagh's house, cooling my heels in a small, airless antechamber rendered stifling by the sun shining brightly through a high, unopened window. Séamas's housekeeper, Oonagh, had unhappily thrust me in there, explaining, "Himsel' be tellin' me to put yers in here. Until all them poor tenants of his be done bitin' his ear in the front room. Praise God that it be over in a brace o' shakes."

With that, she disappeared, leaving me to contemplate seeing my only relative for the first time since I was a small boy—and to contemplate Father dead and buried in some potter's field, and poor Murray lying unconscious in his sick room. For reasons that had remained entirely obscure to me, Séamas and my father had never gotten along. Séamas was a middleman, the chief tenant of some titled member of the Protestant Ascendancy who was enjoying the Season in London, no doubt. Or was it to Bath they went for the Season? I'd heard my father mutter darkly about such families, headed by the privileged scions of lieges of Cromwell and Elizabeth who'd wrested the land away from the Irish in centuries past, men who drove their great holdings into the ground to pay for their extravagant lives in England, while leaving it to the likes of Séamas and his ilk to extract every tuppence they could from the poor tenant farmers who ate potatoes so that they could sell the best of their produce into market just to pay the rent.

I could hear Séamas holding court. I tried to shut out the bursts of Irish invective that Séamas was heaping on his poor tenants by burying myself in my favorite book, *The Last of the Mohicans*. My father had given it to me as the carriage waited impatiently at our Dublin house on that cold and rainy October morning to take him and O'Connell and the others to surrender themselves to our Saxon overlords. As Father had hugged me tightly to him, the last thing he'd said was that, when he came back, we'd go to America and find the Deerslayer together, for Repeal was dead, and it was high time for the two of us to flee across the Western Ocean to escape the mighty and harsh hand of the *Sassenagh*. I never saw him again.

"Well, Billy Gogan, what are you doing, darkening our door after so many years?"

I looked up at the shadow looming over me. It was my second cousin, Eibhlin O'Creagh, Séamas's only daughter, who had that very morning returned home from her proper finishing school in England. How Séamas could afford such a luxury I had no idea. Oonagh had sniggered to no one in particular that Miss Eibhlin's arrival home had been every bit the clattering and complicated evolution to be expected of the privileged daughter of a wealthy man. What was worse, she sniffed, was Eibhlin's insistence on now being called "Evelyn," apparently proclaiming to Oonagh, "Can't be seen as too Irish at that proper finishing school, don't you know."

I stared at Eibhlin—Evelyn—for a moment too long, drinking in her golden ringlets and her luminous aura of having a worldly knowledge infinitely superior to that of any mere boy. Our eyes locked, and she smiled tolerantly at me. I stumbled awkwardly to my feet, pitching my beloved book to the floor. I bent over to pick it up, brushing against her, intoxicated by her scent. I apologized. She brushed it off, her eyebrow arched with amusement, apparently attributing my clumsiness to the cramped meanness of the stuffy antechamber. I became conscious of the sweat prickling damply against my chest and prayed that it would not come streaming down my face.

"Come for a walk with me." Eibhlin swept regally from the room and out onto the pleasant terrace at the back of the house. I followed involuntarily. From the corner of my eye, I could see Séamas through the drawing room window. He was gesticulating imperiously at a wretched-looking *spalpeen* standing before him, hat in hand, a woman and child quivering behind the poor man. "Oh, pay him no mind," Eibhlin said, and we ambled from the terrace onto a garden walk. "He is utterly tiresome in how he treats those poor devils. I shall be very happy to be back in school in England."

"You like it in England?" I felt foolish for asking the obvious.

"Oh, yes," she breathed dreamily, "I am to be invited to go with Cecily de Tyson to London next fall. For the Season. I shall be introduced ..." To whom, I dared not ask. "And that's why I have asked Father to call me 'Evelyn.' If I am to find a wealthy English husband, I cannot be having an Irish name."

"'Evelyn' ... it's beautiful."

The silence lingered between us, and I could not bring myself to meet Evelyn's eye.

After a moment, she asked me in an all-too-airy tone, "What're you reading, then?"

"Oh ..." The words I wanted were thick upon my tongue. I glanced involuntarily at my book and then clutched it tightly.

"Forgotten already?"

The dam broken, I said in a rush, "*The Last of the Mohicans.* It's about America in the colonial times. All about English and French soldiers, brave frontiersmen such as Hawkeye and red Indians. James Fenimore Cooper wrote it. He's an American."

Evelyn proclaimed, "Father thinks that Americans are all illiterate savages, little better than the red man, himself. He would never have a book by an American in the house."

"Hawkeye's not a savage."

"Really?" She sounded unconvinced.

"He's the hero," I said defiantly. "He rescues the Scottish Colonel Munro's daughters, Cora and Alice, from the savage Indian, Magua. But Magua captures them again and ..."

"Who's the heroine? Do she and Hawkeye live happily ever after?"

"No."

"Well, what happens, then?"

"It's complicated. But Cora falls in love with Uncas. He's the last of the Mohican Indians."

"A Scottish colonel's daughter falls in love with a red Indian?" Evelyn was utterly disbelieving of such an ungodly proposition.

"Yep. But there's more to it than that. Cora's a mulatta," I replied. "A mulatta, 'with tresses shining like the black plumage of a raven and a complexion charged with the color of rich blood that seemed ready to burst its bounds'," I quoted, hardly glancing at the book. I looked at Evelyn conspiratorially, "Father explained to me that a mulatta is half Negress and half English—or Scottish or Irish, or whatever. A mulatta's not really a Scotswoman or an Englishwoman, so she can't marry an Englishman—or an Irishman or a Scotsman, for that matter. It wouldn't have been right. That's why she falls in love with Uncas. He's not an Englishman either. But they don't live happily ever after, Uncas and Cora. They both die in the end. Father said that it would have been worse than death itself for a Scottish or English woman—even if she's a mulatta—to marry a red Indian. So Cooper had to kill them off." I looked at her with the satisfaction of having very neatly destroyed a romance.

"How sad."

"Well, Hawkeye lives. Like I said, he's the hero. Cooper wrote other books about him. But I haven't read them yet."

"Tell me more. Tell me about Cora. She sounds so mysterious. Why is she a mulatta?" Evelyn slid her arm through mine, and we walked in lockstep across the broad lawn towards the woods.

"Her mother was the daughter of a slave. So she has Negro blood in her. After she died, Cora's father, Colonel Munro, married Alice's mother, who was an Englishwoman. The two sisters then came to America, where they fell under the protection of Major Heyward, who was under Colonel Munro's command. Heyward falls in love with Alice. But Alice had eyes only for Uncas." Now I was frantically thinking of everything romantic in the book that would keep Evelyn talking with me. But I had just about run out of ideas.

"Ooh," Evelyn breathed. "How romantic. Imagine falling in love with a heroic British soldier or a handsome red Indian savage. How dreamy." She then unlocked her arm from mine, looked at me with a coquettish flourish and flounced toward the house.

Oonagh found me on the terrace, quite at a loss as to how to return to the stuffy little antechamber. She said, "Himsel' be after invitin' yers to dinner this evenin'. Apparently, ye be stayin' the night with us."

I began thanking Oonagh, but she interrupted me, "Oh, and there's a Father O'Muirhily to see you and to see himsel'."

⌒

"Cousin Billy." Séamas strode onto the terrace where Father O'Muirhily and I had been talking of inconsequential matters. Poor Murray and Father hung heavily between us, notwithstanding the fact that I was so very glad to see him. Father O'Muirhily seemed equally glad to see me. "*Me bouchal.*" Séamas embraced me and then held me at arm's length, the better to survey me. "Why ye'll be all grown. Almost, that is." He embraced me again and then looked askance at Father O'Muirhily.

"Cousin Séamas, please allow me the honor of naming Father O'Muirhily. He is … was … my Latin and Greek Master at school. St. Patrick's."

"Honored, sir." Father O'Muirhily extended his hand to Séamas.

"Father." Séamas eyed us both skeptically as he and Father O'Muirhily shook hands.

"Billy is one of the finest students I've ever known," explained Father O'Muirhily. "I did not have the opportunity to bid him farewell when he was so abruptly sent down from school." I flushed with secret pride. Father O'Muirhily smiled disarmingly. "I've been tutoring young Master Gogan since the day he arrived at St. Patrick's, and I could not bear the thought of him leaving without my having bid him a proper farewell."

"Aye," Séamas muttered, still eyeing Father O'Muirhily with undiminished suspicion.

Mercifully, Oonagh cut the moment short by announcing rather loudly that dinner was served. Once we were seated, Cousin Séamas scowled dyspeptically at his soup, saying hardly a word. Evelyn also seemed subdued, sitting primly and making eye contact with neither her father nor me, and casting only the shortest of curious glances in Father O'Muirhily's direction. Father O'Muirhily, on the other hand, was positively expansive, recounting stories of the latest gossip from Dublin (not the racy kind, mind you), carefully avoiding news of the newly freed O'Connell and his having apparently aged into a man older than his years during his sojourn in Richmond Gaol, nothwithstanding the reputedly luxurious setting of his imprisonment. He also avoided mentioning St. Patrick's and my dismissal therefrom.

But in avoiding such topics, Father O'Muirhily soon lapsed into a silence from which I could not rouse him. When dinner was over, Séamas flicked the merest glance at Evelyn, who wordlessly withdrew from the dining room, her back already to the table by the time Father O'Muirhily could rumble to his feet and pay her the kindest and most flowery of compliments with an elegant bow. She pirouetted and curtsied to him as pretty as you please, beaming a smile of genuine pleasure that would have melted a thousand of the stoniest of hearts. Séamas made a face.

He recovered quickly enough, though, for he offered Father O'Muirhily a good port and a better cigar. Séamas and Father O'Muirhily offered each other one or two more platitudes as they lit their cigars and contentedly puffed them. Then came a moment of heavy silence, after which Father O'Muirhily addressed me.

"I told you that I would come, my son. My only regret is that I could not keep you up at school, where you so richly deserve to be."

I gave him a questioning look.

"Headmaster was quite adamant. And he would not explain why, merely repeating *ad infinitum* that it 'was impossible'." I waited for Father O'Muirhily to mention poor Murray, but he did not. He instead said, "I fear, my son, that I committed the sin of intemperance and had words with Headmaster. I only hope that he sees fit to be a Christian man and forgive me my transgression. It was this senseless waste of a fine young man's education that drove me here to talk with you both."

Séamas blurted, "Is it a matter o' mere rhino, Father?"

"I fear it may be something more. But sufficient funding for young Master Gogan's schooling, or rhino, as you call it, would almost certainly solve the matter immediately at hand, which is what is to become of Master Gogan, now that he has been sent down."

"Aye, and so it always is," Séamas grunted.

I looked at him expectantly.

"But I cannot be helping the young squireen with no rhino." He gestured at me dismissively.

Father O'Muirhily looked mildly at Séamas. "I would have thought that your direct pecuniary assistance would be unnecessary, at least in the longer run. I have been given to understand that Mr. Gogan *pére* was, shall we say, not penurious. So there should be an inheritance. His father was a barrister, you know. And not an unsuccessful one, I might add. That is, when he was not with Mr. O'Connell, campaigning for Irish freedom. Ancestral lands, as well, I believe."

Séamas snorted.

Father O'Muirhily reacted as if he'd been slapped. In all my years, I had never seen this saintly man act as he had ever since Father had died.

"What I mean to be saying, Father, begging yer pardon, is that Billy, m'boyo's, father is *anfoltach*."

I stared at him at first, curiously detached, then remembering with an inward jolt how I'd reacted to Murray when he'd said the same thing about my father.

Father O'Muirhily was more sanguine. "Pray tell, sir, how that may be?"

"Himsel' wrote to me from his death bed, now, didn't he? *Ar dheis Dé go raibh a anam*." May God bless his soul, I absently translated for myself. With that, Séamas looked away, almost embarrassed, from both Father O'Muirhily, who reflexively crossed himself, and me. He then looked us both in the eye as he said with renewed vigor, "As himsel' lay dying of the gaol fever. Entreatin' me, he was." He lingered over the words. "Aye, that be in his missive. Himself entreating me to take yonder gossoon under me wing. Commending his only son to me, on account of himsel' bein' *anfoltach* and unable to provide for his heir. Damn him for it." Séamas offered no apology for this last bit.

"So you can do nothing for the lad?" Father O'Muirhily's opprobrium was palpable. "He has promise, you know. Great promise. That is, Mr. O'Creagh, if the lad finishes his education."

I interrupted, no longer able to restrain myself. "My father was no criminal, sir." Séamas whipped around to stare at me. I continued, "And he was no debtor, sir. For the love of God, he was a wealthy man."

"But surely ye knew that the *Sassenagh* didna' try him with O'Connell?"

I stared at Séamas dumbly. Father O'Muirhily's unhappy look confirmed the point, and the time for righteous indignation had passed. "Why not?"

"Them bastard *Sassenagh* be havin' a special place in hell to send yer Da', so he could be the one to be atoning fer O'Connell's sins. They could'na be seen to be crucifying O'Connell. So they be convicting yer Da' simply fer bein' the most loyal of all the O'Connell men. If O'Connell had died in prison like yer Da' … well, that would've lit a fuse to the powder keg and blown this island apart. So them *Sassenagh* bastards be after making yer Da' pay for O'Connell's supposed sins."

"I don't understand, Cousin Séamas. I don't understand. Father O'Muirhily?"

"Let him finish, lad."

Séamas continued. "It be a well-known matter that my cousin was a great patriot. Indefatigable, himsel' was. Sacrificed everything he had—excepting yersel', lad—and now he's even done just that."

I stiffened as if I had been struck a blow.

Séamas said in a faintly mocking tone, "All the world be thinking it be the Liberator who organized all them Monster Meetings last year." He paused and fixed me in the eye. I looked to Father O'Muirhily, who remained content to let Séamas unfold his story. "Well, he didn't. Your father did, God bless his soul. Them monster meetings could hardly have happened without what your father did. But himsel' did so much more by giving everything he had to the cause."

"What do you mean?"

"It takes a right big bank to run a revolution—even a peaceful one. Yer Da' wasn't the only one to spend his wealth, nor even one of the biggest. But spend he did. Every last ha'penny he had—and more. He mortgaged everything he had for the cause."

Father had never breathed a word of this to me. I looked once more to Father O'Muirhily for some solace. He offered none, and Séamas continued as if the good Father was not there in the room with us. "So, when they arrested him, they didn't put him on trial with O'Connell—they did something worse … far worse. They took away his respectability. Tossed himsel' into debtors' prison, and left him there to rot."

"Father O'Muirhily? Can this … can this be true?"

Father O'Muirhily nodded unhappily. "I feared that at least some of this might be true. There have been rumors." He turned to Séamas and asked, "So what can be done for the lad?"

Séamas stood, framed by the flickering fireplace. "The young squireen's life, as himself be knowing it. It be over. I na' be rhino-fat. So I cannot be spending me chink educating the young buckeen."

Father O'Muirhily interjected forcefully, "Then there's naught to be gained by talking of this any further. I shall take the lad tomorrow morning, at first light, if you would be so kind as to arrange to transport us to Cork."

"Aye," Séamas said dully. "Aye. That I can do." He then gave us each in turn a sly look.

"Ye can take the buckeen to the quays."

Father O'Muirhily and I stared at him.

"I'll be doing the right thing by yers," he explained. "I be staking yers to emigratin' to the New World. I wrote away to a shipping agent I know, and he tells me that there be a Western Ocean packet ship, *Maryann*, that be leaving in the next day or two. I be giving yers some spending money, as well." I looked at him oddly, and he explained. "I did it all when yer Da's letter came. There was nothin' else for it."

22

Father O'Muirhily looked thoughtful, but said nothing as I thought to ask for my father's letter. But I decided not to. There was no point, and anyway, it would have been too painful by half to read. I looked at Father O'Muirhily, who seemed to reach a con- clusion of some sort. But he did not share it with either of us, for all he said was, "Right, then. I shall take the lad to the quays as you ask, Mr. O'Creagh." Father O'Muirhily rose and gave me a look that told me to stay quiet. "I shall bid you both good evening. If your housekeeper could be so kind as to—"

Oonagh appeared as if from thin air. "Right this way, Father. We be after havin' a nice bed for yers." She tossed a glance at her employer and led Father O'Muirhily from the room, who said to me as he passed, "We shall talk further in the morning, my son. You have nothing to fear."

With that, Séamas and I were left staring at each other in the flickering candlelight, there being no gas lamps in this remote, rural region.

"That na' be all, lad."

"Sir?"

"Even if I were of a mind to be funding yers, I still couldn't be letting yers stay on here."

"Sir?"

"I've got *mi colleen bawn* to be thinking about. *Mi* girleen, Eibhlin. So ye have to go. Ye've got to be leavin'. Whether it be leaving Ireland or going with that *patrico* of yours, Father O'Muirhily, or whoever the devil he is." This last, Séamas seemed to spit. "Wherever himself be after wanting to take yers. I cannot have ye be keeping company with *mi* precious Eibhlin. I don't know what daft nonsense ye be putting in her head. What the devil have yer been telling her? Herself be mooning over heathen red savages and slave girls falling in love. T'ain't natural." He turned and took a few steps towards me. "An' the two of yers, walking arm in arm.

Sweet loving Jaysus! She's yer second cousin, for the love o' Christ Almighty. An' she only be fifteen. *Mi colleen bawn.* A little girleen, she is. Damn yer hide."

Séamas lurched to a halt just short of me. I could hardly meet his eye, but I did, even though all that had befallen me in these past days caught up with me and threatened to start me crying like a child. It was only the male pride of being fifteen that stopped me.

Séamas was speaking again. "I'll be saying *slán leat* now."

With that, his farewell to me, and his blessing—such as it was—Séamas turned and left me to my thoughts.

⌒

I went upstairs to my room in the garret, which Oonagh had shown me earlier, hardly seeing anything. Father O'Muirhily had also withdrawn with a terse "good night" to me, and disappeared in another direction.

Evelyn was standing in the gloom, waiting for me.

"Billy," she said in that soft, aristocratic tone of hers. "I'm so sorry. I have been absolutely beastly to you."

I drank her in once more, perfume, luminous aura and all, and Séamas and his blarney, poor Murray and his cracked head and even my poor, dead father receding into a distant memory.

"I never even asked you why you were here. It's a terrible thing, what the *Sassenagh* did to your father."

It struck me oddly, her saying that, after what she'd said to me about being introduced into society next Season. Held in London, she'd told me. The very cockpit of the mighty Saxon empire.

"Life there, in England, it's wonderful," Evelyn said, as if by way of explanation. "But what they do here, in Ireland ..." she murmured. After a moment, she continued, "I should never have spoken to my father about the book."

"You're not to blame," I said. "He's been—"

"No," she cut me off. "It's my fault. If it weren't for me, he'd have found a way to keep you here. He really likes you."

I snorted involuntarily.

"No, really." She paused, and moved closer, her perfume diz-zying me. "It's me," she said. "You see, he doesn't trust me around you. Ever since Mother died. He doesn't know what to do with me." She hovered so close that we almost touched. "But he's right. He shouldn't trust me. I ..." Evelyn left the thought unfinished and turned to leave. Then in a rush, she turned back, leaned into me, and gave me a lingering kiss on the lips. Her perfume once again overwhelmed me. But she vanished into the gloom before I could process even a single thought. The last thing I heard her say was, "Promise that you'll write to me."

I said nothing.

"Promise," she whispered.

I looked into the gloom at her spectral presence, aching to kiss her back. "I promise."

CHAPTER 3

If No One Sees It

⌒

It was mid-afternoon when Father O'Muirhily and I alighted from Cousin Séamas's ramshackle shandrydan into a seemingly endless sea of pigs milling about on Merchant's Quay in the heart of Cork City. As we left the pig-locked shandrydan behind, we could hear Séamas's stableman, Breandán, complaining that the presence of the pigs was naught but a plot by the Apostle of Temperance himself, Father Mathew, to keep him from his favorite lushery, which he had taken pains to point out to Father O'Muirhily and me in the dawn gloom as we had creaked our way to the turnpike from Cousin Séamas's house. Father O'Muirhily shrugged himself out of the voluminous black rubber cloak that he had rather mysteriously produced from the bottom of a small valise as we'd set out that morning. I, too, was still damp from the chilly, misting rain that had hung over us for hours after decamping from Cousin Séamas's house before dawn. This despite my oilskins, which comprised a great stiff canvas coat stretching nearly to my ankles and its accompanying sou'wester. They had been Father's since time immemorial, and they were redolent of him, even through the stink of the freshly-applied linseed oil, and I'd been almost lost at the thought of him and his absence when I donned them. It was beyond me how the oilskins had come to be at Cousin Séamas's house for Oonagh to produce just as Father O'Muirhily and I were leaving. Unaccountably, Oonagh had hugged me after she'd thrust the oilskins at me, crossing herself and muttering "*Dia leat,*" or

"God help you," presumably referring to me. She'd answered herself, saying: "*Dia leat is Muire*," or "God and Mary be with you," all of which somehow comforted me through a suddenly upwelling sense of trepidation.

Séamas had not troubled to break out his pony trap for us, the one that he'd taken to Cork just a few days earlier to fetch Evelyn home. That would have kept us dry, or at least drier than the uncovered shandrydan, which was little better than a beggar's cart. Séamas also hadn't seen fit to see us off, for not a light had shone from any window in the house as the shandrydan creaked away towards the turnpike to Cork. But I was certain as I took a last look back that I saw the shadow of the curtain in Evelyn's window being drawn back, and I was equally certain that I felt her eyes following me as the rickety, old shandrydan rolled away. Her kiss still lingered as strongly in the predawn cold and damp as it had through the night, and the sight of her at the window helped me stanch a welling fear of venturing alone into the great unknown—just as it had as I tossed and turned through the night, in turn quickening me and then begetting a dread that she might never kiss me again.

In the hours that followed, we ate the morsels of cakebread that Oonagh had thrust into our hands as we made to depart, and Father O'Muirhily and I spoke of nothing much, in English, Latin and Greek, almost as if he were exercising me to ensure that I had not entirely shed the benefit of education in the few days since I'd departed St. Patrick's. Breandán affected not to hear us as he muttered darkly about finding his lushery even if Father Mathew's adherents, all 130,000 of them, stood in his way. When we finished, Father O'Muirhily cleared his throat portentously and said in Latin, "You've a hard choice to make, my son, as to whether to stay in Ireland or emigrate, as your cousin, Mr. O'Creagh has directed you to do."

"He gave me sufficient wind for a steerage ticket, sir, and a bit extra for my keep. I see no other choice."

Cousin Séamas had come to my room last night, after I had gone to bed, and handed me an envelope containing a letter from him to the shipping agent regarding my ticket for passage on the *Maryann*. "Only steerage, now, mind you," he cautioned. "I can't be sending yers like a flash cove, master of his cabin, and eating wi' the captain at his table wi' his missus."

Séamas had then given me a small purse with a few gold sovereigns and 20 shillings. A small fortune to me. But as Cousin Séamas had said, it would need to be husbanded if I was to have anything left when I arrived in New York. Séamas had refused to tell me where the money came from when he gave it to me, saying only, "Ye'll be needin' the money, lad," before looking away. He then said without looking back, "Ye be minding them pinchers. They be after taking yer rhino if they can."

"That was very Christian of him under the circumstances," Father O'Muirhily said drily. "But you have an alternative that might just allow to you live in Ireland—eventually, that is."

He let that sink in for a moment. I thought about what my prospects in Ireland might be, and was quite unable to conjure even a remotely plausible scenario. But of the New World, I could have dreamt for hours, my terror of the night before notwithstanding, what with dark forests filled with bloodthirsty savages, brave frontiersmen armed with deadly flintlock rifles as tall as a man, soldiers on the march and villages of settlers to be protected. I was sure that I could befriend a red Indian like Uncas, who could teach me how to be a great frontiersman. I'd have to be careful, though … trusting such a savage. He could just as easily be Magua, the untrustworthy Mingo, and not a noble Mohican like Uncas.

Well, perhaps I could be a mountain man instead: self-reliant and beholden to no man. One day, when my father was visiting me at school in Dublin, we had gone for a walk. He pointed to a gentleman with a tall hat, and said, "D'you know, that fantastical hat is made of beaver. And, d'you know where beaver comes from?"

My father then told me tales of great explorers called mountain men who would spend a year in the highest mountains in North America. The "Rocky Mountains" he had called them. These mountain men passed their days by themselves, Father said, in the deepest snow and coldest temperatures, with the sun blazing on them all the while. They trapped beaver by the hundreds to sell at a market at Bent's Fort called a "rendezvous," all because rich men like the flash dandy in front of us in Dublin wanted to wear the tallest and finest hats in Europe.

Father had said excitedly, "The most famous of the mountain men was a man named Jim Bridger. I read a book about him last year. A fantastical tale. What a country America is. You and I will go there one day, Billy. To the Rocky Mountains. We'll see the beaver. We'll visit Bent's Fort. We'll have a grand time of it. What do you say?"

I don't know that I said anything then. But as the rain trickled down the back of my neck and the iron wheels of the shandrydan squelched through the mud of the forlorn and bumpy turnpike, I resolved that this would be the life for me. I would strike for the frontier as soon as I reached New York.

I then wondered where the frontier really was. All I knew was that America was a huge and empty wilderness filled with great rivers. Well, someone would tell me where I would need to go to find the frontier. I would become a noble explorer, discovering new countries all by myself—a Captain Cook of the Americas, as it were, and perhaps one better, as I was an Irishman and he had been a mere *Sassenagh*.

Father Muirhily brought me back. "This is an important choice, my son."

"Sorry, Father."

"Yes, quite. Not the first time I've seen you drift off. Happened in Lecture all the time. You were one of the more accomplished practitioners of that fine and ancient art of wool-gathering." I gave a sideways glance at Father O'Muirhily. He wore an amused expression. "As I was saying, I can offer you a way to stay in Ireland—eventually, in the years to come. That is, if you desire it. I, for my part, desire it very much, for I see great things ahead for you in leading this poor country of ours from its current state of perdition at the hands of the *Sassenagh*."

"I've no money to stay here with, sir. No way to become a barrister like my father."

"That is true, my son. But there is another way. One of which I have spoken to you many times in the past. You could go directly to seminary, perhaps even in Rome itself. Become a prelate of the first order, with the finest education available anywhere in Europe."

There it was. The offer of a lifetime. And I said no.

Father O'Muirhily seemed to expect me to decline, which is not to say that he'd made the offer out of some perfunctory sense of duty. Rather, it seemed that he genuinely wanted me to become a man of the cloth, which I found curiously gratifying. There was something else on his mind, though, which began slowly to surface as we departed the turnpike's dreary sea of mud and ruts and clattered down Blarney Road towards Cork, past fine mansions visible through carefully tended rows of trees, about which were scattered rows of dirty cabins, each of which was surrounded by a forlorn garden. But I did not ask Father O'Muirhily what was on his mind until we had passed slowly by the City Gaol's formidable three stories of crenellated stone and we could see Cork City spread before us on an island in the middle of the River Lee, surrounded by the masts and crossed trees of scores of ships being unloaded—and then loaded back up—by armies of navvies. Downriver from the city, a *Sassenagh* frigate was moored, her pennants—the naval version of the hated Union Jack among them—starting to stir as the wind freshened and the rain gradually stopped.

It was only as we passed over St. Patrick's Bridge into Cork proper that Father O'Muirhily finally spoke up over the din and ceaseless movement of the dozens of cadgers lining the bridge and smoking and talking, dancing silent jigs and fishing the filthy waters of the River Lee. He spoke in Latin, as if conscious that there might be listening ears. (Although only God knows how Breandán, let alone anyone else, could have heard anything over the katzenjammer played by the shandrydan's iron wheels on the bridge's cobblestones. I could barely catch every third word, even though I was hunched close to him.) "... Important that you do not remain in Ireland ... has nothing to do with the foolishness your cousin, Mr. O'Creagh, was palavering ... last night ... Headmaster is very upset ... will not countenance your remaining at school ... nothing to do with fees, mind you ... That man ... don't know his name ... visited Headmaster ... you may have seen him ... Young Irelanders ..." And after a particularly heavy rumble of the iron wheels, I heard him finish, "simply not safe here in Ireland for the foreseeable future."

Before Father O'Muirhily could say more—or I could ask him about what he'd said, the shandrydan lurched to a halt in the middle of Merchants Quay, a long cobblestoned dock lined with warehouses and offices running along the river on either side of, and under, St. Patrick's Bridge. We each thrust a tuppence into Breandán's grateful hands and alighted into the midst of a large drove of unhappy and noisily protesting pigs being guided with mixed success onto a sidewheel steamer moored nearby. The commotion raised by the pigs had focused all eyes on them—save those of a company of redcoated *Sassenagh* soldiers standing to attention in three ranks. At a hoarse and unintelligible command, the company turned as one to the right and tramped away to the beat of a single drum and the thin skirl of a flute, flags and ensigns streaming in the freshening wind. They marched right through the squealing pigs as if they did not exist, scattering them hither and yon to the vast amusement of onlooking sailors, stevedores and cadgers alike.

"Well, my son," Father O'Muirhily said to me in English once we were sure that we would not be swept away by the seething mass of pigs, "I am confident that we shall both have our hearing back in no time at all. But," he switched to Latin, "it was fortuitous to have such a hurly-burly while we spoke of sensitive matters. We shall speak of them no more." Switching back to English, he asked, "Where is Mr. Ryan's fine establishment?" Stephen J. Ryan, Esq., was the shipping agent to whom Cousin Séamas had directed me for my ticket to the New World.

We looked blankly at the seemingly endless row of warehouses and offices and trudged up to the closest one. As we went, Father O'Muirhily said, "I will feel much better with you safely onboard … what's the name of the ship?"

"*Maryann*."

"Yes, quite. Thank you. *Maryann*. Then I shall be off to my lodgings, and in the morning on the steamer to Dublin and thence back to school." He looked at me directly, "I've been thinking, you know, and I believe you are making the right decision, as much as I shall miss seeing you grow up."

"Not joining the Church, Father?"

"I have been wrong about you for a very long time. You have a different path to follow than that of the Church. I don't know where that path will lead you. But I do wish you Godspeed."

We said no more to each other, for we had found the shipping agent's office. As the door's bell tinkled discreetly behind us, I handed my letter of introduction from Cousin Séamas to a sallow clerk, who disappeared into an adjoining office, closing the door behind him. The door opened again, and a small, red-faced man of thirty-five issued from within, spectacles perched on the middle of his nose, and wearing a high winged collar, black frock coat and magnificent red silk weskit, all befitting a fine and respectable shipping agent.

He bowed in turn to Father O'Muirhily and then to me, introducing himself with a flourish as the shipping agent, Stephen J. Ryan, Esq., and then urged Father O'Muirhily to take a seat in the single worn chair and saying to me in a conversational voice redolent with the blarney brogue that one seems to find spoken only on the stage these days: "Bring yer arse to anchor, lad, right here," "here" being a rickety stool, which I perched upon with trepidation. "I be with yers both when I be finished with this *fuadh bocht*."

Ryan turned back into the room without seeing whether Father O'Muirhily had heard him. Father O'Muirhily and I glanced at each other without comment. Through the still-open door, I saw Ryan slip behind a great oak desk. Standing in front of the desk, in between two fine and commodious leather chairs apparently reserved for honored guests, was a gaunt man of about thirty, dressed in little more than rags, and holding his hat in his farmer's hands, looking every inch the *fuadh bocht*—a poor and wretched man.

Ryan dropped the blarney brogue for a much more business-like tone as he spoke to the gaunt man. "Well sir, for four tickets to America, to the great city of New York, on the *Maryann*, on which we are just now embarking passengers for the swiftest voyage available from Ireland, it will be … let me figure … yes …" Ryan looked to his clerk, who whispered quietly into his ear. "Yes, of course."

He looked at the supplicant *spalpeen*, who could do no more than stare back at him, and said, "It will be £4, 10 shillings, per passenger. Yes, I am aware that this is somewhat more than the £2, 10 shillings per passage paid for in advance by Mr. Lamb, your land agent. But these are difficult berths to obtain. They are much in demand, sir. Much in demand. I am merely passing them along to you at my cost." Ryan glared over the top of his spectacles, which were now slightly smudged. The gaunt man met his gaze for just an instant before he looked quickly away. Ryan said unctuously, "I am glad that you appreciate my position. I thank you for that."

Having achieved his victory, Ryan continued with hardly a pause, "You will also have to attend the chandler, Mr. Hopkins, to properly provision yourself and your fine family. You may find him past the bridge … St. Patrick's Bridge … on Lavitt's Quay. You must provision yourself for a minimum of 60 days of food for yourselves. A substantial undertaking, that. Mmm." Ryan consulted a pamphlet. "For each person, that requires, well, let's see, fuel for cooking, twenty pounds of flour per person, tea, coffee, suet, pickled tongue, salted pork, salted beef, peas, oatmeal, and the list goes on, sir. That is, of course, sir, according to the *Circular of the Irish Emigrant Society to the People of Ireland*, just published in February of this year. An unimpeachable source of information. A fine society it is, the Irish Emigrant Society. But not eleemosynary. No sir. They cannot assist you financially." He put the pamphlet down and continued. "But fear not, for Mr. Hopkins will advise you further. You should be prepared to spend—how much did you say Mr. Lamb has given you for the four of you as further allowance for passage? £5, 6 shillings, each? Yes, well, I know that leaves you with only 4 shillings for you and your family. But this voyage will pass you across the great Western Ocean—3,000 miles—in the greatest of comfort on the most modern packet ship in the Western Ocean trade—this is a most expensive undertaking, sir. The most important in your life."

Ryan looked up again at the man, who remained unmoving and wordless. He said, briskly, "Yes, good day to you, sir. Very nice to have met you and assisted you in such a complete manner. Yes. Good day."

The gaunt man retreated wordlessly into the front office, where he consulted briefly with Ryan's clerk and disappeared through the front door, leaving the faintly ringing doorbell as the only reminder of his existence.

Ryan looked up and called to us through the open door, his bluff and blarney brogue evident once more, "Father O'Muirhily, Mr. Gogan. Please do come in and put yersels' t'anchor right here."

I entered and he gestured to the leather chairs opposite his desk. "Mr. Gogan, how is Mr. O'Creagh? He be a great friend to me, indeed." Ryan scrutinized Séamas's letter, and said, "He says here ye'll be after the great journey across the Western Ocean to the New World." He looked at me expectantly, gesturing to the letter. He then looked at Father O'Muirhily, who smiled politely.

"Y-yes sir," I replied. "A great adventure it is, too, sir. I cannot wait."

"Quite." The blarney brogue disappeared once more. "Your cousin has purchased you passage in steerage. That is most unfortunate. No gentleman such as yourself should be travelling in steerage. Oh my. Never. It'd leave you in the suds, if you'll pardon the expression. Very uncomfortable. Very uncomfortable, indeed. And you won't be dining at the captain's table with fine wines like a flash cove. No, sir, no, indeed. All the ship'll give to eat is a bum charter. Worse'n the *Sassenagh* victualling at Richmond Gaol, I should think."

I winced inwardly.

"Not good. Not good at all."

After seeming to reflect for a moment, he said slowly, "Perhaps there has been a mistake." Then he continued more briskly, "But there's no time to send a letter to *mo comhbhrathair liom* to allow him to rectify this unfortunate circumstance. *Maryann* sails on the evening tide."

Ryan then paused again for a moment, and conferred with his clerk, who was still standing at his shoulder. He looked back at me and murmured collusively, "You know … I think that I may just be able to book you a second-class cabin for a mere £6 more. £8, 10 shillings for a second-class cabin on such a fine packet ship as *Maryann*, well …"

I thought of Cousin Séamas's admonition about pinchers, and replied, "I cannot afford that, sir, unless Cousin Séamas were to fund me."

"Ah, yes." Mr. Ryan sighed, looking pointedly at Father O'Muirhily. "He—Mr. O'Creagh—was quite clear in his letter that he was authorizing the expenditure of only the £2, 10 shillings—which is sufficient only for a steerage passage. Hmm. I do wish there were time to rectify this tiresome error. A fine lad such as yourself cannot be left in steerage."

Father O'Muirhily cleared his throat.

Ryan responded, "Father, with all due respect, my hands are tied."

"But surely, Mr. Ryan, something can be done. Young Master Gogan is a man of quality, who happens to find himself in unfortunate circumstances. I would counsel him to wait for the next ship. When is that, by the way?"

"*Dorchester*. Two weeks," Ryan replied without looking up from the desk. "Be more expensive. Far, far more expensive." Father O'Muirhily's response was no word of any language, but it was far from inarticulate in expressing his view. Ryan looked pleadingly at Father O'Muirhily. "'Struth, Father, I have no say over prices. They are set by the company. In London," he finished, querulously.

"I may be able to help," Father O'Muirhily said slowly.

"Father," I interjected. "I cannot possibly—"

"My son, it is the least I can do."

"Father, please. I cannot accept your offer. You have little enough, yourself. And I must preserve my capital."

Father O'Muirhily nonetheless reached into his pocket. I put my hand on his arm. Finally, he relented. "Well," he said gruffly, "perhaps for the best."

Ryan's face fell at the lost prospect. He scribbled for a moment and then handed me an envelope addressed to the master of the *Maryann*. "Here is your ticket, sir. The *Maryann*'s master has informed me that he will commence boarding at four o'clock, this afternoon. He intends to catch the evening tide, and commence passage to the New World post-haste. You will proceed there directly, I should think. But you must first secure your comestibles. Mr. Hopkins can assist you with your needs in that regard."

Ryan scribbled something further on a piece of foolscap and then folded it and sealed it with wax. He handed it to me, and said, "You may rely upon Mr. Hopkins's advice on all matters pertaining to your comestibles, Mr. Gogan." He looked me in the eye, and said evenly, "You may depend upon it."

"Thank you, sir," I replied just as evenly.

"Do not think of it," Ryan waved his hand. "The pleasure was entirely mine. Good day, sir, and a good swim to you. Good day, Father."

It was approaching four o'clock by my pocket watch (a gift from my father almost five years earlier, on the occasion of my departure to St. Patrick's), the hour appointed by the master of the *Maryann* to begin boarding, when Father O'Muirhily and I left Mr. Hopkins's chandlery and started to make our way to Lavitt's Quay, where the *Maryann* was berthed. As Ryan the shipping agent had promised, Hopkins and his clerk were honest. Even better, they were matter of fact about what I would need to do to survive. I intended to heed their words, and hoard my precious reserve of food for the harder times that inevitably lay ahead if—or perhaps, God forbid, when—the voyage stretched beyond the expected 50 or so days.

"First," Hopkins had said, "the ship be after feedin' yer the bare minimum required by law, which is just a meal at noon, hardtack and salt beef, and three quarts of water a day. Half of yer meat'll be rotten, the hardtack lousy with weevils and the water will be positively vile." But he cautioned me against trying to take water with me. Too heavy, he said. "And ye won't be able to store it safely. Some *spalpeen*'d just drink it the minute yer back be turned.

Thieving *bastúns*. Beggin' yer pardon, Father." He spat every bit as well as Cousin Séamas.

"What ye can do is take the right food." The list seemed endless—much as Ryan had described to the gaunt man—and the price seemed so very high. Fortunately, I thought, I am responsible only for my own well-being, and was not burdened with a family like the gaunt man. I could trust myself to husband my resources. I had to. I had no other choice.

Then there were the cooking utensils! I had never used a skillet, a cooking pot or bastable in my life—what was a bastable, anyway? That was what cooks were for. I stopped—that part of my life was over—for now, at the very least. I wondered how my skillet, cooking pot and flour were to produce breads. Well, time enough to learn. I also reflected that perhaps I was not quite so self-sufficient as I might have otherwise imagined.

The final insult was to learn that passengers had to supply their own mattresses—ticks as they were called. Straw ticks that could be shaken out topside during "titivate the ship." Apparently, passengers in steerage were responsible for cleaning their own quarters. Something to do with bedbugs and lice.

When the clerk had finished preparing my packages, I began pulling the necessary coins from my purse. Father O'Muirhily laid his hand upon my arm as I had done to him at Ryan's. "Allow me, lad. You would not allow me to make your life easier before. Let me do this for you now."

⌒

As we left Hopkins's shop, Father O'Muirhily held the door for me. I was staggering under the load—it is amazing the bulk of food required to keep one young man from starvation for fifty days or so, even on short rations and even in the form of tea, salt, flour, potatoes, prepared milk, a small quantity of tinned ham (a very new-fangled luxury in those days) and well-cured bacon, and it was all I could do to carry it. As I maneuvered my way through the door, a big-bellied shambling clown of a fellow brushed past me, all hot breath and the sour smell of not having bathed in a very long time. He knocked my packages to the ground without so much as a by-your-leave, and I could have sworn that the dastard sniggered, even as he muttered, "Beggin' yer pardon, Father." He did not offer to help pick up the packages.

⌒

It was bedlam quayside next to *Maryann*, and my arms were screaming with the fatigue of having carried the bulk of my provisions the better part of a quarter of a mile. Father O'Muirhily—thank God he was with me—was carrying the rest. He was visibly suffering, but he said not a word. People of virtually every walk of life were milling about on the quay next to the ship—from the poorest *spalpeen* to what appeared to be a pair of well-dressed gentlemen alternately manhandling baggage (there was a *spalpeen* aiding them, but he was being perfectly useless) and shooing along a pair of crying girls of five or six years of age. The wives were at a disdainful distance. Quality, the lot of them, and useless as such, as my father would have said. There were also quite a few families, each of whose members clustered around a matriarch ensconced on a pile of baggage, and whose children sometimes listlessly stood there, and at other times flitted about heedlessly as children will do. These families were scattered throughout the crowd in such a way as to perfectly impede progress up and down the quay.

To one side of the quay, near the *Maryann*'s bow, a trio of merry fellows, a fiddle, a flute and an uileann pipe, were playing one of those vaguely recognizable tunes that you always hear, wherever there is an Irishman playing music. A fourth man was briskly dancing a jig just in front of them. These four fellows, at least, were happy. On the quay opposite the middle of the ship, a table and chair were being set down for use by the medical officer—so said the sign that a sailor-looking fellow was holding over his head. Another sign said that every passenger was required by law to have his or her hand stamped by the medical officer before boarding the ship.

Not surprisingly, as soon as the table was set down, and even before a gentleman—presumably the medical officer—could sit in the chair, the crowd instantly enveloped the poor man and his table. The two sailors escorting him began to angrily shout "belay that" and "make way" in a futile effort to stop the prospective passengers from swarming around. Two more sailors rushed from the ship and began helping the first two herd the crowd into a long line. The effect was not unlike the drovers with the pigs on Merchants Quay earlier in the afternoon—except, this time there were no bloody lobsterbacks marching through the crowd to the beat of a drum and the wail of a martial flute.

We made our way to the back of the line, which now extended past *Maryann*'s stern. I resigned myself to being one of the last to board. As we stood there, I gave Father O'Muirhily a tentative smile, barely holding back some unbidden tears. "Half of me wants to take you up on the offer to go to Rome," I said to him. "Even a monastery might offer greater creature comforts than that old scow."

Father O'Muirhily looked appraisingly at the *Maryann*. "I dare say you're right about the monastery." He waved at the ship and said, "She's not likely to be a charter member of the Black Ball Line." He grabbed me by the shoulders with a look of genuine affection in his eyes. "My son, I will miss you. I do wish you could stay, finish school and help in the struggle to free Ireland. But it is better—and safer—if you leave for a very long time."

"Father." A man who appeared to be a sailor from the *Maryann* was looking solicitously at the priest.

"Yes, my son?"

"Ye shouldn't be at the back o' this line," the sailor said. "Let me help yers and the greenhorn board the ship with all them supplies."

Father O'Muirhily looked at him in surprise. "Oh, I'm not going. But my young friend is."

"Oh, well, Father, this line be only fer passengers. Steerage passengers, that is." The sailor addressed me, "Young 'un, I 'spect from the looks of you that ye'll be a deck passenger?"

"Steerage."

"Oh." The sailor studied me for a moment. "Well, then, ye'll be boardin' after all these folks," he said, gesturing to the line."

I nodded.

The sailor said, "Father, I'll have to be askin's yers to move along, as this line is for passengers only."

Father O'Muirhily and I looked at each other. There was nothing more for it. He embraced me, and muttered, "The best to you, my son, and Godspeed." Then he turned and vanished into the swirling crowd. I felt bereft. Shorn of the only man in Ireland who gave a damn as to whether I lived or died. Such thoughts brought Evelyn to mind as the only other human who gave a damn, and I missed them both terribly, the terrifying prospect of the New World looming behind my loneliness. I closed my eyes for a moment and then rejoined the bustling quay.

The two Quality families I'd seen earlier were ushered by a colored man—the first I'd ever seen—as quickly as dignity would allow to the head of the seething and roiling line of prospective passengers. I heard one of the Quality men say mockingly to the other as they passed me by, "I say, but there's a lot of them going in steerage. At this rate, with a few more ships, the sight of a Celt on the banks of the River Lee will soon be as rare as a redman on the banks of the River Hudson." One of the women asked querulously, "There are redmen on the Hudson? I thought the murderous heathen had long been cleaned out. Thomas, are we going to be safe in America?" I did not hear his response. The medical officer looked briefly at them, and they were whisked on board without further ado. I thought for an instant that perhaps

I should have allowed Father O'Muirhily to have paid for a second class cabin, as I was now trapped in this line of what must have been two hundred people and all their worldly possessions, one of whom was that damned big-bellied hayseed—*ina bronnadh cábóg*, Oonagh would have sniffed contemptuously—who'd knocked my packages to the ground outside Hopkins's chandlery. Fortunately, the lout did not turn around. But I had a feeling about him rather like a new boy does about a boorish bully of an upper classman.

Behind me in the line was a large family of several generations, positively vibrating with energy. Each was busy conversing with another and helping shuffle the family's great mound of possessions along as the line to the medical officer slowly moved forward. In front of me was a young woman with a small child, a girl of perhaps three or four. She seemingly had few possessions, just a couple of sacks hanging from a leather strap slung over her thin shoulder. Her daughter was clinging to her opposite hip. As the woman stepped forward, the strap holding the sacks over her shoulder slipped and caught at her elbow, almost knocking her over as her child's weight shifted involuntarily.

I couldn't help myself, and leaned forward courteously, "May I help you with your bags, ma'am?"

The woman turned to me, shocked at being addressed. Her isolation from all save her child had until now seemed complete, even on this quay swarming with humanity.

"Oh." The woman seemed to have difficulty finding her voice, as if she had not used it for some time. She then replied to me in as thick a mixture of Irish and English as you could find in an English-speaking Irish woman—or man, for that matter—"I be fine, an' ye'll be bowed down with all yer belongin's."

But the woman did not look as if she would be fine by herself. Her sacks had now slipped to her wrist, forcing her to drop them to the none-too-clean cobblestones of the quay. Her daughter twisted violently on her hip, almost knocking her over. I steadied the woman by the elbow.

"Please," I said. "I'll just take them with my bags until we get to the medical officer."

"The what?"

"The doctor, ma'am."

"Why we be seeing a *dochtuír*?"

We inched forward again, and I ignored the murmurings of the family behind us as I dragged our belongings. The child kicked down, and the woman put her to the cobblestones, admonishing her in Irish, spoken too quickly for me to follow. The little girl stood obediently by her mother's side, holding her hand and staring at me appraisingly.

The woman apologized to me for her daughter distracting her, explaining in her patois, "She be a regular *bairneach*, clinging to me, 'cept when she be wanting to be wanderin' about. And this place bein' so black wi' people." She flashed me a smile, revealing herself to be very pretty—beautiful, even, in a winsome manner— beneath her curly black hair, which gleamed in the weak sunlight. I looked at her closely. She could hardly have been twenty, even given her daughter, who was indeed clinging to her like a limpet. But she looked terribly tired, careworn even, when she wasn't smiling—although, as I studied her, there was something else there, a strength I could not quite define.

"But, of course, ma'am. The doctor has to look at you before you'll be allowed to board. Your daughter as well. The ship's captain is not allowed to board anyone who is sick."

The woman muttered quietly in Irish. I looked at her with a smile and hoped that she was right about her and her daughter being fine or healthy, or whatever exactly it was she had said.

We slowly moved to the front of the line. At the table, we were asked for our tickets, which were duly inspected. The medical officer looked at the three of us in one go, and waved his hand. A sailor reached out and marked each of our left hands with an "X" with a piece of charcoal. As he did, I could see my new companion look visibly relieved at having passed the medical officer's scrutiny.

Another sailor motioned us over to a group just to the side of the gangway leading to the ship. The family behind me clattered around us and over the gangway onto the ship with a great fuss and manipulation of children, bags and other possessions.

The sailor said to us, "Stay here, with these people, and we'll board you in turn."

With that, he departed. We waited with this group for about a quarter of an hour. The quay was much less crowded now as most of the passengers had already boarded. Finally, we were led onto the ship, and then forward, toward the bow. As we moved, I picked up my companion's strapped–together sacks with the rest of my belongings, conscious that I could barely pick it all up. She did not stop me, but instead swung her daughter to her hip and flashed me a smile of thanks.

We descended through the main deck hatch onto a steep ladder or set of stairs (it took me two trips to move everything, much to the consternation and impatient whispers of those behind me), and thence down into an instant, gloomy fug of the unwashed that overlaid a deeper, more ancient foetid smell I could not quite place. As the sailor leading us admonished us to "mind yer noggins," I instinctively ducked my head to avoid clipping it on a massive beam running the entire width of the ship. I wasn't tall, hardly more than five-and-a-half feet, but even I had to duck to avoid knocking my head on the deckbeams.

I jumped a little as the planks underfoot seemed to quiver as I walked over them. I looked down, and the planks seemed to have been placed over the beams below without being properly secured. Bunks were set in long rows, two high, and they appeared every bit as temporary as the flooring (the "decking," as I later learned) underfoot. The fug fully enveloped us as we moved farther aft and away from the hatchway, the way lit only by a flickering tallow candle in a glass jar held by the sailor guiding us. I noticed through the flickering gloom that small groups of people seemed to be sharing individual bunks.

As we proceeded aft, members of our group were peeled off and assigned bunks. Finally, as the compartment began to narrow, and ended in a rounded bulkhead that I realized was *Maryann's* stern, the sailor motioned to a bunk in the darkest corner of the hold. (The only natural light—and fresh air—in the entire compartment came from the main hatch many score feet forward of us.) He said to my companion and me, "This be yourn'. Plenty o' room for yers and the bantling."

With that, he was gone. My companion and I looked at each other. I flushed with embarrassment. The sailor had clearly thought we were a family, and had assigned the three of us to just a single bunk.

"I'll find somewhere else." I gathered my bag and my oilskin coat and turned to walk away.

As I realized that I was leaving behind every foodstuff that Father O'Muirhily had purchased for me, my companion grabbed my elbow and said, "There na' be nothin' else. Ye'll be stayin' here with me and Fíona."

"I couldn't ..." And I really couldn't. Sleep in a bunk with her? She was a woman, and one with a child. Where was her husband, for the love of God? I could hardly think of staying. What would my mother have said (had I known her when I was old enough to have understood her to express such a sentiment)? My companion touched my arm and said quietly, but firmly, "Ye'll stay, 'cuz if ye be *cúthail* wi' me, ye be after sleepin' up there, on deck." She gestured

46

to the overhead and smiled slightly. "Anyway," her smile broadened as she gestured to the packages sprawled upon the bunk, "what on earth would you do with all of this?" She continued, "Me name's Máire. Máire Skiddy. And this be *mo* wee *wain*, Fíona." Máire affectionately smiled down at Fíona and then kissed her quickly on the top of her head. Fíona looked up at me shyly, and smiled.

I was speechless. But I looked around at the crowded compartment, and reckoned that she was right—this bunk of Máire's was the only place I could sleep, and if I were too bashful—*cúthail*—to do so, and tried to sleep on deck, I'd probably be tossed from the ship as a stowaway. There truly was nowhere else for me to go.

"Thank you," I said.

Máire replied briskly in Irish, forcing me to translate slowly—something about my not needing to thank her. She continued, blithely unaware of my difficulties, "*Cén t-ainm atá ort?*"

"My name? What's my name?" I asked in surprise. Her Irish really was taxing my slender resources. "Billy. Billy Gogan."

Máire flashed her brilliant smile at me, and my heart unaccountably jumped. She mercifully switched back to English, "Nice t'be meetin' yers." She extended her hand as prettily as any lady of breeding. I took it and met her eye as I gently grazed the back of it with my lips. With another smile, this time small and inscrutable, Máire said to me, "An' ye be after callin' me 'Mary,' won't you? It's what all the toffs do."

"What's that?" I tried not to sound surprised.

If I did, she ignored me. "Use the *Sassenagh* instead of their given Irish name. Makes it easier to get on in the New World."

"I ..." I stopped and thought about Evelyn for a moment, and how curiously alike the two of them were, albeit from two entirely different worlds. But very alike, nonetheless. I smiled inwardly as I said earnestly, "I'll call you 'Mary,' then."

"Thank you, Billy." Mary gave me a huge smile this time, which was nonetheless tinged with shyness. Then she turned and looked at her few possessions and said matter-of-factly, "It's no' as if we've no room f'yers, Billy Gogan. I na' be after havin' a tick for Fíona' n'mesel'."

I said quickly, "I have a tick. You and Fíona will have it." I took my straw tick, which the chandler's clerk had rolled tightly for me and secured with twine and handed it to Mary, still not resolved about whether—or how—to share the bunk.

Máire looked at me solemnly, and said, "We'll share. I did wi' me brothers an' sisters 'afore I be married."

She then smiled at me, her eyes dark and amused under her curly hair, and very fetching. "I reckon ye had a feather tick growing up—and all to yersel' to boot." Her smile turned even more playful as she said in Irish, "a fine little rich maneen like yersel' in tha' big house." She then touched my coat lightly and finished, "And such fine clothing."

"I'm not rich," I replied in a whisper, looking away from her. "I wouldn't be here if I were. I don't have any family. I'm alone." I flushed with an empty despair. "My father is dead, and I've been sent away." I tried to recover my dignity a bit by muttering, "The clothing's decent enough, though."

Mary ignored my attempt at being a wiseacre, and apologized to me in Irish. She then drew her breath in and said to me in a rush, "Well, ye've got a family now, fer a while at least."

We stared at each other for a moment before Mary broke the silence, gesturing to our now-pooled possessions, "Let me arrange all of this. Can ye take Fíona from me for a moment?"

I looked at her curiously, trying to comprehend the concept of having acquired a family today—even if only temporarily. I was also trying to comprehend the prospect of sharing a bunk—and a tick—with Mary (or any woman, for that matter) and her daughter. Indeed, despite my maudlin response to her, Mary had been exactly right: I had never shared a bed with anyone. My mother had died when I was born, my father was a very proper gentleman who would never have shared his bed with anyone, and I certainly wouldn't have shared a bed with the housekeeper or with anyone at school. And what would Evelyn think of me, sharing my bed with a woman? The thought that Father O'Muirhily would understand, and perhaps even approve—he knew I was a gentleman, after all. So, too, perhaps Evelyn might appreciate the circumstances.

Mary was looking at me equally as curiously, and I realized that I must have been standing there, not responding, for quite some time. "Of course. I'll take Fíona on deck and show her the city—right now."

I swung Fíona up, and she sat compliantly, clinging to my shoulder as if she belonged there. We made our way on deck, where I put her down, and walked hand-in-hand to a spot on the side of the main deck away from the quay that seemed to be out of the way of the sailors who were bustling about, slamming shut the hatches to steerage and gradually coalescing into small groups beside the lines that secured *Maryann* to Lavitt's Quay, and in a larger group on the foc'sle. Just a few feet away from us, the three fellows who had been playing the fiddle, flute and uileann pipe on the quay earlier were playing once again, although nobody was dancing now. The few other passengers who had escaped the foetid compartment below before the hatches were secured were beginning to crowd between us and the fiddlers, watching the proceedings and doing their best to stay out of the way as *Maryann* prepared to leave her berth.

I looked across the waist of the ship to the quay, which was virtually empty now, save for a couple of navvies standing by the lines securing *Maryann* to the quay and a few hucksters who had not moved on from trying to sell useless trinkets to penniless emigrants before they boarded. A man with a tremendous handlebar moustache and wearing a battered blue felt cap and a long, dark blue wool coat—unbuttoned to reveal a nondescript and rather dirty white shirt above equally disreputable denim trousers—swaggered by, softly slapping a short, knotted whip in the palm of one hand—a starter, it was. I remembered my father having once told me about them when we visited the quays to look at the tall ships. Used to "start" laggard sailors, he'd said.

Just as the mustachioed sailor passed me, he produced a small, silver whistle and blew it loudly. Then he bawled a series of orders in a harsh voice that likely could have been heard across the harbor. An Englishman, he was, by the sound of him. Every sailor on the ship burst into action, retrieving the lines thrown over from the quay by the navvies who had been standing by. Behind me, a paddlewheeled steam tug secured by two lines to Maryann's bow blew her steam whistle in seeming acknowledgment, because her paddles began thrashing and Maryann shuddered gently as she pulled away from the quay. Every passenger on deck jumped at the blast. Even the fiddle, flute and uileann pipe players stopped momentarily, if only for a beat or two. Fíona squealed with delighted terror and put her arms around my neck as I knelt to comfort her. The tug pulled Maryann clear of Lavitt's Quay into the center of the river, and after a complicated maneuver, stood just a couple of yards off Maryann's bow.

Forward, a deep bass voice began singing:

> Oh! blow, me boys,
> I long to hear you!

Forward and aft, his shipmates chanted in reply in time with the hauling in of the lines:

> Blow, boys, blow!

The first sailor sang again:

> Oh! blow, me boys,
> I long to hear you!

Once again, the sailors replied:

Blow, my bully boys, blow.

As Fíona clung to my neck, I looked back over at the now almost completely deserted quay (the navvies and the few remaining peddlers had vanished seemingly into thin air). There were only two men standing there. One was Father O'Muirhily. He must have been virtually the only well-wisher seeing off the *Maryann* and her passengers. He was standing at the quay's very edge, his hand shading his squinting eyes, as if to catch one last glimpse of me before the ship disappeared down the River Lee. The other was a short man, clad head-to-toe in funereal black. He looked familiar, but it took me a moment to place him. I shivered to my very core when I realized where I'd seen him before—at St. Patrick's. Why I reacted so, I couldn't say. But it drove me to think first of poor Murray. Did he live, still? Then I remembered what Father O'Muirhily had said of the Young Irelanders and their fury at the Repeal Year's failure, although truth be told, what with the noise and the rambling nature of Father O'Muirhily's soliloquy, I'd not fully grasped what he'd been trying to tell me.

As I watched in curious fascination, the man in funereal black sidled over to Father O'Muirhily and almost pressed against him from behind. Father O'Muirhily lowered his hand and looked with seeming irritation at the intruder. Then he staggered a bit and toppled off the quay into the water. The man stood there, as if nothing untoward had occurred, looking right at me, it seemed, and I could have sworn that he acknowledged me with the merest tip of his top hat. Then he was gone. I looked around wildly at the hundred sailors and passengers on the ship and then back at the deserted quay and then back at the sailors and passengers crowding the deck. Not one of them had reacted. I looked again at the water. There was no sign of Father O'Muirhily. I lurched forward, suddenly conscious of not wanting to drop Fíona.

A sailor practically tackled me, snarling, "Ye fuckin' daft mick. Watch yer great galumphin' hooves."

"Did you see the man on the quay fall into the water?"

"What're ye sayin', ye bloody oaf?"

"A man fell in the water. A priest. I can't see him anymore. We must rescue him."

"Bloody hell. There ain't no man in the water."

"We have to stop. We have to go back to the quay."

The sailor grabbed my arm roughly. I almost dropped Fíona. "Get back, ye daft buffle-head. We ain't doin' nuttin' but puttin' t'sea an' sailin' the Western Ocean."

"I must talk to the captain. The first mate. Anyone!" Fíona clung tightly to me. I was conscious of acting the utter fool. The man on the pier had murdered Father O'Muirhily as surely as the sun had risen that morning, and literally no one other than I had seen it. I looked again at the water. There was no sign of Father O'Muirhily. Dear, loving God.

"What's this?" The handlebar-mustachioed Englishman I'd seen earlier was sticking his face in mine. "What's this about a man falling in the water?"

"There." I pointed. "Right there. I cannot see him anymore. We must save him."

"Lad," the Englishman was starting to get exasperated. "T'ain't no one there. If a man had fallen in, he'd be thrashing about and we'd save his fool carcass. Happens all the time. Careless sand crabs are always falling overboard. Silly bastards."

"Sir—"

"I ain't no 'Sir', laddybuck. You may call me Mr. Mounce. I be the first mate."

"Mr. Mounce, I believe I knew the man. Father O'Muirhily. He—" I choked involuntarily, tears burning my eyes. "He's a friend of mine."

"Look, laddie, ye don't seem the run-of-the-mill simpleton like the rest of these paddies. But what in tarnation are ye talkin' about?" He grabbed my shirt collar and thrust me to the gunwale. I almost lost grip of Fíona in the process. "There's no man in the water. See?" I stared at the choppy, murky water. There still was not a single sign of Father O'Muirhily. "Now, lad, we'll have no more of such foolishness. Get back with the others."

With that, I was thrust back to the lee side, and I stood numbly, watching the steam tug take a towline and slowly tow *Maryann* down the River Lee, Cork City slowly receding into the distance.

It was some time later, after the sun had set and the sky was deepening into night, when Fíona snuggled up against me and whispered in my ear, "Billy? I saw the priest fall into the water. An' then I didn't see him anymore after that. Was he your friend?"

$\backsim$

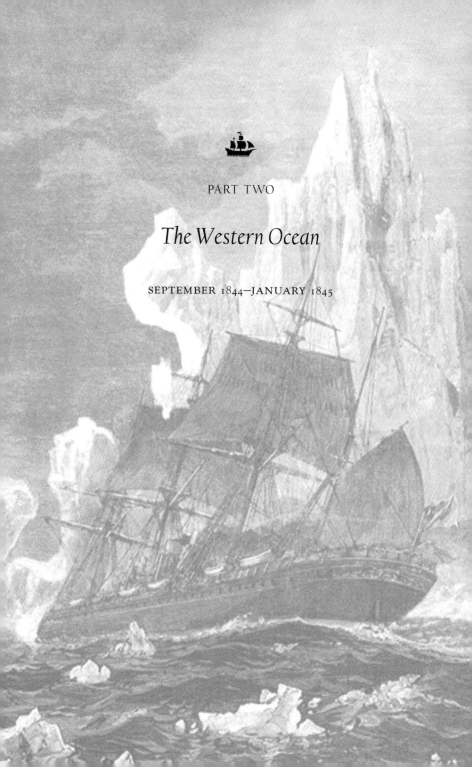

PART TWO

The Western Ocean

SEPTEMBER 1844–JANUARY 1845

CHAPTER 4

Anchored

⌐

THE TUG TOWED US SLOWLY PAST BLACK ROCK CASTLE and into Lough Mahon. I did my best to entertain Fíona, but my heart wasn't in it. By and by, I found a comfortable place out of the way and sat on the deck, my back against the skylight venting the steerage compartment. Fíona, bless her soul, sat with me, content to let me brood. The only man who had cared a whit about whether I lived or died was dead. I had watched him be murdered, and I had done nothing to help him. My ineffectual exchange with the first mate did nothing to assuage my overwhelming sense of helplessness— and downright incompetence, if the truth be told. I should have leapt over the side to save him. Done something. Anything.

It didn't occur to me for a very long time, so well was I stewing in the juices of my own inadequacy and grief, to question why Father O'Muirhily had been murdered in so brazen a fashion. And then I became seized by a fit of paranoia—the man in funereal black had looked directly at me as he murdered Father O'Muirhily, which must have meant that I was somehow implicated. The renewed realization that the man in funereal black had also been at St. Patrick's the day I learned that my father died and I had been sent down from school only further cemented the fantastical sense of paranoia that paralyzed me. I could feel myself sweating and shaking, my heart pounding. It was only very gradually that the urge to scream in frustration (or fear, I wasn't sure which) didn't overwhelm me. But whether I should—or even could—have done something to save poor Father O'Muirhily remained a burden that I could not resolve. Fíona remained wordlessly glued to my leg, her face buried in my thigh, and there was naught I could do to cheer her up.

After some hours—the sun long since set—the crew opened the hatches, and those of us on deck were peremptorily commanded to go below. Fíona and I had hardly even cleared the combing when the hatches slammed shut above us. Fíona huddled closer to me in fright, but didn't utter a sound. I found Mary sitting on the bunk, where our belongings were neatly stowed, and the tick was covered by my father's oilskin. Mary seemed not to notice Fíona's or my distress. I was thankful for that, for I didn't have the words to describe to my traveling companion what had just happened. I hardly knew her, and with every moment, I was becoming increasingly aware of her as a woman. Instead, Mary explained apologetically that the oilskin was the only blanket we had. "But the pot and bastable and frying pan are perfect," she enthused. "Much nicer than mine." She paused a little uncertainly.

I looked at Mary sharply. She had had no pots in the sacks I had carried on board for her. Then it dawned on me: she'd lost most of her possessions. The scope of her apparent disaster hung between us.

"You don't have any food either, do you?"

"*Chaill mé teaghlachas*," she said softly, confirming that she'd indeed lost most of her things, if I understood her correctly.

"Well, you and Fíona'll share my food with me."

Mary retreated to Irish in responding to me—as if to protect herself. I followed her only with difficulty, gleaning that she and Fíona would not share my food.

"No." I reacted curtly to her protestation. "Sharing is exactly the right thing to do—the Christian thing. We'll make do. You and the child cannot starve, and the ship's victuals won't be enough."

Tears started at the corners of her eyes, and she crossed herself as she muttered in Irish some blessing or another from God. Then she said, "*Is tusa mo chúisle.*" You are such a dear.

At that moment, a sailor came through the compartment bawling: "Lights out. All lights out. Passengers must stay below until you muster in the morning … lights out …" He moved forward, continuing his chant.

In the sudden near darkness, it seemed as if there was no one in that compartment but Mary. I could feel her presence rather than see it. I stood stock-still for a moment, very unsure of what I should be doing. Fíona squirmed by. Mary said to me very matter-of-factly, "Fíona … *Beidh sí ag codladh eadrainn.*" Fíona will sleep between us. "But you get in first," she said softly. I brushed by her, my mind in a state it had never been before. Fíona clambered in next, and lay there, seemingly asleep before her head had even touched the tick. I lay there for a very long time, very conscious of Mary and her nearness—even though the squirmy box of energy that was the sleeping Fíona lay between us. Mary shifted, and our feet inadvertently touched. She withdrew her foot as if she'd been stung. But her touch lingered on, reinforced as the night wore on, and Mary once again shifted in her sleep in reaction to Fíona's movement and our feet touched yet again. Unbidden thoughts came to my mind, and left me very discontented with myself.

⌒

I awoke to the piercing twitter of a pipe and bawling cries of, "All passengers on deck. Get a move along now. Look lively."

Hardly had the cries finished than several crew members, who must have slipped down into the berthing compartment the instant that it was opened, began swearing at us and punching and shoving us up the ladder and onto the main deck, and herding us aft with much commotion until we were looking up at the quarterdeck. Amidships, his hands on the beautifully polished railing at the forward end of the quarterdeck, and dressed in a magnificent—and immaculate—fawn-colored greatcoat, stood a big man, hard-faced with harder eyes, lord of all he surveyed.

This, then, must have been the captain. As a pipe whistled harshly, the captain raised his arm, and we passengers quietened expectantly. "I am Aloysius Quincy Urquehart, and I am the master of this fine barky." He sounded American—or what I thought an American should sound like, and his voice had a hard quality to it that matched precisely the hardness in his eyes.

He looked over the passengers as he spoke, "Disobey me or disobey my mates, and I'll have you clapped in irons. Mutiny, and it'll be the death of you. These are my mates." He gestured to three equally hard-looking men standing on either side of him, arms folded, one of whom was the mustachioed Englishman.

The captain looked over the passengers once more, and said, "We anchored last night in Lough Mahon, to await a fair wind. In the meantime, my first mate, Mr. Mounce, will acquaint you with a few of our rules. Follow them, and all will be well. Disobey them and ... Perhaps it is best for you to just remember that I am the master of God, and Mr. Mounce stands at my right hand."

Out of the corner of my eye I saw the *bronnadh cábóg* who'd knocked over my packages outside the chandlery smirking to himself. I also saw one of what appeared to be the mates (he was standing at the captain's left shoulder) frown at the fellow's bad manners.

With a flourish, the captain bowed to the mustachioed Englishman, who said in that harsh, stentorian voice of his, "First, this is the quarterdeck. No steerage passengers allowed up here. Ever. Second, go on the fo'csle, an' I'll have you flogged. Third ..." and he began to drone on reciting lists of rules and regulations for above a quarter of an hour. I drew a certain satisfaction from how the *bronnadh cábóg*'s face fell as each succeeding rule presumably further crimped what he seemed to feel were the rights and privileges due him.

We were to be confined to steerage at night. Access to the weather decks—the topside decks—was to be restricted in bad weather. When we could—and could not—go topside was to be communicated to us via the mate's pipe. We received a sudden and lengthy demonstration of the shrilling pipe which had roused us from sleep and herded us to deck. There was more: we were to be fed once a day, at eight bells of the forenoon watch—mid-day to us lubbers. Each afternoon, we would also have access to the ship's galley—in shifts of twenty, one representative for each family or travelling party—to cook the second meal of the day. If someone was not with a travelling party, then that *fuadh bocht*—my words, not Mr. Mounce's, as I remembered the gaunt man at Murray, the shipping agent's office, and wondered what had become of him— had better join a party post-haste.

Mr. Mounce also announced to us that we would be electing a representative from steerage to communicate with him. No one else was to communicate with Mr. Mounce, and no one was ever to communicate with the Captain, not even our representative. "Is that understood?" The question was as equally rhetorical as it was belligerent.

Our representative apparently was to be a man of considerable power. He was to be in charge of us in every way. He was to direct us in keeping steerage clean. Sweepers would be piped every day. There was another sudden demonstration of the mate's pipe.

And on it went. Eventually, Mr. Mounce dismissed us. The men from steerage gathered around, and with a great debate and harrumphing elected as our representative one of the apparently few men who could read and write, a thin little fellow named Mr. O'Hurley, who had once been a parish clerk. The *bronnadh cábóg* had been a vociferous supporter, extoling the learned Mr. O'Hurley's qualities as a brave and virtuous man who would help us all in *ár slíghe go Mheiriceá*, our passage to America, the prom- ised land.

Mr. O'Hurley's first act was to lead us in prayer, and *ina bron-nadh cábóg* was chief among the prayerful. We then had to clean steerage, which apparently meant that the men stood around and the women-folk did all the work in the curious half-light of flickering lanterns and shadowed beams of light from the vents and hatchways. As the women worked, the children coalesced to play, and some began running around wildly until one irritated mother said to another, "Ha' ye no' *smacht* o'er yer childer?"

Thus did the day start, as did each of the next three days (with our being harangued for our collective shortcomings by Mr. Mounce, rather than the ship's master, whom we saw only sporadically at most, and then only as he paced the quarterdeck, God-like in his isolation). During those four days, we endured squalls of wind and rain that rocked the ship at anchor and caused many to be violently ill. At night, the stench in steerage was almost unbearable. In the mornings, the women-folk cleaned the compartment as best they could while the men watched. I tried to help Mary on the first morning. She simply shooed me off, directing me to take Fíona with me. She didn't care where we went, just so long as we were not underfoot.

But even after the women cleaned and organized, the passenger compartment remained horribly crowded—and fetid. The situation in which Mary and Fíona and I found ourselves—the three of us sharing a bunk—was no different than in virtually every other bunk. Entire families shared a single bunk if the children were small enough. Sometimes, they shared even if the children were not quite so small. Single passengers also shared, men with men and women with women, with two or three to each bunk.

Then there were the supplies and the baggage. Mary had packed our belongings very neatly—and well out of the way. Others were not so efficient. Bags of foodstuffs, pots, pans, and every other manner of flotsam and jetsam were stacked in every passage between the long fore-and-aft columns of bunks, often occluding them. Such a situation was intolerable to the neigh-boring passengers, who would quickly rectify it by heaping moral opprobrium upon the offending family or party of passengers. Occasionally, a little rough justice came into play—the offend-ing goods were simply stacked on the offending party's bunk. Only once or twice did I see Mr. O'Hurley become involved. And the result was little different: the swift execution of rough justice—with in*a bronnadh cábóg* serving as a righteous enforcer—a bit of grumbling and an occasional muttered threat by one or two of the men of the offending party.

The relative peace in the overcrowded compartment was greatly aided by the lack of poteen. Some of the men, particu-larly the younger ones—Mary tartly referred to them as *reathaí* or "wild men"—had brought onboard quarts, and in some cases gal-lons, of the smoky peat-flavored liquor to keep themselves well peloothered during the coming voyage. In one of his first acts as the passengers' representative, not long after he had concluded his prayer of thanks after being so installed, Mr. O'Hurley, a teetotal-ling adherent of the Apostle of Temperance himself, had conferred with Mr. Mounce regarding the poteen and the *reathaí*.

Within the hour, the two of them had promptly instituted a search of the compartment for all liquor, confiscating many doz-ens of bottles, canteens and flasks as well as scores of every other sort of container capable of holding liquor. The second and third mates and the couple of other sailors whom Mr. Mounce could trust to help him and Mr. O'Hurley in their stem-to-stern search may have been seen as reliable men, but they had not been happy about having to help. I am sure, though, that life in steerage ended up being quieter (and far less violent) than if the liquor had been consumed by the *reathaí* late at night, keeping every other living soul in the compartment wide awake and seething with resent-ment and anger. I supposed that some of the poteen, at least, must have been thrown overboard. But I was quite confident that much of it ended up in the foc'sle—where the crew's quarters lay—to be used (medicinally, of course) to ward off the chill of the autumn nights during the voyage.

The deckhouse was home to the six people of Quality we had seen hustled onto the ship before everyone else. Their every whim and desire was catered to by the colored man I'd seen escort them onboard the ship when we all boarded at Lavitts Quay. They ran him him from dawn until dusk with their petty demands, treating him worse than I'd ever seen even the most miserable of servants treated in Ireland. He seemed to rarely speak to anyone in the crew, and then only to apologetically tug at his forelock at communicating some demand or another from the Quality. Captain Urquehart ignored the poor man, even when he brought coffee up to the quarterdeck.

Unlike us steerage passengers, the six Quality could spend their topside hours on the quarterdeck—just as long as they steered clear of Captain Urquehart and Mr. Mounce. The two couples mostly feigned to ignore us as if we weren't there. On the odd occasion when proximity forced social intercourse, the two women, a pair of frozen witches enveloped by their starched cabriolet bonnets fringed in lace and ringed by their icy Anglo-Irish disdain as they scolded their respective beribboned daughters about, treated those unlucky enough to cross their paths as mere vermin underfoot. Their husbands spent their time unctuously kowtowing to their wives when they weren't strolling about, endlessly talking with each other. One of the men persisted in wearing his top hat until the wind blew it overboard on the second or third day. In my former life, I had been the social superior of these people. But here, I didn't quite know what to think about where I stood with them. Mary sniggered derisively in an unguarded moment, calling the two women *badhbh craythurs*.

We also learned during these few days how little food we would receive from the ship's cook—who was known to all as "doc" or the "doctor"—small helpings of watery soup, occasionally weevilly ship's biscuit and hard cheese or salted meat. Mary was amused when I explained to her that there was no real doctor on board, so the ship's cook was our source of medical help. The comestibles that Mr. Hopkins the chandler had pressed me to buy allowed the three of us to meagerly supplement what we received each mid-day—and I do mean meagerly, as there were now three of us. Mary prepared our food in the ship's galley, which was just forward of the mainmast, competing with three-score or so other women, who cooked in shifts all afternoon long. The galley was a tiny affair, surrounded by three goats in one pen, two sheep in another and a flock of hens in the poultry pens, which supplied fresh eggs for the captain, his three mates and the six cabin passengers.

Mary conjured more cooking miracles than most, producing delectable cakebread made in the bastable forced upon me by Mr. Hopkins the chandler, as well as tea (hot, if we were fortunate, usually it was merely tepid and full of tea leaves), bolstering it with a bit of tinned ham and potatoes fried to perfection in grease or lard—when we could get it. So it was quite unremarkable that, on the very first day, she shooed me away from my rather pathetic attempt at cooking in the galley, telling me to the vast amusement of the other women there that cooking was a woman's work and, anyway, I didn't have the faintest idea what I was doing—which was true enough. I was happy to leave the cooking to Mary. My only worry—save one—was whether we would consume all of our own food before the ship could depart Lough Mahon and the distant sight of Cork City up the River Lee.

⌁

I was surprised during those few days to find that the wreckage of my childhood seemed very distant. Perhaps it was the isolation in the alien environment of a ship far from the rest of the world—even if I could see a smudge of land on the horizon when the weather was clear. But I think it had much to do with Father O'Muirhily's unjust and unwarranted murder being the very essence of Ireland having forsaken me. I had thus resolved quickly to forsake Ireland and make my way in the New World, come what may. My only lingering obligation to the Old World was my promise to write to Evelyn, and I didn't see that as an obligation, but more paying homage to an ethereal being whom I was unlikely ever to see again.

My father had always been a constant in my life. He was still, but I now found him coming to mind in the things I did and said, and even in my very mannerisms. I found it comforting, rather than sharpening my grief at his death, alone in that *Sassenagh* jail. By contrast, poor Murray and the vision of the red cricket ball striking his head with a sickening crack seemed to have become a story told by someone else, although truth be told the awful sound of Murray's skull cracking did seem to worm its way into my consciousness late at night, as Fíona squirmed next to me and I listened to the night sounds of the crowded and noisome passenger compartment. But a touch of Mary's foot against mine as she turned in the night was always enough to banish all thoughts of Murray and I inevitably lay awake, confabulating with myself over the wonder of it all.

A more immediate worry was the *bronnadh cábóg*, all sour breath and toadying to Mr. O'Hurley. I had spotted him one day, a sickening smile on his face, apparently saying something to Mary while she was cooking. Mary flushed. When I asked her about the dastard later and whether I should confront him about his rudeness, she told me in Irish, "It be nothin', *mo chúisle*," and not to worry myself about him. When I tried to argue with her she glared at me, and I concluded that she would brook no further discussion.

CHAPTER 5

An t-Anfa Mor
(The Great Tempest)

⌒

THE WINDS MUST HAVE TURNED FAVORABLY during our fourth night at anchor, because on the morning of the fifth day, when we passengers were mustered on deck for our morning roll call, the coast of Ireland was on our starboard side as the ship sailed in a gently rolling sea, southwest to the Atlantic. I spent the day with my book topside. I had found a quiet, out-of-the-way place to read under one of the two ship's boats that *Maryann* carried on her main deck. They were secured bottom up by strong lines to a frame over the skylight, which vented the steerage compartment. The oars were lashed to the bench-like seats in the boat, ready for use. I found that, even in rainy weather, I could slide unnoticed underneath one of the boats, and quietly read to my heart's content. When Mary was producing one of her wonderful concoctions in the ship's galley for the afternoon meal, I watched Fíona, which usually meant watching the seas and the sky with her or reading to her from *The Last of the Mohicans* as she sat in my lap. After a day or two, she was able to pick out letters and words, and was well on her way to learning to read. I took an immense pleasure in her progress.

One night, just after lights were out and the hatch to steerage battened down until morning, Mary asked me in a whisper about *The Last of the Mohicans*. I gave her an overview. She asked me what a mulatta was, and why it mattered that Cora was a mulatta. For wasn't Cora simply the Scottish Colonel's daughter just like her younger sister, Alice, and thus herself a proper lady with serving girls like her, Mary, at her beck and call in the great house? I was at a loss to explain why. I mumbled something about it being just the proper order of society. White men and colored women simply could not be together, any more than colored men could lie with white women. Mary said that was stupid. She told me that she was glad to have left Ireland where it was the proper order for her, Mary, to always be the servant girl. Not in Amerikay, she declared, trying to say "America" in English, and not in Irish, which was "Meiriceá," and sounded just like "'Merikay." I pronounced "America" for her, and she said that she would pronounce the word just like a proper toff. She emphasized the word when she told me that she was going to be a proper lady in America, just like Alice and just like Cora should have been. And Fíona would be reading a hundred books just like *The Last of the Mohicans*. With that, she snuggled chastely with me, and I lay awake, full of tortured thoughts.

On the third day at sea, though, Mary woke up with a fever and chills: a wee *fiabhras*, as she called it. She tried to brush it aside. But she grew progressively weaker as the day wore on. I left her to sleep through most of the day, keeping Fíona with me. I also did my best with the afternoon cooking. One of the other women helped me make some pea soup, which I fed to Mary in the bunk. I sat with her for some hours, alternating holding her and letting her toss uncomfortably. Finally, she slept again. Fíona slept with her, and I slipped away on deck for some fresh air before we were locked down for the night.

I idled by the railing near the foc'sle, on the larboard side, which was the ship's lee side, away from the wind and sea harrying the ship on her weather side. I was alternately gazing at the iron gray horizon to the southwest and then down at the water roiling and hissing past the gunwale hardly more than a couple of feet below me. The sun, bright if without much heat during the day, had set during the quarter of an hour I'd been standing there, leaving a crisp, chilly blue, almost black, sky to the east—a marked contrast to sunrise that morning, which had been a glorious orange and scarlet haze sweeping the night away.

The ship's boy whom I'd tried to tell about Father O'Muirhily's murder sidled up alongside me, leaning equally as idly against the gunwale. We stood in quiet company for a few moments before he stuck his hand out and said, "You're that greenhorn who saw the man drown as we were pulling away from the quay in Cork town."

I stiffened, ready to defend myself.

"Don't be gittin' all-fired with me, bub." He smiled disarmingly. "You waren't exactly off your thatch about it."

I looked at him, dumbfounded.

"Yeah, I heard tell that one o' the foretop hands might 'a' seed somethin'."

My mind boggled. The ship's boy looked at me with a certain empathy. I finally asked, "Why didn't anyone—?"

"Anyone?" he asked archly. "The only 'anyone' on this barky be the Old Man, an' he's a hard customer, if there ever was one."

"But this was—"

"Accidental?"

"But—"

"You'd be beating your head against the wall. Anyhoos, bub, who's gonna do anythin' about it now?" He swept his hand across the horizon. I shook my head. "Look, man," he said, "you're okay. But there ain't nothin' t'be done about that poor cove, God rest his soul. Whatever happened."

Someone other than myself and Fiona who may have seen something. I didn't know what to make of it. Here we were, hundreds of miles into the Atlantic. What was I to do? The unspoken words rang in my mind as weak and kittenish, and I reviled myself for it. In the next instant, I felt a strange sense of relief, for what Fiona and I had seen was indeed real. Of course, that brought crashing back the almost crippling sense of paranoia about the identity of Father O'Muirhily's killer and the cold, hard fear that Father O'Muirhily's death was somehow related to me. Then it was all so very clear and obvious. When the ship landed in New York, I was going to be far away from whatever had happened on the quay in Cork, safe in the anonymity to be afforded by the New World. I would therefore mourn poor, dear Father O'Muirhily, but I would never speak of him or his murder or my paranoid suspicions to anyone, ever again.

"Hey …" The ship's boy was smiling at me disarmingly as I returned from my wandering thoughts. "I'm Jeremy."

"Billy. Good to meet you." We both reached out and shook hands. As we did, I looked at him more closely, consciously disregarding my inner turmoil and equally consciously resetting my relationship with Jeremy to disregard what had just passed between us. "You're an American?"

"Shore am. A reg'lar Brother Jonathan, I am," he said with a slow smile.

"Brother Jonathan?"

"Ayut. From up Boston-way." He pronounced it "Bahstun," rather than "Boston," which was the name of a largish city in *Sassana*, in a curiously nasal accent that struck me only now, some minutes into our talk. He continued by way of explanation, "You can call me a Jonathan, Yankee, Uncle Sam, downeaster—any o' them names is good. Boston's northeast of Gotham itself, which is where we're headed. Yessirree. That's where we're headed. Gotham City." He stared at the horizon. "'Ceptin', t'ain't gonna be easy. We're in for a right powerful blow. See that?" He pointed to the gray band along the horizon, which blurred imperceptibly into the sea.

I looked again, this time with a more clinical interest.

"That, pal, is a nor'wester gittin' ready to blow, I reckon—as opposed to the nor'easter we see back home. No siree. We're gonna get a blow from over there, pointing northwest to the windward side of the ship, along the starboard bow. It's gonna come in hard, maybe tomorrow some time. Like I said, it'll be a powerful blow."

I had imagined that we would be spending the rest of the Western Ocean passage much as we had done during these past few days: rolling in the swells, some spray as the ship leaned before the wind to her lee side, sometimes almost to the level of the main deck, a little rain and blustery wind—and the bitter edge of chill that cut to the very core. All of it meant hardship at times. Women and babies would get sick and fretful. But it was something to be lived through, to be survived.

"When you say, 'powerful blow'," I asked slowly. "What exactly do you mean?"

"Well," he replied in that nasally voice of his, "it's like this. The Western Ocean is a powerful big place. An' dangerous, to boot. Ice to the north in the winter. Great winter gales in front of us, and the Gulf stream to the south, which we can't go through. At least not direct-like. So we've got to go north, dodging the gales when we can, grinding through them when we can't, and stayin' south of the ice fields. Would've been better in the summer time. But it's fall now, an' it'll be getting on to winter in a few weeks. And the closer we get to winter, well…"

"Not something that bears thinking about," I finished.

"I reckon that's about right, pal. I gotta tell ya, I'd be a hull lot happier in a packet ship. They can weather a nor'wester a hull lot better'n this fine barky."

"You mean a Western Ocean packet like *Fidelia?*" I asked in a conscious display of knowledge, borne of a visit with my father to the quays of Dublin before the madness of the Repeal Year consumed him.

"Ya know about her? A Gotham barky. She's a right likely 'un. Me, I'm a downeaster. So I'm partial to Boston-built barkies. There's this new fella up there, Donald McKay, working with the Enoch Train line. His clipper, *St. George.* They reckon she can do the run in under 14 days, going full chisel. She'll be like greased lightning, I'm figgering." He warmed to his task, "Put them lime juicers to shame. A right lubberly tribe, they is. But they ain't bad folk. They just ain't sailors like us Yankees is."

I piped in, "*Fidelia* was beautiful." I looked around at *Maryann*. "Not like this. The shipping agent told us *Maryann* was the finest packet ship on the Western Ocean."

Jeremy laughed derisively. "That's a bodacious lie if I ever did hear it. You know what this barky is?" He continued without waiting for a reply. "She's a reg'lar one-horse scow. She's older than Methuselah hisself. Been hauling timber this past 20 years or more. And ya know what really beats the dutch?"

"What?" I asked, slightly stupified.

He laughed again. "She ain't never hauled paddies 'afore. First time. Who'd 'a thunk that?"

"So that's why the passenger compartment looks all thrown together?"

"Ya mean that it's all ahooey?" Jeremy smiled.

"Ayut," I imitated him.

"We'll make a Jonathan of you yet," he cracked. "Yeah, that's exactly why. Soon as we dump all them paddies in Gotham, all that lumber gets torn out and we ship timber outta Halifax 'n' back to Liverpool."

"Yeah. I guess that ain't no brown salve," I said, using my best public school slang to indicate my marked lack of surprise at Jeremy's news that *Maryann* was no regular packet ship, but instead was a cargo ship hauling timber from the New World to the Old and, until now, God knows what back to America.

Jeremy ignored my effort and asked, "What do you think of the Old Man?" He looked up at the quarterdeck, where the captain, resplendent in his immaculate fawn greatcoat, was pacing steadily, hands clasped behind him, from one side of the ship to the other between the ship's wheel and the quarterdeck railing.

I shrugged.

"He don't care about *Maryann* bein' a one-horse scow an' all, an' he don't care whether he's hauling timber to Liverpool or paddies to Gotham, I reckon. He figgers he'll bring her to Gotham an' home to Liverpool which whatever way." Jeremy fixed his eye on me and said, "That Old Man is one hard citizen, though. Has to be—a Yankee running with them lime juicers on this Liverpool barky."

We both leaned back over the railing, eyeing the horizon and contemplating the morrow and, on my part at least, congratulating myself on my decision to bury my past.

"So, what about this storm?" I asked.

"Red sky in morning, sailors take warning; red sky at night, sailors delight," Jeremy quoted. "Ever heard that?"

"Sure. Even farmers and shepherds know that," I said with an air of knowledge.

"Yeah," Jeremy responded slyly. "Ever'body knows it. But not many unnerstand it, does they? It's from the Bible. Matthew:

> The Pharisees also with the Sadducees came, and
> tempting desired him that he would show them a
> sign from heaven.
>
> He answered and said unto them, When it is
> evening, ye say, It will be fair weather: for the sky
> is red.
>
> And in the morning, It will be foul weather today:
> for the sky is red and lowering."

"Sure you ain't Catholic?" I joked. "You know the Bible better 'n' a prating Levite at the local cathedral."

"My ma beat it into us when I was young, 'afore my old man picked up and absquatulated, and she took to the bucket shop and croaked from the foot juice," Jeremy said flatly. He didn't look at me, but instead looked over the railing and contemplated the hissing wake for a moment.

"Sorry," I said instinctively.

"It don't get my Irish up nohow. Been a coon's age since she croaked," Jeremy replied bleakly. "You're lucky you have family, the woman and the wee one."

"Family? No, they're not family. I met them on the quay before boarding."

"That so? But you're traveling together?"

"Seems so."

Jeremy gave that a moment's thought, then said, "You don't have no family neither?"

"No," I replied heavily. "My father died earlier this year. That's why I'm headed to the New World." I smiled as bleakly as Jeremy had. "My mother died when I was born."

"Sorry to hear that."

We lapsed into silence for a moment, and then Jeremy shook it off and said, "When the sun rises in the morning and it shines blood red, that most o' the time means bad weather because the good weather has passed to the east in the night. If the sky's red at dusk, then, well, maybe good weather be coming. 'Member yesterday's sky? All them high clouds 'n' such?"

"Yeah."

"Well, them mare's tails was another sign of a blow coming."

"So, we 'batten down the hatches'?" I asked.

"Ayut," Jeremy replied.

The next day, we awoke to freshening seas and rain squalls coming from the northwest, off *Maryann*'s starboard bow. I soaked a dirty shirt of mine in the rain and used it to cool Mary's burning forehead. I held her close as I lay the cloth on her head, and she slept in my arms. When Mary awoke some time later, she seemed much better. She smiled and called me "*mo ghrá*" in the way that a mother praises her child. She then slept some more.

We couldn't cook that day, as the weather had turned too rough to light any fires. Sweepers was a mess as well. A few people more were becoming seasick now, and the womenfolk were struggling to keep up. As usual, the menfolk were largely absent from the housekeeping efforts. And it was getting noisier in the compartment: babies were crying, toddlers were fussing and even the older children were looking a little apprehensive.

The woman who had helped me cook yesterday asked me how Mary was. I told her that Mary had a touch of *slaghdán*, a bit of a cold, but that she was on the mend. I didn't know what was wrong with Mary, but I surely didn't want to raise any alarms. The woman offered to look after Fíona, who was playing with one of her children while Mary slept. I readily agreed, and then escaped topside to my sheltered spot under the ship's boat. On impulse, I took my oilskin. Mary had bartered for a proper blanket some days earlier, and was now swaddled in it as she slept.

When I emerged topside, I was surprised by how much angrier the seas had become, smashing up broad on *Maryann's* starboard bow. Her sail was shortened—partially reefed—and heeling her far over to larboard, and she was plowing across the waves, her bow pounding up and down like a restless horse. The resulting foam hissed insistently by the lee side, almost broaching the gunwale.

Jeremy ran by me as I was heading to my hiding place and called out to me: "We are in for a blow—jes' as I said."

Any reply I could have made would have been lost in a sudden gust of wind, which heeled the ship over even further. The foam from the lee side kicked over the gunwale and splashed me as I made my way to the ship's boats and slipped under them, out of the rain. I was glad I had left my book below in my bag with my clothes, because I would have ruined it otherwise.

No sooner had I reached my spot than the crew began closing the hatches to steerage after having shooed back down into the compartment a couple of brave souls who were still on deck, getting drenched by the sea spray and rain. They then battened down the hatches, securing them tightly, rolling tarpaulins over the top of them and nailing thin pieces of wood—the battens, I later learned—into the hatch coaming to hold the tarpaulins in place. The skylight below me had already been battened down, and the boats tied down with extra gripes. I could no longer go below to what I thought was the safety of the passenger compartment—and no one from there could come on deck—not that I thought anyone would want to in view of the deteriorating weather.

Packet rats—as Jeremy had called them—raced aloft to "shorten sail," clinging to the yards as they plunged, rose and rolled viciously in the rising seas as they furled every sail except the foretopsail at the very top of the foremast, which was reefed to the merest scrap, just enough to maintain enough speed to control the rudder. Jeremy had told me that this was called maintaining bare headway. The mainmast was now a bare pole, the mainsail boom had been lowered, and it, the crossjack yard and the gaff were secured on the quarterdeck. The crew also put extra lines out—preventer stays—to reinforce the rigging and rigged lifelines along the deck to hold onto as they moved about. Sailors were tying themselves to the lifelines as they moved around so that, if they slipped or fell, they wouldn't be instantly swept overboard.

The gale announced its arrival with a single, terrible blow, wind shrieking and rain driving, still from the northwest, and it laid the ship over to larboard, almost onto her beam, it seemed—further than I thought would have been possible. In the instant before I was tossed from my perch upon the frame holding the boats, I thought that the ship must surely be lost. In the next instant, I smashed into one boat, and then the other. I instinctively grabbed at one of the lifelines and hung on for dear life. But I didn't recover myself until I was at the gunwale and nearly washed overboard. Green water flooded over the gunwale, burying me up to my chest. Slowly, the ship righted herself, and I scrambled back under one of the boats. I loosened the boat's painter and tied the slender line around my waist at one end and around the frame holding the boats at the other. Although I was safe for the moment, I was also teeth-chatteringly cold from the soaking I'd received.

I looked aft to the quarterdeck and saw two men at the ship's wheel instead of the usual one, one lashed to the wheel and one not. Captain Urquehart had lashed himself to the frame holding the ship's wheel and was calling through his tin megaphone to Mr. Mounce near the quarterdeck, who was attached to the larboard lifeline and cupping his ear trying to hear.

Maryann was lying to under her storm-shortened sail, her bow pointing more or less westerly, only slightly to the larboard of the wind and seas, which were still punishing her broad on the starboard bow. Jeremy had told me that this was as safe a maneuver as there was during a storm—if the helm were well handled and the proper sails set. The alternative would have been to scud, or run before the wind with the seas deep on one of the quarters. But that would have sent us back towards Ireland, all the while at risk of the ship being pooped by some massive graybeard of a rogue wave, which could sink the ship and kill us all.

The wind shrieked through the rigging, and the two helmsmen were struggling with the wheel. Time seemed to be suspended in this little world of mine, huddling under the ship's boat, so I have no idea how long I was there, whether it was many hours or merely minutes. But my teeth were no longer chattering, as I was building a little warmth back under my oilskin, and my hands were no longer quite as numb as when I first lashed myself to the boat frame.

Everything changed in an instant as another squall tore at the ship. Pebble- and cricket-ball-sized hail smashed down, pummeling anyone not under cover. I watched even Captain Urquehart flinch as hail hit him in the face, drawing blood, which the spray instantly washed away. I was thankful for the shelter of the overturned ship's boat. But the dashing of the hail above my head sounded for all the world like the Earl of Hell's coach and four-in-hand racing through central Dublin's cobblestoned streets.

I was brought from my reverie by the most horrible cracking sound, and some unnamed premonition drove me from the safety of the ship's boat to see what the noise was. That premonition saved my life, for as I slid clear of the boat, what I realized later was the fore topmast had come crashing down, smashing both boats into little more than kindling, and finally tearing into the skylight, rending the tarpaulin through in places and smashing the glass panes underneath. I looked down through the splintered skylight and glimpsed terrified faces below—steerage passengers who could not know what had just befallen the ship, but who must have thought the very worst. One of them was the big-bellied *cábóg*, staring up with a look of sheer terror overlaid by an expression of utter outrage, why I couldn't say, for I was being bludgeoned by the foaming green waves breaking over the deck and blinded by needles of rain driven by howling winds. I then looked up and found myself surrounded by broken splinters, twisted cordage and blocks from the ruined rigging—all of which had missed me, but which had trapped me where I stood. I was so stunned that it didn't occur to me to thank my Maker for leaving my head undamaged and attached to my shoulders.

I looked aft. Mr. Mounce, huge axe in hand, and four or five packet rats were making their way forward to me as quickly as they could, staggering along the two lifelines, heads bowed before the hail whipping into their faces. Mounce reached me first. A single, powerful two-handed swing with his axe parted the cordage binding me into place. He gesticulated to me, and I grabbed his hand. He tore me free of the torn cordage still cloying at my legs. I grabbed the lifeline and hung on.

Mounce staggered as the ship jerked unnaturally. I instinctively looked aft. The helmsman who had not been lashed to the wheel was flung to the larboard gunwale like a discarded rag doll. The helmsman who had lashed himself to the ship's wheel had also lost his footing, and was being thrown around like a sideways top as the wheel spun, untended. The ship's head started to fall off to larboard, away from the wind, presenting her broadside to the storm's full fury. Even I could see that, if we did not act quickly, *Maryann* would quickly broach and capsize, sending us all to a watery grave.

I saw this all in the merest instant, and turned back to Mounce. But he wasn't there. I glanced about wildly, looking for him. I was alone. The packet rats who had been following Mounce had also seemingly disappeared. The ship continued to heave and jerk unmercifully, as if she were desperately trying avoid her—and our—inevitable fate, and I almost pitched headlong into the roiling seas, saved only by my death's grip on the lifeline. As I crashed back down on the deck, I saw Mounce. He had slid to the gunwale, and was hanging half in the water, one arm hanging uselessly. A loop of cordage had ensnared his ankle and he was hugging a stanchion with his good arm. But his grip seemed to be beginning to loosen, and if he lost it, he was in danger of slipping over the side, his ankle still ensnared. He probably wouldn't have drowned, but he would likely have been smashed to death against the ship's heaving tumblehome His eyes met mine, with an imploring look.

To save him, I was going to first need the axe with which he'd freed me. But he was no longer holding it. I strained my eyes against the lashing sea spray and the wind and the rain and deepening gloom. I couldn't see it. I looked back over at Mounce. I had no time. I signaled a chopping motion in the vague hope that he knew where the axe was. How I could have expected him to understand, let alone point to the axe (as he didn't have a free limb with which to do so), wasn't apparent, and I felt a spasm of uselessness surge through me. Then I saw him looking at something, and I saw the axe entangled in the cordage, miraculously hardly a yard from me. I shinnied and slithered my way to it, thanking my Maker that I didn't have to loosen my grip from the lifeline.

But I was going to have to loosen my grip to save Mounce. I froze in fear, looking as imploringly at the quarterdeck as Mounce had looked at me. But the quarterdeck remained chaotic. There would be no succor from that quarter. I steeled myself, gripped the axe to my body and loosed my grip from the lifeline. I was vaulted to the gunwale by the ship's wild kicking and jerking. And then I was at Mr. Mounce's side. Without acknowledging him, I slid down to the line wrapped around his ankle, at first wondering how I could part it with the axe without injuring him. As I clawed at it, the line loosened just enough for me to pull it free.

I'm not to this day quite sure how we did it, but Mounce and I lurched back to the lifeline. He was so close to me as we wrapped ourselves around the lifeline that I heard him mutter "Jaysus, Mary and Joseph." I realized that he must have roared at the top of his lungs because the din from the storm was overwhelming. I also reflected wildly—funny what'll pass through your mind when you are in extremis—that I must have been wrong about Mounce: He was as Irish as I was, and not English. No Sassenagh could ever swear so beautifully. I also realized in the same instant that Mounce passed himself off as an Englishman so as to better control the English packet rats, who would look down on him if he were a mere paddywhack.

He muttered into my ear (he probably yelled, but that was how bloody loud it all was) what sounded like his thanks, and then we were no longer alone. Three packet rats were hovering. God knows where they came from, or even whether they were the same ones who had been following Mounce. Mounce turned to the two sailors next to him and gesticulated wildly. They moved off laboriously towards the mainmast. He then leaned over to a third sailor—Jeremy—and shouted something into his cupped ear. Jeremy nodded and absquatulated with amazing speed to the quarterdeck, where the captain was laboring with the remaining helmsman to regain control of the ship's wheel.

Mounce turned back to me, leaned close and cupped his hand about my ear, "Take the axe, lad." I wondered why he didn't use it, and saw that he had a huge knife in his hand. "You 'n' me gonna be cuttin' the rest of this clear. God help the Old Man and us. We might just live if we can clear this—and if the lads can get a scrap of sail up." What went unspoken was the fact that the foretopmast carrying the scrap of sail that allowed the ship her bare steerageway was gone, and so was any control over the rudder. The sail had to be replaced if we were to survive.

Mounce and I labored for many minutes. Part of the mast lay over the larboard side, weighing the ship down like an anchor. We directed our blows at parting the lines and cable securing the mast to the ship. Finally, after what seemed to be an agonizingly long time, Mounce took a huge swing at a straining line, which popped audibly, even above the howling wind and driving rain. The wrecked mast and rigging slipped over the side and the ship righted herself.

I looked up. We were still dangerously close to broaching. But the Old Man and the remaining helmsman finally had the ship's wheel under control, and at long last there was a scrap of sail showing from the mainmast—the main staysail, as I later learned, the best sail for the conditions—no strain on the ship, and perhaps the best sail with which to lie to the wind with—better, according to some than the foresail the captain had set as the storm started.

Someone grabbed me by the sleeve, and I stumbled forward with two or three other sailors to the foc'sle hatch. Down inside we plunged to an enormous locker, from which we pulled a great cable and began dragging it up topside to the foc'sle, and then laboriously down the main deck to the quarterdeck. As we progressed, more and more packet rats joined us, and we heaved the cable onto the larboard (and still lee) side of the quarterdeck. One end was made fast to bitts in the very stern of the ship. To the other we attached a buoy. We then heaved the heavy cable over the starboard quarter as the wind and rain once again lashed us with renewed fury. The line paid out and then pulled taut very quickly, causing the ship to jerk—as it did, I realized that we had put the line out so that it would act as a pivot to help the ship come about in the heavy seas. The Old Man and the helmsman put the helm 'a' lee, which meant that the Maryann's bow began to fall off to larboard, away from the wind and weather. We all prayed that Maryann would wear 'round to larboard smartly until she was running before the wind. If she hung up and broached, beam to the weather, then we would hardly have time to say our last Dia Uas!, as Cousin Séamas would have said.

Slowly at first the ship's head began to fall away to larboard and farther from the weather. We then went quicker, pivoting on the line and buoy, almost racing through the critical phase where Maryann was exposed beam on to the seas, and was at the greatest risk of broaching. Then we were through, and the seas settled on Maryann's larboard quarter. We were safe for the moment—as long as a giant "widowmaker" wave didn't crash over us from astern and instantly swamp us. We had, as Jeremy would later tell me, "worn the ship with bare poles," a maneuver that brooked no margin for error. It was a most desperate measure undertaken in the most desperate of circumstances. But at the time, I had no chance to reflect on what we had done for we were now hauling in the cable and buoy, which had outlived their usefulness and could pose a danger if left deployed too long. There was no sea shanty, for no one would have heard it through the noise of the storm, just a quick, rhythmic pulling in of the cable. My arms and back instantly screamed with fatigue, but I dared not stop, sensing that to slacken our efforts would be to fritter away the small advantage we seemed to have gained over the storm. Finally, we had the cable aboard and neatly flemished (or laid out in flat concentric loops) along the larboard length of the quarterdeck, its bitter end still attached to the bitts at the stern.

Jeremy was at my elbow, cupping his hand about my ear, "Reg'lar barrel o' fun, ain't it?"

I couldn't reply.

"We's gonna pay the hawser out," indicating the neatly flemished cable, "in a giant bight."

I looked at him questioningly.

"Like a big loop. It'll break the waves." He said as patiently as one can when yelling into the ear of another during a storm.

I nodded without fully understanding, and we passed the free bitter end of the cable through the larboard stern hawsehole and struggled with it to the starboard hawsehole. Mounce pushed me into a party of three more men, and we slowly paid out the cable— if we paid it out too quickly, the cable would drag in the water and we would have to consume precious time in recovering it—time during which we ran the risk of being pooped before we could set the bight in place. But if we dawdled too long keeping the bitter end out of the water, we ran the same risk.

From over my shoulder, I could hear Mounce roaring instructions. I leaned over the taffrail and moved crabwise to the starboard hawsehole, clutching the bitter end to my breast for dear life. After what seemed an eternity during which my arms and back screamed with the effort, we fed the bitter end through the starboard stern hawsehole and secured it to the bitt. We then quickly pulled enough additional cable to neatly flemish equal amounts on the deck by each hawsehole. We slowly paid out the cable through both hawseholes simultaneously, and it quickly formed a growing bight that instantly smoothed the roiling seas within its ambit to a mere mass of hissing foam. We were now safe from being pooped—as long as some great monster of a graybeard wave didn't overwhelm the bight—and us.

I hovered for a moment, seemingly forgotten in the bustle on the quarterdeck and conscious of the strictures regarding steerage passengers being there. As I made my way to the ladder to slip away unnoticed, Mr. Mounce grabbed me roughly by the shoulder. "I ought t'thrash yers fer bein' so daft. Stayin' on deck an' all. But I'll thank yers proper like. Ye saved me bacon. An' ye did a tolerable job after that."

He strode off without another word, bawling at one packet rat and lashing his starter at another.

⌁

The weather had eased a little, each successive squall seemed to envelope us with just a little less enthusiasm than the last, and as Jeremy put it to me as I lounged with him in a moment's lull just before the battens were pulled from the hatches and steerage opened to give the terrified passengers some level of succor, "We's all right now, I 'spect, for now, scudding 'afore the wind. We'll be in old Ireland 'afore too long. We gotta find a safe haven somewhere. River Shannon or Galway, I reckon. Never beed to either o' them ports. We shorely can't raise a proper new fore topmast here at sea. Not to go 2,000 miles all the way to Gotham. We ain't got the spars and cordage."

"How far's Ireland?"

"Couple hundred miles, give or take. 'Pends on where the storm blew us, exactly."

"Passengers won't be happy."

"They ain't got a say. Anyhows, the Old Man's given the word not to say nothin' to them 'til we get there."

"You told me."

"You know enough to keep shut pan."

So it seemed that we had dodged the graybeard's efforts to send us to Old Nick for now. Back to the refuge of the western coast of Ireland to refit seemed a small enough price to pay for that. But it turned out that we weren't quite yet saved, for we were sinking. Jeremy subsequently told me that the second mate had reported to Mr. Mounce that he had sounded the well—which told us how much water was in the bilges at the very bottom of the ship—and it was a foot and rising fast. *Maryann* had sprung a leak during the worst of the storm—and a bad one at that. Until Mr. Mounce and the carpenter discovered the source of the leak and plugged it, we were going to have to pump the bilges, every manjack of us, packet rat and passenger alike. Our lives depended upon it. So below we went, in one-hour shifts—one hour on and one hour off.

The two pumps were in the bilge, where it was dank and dark. Each pump had two big reciprocating arms called brakes. On one side, two men stood on the spur-shoes, which were the big timbers abaft the pump well, and pushed down on one brake, raising the opposite brake (and forcing a quantity of water over the side), which two other men standing on the strakes (the very ribs of the ship to which the hull's planking and copper were affixed) then pushed down—all in time to a shanty (over the next several days, we sang dozens of shanties, one after the other—the choruses, at least, as only the sailor in charge of the pumping detail sang the verses).

One shanty, called *"Across the Western Ocean,"* was a great favorite of the packet rats, and it articulated my own fond desire to see the frontier.

> O, *the times are hard and the wages low*
> *Maryann, where you bound?*
> *The Rocky Mountains is my home*

Chorus: Across the Western Ocean.

It's a land of plenty there you'll see
Maryann, where you bound?
I'm off across the Western Sea.

Chorus: Across the Western Ocean.

To Liverpool I'll make my way
Maryann, where you bound?
To Liverpool that Yankee school.

Chorus: Across the Western Ocean.

There's Liverpool Pat with his tarpaulin hat
Maryann, where you bound?
And Yankee John the packet rat.

Chorus: Across the Western Ocean.

Beware those packet ships, I pray,
Maryann, where you bound?
They'll steal your stores and your clothes away.

Chorus: Across the Western Ocean.

Wives and sweethearts don't you cry
Maryann, where you bound?
Sons and daughters wave goodbye.

Chorus: Across the Western Ocean.

Oh the jobs were bad and wages low
Maryann, where you bound?
The Rocky Mountains will be my new home.

Chorus: Across the Western Ocean.

We chanted and pumped—and pumped and chanted—until the storm finally blew itself out nearly two days later, and *Maryann* stopped tossing about enough for the ship's carpenter and Mr. Mounce to find the leak.

At one point I was manning one of the pumps with the Quality deck passenger who had lost his top hat over the side on the second or third day we were at anchor in Lough Mahon. In the hour we spent together, he never once spoke to me, or even looked at me to acknowledge my existence, his icy Anglo-Irish disdain remaining in place to the end—even after I cheekily muttered into his ear that he was a "natural for afternoon tea"—a well-known public school expression meaning that some boy (clearly a born fool for having been caught by a prefect or schoolmaster) was ready for afternoon detention at 3:00 p.m. for some transgression or another (thereby causing the miscreant to miss afternoon tea, which merely reinforced his fundamental incompetence).

When the Quality didn't respond to my bodacious cheek, I reckoned that he was no public school boy, because he didn't understand how I had insulted him. And I know he heard me because I could smell his sweat as I muttered into his ear. In any case, any real Quality would have been to a public school, and thus well-acquainted with my cheek, and would have responded in haughty and disdainful kind. So, to great hosannas from above (I silently crossed myself in thanks to the Good Lord himself), I realized that this fellow was no more than a mere knight of the barrow pigs with airs far, far above his station. In other words, he (and each of his equally miserable companions) was, as Jeremy later put it, just a bit of codfish aristocracy "what reckoned they war huckleberries above the rest of us persimmons." I smiled at Jeremy when he said that, and damned that jumped-up Anglo-Irish codfish aristocrat and his false airs to hell.

But my amusement at the Quality's expense came at a cost, for on the very next watch, the *cábóg* was working the brake with me. I ignored him as best I could, and he initially ignored me. But little by little, I could feel him slacken his effort, which meant I had to work all the harder to maintain the implacable rhythm to a shanty. This went on for quite some time, and my back and arms were fairly screaming at me.

Then he muttered into my ear, much as I had done to the Quality a couple of hours earlier, "Pretty little *giobstaire* ye been playin' house wi', me foin little *cábún*."

I ignored him, even though he'd all but called me a sodomite and called Mary something even worse. He also said a few other choice things to me over the remainder of our spell on the pumps, all of which I frostily ignored. Not that I had much choice in the matter, what with him slacking at the brake and my being bound and determined to keep pace.

At the end of the watch, as we were being relieved, he leaned into me from behind, all sweat and hot sour breath, whispered, "Bog Irish penny-toff," and then punched me hard, twice, in the small of the back. I staggered and almost fell into the man in front of me. I started to whirl around to confront my assailant, but I was hemmed into the maul exiting the bilges. The *cábóg* punched me again and whispered, "Ye'll na' be standin' in my way wi' the *stachaile*, will ye, me bucko?" I whirled around again to respond to his suggestion that he was going to have his way with Mary, and he gave me a good uppercut into the breadbasket. I collapsed to my knees at the bottom of the ladder, unable to breathe.

When I arrived back at our bunk, Mary was looking at me with a worried expression.

"What's wrong?"

I could feel the *cábóg*'s eyes boring into me, and I could hear his sour-breathed snigger.

"Nothing. Just tired."

It turned out that we had been saved from foundering by the merest strip of seaweed. Jeremy told me later that Mr. Mounce reckoned that without the seaweed plugging a badly sprung plank until he and the carpenter found it, the good barky *Maryann* would surely have foundered. We all were mighty pleased with that strip of vegetation, which I believe ended up in the Old Man's cabin, where it dried and remained as a reminder of our missed date with Old Nick. I was sleeping when Mr. Mounce and the carpenter found and fixed the leak, and so didn't have to return to the bilges to pump. I lay in our bunk, next to Mary, luxuriating in my idleness. The *cábóg* and what he had said to me seemed to be unreal, so I strove to dismiss it from my mind as no more than mere bullying of the sort endured by every new boy at St. Patrick's. At some point, Mary disappeared, and later woke me with her wonderful cakebread and some tepid tea—the galley fires having been lit once again. We then sat in the bunk, quietly talking as Fíona played with one of her companions. It was then that she told me of my book, which she had discovered ruined among our clothes as she and the other women-folk were busy titivating the steerage compartment, which the storm had left an utter tip. I bade her not to show it to me and to merely toss it overboard when she had the chance, which she did, sight unseen, God bless her soul—or, as she would have said it, *Go mbeannaí Dia a hanam.*

A few days later, after another, thankfully minor, blow, we heard a great commotion after we had been secured below in the passenger compartment for the night. Nobody cried out in terror, but we were all very much awake and listening to every sound. Eventually, the third mate came below and explained that the binnacle lanterns of another ship had been spotted. The Old Man had caused red rockets to be shot and blue lanterns to be hung from the yard-arm.

At daybreak, as we were mustered, we saw the other ship—*Constitution*, people whispered excitedly, a famous Western Ocean

CHAPTER 6

Sceal Mhaire (Mary's Story)

It WAS SEVERAL DAYS BEFORE WE SAW LAND AGAIN. *Constitution* kept us company the entire way as we plodded our way east, just as Captain Britton had promised. I and every other passenger in steerage was glad of it. Each morning as the hatches to steerage were opened and morning muster taken, I and just about every other passenger on Maryann quickly located the *Constitution* as she accompanied us through the trackless wastes of the Western Ocean. We were equally thankful that the weather stayed relatively calm as we scudded along before the seas to a refuge where the ship could be repaired.

One morning after many days of this almost religious act of observance, we emerged from our fetid cocoon to the sight of land. It was little more than a dark line thickly drawn on the horizon off our larboard bow below a cloudless, brilliantly sapphire sky. A biting wind from the northwest pushed us steadily closer to shore as the morning wore on. Mary had joined me, looking thin and wan and shivering in her shawl. But she was grinning broadly nonetheless at the welcome sight of land. Despite their teeth chattering from the cold, neither Mary nor Fíona would go below. I wrapped them both in my oilskin, and they gradually grew warmer in the weak, if brilliant, sunshine. Scores of other passengers crowded around us, their excitement barely abated as the first smudge on the horizon began to gradually take shape as a bleak and inhospitable-looking island that terminated at a lighthouse atop rocks, against which the ocean was relentlessly breaking. Jeremy bounced by on some mission or another and told us that it was Inisheer Island. "We's going to Galway, at the very back of beyond of Ireland, so Mr. Mounce says."

Off the starboard bow, the coastline terminated in a headland even more inhospitable than Inisheer—the Cliffs of Moher, Jeremy told me: jagged rocks defended the foot of the cliffs from all comers. The cliffs themselves, all sandstone colored with flashes of pale green here and there, rose some hundreds of feet into the air. After a while, we saw a castle perched atop the cliffs, looking for all the world like a dollhouse flung there by some forgotten Titan. *Constitution* began to forge ahead of us now, heeled over in a tall cloud of sail and a flash of copper at her waterline, as we moved into the huge bay, past the Scylla of Inisheer and the Charybdis of the Cliffs of Moher and the tiny castle on top. The cliffs grew higher still as *Maryann* passed farther into Galway Bay, stretching 1,000 feet into the air, as bleak and uninhabited as could be.

All of a sudden, the quiet fever of the steerage passengers erupted into cheers, huzzahs and clapping. The cry went up: "*Táimid tar éis Meiriceá a shroiceadh! Labhair Dia linn agus bheann-aigh Dia muid!*"

Mary translated for me, "They be saying: 'We've arrived in Amerikay! God has spoken to us and blessed us!'"

That shocked me. I thought everyone knew what the crew from first mate to packet rat knew and what I, Mary and Mr. O'Hurley knew: the Old Man had pointed *Maryann* east, in the direction of the rising sun and running before the seas, to the western coast of Ireland, seeking refuge where the ship could be repaired. Where exactly, nobody had yet said until Jeremy had told me this morning. But how could these people not have known we were headed to Ireland? We had almost died in the storm, and there was no way for the ship to have continued her voyage to New York.

But equally as quickly, the cheers were shouted down by a chorus of "*Tá muid in Éirinn*"—"We're in Ireland."

And in the silence that followed this revelation, some wit said
something loudly and derisively Irish. Mary laughed when she said,
"Tha' man be saying 'it's you who speaks of America. God hasn't
said anything to you or to anyone else, yer *bastún dall*'." The last bit
needed no translation from Mary. "You ignorant lout."

In the deflated quiet, many of the passengers left the deck, and
moped back into steerage. For them, it was all too much to bear.
Separation from all they had known and the excitement attendant
to leaving, with jigs merrily danced and violins plangently played.
Then they had endured the terror of the storm, and now this—
Ireland again.

Then someone was saying in Irish, "We'll be going home, then."

But his suggestion was met by yet another caustic reply in broken Irish and English, "Galway be on the far side of the earth from
Cork, all the good it'll be doing you, yer daft *ruais*—there na' be
no roads back to Cork from there—there be roads to hell probably,
but nowhere else."

The man was right. In those days, the railway had yet to come
to Galway, and the only overland route was by muddy tracks that
made the turnpike to Cork seem like Dublin's High Street. The
only way from Galway to Cork was by ship, and *Maryann* was not
about to sail back. Not if her master had anything to say about it,
so Jeremy informed me.

⌒

The next morning, when the hatches opened and we were herded
amidships for morning muster, we were quayside. Mr. Mounce was
at the quarterdeck railing. "All passengers," he began in his flat,
harsh English-accented voice (with whatever Irish he had having
been safely hidden away after the storm). "You will be required
to vacate the ship no later than four bells of the forenoon watch

tomorrow. That is mid-morning for you lubbers. You will need to obtain lodging in town for at least a week while we replace the mast. You must stay in regular contact with your representative, Mr. O'Hurley, concerning re-embarkation. Mr. O'Hurley will make known the location of his lodgings before midday tomorrow. That is all."

And with that, we were unceremoniously cast ashore the next morning to subsist on my rapidly depleting store of gold sovereigns while the ship was being repaired.

◦

We left the ship as early as we could, with all of our meager posses-sions in hand, determined to be among the first passengers to find lodging. Galway was not a big town, well less than half the size of Cork, and a mere trifle compared to Dublin itself. Mary and I were concerned about the availability—and price—of lodgings. Even having mustered her few shillings with my all-too-small store of gold sovereigns, I didn't think we could last long before we were completely destitute. And we had no means of replenishing our slender store of chink. We were also very hungry, what with the ship having berthed in Galway the night before after two days of limited access to cooking fires, no food being served to the steer-age passengers yesterday and this morning's bedlam of 300 steer-age passengers making ready to depart the ship more or less at the same time.

When we stepped onto the bustling and crowded quay, it was all Mary and I could do to keep Fíona's mind from her growling belly. The quay, along with all the other quays in the New Dock, were virtual cornucopias of pallets of butter, oats, eggs and sides of beef and ham, all waiting to be loaded onto the half-dozen wait-ing cargo ships that I imagined would be bound for England, just like the merchant ships departing Cork were almost all bound for Liverpool or Bristol. Hundreds of bales of wool and freshly

produced linen cloth were also on the quays, presumably also awaiting export to England. The quays were further encumbered with
ploughs, scythes and other farming implements that had probably
just been unloaded from the same cargo ships. They were awaiting
shipment, I later learned, to the very farms of Connaught from
which had come all of the bounteous produce found on the quays.

We departed the quays, and were soon directed to the meaner
streets of Galway. After several inquiries, and the extraction of
two shillings from our already too-thin wallet wrapped around my
waist, we had secured lodging for the next week. We then splurged
some more of our all-too-few pennies—at my behest—on fresh
bread, freshly cooked potatoes and great draughts of milk, and ate
to our hearts' content, which I had not done since I had left my
cousin Séamas's house. Mary later told me that the meal had filled
her more than any other in her life. I did not think that she was
exaggerating when she told me that. Our final indulgence that
day was to clean ourselves and the few remaining clothes we had,
and replace at least some of the clothing that had been ruined in
the storm. Mary shooed me from the room for an hour when she
cleaned herself, long after she'd stripped me with barely a raised
eyebrow and made me scrub myself nearly raw, and seen to Fíona.

When I returned, she and Fíona were fast asleep, and I lingered over Mary's slightly déshabillé form, drinking in the sight of
her for a moment. Sleep came quickly, and it was never sweeter to
me than it was that night.

The next few days were ones of comparative luxury. Mary slowly
recovered her strength and at least some of the weight she had lost
during her illness. Fíona once again became lively. We took walks
for hours at a time, about town and far into the countryside, for the
sheer pleasure of it after having been cooped up on the ship for so
long. We also spent quite a few hours promenading up and down

the Long Walk, which was the row of houses on the quay facing the River Corrib we had seen as *Maryann* entered Galway Harbour.

As I no longer could read to Fíona from *The Last of the Mohicans*, I slipped out by myself one morning to a tiny bookstore in Eyre Square, "The Square," as it was called in Galway. When I asked for a proper children's book, the proprietor directed me to a book called *Goody Two-Shoes*, and told me that it was the very best book for teaching young children how to read, because, as the author himself said, it instilled:

> *precepts of activity, gentleness, and morality; that it may enliven and animate the rising generation, and lead them forward in the practice of those virtues that at once ensure respect and success through life.*

I talked with the bookseller for a while after he read me this passage, and was able to obtain a copy—albeit well-used—for just a few more precious pennies. But I was determined—regardless of the pennies or shillings spent—that Fíona would be reading by herself before we reached Amerikay, as both Mary and Fíona pronounced it.

I was sitting outside the boardinghouse with Fíona later that day, reading to her from *Goody Two-Shoes* about Margery Meanwell's idyllic existence in her father's house upon that "certain village green," when Mary found us. She took the book gently from me and asked where it was from. I told her.

"Ye can na' be doing that," she replied. "We can na' afford it." Tears started at the corners of her eyes, and she shooed Fíona into our room, away from our disagreement.

"Mary," I said, "you want her to read, don't you? You've told me that, how many times?"

"*Go deimhin.*" Of course, she acknowledged quietly. "Lots of times. But what about the money?"

"We'll be all right. No more luxuries. Anyway, we'll be back on the ship in two days' time, and on our way to Amerikay."

⌒

I soon had the opportunity to rue my confidence. The very next day, I made my way over to *Maryann*, and was stopped cold by the sight of the foremast completely missing, and no work taking place anywhere that I could see. I boarded the ship—there being no one on deck to stop me—and I wandered about until I found Jeremy working quietly below on some task that the ship's carpenter had set him to.

"Well," he said, referring to the missing mast in that nasally Yankee voice of his, "that ain't the half of it. The Old Man, he 'n' the shipwright're fighting over the chink to pay fer it, and the Old Man sent a letter to the ship's owner informing him of the turn of events, and asking fer authority to pay the shipwright. We could be stuck here for weeks if we left it up to the Old Man."

"So what happens now? There are 300 people stranded here—most of 'em without a farthing to their names."

"Oh, yeah, well, the story gets better. You remember Mr. O'Hurley, 'the elected representative'?"

I nodded.

"What a fine old coot he is. Mr. Mounce says that O'Hurley thinks he's the King of Ireland's right-hand man—whoever the Sam Hill 'the King of Ireland' is. I thought you guys was ruled by them lime juicers and their queen. Anyway, him—Mr. O'Hurley—and Mr. Mounce had a big meeting a coupla days ago. And turns out, a whole bunch o' them micks ..."

I glared at Jeremy, offended by the slur.

He flushed. "Sorry, buddy, but you ain't one o' them coots."

I shrugged, and he continued, "Well, anyway, them poor slobs in steerage what ain't got no rhino got theirselves put into the workhouse."

"Good God. No getting out of the workhouse once you're in."
I shivered as I said it.

The workhouses had been around since I was a child. Everybody had heard of them. Nightmarish. The sort of place a nanny would threaten a misbehaving child with. Crowded. Starvation diet. And, once you were admitted within the workhouse's walls, the wardens would not let you leave until you could demonstrate some visible means of supporting yourself—which, of course, was a practical impossibility.

"Ya don't say," Jeremy replied. "That'd be bad to happen t'anyone. Well, as Mr. Mounce tells it, he got the Old Man to tell the mayor about it. Well, it turns out that the mayor and the good city burghers—that's what Mr. Mounce called 'em—don't want them micks—sorry, again—whaddya call 'em?"

"Emigrants, I should think," I said formally. "We'll call ourselves micks and paddies. Oh, and don't even think of calling us paddywhacks."

"Emigrants. Yeah, I'll keep that in mind, buddy," he replied cockily. "Well, the good city burghers—as I was saying—don't want them *emigrants* in their workhouse. It's costing them—the good city burghers—money to keep them emigrants in that workhouse. Real gold sovereigns—or bucks or dollars, as we'd say in the States. Go figger."

"So? How does that help us?"

"Well, them city burghers don't wanna pay t'keep them emigrants in the workhouse. So they're putting pressure on the shipwright—Manning's his name, I think—to hurry up and fix the good barky *Maryann*, and get her absquatulated right on outta here, and on to Gotham itself—with all 300 of them emigrants—you included, ya durn mick."

"Well, that'd be good, buddy," I replied, casually ignoring the gibe and fumbling for a suitable rejoinder.

"So, hows ya been, bucko?" Jeremy changed the subject, and we spent the next twenty minutes as a pair of fifteen-year-old boys who like each other will—alternately boasting and feigning to disbelieve the other's boasts. Eventually, the carpenter returned, and I skedaddled.

A few days later, Jeremy's prediction seemed to have been as good as his word, because cranes were erected, and a great long mast was "stepped in." I spent quite a few hours each day watching the operation. Sometimes I was by myself. But more often, I had Fíona with me, as Mary would tell me that she had an "errand" of some sort to run. She made it clear that I was not to inquire further about her errands, and I did not. Nor did I give them an ounce of thought, because I was captivated by the mast being replaced.

Finally, the shipwright and his men were done, and word was passed from Mr. O'Hurley, who now thought of himself as the veritable right hand of the great Daniel O'Connell on account of what he'd done to help save some of our more destitute brethren from the workhouse, that we would be departing on Wednesday week, and that we should present ourselves quayside at 9:00 o'clock on the preceding day to embark.

Mary and I danced for joy when we heard the news. We promptly went to the chandler and replenished our diminished foodstocks with enough, the chandler said, to last sixty days over the Western Ocean to the New World, which thinned my wallet terribly. I despaired privately of what I—we, Mary, Fíona and I—would do when we arrived in New York. I would have to work. But at what? I was a mere schoolboy with no skills. But I dismissed such concerns when Jeremy and I met up that afternoon and traded still more stories.

The night before we embarked, Mary gave me a present, wrapped in brown paper. She told me to put it in my bag, and open it on the ship. I thanked her, and forebore from asking her about the bruise on her cheek and the cut on her lip. It wasn't the time to ask, and the look in her eye told me that I shouldn't be asking in any case. We sat quietly for a time in the shadows of the flickering tallow candle we allowed ourselves for half an hour or so each night as Fíona fell asleep.

When the little girl's breathing turned regular, Mary told me her story, of how she and Fíona came to be on the quay the day we boarded *Maryann*.

~

"I was so heartbroken the day we arrived in Galway," she began. "Even though I be grinning at yers. Ye was standing there so excited, looking at the land … and so sweet to wrap me and *mo wain* in yer oilskin—Fíona was so cold." She smiled briefly and then said that as we made our way up Galway Bay, she thought that she and her daughter had lost everything because she didn't think that *Mayrann* would ever leave Ireland again—or if the ship did leave, it would not be with her and Fíona on board. She knew that I was right to say that we were all lucky to be alive, and that we eventually would get to *Meiriceá*. But that didn't change how she felt, because she and Fíona had nothing to go back to in Skibbereen. Everything they had there was gone now.

I must have had a blank look of incomprehension on my face as I struggled to understand Mary's Irish, because she stopped her story and apologized to me—in Irish—for not always speaking proper English. Despite—or perhaps because of—her apology, Mary told the rest of her story in both Irish and English and every stage in between as she stared off into the darkness beyond the flickering halo provided by the tallow candle.

"You must have wondered," she said, "why I never spoke of my husband."

I shrugged.

"He died ... the week before Fíona and I met you on the pier next to *Maryann*. A fever killed him." She smiled bleakly. "He never got a chance even to see the Western Ocean, let alone *Meiriceá*. The poor man. He was a good husband ..."

Mary's voice died away for a minute or two in remembrance. I left her quietly with her thoughts, her beautiful face silhouetted in profile by the candle.

Eventually, she resumed, saying: "*Muid*—Liam, *mí* and *mo wain*—we were forced to leave Skibbereen. The land was no good and we were slowly starving to death ... and the landlord's agent made us an offer we couldn't refuse ... an offer that eventually was the death of Liam. But it wasn't always like that in Skibbereen. My mother and father used to tell me how things were so much better in the old days. Skibbereen used to be a good place to live. It still was a good place to be living—sort of—even five or six years ago ..."

She paused and sighed. "... when Liam and I were married. I was fifteen. I had been up at the big house as *an bhean sclábha*—a maid-servant—for about a year when Liam came a' calling. When I was there, at the big house, the housekeeper taught me English. And it was she who told me to call myself 'Mary'."

Mary smiled proudly when she said this last bit in perfect English. But she slipped right back into Irish. Despite my difficulty following her, it was clear to me how Mary and Liam had gotten off to a promising start. Liam had a small farm, which was half of a larger farm he had inherited when his father died—his younger brother had inherited the other half through the ancient practice of rundale, which could easily split a man's farm into six or eight or a dozen tiny plots, which would force the farmer to raise his potatoes on one of three different plots, keep his chickens on another, and raise vegetables on still another—if he was lucky. Often, rundale could force a farmer to abandon his farm tenancy simply because it was too broken up to be economically viable by any standard—even that of bare subsistence.

What's more, Liam's mother, who had still been alive when Liam and Mary were married, apparently was supported by Liam's younger brother—the unlucky soul. Indeed, it was not unusual— even nowadays—that such a young man might be obligated to look after his mother for years if she were a widow—perhaps even decades, and it could mean that he might never marry, ever. And that would doom him to eternal bachelorhood on the farm with the cold comfort of a mother who might die when he was middle-aged and dried out from a lifetime of isolation. In such a circumstance, marriage would be simply out of the question.

Mary continued, recalling me to her story: "Mo *mháthair* gave me *a libheadhan* …" She exclaimed in frustration: "What's the word? A chest with some linens and some chickens."

"A dowry for Liam when you got married?" I suggested.

"*Cinnte*," she whispered. Exactly. "*D'fhan mo dheartháir sa bhaile chun aire a thabhairt do mo mháthair i ndiaidh do fuair m'athair bás*—I'm sorry—my brother stayed at home to care for my mother after my father died." Another brother left behind to care for a widowed mother, just like Liam's younger brother having to care for their mother. I wondered what had happened to Mary's father, but I didn't want to interrupt her. Mary stopped her story for a bit as she became lost in thought again, perhaps wondering about them—and also perhaps grieving just a little that she'd likely never see them again—and they'd never know whether Mary and Fíona— and Liam, God rest his soul—lived or died.

Mary continued in Irish, "At the wedding, before the priest married us, my brother said to Liam: 'Be good to my sister. She'll be your wife 'afore the sun sets, please the heavens.' And for a while, Liam was good to me." She began to lose me as she lapsed into her patois. "Fíona came quickly. But nae more wee *bunócs* after that," she said a little sadly, and without elaborating. "Then it all began to change. We was still eating enough. But we couldn't sell our flax and linen anymore. *Na ceannaithe*—the merchants—they weren't buying. The *Sassenagh* factories was making the flax and linen cheaper than we could, so the merchants told us. They were buying only butter, cheese, vegetables, poultry and hogs—the very things we saw on the quays the other day—and the very food we were eating when we could. So we sold all we could to make ends meet, and we began eating praties, most of the time without even any milk, because we used it all to make cheese for sale to the merchants."

What an existence, I thought—reduced to eating only praties, which is what everyone called potatoes.

"And the rents ... The middlemen and land agents was charging twice as much as they used to—and that was without the manure we needed for fertilizer. So Liam gave up some of his land and took some other land for a lower rent. But it wasn't near his old plot. So himsel' was now running around something awful. And there wasn't enough praties, even at the best of times. And then, on the meal months, there was almost nothing.

Meal months were the final cruel trick played on those who were so bold as to subsist on potatoes and nothing else: Potatoes were harvested in September each year, and lasted only nine or ten months before they became too mealy to eat. Moreover, some potatoes had to be set aside for next year's harvest. So, by June of each year, there would be virtually nothing to eat, and the succeeding summer months until the next September became known as the meal months during which everyone either starved or nearly starved.

"And there was no other work in Skibbereen for no one. We heard tales of lads going to Cork searching for work, and then ending up starving on the streets. And some *spalpeen* traveled even farther—to Merseyside and such, looking fer work. I remember one *scolbanach* coming back wi' his shillings sewn in his trousers. A *mháthair*—his mother—was so happy when he handed her his trousers 'cuz he'd given her the year's rent."

Mary was quiet for a while. The tallow candle had gone out, and we could barely see each other in the faint moonlight. I thought that there were tears on her cheeks. But I couldn't be sure, and I wasn't going to ask.

"And Liam, God rest his soul, himsel' be drinking. Reg'lar falling-down peloothered. And himsel' was no' listening to the likes o' no parish priest—let alone to the likes of Father Mathew, the temperance man, neither. Too bad," she said flatly. "Tha' poteen be after killing him.

"But we was still able to make ends meet—barely. I spent my days planting the pitaties, digging turf, in addition to raising the chickens, slopping the hogs and weaving frieze for our clothes. I even rethatched the roof by myself last year. We was still better off than many. Lots of our friends and neighbors was just simply ejected—and that was 'afore the middleman died, and that land agent came in—a terrible man, he was. The middleman's drivers was coming 'afore dawn, sometimes t' flatten the cottages, *spalpeen* 'n' all still inside. Them poor *créatúrs* was without a chance. I remember one ..." Mary stopped for a moment.

"I remember one family ..." she started again. "Naked them *wains* was—and no' clothing to put on them. They all be setting in the ditch."

Mary paused, and resumed again in Irish. "*Do bhí an sirriam agus an meáncheannaí ar dhroim capaill.*" The sheriff and middleman were on horseback, she said.

I could picture the scene as I slowly translated Mary's story: the heartless sheriff and middleman, with warm hearths to go home to, there on horseback with the sheriff's bully boys to enforce the law as the tenants—in this case, a widow, a grandmother and several naked children (there being no man in sight)—were ejected and their hovel flattened. The middleman was there, self-satisfied and righteous in having done his duty, to see his tenants off. Both he and the sheriff were lording over the cowering family—naked children squawling, and the mother and grandmother keening. *Dia Uas!* The frightened neighbors had gathered in the muddy road to watch in horrified silence, each of them probably thanking God himself that he and his family were not the ones being ejected.

"Worse than that were the daid bodies that be lying in the ditch," Mary continued matter-of-factly. "One day, me 'n' an *mo wain* saw a whole daid family a hundred yards from a ruined cottage. Three of 'em, there were. *Athair, máthair agus a wain.*" A father, mother and their child. All of them dead. Sweet Jesus.

She stopped for a moment to compose herself, and then continued, this time mostly in English, "The good Lord himself only knows where those poor people were going. On the road, I suppose. Where? Merseyside like the travelling *spalpeen? Na daoine bochta.*"

As I followed, she told me these poor people who were starving to death alongside the road were simply buried where they fell. Others—the lucky ones, if one looked at such a miserable existence as "lucky"—went to the workhouse. Still others lived in what were little more than dogholes dug in ditches on the side of the road—entire families in one little hole. No food. No shelter.

Mary crossed herself in the dark. "God save their souls." I was surprised that she said the blessing in English.

Mary continued, her voice a little stronger now, and her words coming faster, "The old middleman died right after that." She smiled slightly in satisfaction in the rising moonlight.

"I remember," she said. "Them *spailpíní* were so happy when himsel' died. It was like when *Maryann* came to Galway, and everyone thought we be in *Meiriceá. Bastúns dall.*"

She was right—the estate tenants were foolish for thinking that things would get better simply because the middleman had died.

"They were lighting bonfires on every hill to celebrate that man's death." Mary chuckled mordantly, and her tone darkened. "But, it soon was worse than ever. There was this land agent who came—I don't really know the difference between a land agent and a middleman. But that's what himsel's lordly title be when himsel' be after telling us that *spailpíní* would be treated fair-like. Fair words indeed. And so it seemed right that a lot of us *spailpíní* went to the land agent and asked that the rent be reduced."

She almost laughed at the recollection. "Himsel' said he was talking to the landlord on *Sasana*. So himsel' asked us to wait for a month. So, we waited. And a month went by, maybe more. A group o' *spailpíní*—a deputation, what them *créatúrs* called themselves— went up to the big house when himsel' came back from *Sasana*— Liam was one of 'em. Himsel' refused to see the deputation." She said the word with care. "Himsel' sent his *buachail*, instead. His fancy servant in his fancy livery," she spat. "To tell them that the rent was going up—and not down. Well, that wasn't the end of it." She shook her head at the memory. "*An t-eirghe mór* gathered that night, with torches, and themselves be right bulling with rage."

I stopped her and asked, "*An ergha*. A mob, you mean?"

She hardly acknowledged me as she continued. "Bonfires were set. Speeches made. Then the *erghe* burned down the land agent's house. Chased the land agent out the back, running fer his dear life. That *buachail*, himsel' wasn't so fine now in his fancy livery. Kneeling, he was, on the lawn in front of the house. Begging after his life, himsel' was.

"Well," Mary chuckled sardonically once more. "That land agent didn't stay gone. Himsel' got the *Sassenagh* troops rounding up them poor *spalpeen* in the deputation—and then he had them all hanged. But not Liam. The *Sassenagh* missed him—why the sheriff never caught him, I never did know. *Moladh le Dia.*" Mary crossed herself again as she praised God for sparing Liam "*Na mná céile an fir crochadh …*" She translated, "the hanged men's women-folk. The sheriff and his drivers had an escort of *Sassenagh* soldiers to protect them. And they ejected them *mná bochta* from their cottages the very day their men were hanged. Them *mná bochta* were by the roadside with nothing, not hardly even the clothing on their backs. And them *Sassenagh* galoots and peelers. Themselves just be laughin' at them poor *papul* standing in the ditch with naught but the rags on their backs, and called their dead menfolk 'fruit of the gibbet.' Even the *Gaels* what took the *Sassenagh* shilling and what knew better, laughed. And them poor *papul*? Well, it be off to the workhouse for them. Or they be dyin' by the roadside."

Mary looked at me in the gloom as she continued her story mostly in Irish. "Then, a few weeks later, everything changed. There was a new land agent, and he offered to pay for our passage across the Western Ocean—to the New World, himsel' said—to Canada. 'Assisted emigration', himsel' promised us. Two hundred farmers and their families, including Liam, Fíona and me, we were to go to Canada on board a big ship—the *Rose Tremayne*. We had to go to Liverpool to board her. We even received 20 shillings to spend for food and other necessaries on the journey. A few days later, the land agent let us leave with our belongings before his boys flattened our cottage—himsel' being such a generous soul. We didn't look back as we left." She said it simply, a sudden air of melancholy in her voice. "We walked all the way to Cork City. In the rain, with the land agent's man—God rot his wicked soul." She crossed herself a third time.

I started because I'd never heard her take God's name in vain quite like that before.

She switched entirely to Irish, saying that Liam was sick when they finally arrived in Cork, and the medical officer on the quay who was screening passengers for illness would not allow Liam onboard the ship that was to take them to Liverpool. So now I understood why Mary had reacted on the quay in Cork when I told her that a medical officer was going to screen us.

She had been afraid that it would happen again. Indeed, she might even have already been coming down with the fever, and so had worked to hide it.

Then she said something about *an galtán*. I looked at her questioningly.

"*An galtán? An bád* ..." She searched for the English word, but couldn't find it. So she said, "Just like the tug that saved us in Galway Bay."

"A steamship?" I asked.

She nodded. "The ship was leaving right then, the land agent's man told me. So, me and *mo wain* were sitting on the quay, on the cobblestones, with Liam lying at our feet—and we were saying good-bye to our neighbors and friends—everyone we knew. I couldn't leave Liam."

What a disaster, I thought—her husband dying on the quay as everyone she knew left her. No one stayed behind to help. God help a soul in a jam like that.

"Liam died that night, on the quay," Mary said quietly. "He simply gave up." Her English improved as she remembered her husband dying. "I held him as his soul departed. I was so lost, that I was hardly aware of anything other than him—I do na' even know who 'they' were, the ones who took him away."

After a moment, Mary gathered herself and resumed in English. "I never even saw him again. To this day, I don't know where he's buried. Some potter's field, the land agent's man, himsel', told me. It'd be impossible to find him, buried in an unmarked grave ... or worse ... The greatest shame of it all is that I should have prepared himsel' for his own great journey."

She held back the tears by sheer dint of effort, saying, "And I na' be after sendin' him proper-like to the next world." Now the tears did flow—but only for a moment.

Not being able to prepare her husband for burial, and not being able to mourn him properly, must have destroyed her. It was a wife's duty to properly bury her husband. In her own eyes, she had failed—regardless of the circumstances.

Mary abruptly stopped herself, sighed, and then continued. "The agent's man came to me after Liam died." She snorted bitterly in her recollection. "Himsel' said that there was going to be another *bád*. The *Maryann*, *Beidh sé ag imeacht i gceann seachtain*." Mary looked away when she said that, and stopped talking.

Mary had almost lost me as she veered back to Irish. But I think I understood her: *Maryann* was to leave a week later, and the land agent's man had agreed to buy her a ticket on that ship. But that delay left her and Fíona stranded in Cork City, friendless, for a week. She probably thought that she and Fíona were lucky to have escaped the workhouse.

Mary continued tonelessly, her shoulders slumped in the gloom. "The boardinghouse, *a ghrá*. Himsel' the land agent man took me to a boardinghouse." I still had not gotten used to her calling me "*a ghrá*"—my dear. It was as if I were her favorite nephew, or younger brother. That knowledge didn't sit well with the thoughts I'd had about her.

"Himsel' knew that horrid clart who kept the boardinghouse."

A clart, I thought, a dirty old woman. The boardinghouse couldn't have been a very nice place.

"An' himsel' stayed a while with me."

This time, she stopped for quite a few moments. I knew enough to let her be, and to let her finish her story in her own time, because she was almost done now.

Finally, she spoke again in her broken patois, saying that she and Fíona had stayed a week in the boardinghouse room, waiting for the *Maryann* and hardly going out, even to find food. But they had had a tick to sleep on, and so they had been dry—and safe—for the moment.

Mary paused briefly, before murmuring with a ghost of a smile that she had heard a saying once, "There are three things that leave the shortest traces: a bird on a branch, a ship on the sea, and a man on a woman."

Then in an even softer whisper she told me that this was how she had been when she and Fíona boarded the *Maryann*—there wasn't a trace of that *get*—as she called the land agent's man—left on her, and she had been very happy for that.

Mary sat quietly for a few minutes after she finished, and then smiled broadly at me in the moonlight. "And that be when *mé* be finding ye, *mo ghrá*."

But she turned serious again, looking at me directly in the eye, saying in Irish, "I'll never marry again—ever. Marriage and men are for fools." She then spat, "Begob."

That shocked me. But, then again, Father hadn't married again after my mother died. Still …

"What can Fíona be looking forward to in a marriage, after all of this?" She answered herself almost without pause, "*Mé* be tellin' yer what. She be learning *a léamh*—to read." She looked at me again, urgently this time.

Conscious of the open-ended nature of my commitment, I replied, "I'll have her reading in no time. And doing her sums. She can be a schoolteacher herself, just like Margery Meanwell in *Goody Two-Shoes*."

"I be liking that. Fíona hersel' being an *ardollamh*." She smiled. Fíona becoming a professor? I thought it a little strange that Mary wanted Fíona to be a professor, because only men are professors. I thought it even stranger that Mary knew what a professor was. But then I thought, why not? We'll make her a professor. That's better than being a mere schoolteacher.

Mary didn't say anything else after that, and she didn't invite any more comment from me. After a while, she slept and didn't awaken until dawn.

I spent an hour in the moonlight writing a letter to Evelyn, the first one I had written, telling her of our adventures and our unexpected return to Ireland for repairs. I told her of Fíona and teaching her to read. But Mary hardly figured, and I certainly didn't mention Father O'Muirhily or his murder at the hands of the man in funereal black.

I then wrote a letter to my former headmaster at St. Patrick's. This time I did write of Father O'Muirhily and the man in black. I must have started the letter three or four different times, both because I found the task of writing about his death exceedingly difficult—I couldn't bring myself to use the word "murder," but what else could Father O'Muirhily's death have been?—and at least once because the tears I had never shed for the poor man whom I'd loved more as a child than anyone else except for my father flowed uncontrollably (if silently so as not to disturb Mary and Fíona as they slept) fell on the paper and smudged the ink.

I posted both letters the next morning, just before we boarded *Maryann*.

~

The last of the passengers had hardly straggled aboard *Maryann* when the bosun's pipe twittered and we were herded to the waist of the ship. Mr. Mounce quieted us for an announcement from Captain Uquehart, who was accompanied by a constable who by the look of his uniform was no mere "peeler." Mary and I exchanged glances, her eyes bland and mine questioning. I caught a glimpse of Jeremy, who when our eyes met gave me a barely perceptible shrug. Then I remembered the *cábóg*, whose eye always seemed to find me at times like this. I craned my neck briefly, but didn't see him.

Urquehart pulled back his fawn greatcoat, hooked his thumbs in his waistcoat and said, "I am sorry to report that one of your fellow passengers has been found most foully murdered and robbed of what few possessions he may have had." He paused for the inevitable gasp and ripple of shock that ran through the maul of passengers. "We have been asked to cooperate with the local constabulary so that they may undertake inquiries as may be necessary to apprehend the culprit." The Quality, who were milling about the quarterdeck behind the captain, his mates and the constable seemed to quiver at this suggestion of delay due to a criminal inquiry. Urquehart reassured them—and the rest of us—that, "We will endeavor to sail at our earliest convenience, just as soon as inquiries have concluded."

Mounce stepped forward and introduced the Head Constable of the Connacht constabulary. The Head Constable nodded with vast dignity and addressed us. "We do not know the name of the murdered man, but we are sure that he is not a Galway denizen, and as *Maryann* is the only ship in port, we believe him to be one of her passengers. We will therefore ask each man and woman to view the dead man. Captain Urquehart and his mates will direct you to form a line. We will then proceed further with our inquiries."

Mounce stepped forward once more and bawled his orders. There was a flurry of bosun's pipes and activity and we passengers (other than the children, who remained onboard and away from the gruesome proceedings) found ourselves posthaste in line on the quay, shuffling past what appeared to be a coffin propped upright. Mary was beside me, looking straight forward, her face serene as we shuffled along towards the coffin. Uncharacteristically, she was holding my hand. We didn't talk, nor did anyone else, aside from a furtive whisper or two. Nobody'd forbidden us from talking, but it seemed wrong in view of the solemnity of the occasion.

When we reached the coffin, I gasped, for upright in it, his arms crossed over a shirt encrusted with dried blood, was the *cábóg*. It struck me as grimly amusing that here he was, dead, and for all the bullying of the past several weeks, I didn't even know his name. Mary was pale, but composed. Other women had pulled their shawls tighter, crossed themselves and muttered some prayer or another as they saw the dead man. In some hands, I could see rosary beads being worked. But not Mary. She looked at the dead man levelly, glanced at me and we moved on silently to a waiting sub-constable, who asked, "Can you identify the decedent?"

I answered first, "I can say that he is—was—a passenger, but I never knew his name."

"You, Miss?"

"I spoke to him once or twice, but I never knew him. He wasn't very nice."

"How's that, Miss?"

"He was …" Mary paused. "Suggestive. In an unwelcome way."

"I see, Miss. Where were you the night before last?"

Mary opened her mouth, but I interjected without thinking, "She was with me all night, at our lodgings."

"Yes, Mr. …"

"Gogan. William Patrick Gogan. Late of St. Patrick's College and bound for the New World to seek my fortune."

"Quite," said the sub-constable. He appraised me for a brief second, and then said, "Thank you for your assistance."

And we were done and headed back to the ship.

"What did he say to you?" I asked.

"Ye'd rather not know, mo chúisle."

"Mary, the man's dead. Did he threaten you?"

"It be over, now, a ghrá. There be nothin' t'be worryin' yersel' o'er."

I didn't ask Mary where she'd been for several hours that day. I'd asked before, and she'd cut me cold.

⌒

A couple of hours later, Jeremy skittered by as I was reading and said to me excitedly, "They know his name. Sean O'Hara."

"Does anyone know him?"

"Jes' his bunkmates, who the story goes, are as glad to see him gone as circumstances permit."

I looked at Jeremy quizzically.

"I heard one o' them constable big bugs say it."

"They know who killed him?"

"Nah. An' I hear tell they ain't gonna try t'figger it out."

"Why not?"

"The city fathers want to see the back of the good barky *Maryann*. Havin' a hunnert or more o' them passengers in the workhouse ain't sittin' well with 'em. And another couple hunnert without jobs and joining their compatriots in the workhouse within a week or two? Think of what it'd do to the poor rate. That ain't somethin' the city fathers want t'be contemplatin'. Leastways, that's how Captain Urquehart and Mr. Mounce have put it to them."

"Thank God. We've spent long enough here."

Jeremy looked at me. "You weren't the only one he bullied, y'know."

I flushed and muttered something about it being no more than what I put up with as a new boy at school.

⌒

As the sun rose gloriously the next day, the ship left Galway, just as promised by the Captain, leaving unsolved the murder of Sean O'Hara, the itinerant *bronnadh cábóg* whom nobody would admit to knowing, not even his erstwhile bunkmates.

⌒

CHAPTER 7

Slighe go Mheiriceá—Arís
(Passage to America—Again)

◦—

THE SHIP POSITIVELY VIBRATED WITH EXCITEMENT as she left Galway Harbour, and the Old Man strode the quarterdeck in his immaculate fawn greatcoat, flourishing his speaking trumpet to great effect. The day was chilly, even for early November, with a bitter wind blowing from the northwest, and it was as startingly clear as the day we had arrived in Galway some four weeks earlier. Oblivious to the biting wind, we steerage passengers were crowded amidships, craning to watch the paddlewheel steam tug ease *Maryann* from her berth and take her under tow. It was a highly complex maneuver that I couldn't observe well, although we could hear a sea shanty being sung on the foc'sle as they first cast off the lines that bound *Maryann* to the tug, and then brought a separate towline aboard and affixed it to the foc'sle bitts. As *Maryann* passed the Mutton Island lighthouse, the steam tug stopped, and a detail of packet rats on the foc'sle cast off the towline, which the tug's crew began hauling aboard. Meanwhile, another detail mustered aft on *Maryann's* quarterdeck, making ready, as Jeremy had explained to me in Galway, to hoist the great gaff-rigged fore-and-aft mainsail.

As the detail mustered, a call came from the quarterdeck—it was the second mate, I think. "All right, lads," he commanded, "*Oh, You New York Girls, Can't You Dance the Polka?*" Throughout the ship, the crew, whether on the foc'sle casting off the towline, on the quarterdeck raising the mainsail or aloft setting the other sails, began singing a rhythmic chorus together:

And away, you Santee
My dear Annie
O, you New York Girls
Can't you dance the Polka?

As the chant commenced, the quarterdeck detail began the hard labor of hoisting the main gaff 60 or so feet up the mainmast by rhythmically hauling on the throat halliard. Each spasm of the gaff ascending the mainmast commenced in perfect time with the last syllable of each line of the shanty's chorus, and was accompanied by a single stamp of the foot of each sailor on deck.

The chorus ended while the steam tug ran down *Maryann's* starboard side with one last blast from her steam whistle and a final wave good-bye from her master, who raised his pipe, as resplendent in his blue greatcoat as he had been when we arrived in Galway. The whistle blast concluded, and the second mate began to sing from the quarterdeck in his strong bass voice. At the end of each line, the main gaff was hauled another few feet up the mast to the accompanying foot stamping:

As I walked down the Broadway
One evening in July
I met a maid who asked me trade
And a sailor John says I.

To Tiffany's I took her
I did not mind expense
I bought her two gold earrings
And they cost me fifteen cents

As soon as he finished this verse, the rest of the crew began to sing the chorus once again.

> *And away, you Santee*
> *My dear Annie*
> *O, you New York Girls*
> *Can't you dance the Polka?*

Then the mate sang:

> *Says she, "You Lime Juice sailor*
> *Now see me home you may"*
> *But when we reached her cottage door*
> *She this to me did say.*

> *"My flash man he's a Yankee*
> *With his hair cut short behind*
> *He wears a pair of long sea-boots*
> *And he sails in the Blackball Line*

By now, as the chorus was sung for the third time, the mainsail had been hoisted halfway, and the foc'sle detail was securing from its towline tasks and turning to assist the rest of the crew in setting the other sails. The mate began the third verse as the chorus died away:

> *"He's homeward bound this evening*
> *And with me he will stay*
> *So get a move on, sailor-boy*
> *Get cracking on your way"*

> *So I kissed her hard and proper*
> *Afore her flash man came*

And fare ye well, me Bowery gal
I know your little game

Once more, the crew sang the chorus as the main gaff was hauled home, and the mainsail billowed, catching the breeze. The second mate began the final verse:

I wrapped me glad rags round me
And to the docks did steer
I'll never court another maid
I'll stick to rum and beer.

I joined a Yankee blood-boat
And sailed away next morn
Don't ever fool around with gals
You're safer off Cape Horn.

The packet rats sang the chorus one last time as the quarterdeck detail secured and the last sails were unfurled and their courses set. The Old Man set *Maryann's* head to west by southwest so as to pass south of the Aran Islands and into the great Western Ocean beyond.

The excitement of leaving harbor ebbed quickly away among the watching passengers. Many of them disappeared below into the steerage compartment to get out of the biting wind. Mary smiled at me and made her way to the galley to begin preparing the afternoon meal. I leaned against the leeward rail, studying the water coursing by just a few feet below me. Fíona wrapped herself inside the open flaps of my oilskin and leaned against me. Presently, Jeremy sidled up alongside.

"How do, buddy?" He clapped me on the shoulder and looked out over the water. "Man alive! It shore is good to be underway again."

I agreed with him, and then asked, "In the shanty, you were singing about a 'bowery girl'. What's that?"

"Oh," he replied. "You mean a Bowery g'hal?" He chuckled and continued, "That's how them Bowery b'hoys say it in Gotham, and them city swells chasing them g'hals through the Bowery dancehalls say it that way too. That way, they don't get crossways with them Bowery b'hoys. They's just about the orneriest critters you ever did see. Jes' as soon stomp a mick's face in with them boots o' theirs or start a fire jes' so's they can put it out with their own fire brigade as they would liquor up. So them uptown swells know to call them gals, Bowery g'hals."

I was fascinated. "Where's the Bowery? In Gotham?"

"Ayut," he grunted in that curious downeast manner of his. "Right cheek by jowl with the 'Points—which is where all the poor micks end up—right there with the darkies—and just south o' the Hook—where *Maryann*'ll tie up or anchor out."

"Darkies?"

Jeremy looked at me quizzically. "Yeah … like the cabin boy. 'Ceptin' he's from Jamaica. Anyway, the 'Points is the Five Points, which is the toughest slum in all Gotham. Makes the Hook—Corlears Hook—look good by comparison. Still, iff'n yer gonna be starting out in Gotham—I 'spect the 'Points're where you'll end up."

"Well," I countered, testing my drawl just a little bit and self-consciously breaking every rule of grammar so laboriously beaten into me at St. Patrick's by cane and rote memory, "I'm going west. I ain't gonna be stuck in no slum such as the 'Points. I reckon I'm gonna go where the sky opens up as big as it does here on the Western Ocean." I gestured to the winter sun slowly descending over the mouth of Galway Bay, towards which *Maryann* was sedately progressing.

"And where will that be?" Jeremy asked in an amused tone. He knew very well, because we had engaged in this self-same routine numerous times during our Galway sojourn.

"I'm headed to the Rocky Mountains. I'm going to be a famous mountain man," I replied defiantly. "I'm going to trap beaver and meet Jim Bridger and trade at Bent's Fort. And," I said dramatically, "I'm gonna have me a long rifle called Killdeer."

"Well, that ain't for me, pal," Jeremy replied. "It's like the 'Polka," he said, referring to the shanty. "I ain't gonna grow no barnacles and let some ruffian Bowery g'hal capture me. And I shore ain't gonna foul me anchor on some cherry pie that'd truss me to a plow on some farm somewhere."

I reflected to myself that I, too, was inclined to the sentiment of the pumping shanty I had gotten to know so well when we were keeping the ship afloat after the storm. Except I wanted to go to the Rocky Mountains. Jeremy could have the seafaring life. It wasn't for me.

Jeremy talked through my thoughts. "I'm a Jonathan," he concluded. "But I'm adopting that Lime Juicer's view of it. I'd be safer off Old Cape Stiff in a winter gale than barnacled in port with some ruffian g'hal who'd jes' kick me to the gutter when my brass was spent."

"So, what'll you do?"

"Waal," he drawled expansively. "Lemme tell ya. I'm gonna find me a right fine barky and ship out as a reg'lar packet rat. Go the whole hog on the best packet on the Western Ocean. Ship on a fast sailer like *Constitution* or that barky you like, *Fidelia*. I ain't shipping on nothing like this scow." He sniffed contemptuously. "If I'm shipping with a hard citizen like the Old Man and a bucko mate like the good Mr. Mounce, I want to be on a fast barky. None o' this shipping timber from Nova Scotia on 60-day passages, and runnin' outta water and such like. What I'd really like is one o' them 1,000 tonners that Donald McKay be building for the Enoch Train line outta Boston. They're gonna break 14 days' passage Liverpool to New York. Just you watch. And I want to be the fore-top captain when she does."

The fore-top captain, Jeremy had explained to me as we had sat in some quiet corner in the New Docks out of the way of the carpenter's demands and Mr. Mounce's wrathy fists, was the surest-footed sailor on the ship, with the most experience at the highest point on the foremast, where the last scrap of sail would be set in the worst storms—and which was thus the most dangerous, and most glamorous, packet rat's billet.

We idled for a few more minutes, staring quietly at the sinking sun and the low dark line of the Aran Islands as they began to pass on our starboard side. We, and every other soul on board were happy to see the last of those islands and the bleak Cliffs of Moher on our larboard side, and we all were equally happy to greet the three thousand miles of desolate Western Ocean between us and Gotham.

Jeremy skittered away before he could draw Mr. Mounce's ire—and his starter.

⌒

The weather continued to hold in our favor over the next many days, and we were all happy for that. The winds, as Jeremy explained to me, were not at their best for a swift passage (even by *Maryann*'s modest standards), but we were steadily plodding our way towards the setting sun. We were going to America, and we were going to get there—eventually.

I spent much of each day reading to Fíona from *Goody Two Shoes*. She could now pick out letters and even certain words, and she seemed to identify with Margery. We discussed Margery's attributes of being affectionate, frank and free. We compared Margery's affectionate nature to Fíona's own great affection for her mother. Going unmentioned, but not unnoticed, at least by me, Fíona had also been gradually growing more affectionate with me as the weeks had passed. I thought that this must be what having a younger sister must be like. We also discussed frankness and the need to be truthful one day when she slipped away from both Mary and me, and then tried to blame her disappearance on one of the other children. Freedom was a difficult concept for Fíona to understand. But we talked—perhaps I talked and she nodded to make me feel better—about what it meant to be a young man (or young lady) in America, free to make of oneself what one could. I felt a kinship with my father as I spoke, as many of the words I spoke seemed to emanate directly from him (or at least my conception of him).

Sometimes, Fíona and I would have some company in the form of one or another of the many young emigrant children. Some stayed for a while, others flitted in and out. But the constant of these sessions was Fíona and the intense pleasure she took from my reading with her. She and I also spent many an hour standing by the lee railing and studying the clouds on the horizon and the fish and porpoises accompanying us just a few feet away. The porpoises sometimes came so close that we could see their blowholes foaming as they emerged from the midst of a swell, arced through the air and then disappeared into the next swell. I occasionally had the eerie feeling that they were spending as much time studying us as Fíona and I spent studying them.

We learned from Jeremy and others that the porpoises would join us because they were guiding the ship to a safe haven, and their presence portended a good voyage and safe arrival. He also said that he had heard from other sailors, particularly the second mate (he of the deep bass voice and endless supply of sea shanties), many stories about porpoises. The second mate maintained that porpoises could foretell the weather. When they were travelling north, the weather portended fair, and when they were travelling south, the weather portended foul. Jeremy had told me that, one evening when the ship was in Galway, the second mate had said that he'd seen porpoises heading south the day before *Maryann* encountered the gale that had dismasted her. So he was a believer.

One day, Fíona and I were reading when we were joined by the two daughters of the cabin passengers, wide-eyed, solemn and holding hands. I didn't know how the two girls had escaped the clutches of their witchly mothers, but it gladdened me to be able to read to them for a bit from *Goody Two Shoes*. Fíona and I were reading of Mr. Graspel's taking the farm from Margery's father, Mr. Meanwell, and talking about how the mean Mr. Graspel was just like the land agent who took Fíona's home from her and her mother and father.

Fíona said in her English-Irish patois—not dissimilar to her mother's—that her *Daidí* had died just like Margery's father had, homeless and seemingly without hope. I could hear Mary's words as Fíona made the connection between our book and her life. Fíona's lip quivered a bit as she said that she did not want to lose her Ma like Margery lost hers. I hugged her and reassured her that she would not. Anyway, I was sure that Fíona would end up a beloved schoolteacher just like Margery Meanwell. Fíona then brightened, as small children will, and told me that Ma loved me very well, and that she and Ma wanted me to live with them because we could make a good life together in *Meiriceá*. I little doubted that her words ran nearly verbatim from Mary, virtually indecipherable Irish and all. In the telling, I wondered whether Mary saw me as anything more than a mere sexless boy. For despite my increasingly fevered dreams of her, stocked by the occasional touch of the foot in bed, or her hand on mine during the day—and by the occasional glimpse of her near-naked form (which had happened several times in our Galway lodgings, where Mary had been less concerned about revealing herself—so she apologetically said one day when I happened upon her)—she had never once seemed to look at me as anything else than that.

But this peaceful interlude, sheltered from the chilly wind and bright sun by the lee of the ship's boats (freshly repaired and restored to a properly seaworthy condition) was soon ended when the Quality harpies hove into sight, and with a reproving glare at me, scolded their two children into instant tears—all without a single word being uttered. I dismissed this episode—and the harpies and their knight and barrow pig husbands—as being from a former life to which I was never to return.

⌒

A few days later, I found myself sitting in the very same spot, sheltering from the wind and sun with pen and paper in hand. (We had had a beautiful run of almost two weeks now, and everyone was hoping for a swift and safe voyage now that the porpoises had joined us each day for many hours at a time.) I was resolving to commence a second, long-put-off letter to Evelyn. No matter my increasing distance from my former life and my increasing infatuation with Mary, I had not wavered from my pledge to write to Evelyn as often as I could (and, dared I even think about it, to kiss her again). I also looked forward to a time when I could hear from her. And then there were those golden curls, which remained so vividly in my mind's eye. I thought that I would never see such a beautiful girl again. I started writing of our adventures since Galway, elaborating on my growing kinship with Fíona while at the same time reducing Mary to the merest cipher. I also spent much time talking of porpoises, sea shanties (but not Bowery g'hals) and wanting to go west to the Rocky Mountains (with her by my side, of course).

I had just finished writing my letter when I saw Mary standing in front of me, squinting in the sunshine. She wore my oilskin to stay warm most days now when she came topside. But she nonetheless huddled against me for warmth as she handed me the brown paper package that she had given me the night before we left Galway.

"*Rinne mé dearmad ar seo ...*" she began. "I forgot this," she began again, remembering her resolution to speak "proper English" from now on. To that end, each night after we had been confined to our passenger compartment, we had spent many hours talking softly to each other in English in the dark before we fell asleep, lips and ears often but an inch or two apart.

"Open it," she said.

I did, and inside was a brand new copy of *The Last of the Mohicans*. Tears started in my eyes. Mary had inscribed it: "*Do mo ghrá*, Mary." The handwriting was hers, but it was a perfect script. I could only wonder how long she must have practiced. We hugged. I could do no more than whisper my thanks, or I would have flat-out cried. We sat together for a very long time after that, neither of us saying a word.

⌒

The next day, the weather changed for the first time since we had left Galway. The second mate swore to all who would hear him—until Mr. Mounce silenced him with an angry retort of, "Shut your neck"—that we were in for a blow now that the porpoises had fled south. The Old Man must have agreed, Jeremy told me, because we were now headed north-northwest to avoid the storm—if indeed one was coming. I must say that the passengers heartily agreed with the Old Man's decision, and met forthwith to direct Mr. O'Hurley to communicate their pleasure to him. I never did hear about Captain Urquehart's reaction to their pleasure. In fact, I'm not sure that Mr. O'Hurley was ever granted an audience to speak with him on the matter. For that very day, the Old Man ruined his fawn greatcoat.

Fíona and I were in the waist of the ship listening to a young man sing a lament of leaving home:

> *As slow our ship her foamy track*
> *Against the wind was cleaving,*
> *Her trembling pennant still look'd back*
> *To that dear isle 'twas leaving,*
> *So loath we part from all we love,*
> *From all links that bind us;*

So turn our hearts as on we rove,
To those we've left behind us.

The young tenor sent a wave of homesick melancholy through me, and I pined for a lost home and family that I probably never had—that is, other than my father, when he was there. I thought, too, of Evelyn, and whether she was even real, and if she were, whether she had really told me that she loved me. Poor, pure Evelyn. So different from the Evelyn the tenor had sung of just a few moments before:

Oh! Weep for the hour,
When to Eveleen's bower,
The Lord of the Valle with false vows came;
The moon hid her light
From the heavens that night,
And wept behind her clouds o'er the maid-
en's shame.

I could not have imagined my Evelyn putting herself in such harm's way, although I did recall with a shudder what that *cábóg*, O'Hara, had threatened to do to Mary, who had been innocent of all wrongdoing.

A tear started at the corner of my eye, and I caught Fíona staring at me solemnly. I was debating whether to say something to her when the cry came, "Make way. Make way for the Old Man." Captain Urquehart came bounding by, the skirts of his coat briefly flailing Fíona. As the Old Man heaved himself onto the foc'sle on some errand or another, I stared at him in silent fascination, because I'd rarely seen him leave the quarterdeck day or night, let alone venture as far forward as the foc'sle. Indeed, he owned the quarterdeck and left the running of the rest of the ship to Mr. Mounce and his starter.

The ship took a bit of a lurch in the mounting seas as the Old Man strode across the fo'csle with great purpose. His foot shifted, tipping over a bucket full of pitch. The pitch splattered all over the deck and the skirt to his greatcoat. It dried instantly. The Old Man grimaced at his ruined coat, and with a reddened fury contorting his neck, thundered, "God damn your eyes" to the unfortunate sailor who had been patiently caulking the decking with the pitch and oakum (and then very carefully cleaning up after himself to minimize the difficult task of holystoning the deck to restore it to white perfection). The sailor scrambled to his feet, automatically apologizing, but to no avail.

The Old Man raised his voice even further, and lashed at the poor sailor with the back of his hand, exclaiming, "You did this purposeful-like, you wretched gawnicus. Ye'll pay for this…"

He struck the sailor again, this time with an open hand slapping the man's jaw. The sailor lashed out blindly, catching the Old Man on the nose and eye. Mr. Mounce bounded up the ladder to the foc'sle and instantly smashed the sailor to the deck, senseless, with repeated blows from a belaying pin he had snatched up along the way. Mr. Mounce gestured contemptuously at the fallen packet rat and said in a voice that would have cut through the greatest gale, "Take this mutinous *get* below and clap 'im in irons."

The second mate jumped to the task with the greatest alacrity. I saw two packet rats roughly half-carrying, half-dragging their stunned comrade below through the main deck hatchway down to the orlop through the passenger compartment, with blood dripping from his head wounds the entire way.

Mr. Mounce then turned to the three or four sailors standing motionless on the foc'sle and ordered: "You there, you damned crinklenecks, quit dicking the dog and get this feather merchant's mess squared away!"

"Belay that, Mr. Mounce," the Old Man said. "Bring that blasted *get* to my cabin directly. We'll have him square it away."

With that, Captain Urquehart strode from the foc'sle and through the gawking passengers and idling packet rats to his cabin, the flapping skirt of his fawn greatcoat stiff with dried pitch.

Fíona looked at me very earnestly and lisped, "The Old Man was very cruel to that poor packet rat. He didn't do anything wrong."

Funny how children pick up the lingo. I smiled as I replied offhandedly, "Well, Jeremy says that a ship's captain like Mr. Urquehart is the very master of God, and Mr. Mounce sits at his right hand. So I reckon that the captain can do whatever he pleases."

"Does that mean he could hit me if he pleases?"

"Of course not, mo ghrá. Your Ma and I would never let that happen. Anyway, we're passengers, and he's not allowed to do that as we passengers don't mutiny—at least that's what the Irish Emigrant Society says."

"What's a mutiny?"

Within the hour, the unfortunate sailor, his head bound with a blood-stained bandage, had been hustled from the Old Man's cabin under tow from the second mate and a pair of packet rats, and deposited on the foc'sle, where he began laboriously holystoning. First the foc'sle deck, and then the deck amidships to the main hatch where the trail of blood continued below through the passenger compartment to the orlop where he had sat in irons for an hour waiting upon the Old Man—although he did not have to holystone the passenger compartment as the womenfolk had scrubbed those stains to a fare thee well long before he had finished holystoning the topside decks.

As Jeremy put it to me later, the poor sailor spent many hours "saying his prayers," as sailors call holystoning, an uncomfortable and exhausting task performed on one's hands and knees with little more than a square piece of sandstone the size of a bible and a small bucket of water—or sand if water were in short supply, as it often was onboard a sailing ship—scrubbing the deck to snowy whiteness. The second mate, at Mr. Mounce's direction, kept the poor man at his Augean task all night. And when later he collapsed, he was revived with cold seawater and set once more to scrubbing with his holystone.

It was several days after the sailor had holystoned the last of his own blood from the decks before we saw him again. Jeremy told me that the sailor had passed several feverish days in his hammock, calling for his mother in his sleep, before he was once more restored to his duties on the foc'sle. I reflected to Jeremy that the Old Man, the "master of God," didn't look quite so magnificent in the battered dark blue greatcoat that he wore for the rest of the voyage.

⌒

Two days later, we passengers were turned out for our morning muster in the freezing cold before dawn—the days were growing so much shorter the farther north we went and the later in the year it became. As the sun slowly rose in the east into a gloriously clear sky, we were met with a sight from another world. *Maryann* was lost in an endless forest of icebergs, ranging in size all the way from tiny growlers that bumped against the sides of the ship to massive ice mountains protruding many hundreds of feet high and dwarfing *Maryann* into an insignificant interloper in a strange and wondrous world.

We passengers rapidly learned from the crew, all of whom were very subdued in the still water and silence of this other-worldly place, that the icebergs were much, much bigger under the water. More worrisomely, each was a terrible hazard upon which the ship could founder and sink, leaving us all—passengers and crew alike—in the freezing water, hundreds of miles from any possible succor. Adding to the eerie nature of our predicament was the fog rising from the icebergs. This ice fog enveloped us completely on occasion, and then, at the merest breath of wind or seemingly for no reason at all, cleared so completely that we were once again overwhelmed by the vast iceberg forest sparkling under a brilliantly sapphire sky.

After muster broke, Mr. O'Hurley organized the passengers into prayer, and no one was inclined to disoblige him. He searched his memory for a moment as we all knelt with him, and then he prayed at length for our welfare:

> O most powerful and glorious Lord God, at whose
> command the winds blow, and lift up the waves of
> the sea, and who stillest the rage thereof; we, thy
> creatures, but miserable sinners, do in this our great
> distress cry unto thee for help: save, Lord, or else
> we perish. We confess, when we have been safe,
> and seen all things quiet about us, we have forgotten thee our God, and refused to hearken to the still
> voice of thy word, and to obey thy commandments:
> but now we see how terrible thou art in all thy
> works of wonder; the great God to be feared above
> all; and therefore we adore thy divine Majesty,
> acknowledging thy power, and imploring thy goodness. Help, Lord, save us for thy mercies' sake, in
> Jesus Christ, thy Son our Lord.

When he finished, we all enthusiastically replied, "Amen," and crossed ourselves. But we were not quite done. A voice, I didn't know whose, began and we joined in unison: "Our Father, who art in heaven ..." and recited the Lord's Prayer through the concluding doxology, "For thine is the power and glory, forever and ever. Amen." We arose from our knees as one and dispersed wordlessly.

We sat in the iceberg forest, becalmed, for many unvarying days. It was terribly cold everywhere in the ship—leaving a cup of water open on deck for even a few minutes would allow a thin scum of ice to form. Even below deck, in the passenger compartment, water froze nearly as quickly. And we shivered at night under our thin blankets, even when we wore all of our clothing.

But that was not the worst. At muster one morning, Mr. Mounce announced that the daily water ration was being cut in half as the ship was beginning to run out of fresh water—this with more water than all of Christendom could have drunk in a millennium barely beyond our reach in the iceberg forest, unattainable as a mirage, for no boat could safely approach them without risk of foundering on the unseen ice shoals lurking just below the surface. We had only been at sea for a little over a month at this point—Jeremy later told me we were 35 days out of Galway and just a week or two from Gotham, at most, and so we shouldn't have been short of water. Jeremy told me that the ship's cooper discovered that half a dozen casks were filled with brine instead of fresh water. These casks held more than two weeks' worth of drinking water, and were thus a serious loss. If we remained at sea for more than about 50 days or so, we were going to be very short of water. Nobody quite knew why the water casks were bad, but the Old Man was heard that evening at dinner damning the shipowner to the cabin passengers, after the cabin passengers had ventured to complain of the sudden decrease in their water allowances. When I heard this, I did spend a moment hoping that the knight of the barrow pigs was enjoying his thirst along with the rest of us.

Even though it was very cold, I continued to spend most of my days topside, secreted in my lair in the lee of the ship's boats. Fíona likewise passed many of these days with me. Sometimes I would read to her, and other times she simply sat with me while I reread *The Last of the Mohicans* to my heart's content. Fíona had progressed so much with her reading that she could now read many of the words from *Goody Two Shoes* to me. One day, we were approaching the end of the book, and began reading the story of Margery Meanwell's trial for witchcraft—all on account of the jealousy of women in the next village over Margery's helping the farmers in her own village. We compared Margery's trial to our own, becalmed in the midst of the iceberg forest, many hundreds of miles from safety. But Fíona and I agreed that all would turn out very well indeed—just like it did for Margery Meanwell, and we would arrive safely in New York. She and I had both heard the second mate say that the porpoises had swum with us for so many days, and that augured well for our voyage.

But it was not to be quite so easy. Food stocks were running low as well. Many—among them all of those freed from the work-house—had been relying entirely on the miserable ration issued each noontime by the ship's cook ever since the ship had departed Galway. Those passengers who had replenished their comestibles in Galway had by-and-large run out and were now slowly starving on the ship's rations. And the lucky ones, such as Mary and me, had only the slenderest reserves left.

Tempers frayed and those with comestibles constantly kept them physically close. Yet thievery still happened. One night, we awoke to a vigilante mob descending upon the impecunious family in the bunk above us. Mary reacted first, gasping at the thunder of bare feet and hob-nailed boots on the deck. I opened my eyes to the sight and stench of unkempt clothing and unwashed bodies and legs occluding our bunk entirely. Fíona screamed in terror as Mary and I huddled together, shielding her—and ourselves—from the violence above. Cries of terror and pain from the woman of the family and the little boy—hardly more than a spavined tod-dler—were stifled, and I could hear the sickening thud of punches and blows landing, presumably on the man. Then as quickly as it started, the mob vanished. The woman and the little boy sobbed for a very long time. The man, aside from a single, audible groan, made no noise at all. The rest of the nearby steerage passengers stayed as quiet as church mice, except for the fevered whispers of some.

Mr. O'Hurley must have said something to the first mate, for Mr. Mounce bellowed with indignation at muster the next morning. "I will not tolerate lynch mobs, for surely that is what occurred last evening. If there is another such occurrence, I will manacle every male passenger and there will be no rations save for hardtack and water. If there is another reported incident of theft, there will be the same consequence, and if anyone is caught stealing, he will receive twenty lashes."

Fíona asked me if Mr. Mounce's threat meant that there had been a mutiny. I whispered that it was close enough.

We were dismissed below and locked in steerage for the remainder of the day. But there were no more thefts of food.

About a week later, some of the passengers began to exhibit signs of scurvy—a disease I had never heard of, raised as I was in a wealthy and sheltered home. Scurvy can be cured by a little juice from a lime, a lemon or an orange. Mary told me that she had occasionally seen poor *spalpeen* and their families suffer from scurvy when times were bad. Death was never far behind for the afflicted, that is unless they could get themselves to a workhouse—a fate that I had always considered to be worse than death.

We were horrified one morning to see the gaunt man, whom I had met in Murray the shipping agent's office the day we boarded *Maryann*, collapse on deck. He was missing most of his teeth, his face was deathly pale and his gums were bleeding. Someone lifted his shirt, and we could see suppurating sores on his stomach. The ship had no doctor other than the cook, of course, and all that could be done for him was to take him below to his bunk and give him a little lime juice from somebody's precious hoard. He and his family were among the first to have run out of their own food stocks, and they had been subsisting solely on the ship's food for quite a while. I also heard from one of his friends that the gaunt man had been starving himself even longer than that in order to eke out his stocks for his wife and children. Mary and I, along with everyone else with any remaining food stocks, each contributed a little of our lime juice to a central store, which was then doled out daily by Mr. O'Hurley.

A few days later, we passengers gathered and voted to deputize Mr. O'Hurley to ask the Old Man to release more of the ship's food stocks, particularly the lime juice, so as to prevent further starvation. Although he was not terribly pleased about having anything to do with Captain Urquehart, particularly as the Old Man had been in a perpetual dutch fit ever since he had ruined his greatcoat, Mr. O'Hurley eventually fixed his courage to its sticking place and mounted the ladder to the quarterdeck.

About a hundred of us were standing amidships, trying not to stare aft, when Mr. O'Hurley approached the Old Man. Mr. Mounce was nowhere to be seen, so Mr. O'Hurley ventured to address the Old Man directly.

None of us could hear what Mr. O'Hurley said, but we did hear the Old Man respond, "Damn your eyes, Mr. O'Hurley, you will not dare address me on my quarterdeck. You gawnicus … you worthless feather merchant! Now, begone sir, before I horsewhip you myself … Mr. Mounce?" he called. "Mr. Mounce? Oh, there you are. Would you be so kind as to escort this …" he paused, "this … gawnicus from my quarterdeck?"

"Aye aye, Skipper." Mr. Mounce knuckled his forehead briefly, and began escorting Mr. O'Hurley from the quarterdeck, talking to him under his breath. We passengers turned away so as not to witness Mr. O'Hurley's shame as he scurried below into the passenger compartment, looking for all the world like a whipped cur.

As he passed by, a man's voice was heard to say mockingly, "Not at the right hand o' O'Connell no more, are ye', me little *maneen?*" He was immediately "shushed" by the appalled voice of a woman. His wife, no doubt. But that was the end of Mr. O'Hurley as the passengers' representative. He, like the accused thief, hardly departed his bunk for the remainder of the voyage. The only positive thing to arise from this incident was that "Doc," the ship's cook, under the second mate's direct supervision, began issuing tiny quantities of lime juice to the sickest of the passengers, including the gaunt man and his family.

⌒

So it went. Each day, we got a little hungrier and had a little less water. It also stayed very cold as *Maryann* slowly picked her way through the iceberg forest. Every night, the Old Man would heave the ship to. We then spent the night moving with only the barest way on, just enough to keep the bow pointed southwest towards New York—not that anyone (other than Jeremy occasionally whispering to me) told the passengers where in the Sam Hill the ship was. Lookouts were kept at the top of each mast and at the base of the bowsprit in the very eyes of the ship, looking for the ghostly shapes of icebergs that would break through the fog to loom ominously over us, sometimes just a few tens of yards away before they were spotted. The Old Man, Mr. Mounce and the second mate hardly left the quarterdeck at night and kept the lookouts at their vital task in the harshest manner. I only knew about this nightly exercise from Jeremy because we passengers were locked below each night, where we all prayed that we would not hear a grinding collision with the ice.

Finally, the winds began to freshen and the seas swell. Miraculously, over the course of a day and a night, the iceberg forest broke apart and the icebergs simply vanished without a trace. *Maryann* was once more alone on the Western Ocean, under sail, plodding her way towards New York. If Mr. O'Hurley had not taken permanently to his bunk, I am sure that he would have led us in offering our thanks to the Good Lord. I saw Mary privately offering thanks, kneeling with Fíona on the bunk when I came below to relieve her of watching our food stocks so that she could go topside to cook a little something for us in the galley.

In a fine twist of fate, it actually became much easier to cook in the galley in the weeks after Mr. O'Hurley's humiliation. The vast majority of people had run out of food, and those few who were left to burden the small galley fire with their cooking demands had very little to cook with. We were among the most fortunate, and even we now had only a little flour left—and no bacon. We contented ourselves for many days with a single small loaf of cakebread to relieve at least a little of our mounting hunger, which Mary baked every afternoon, squatting before the fire as she shivered almost uncontrollably with the cold. I took over these duties after a while, but my baking efforts were miserable compared to Mary's.

Mary and I had also run through all of our lime juice, and we now prayed that we would reach New York before we too came down with the scurvy that had laid so many others low.

Over the next two weeks, now that we were clear of the iceberg forest, *Maryann* endured three back-to-back howling storms, which drove icy rain into every crevice on the ship. They were nowhere near as intense as the tempest that had dismasted *Maryann* so many weeks ago, and for that blessing we were thankful. But the resulting damp and mildew penetrated every article of clothing and bedding—even our tick dampened and the straw became matted, destroying the last vestiges of dry refuge in our bunk.

Until those storms soaked us, I didn't think that we could have gotten any colder or become any more miserable. But we did. My oilskin failed to help Mary and Fíona very much, even though they spent virtually all day wrapped in it, huddling together for warmth in the bunk, under it and the blanket. When the weather cleared, I was able to get back on deck once again, but it was now too cold to think about sitting, let alone reading either of our books—which had been wrapped in my oilskin cap and carefully stored at the foot of our bunk to avoid any damage. Only constant movement up and down the waist of the ship, from foc'sle to quarterdeck and back again, provided any measure of relief. But I was careful after the first day not to sweat while I exercised, because if I did, the cold became that much worse once I stopped moving.

Christmas Day came with hardly a word from anyone. Neither Mary nor I mentioned it to Fíona. We had nothing with which to even begin to celebrate the holiday, and I rather suspected that Fíona had few if any memories of the holiday beyond the obligatory church service, and that as I understood it Mary's only experience with Christmas—if any at all—would have been during those few months she was a serving girl at the landlord's house.

As soon as I opened my eyes on Christmas morning, I said a prayer for poor Murray—the first time I'd prayed since I was a small boy. But it had been a long time since I'd given Philip Murray any thought, and I felt quite guilty. I then said a prayer for Father O'Muirhily's soul. I spent the remainder of the day thinking of my father, without thinking further of O'Connell, the Repeal Year or any of the rest of that nonsense I'd left behind in Ireland. I instead relived the last Christmas I had spent with him and the ten days after, a halcyon time just before the Repeal Year and all the madness that had followed. We had enjoyed a fine goose and cracklings on Christmas Day, and had walked the hills outside Cork on the couple of fine days during Christmas week. We had rung in the new year quietly, and I had left for school two days later.

Late on the afternoon of the last day of the year, as the bleak, cloudy winter sky began to darken, a call came from the lookout high up on the foretopmast. "Land ho! Broad on the starboard bow!"

The Old Man whipped his looking glass to his eye and studied something we on deck could not see with the naked eye.

He exclaimed, "Mr. Mounce, the charts, if you please."

The two consulted for a few moments, and then agreed on something—I couldn't tell what, and I was condemned to ignorance until Jeremy contrived to skitter by, whispering *sotto voce* into my ear, "Montauk Point. The very tip of Long Island. Right where we should be."

He clattered off to the foc'sle on one errand or another.

I turned to Mary and said to her, smiling, "*Agrá*, I think we can see *Meiriceá*."

She jumped up and grabbed me around the neck and gave me a huge kiss on the lips. As I recovered, she knelt down to Fíona and said, "*Meiriceá, agrá.*" She then picked up her daughter so that she could see the smudge on the horizon Fíona craned wordlessly for a moment, and then shrugged. For her, there was nothing yet to see. But people were crowding around us, asking, "*Meiriceá?*"

I looked around and said, "I'm not sure. But let us pray to God that it is so." With that, a buzz moved about the now-crowded waist of the ship.

No word came from the quarterdeck as we waited breathlessly, and the expectant excitement gradually began to ebb away. But nobody left, and a few latecomers made it more crowded still. Finally, after what seemed an eternity, just as the last light left the horizon and the cold began to deepen, the bos'un's whistle called us passengers to muster.

Mr. Mounce presided over us from amidships at the quarterdeck railing. The Old Man was behind him, indifferent to the proceedings. Behind the Old Man, the six Quality cabin passengers, looking as sleek and well-fed as the day they boarded *Maryann*—if somewhat thirstier and much grubbier from a lack of water to drink and in which to wash themselves and their clothing—affected complete disinterest. But we steerage passengers were anything but uninterested, and as many of us who could leave our bunks surged aft towards the quarterdeck, straining to listen.

"Attention, all passengers," Mr. Mounce brayed at a volume just below that necessary to be heard in a North Atlantic gale. "We have made landfall off the Long Island coast, at Montauk Point, the very eastern end of the island. We expect to be in New York Harbor tomorrow." He paused dramatically. "The cook will issue double rations this evening and a double allowance of water." Cheers and clapping erupted from amidships, so he spoke no further.

Voices came from the crowded waist of the ship, "Hip hip."

We cheered, "Huzzah!"

"Hip hip," the directing voices cried once again

"Huzzah!"

"Hip, hip," came the cry a third time, and we gladly responded one last time, "Huzzah!"

Needless to say, the ship was joyful that night, as bellies were filled and thirsts well-slaked for the first time in weeks, and we all wished each other the best for the coming new year in the New World. Better yet, Mr. Mounce had promised us two sets of double rations and double water allowances on the morrow, the new year's first day, as we made the passage along the length of Long Island towards the great harbor of New York. The gesture was a fine *handsel* for the new year, and we were all very happy for the good luck such a gift would bring.

After we ate, I went below to look out my few possessions. A notion struck me, and I reached under my clothing and pulled out my wallet. It had been weeks since I had looked at it—there had been no need. I opened it, expecting to see one gold sovereign, four shillings and three pence—all the monetary wealth I had in the world. But instead of there being just four shillings, there were eight and twenty—and there was an extra gold sovereign. In other words, I had £2, 4s more than I should have. I was as shocked as I had been since leaving Ireland, and I could not conceive of where it might have come from.

Then I remembered. Mary.

I had given her my wallet during the last storm, when I went topside into the lashing rain to rinse a blanket that had become fouled with sickness from the poor woman in the bunk above us. But where on earth ... I ran topside, and found Mary at the starboard railing, staring into the inky blackness, trying to conjure Long Island into her mind's eye. Fíona stood beside her, clutching her leg.

"My wallet ..." I said.

Mary looked at me coolly, and said in perfect English, "We've been a burden on you, and you want to go west. You'll need the money to get you to the Rocky Mountains."

"What about you?" I wasn't prepared for this. I don't know why. We had been dancing for weeks around the question of what we were going to do once we reached New York. I wanted to go west ... and she wasn't sure what she wanted—that is, not beyond shepherding Fíona to a happy adulthood, as if that weren't enough.

"Fíona 'n' me, *beidh muid ceart go leor linn féin*," she answered, defensively reverting to Irish.

"You'll be fine?" I asked sarcastically—my Irish had improved nearly as much as Mary's English had during the course of our passage over the Western Ocean. "How much money do you have?"

"*Beidh go leor againn chun a theact leis*," she replied defiantly.

"What's enough for the two of you?" I pressed.

"*Ceithre scilling.*"

"Four shillings?" I mocked. I had never spoken to her like this. We stood toe to toe, glaring at each other, intensely private in our whispered discussion in the cold dark of the winter evening, surrounded in the waist of the ship by a hundred oblivious passengers and crew.

"*Tá go leor againn anois, go dtí go dtosaím i seirbhís*," she snapped. She repeated herself in English, "It's enough for us for now." She also said something about going into service. She must have been contemplating becoming someone's maid. Now there was an irony. (Yes, I did occasionally pay attention to my English master back at St. Patrick's.) Mary and her beloved daughter were going to have braved the Western Ocean, only for Mary to go right back into service as the upstairs maid or some such thing for a wealthy American family somewhere, the same situation she had left behind in Ireland—semi-involuntary servitude at the Big House.

"No it's not." I opened my wallet and forced all the money, gold sovereigns and shillings alike—save a single gold sovereign for myself in case of emergency—into her hand. She resisted at first, and then relented, looking at me.

"A *Dhia*," she said in exasperation, holding the money uncertainly. "What about you going west? How're you going to get to the Rockies?"

"I'll figure that out," I said defiantly. "But you cannot be without money—if nothing else, it's for her." I gestured to Fíona.

Mary hesitated and then agreed, "For her."

We both looked down at Fíona, who looked back at us each in turn, and then back again, trying to understand. I couldn't explain to Fíona what had just happened, because I didn't understand it myself. I wasn't going to ask Mary to explain it, and she didn't seem inclined to explain—if indeed she knew herself.

That night, when the hatches had been closed and the lights in steerage doused and the night noises had dulled to almost nothing, Mary and Fíona shifted, rousing me from a deep slumber in which my unbidden thoughts were leading me on a merry chase involving both Evelyn and Mary—and Fíona, although not Fíona as I recognized her, but in some future, almost ethereal self. For the first time since we'd embarked in Cork those many weeks before, Mary was pressed up against me, her head on my shoulder. She said nothing—nor did I—as her hand playfully explored.

Early the next morning, *Maryann* eventually stopped a mile or so from a lighthouse on a sandy spit of land—Sandy Hook, New Jersey, so Jeremy told Mary and me—just as we were mustering amidships and wishing each other the joy of the new year. A harbor pilot embarked from one of a dozen pilot boats milling about, some of them little more than rowboats tossing about in the chop, each with a pilot on board waiting for the opportunity (and the handsome fee) to guide an arriving packet ship or cargo ship into New York or Brooklyn or Perth Amboy in New Jersey, and the ship slowly once more got underway, leaving Sandy Hook behind her as she moved north towards Gotham.

Jeremy flitted by on his various errands and pointed out the sights to us as they unfolded. Staten Island, on our larboard side, and Long Island, which we could just see off the starboard side, were nothing like the dramatic entrance to Galway Bay. The two coasts sat low and unassuming under a sullenly cloudy and cold January sky. As we moved into the narrows proper, we saw small fishing villages and boats dotting the Staten Island beaches.

By mid-afternoon, we were through the narrows, and the bay expanded once again, allowing us our first glimpse of New York, Governors Island and Brooklyn. We were following two other ships, both far more magnificent than the homely *Maryann*. They spread their sails as they proceeded deeper into the harbor, leaving us far behind. The New Jersey shore, now that we were past Staten Island, was increasingly populated, and seemed to bustle. On the starboard side, the Long Island sand dunes had given way to farmland which was just now giving way to the great city of Brooklyn, with its unending piers and hundreds of ships and boats of every description. We could also see ahead of us on the starboard side, between New York and Brooklyn, the castles and forts of Governors Island guarding the harbor and the city proper. The scale of the harbor and its cities and military defenses dwarfed anything I had ever seen. Even Cork, with its magnificent harbor, dwindled to insignificance, and Dublin was tiny in comparison.

Maryann turned to the northeast after having passed Governors Island and the full expanse of New York opened up in front of us: Buildings that went north as far as the eye could see from a nonstop row of piers thicker on the shore than even in Brooklyn, whose size and density of shipping we scarcely had believed. The entire harbor seethed with activity: ships arriving and departing up and down both waterfronts, and innumerable vessels of every type and description plying their ways to and fro in the harbor. Jeremy pointed to a bend to the right ahead of us in what was now the East River, and said that Corlears Hook was on the Manhattan, or larboard side, and that was where we would be mooring, at one of the South Street piers. On the starboard side, Jeremy pointed out the shipyards where the huge 1,000-ton clipper ships were being built by Donald McKay's Brooklyn-based competitors. Jeremy again reflected to me that he was going to ship out on "one o' them fine barkies." There would be no more *Maryann* for the likes of him, he declared.

Finally, we were opposite the South Street piers. But the ship stopped, and did not head in. In fact, with a minimum of ceremony and nary an explanation from the Old Man or Mr. Mounce, *Maryann* simply dropped her anchor in the deepening gloom of the late January afternoon, just 200 yards away from the New World. As the windlass was cranked out, the Second Mate sang a shanty and the windlass crew sang back the chorus, which might have helped them with their work but didn't do much for our spirits, being so close to getting off that ship.

It wasn't until evening that Mr. Mounce caused us steerage passengers to be mustered amidships. While we waited, we saw the six Quality cabin passengers and all of their baggage pass through us to a waiting boat that rowed them ashore.

After we had mustered, Mr. Mounce announced to us, "Immigration authorities will not arrive on board until tomorrow morning. Once immigration authorities have cleared the ship to debark its passengers, then you will be transported ashore before the end of the day. The ship will not be mooring at the South Street piers because of a lack of room due to other ships arriving today before *Maryann*."

And so to bed we went—without any food or water being issued that evening.

⌒

It was brutally cold when we were mustered before dawn the next morning. A passenger steam launch, snorting and belching like the steam tug in Galway Bay, was tied alongside *Maryann* to her starboard side. On the quarterdeck, Mr. Mounce was conferring with a group of men in black overcoats and top hats. The Old Man was nowhere to be seen. We passengers stood restlessly amidships, waiting for Mr. Mounce. Our belongings lay below, packed and ready to go. Mary and Fíona stood beside me as we waited, Mary wrapped in my oilskin and Fíona shrouded underneath the slicker's tails.

One of the top-hatted men descended the ladder to the main deck and began walking through the passengers, stopping to look at a few of them, seemingly at random. The word spread like a wave through the crowd of passengers, "*An dochtuír, an ollamh.*" The medical officer stopped in front of the gaunt man and his family. Seemingly wordlessly, the doctor gestured to an accompanying sailor, who led the family to the foc'sle. The gaunt man's wife was crying. Again the word spread through the crowd, "*Tá tinneas orthu.*" They're sick. Finally, after having the sailor conduct three more passengers to the foc'sle, the doctor returned to the quarterdeck, and the top-hatted men once again grouped around Mr. Mounce in conference.

The pipe sounded muster, and we gathered more closely to the quarterdeck. No one felt the cold—or the hunger of not having eaten since the previous morning. We all craned to hear Mr. Mounce.

"Attention," he began as always. "The passengers on the foc'sle will remain aboard until other arrangements can be made. The rest of you will be conducted below in groups of twenty to gather your belongings and depart *Maryann* on the steam launch."

With that, a group of sailors, Jeremy among them, began conducting passengers below. Jeremy came straight to Mary and me and hustled us below to gather our belongings. Despite Jeremy's efforts, by the time we returned topside, the line to board the steam launch must have been a hundred people long, all of them jostling and jockeying for position. With hardly another word, Jeremy disappeared into the crowd. Mary, Fíona and I moved forward steadily in line. We hardly talked. I was too keyed with excitement, and lost in thought.

Then we were at the head of the line. I guided Mary and Fíona down the ladder to the waiting steam launch, and then handed down all of our belongings, my bag included, to the sailor waiting on the launch. I turned to accompany them, but a hand grabbed me, and a voice said, "Na', lad, ye'll be waiting on the launch's return. She's got her complement. No one else goes aboard."

I turned to call out to Mary, who was mutely looking up at me. Before I could utter a syllable, the same voice said, "Belay that noise. Ye'll see the missus shoreside. Ye'll be going ta Pike Slip. She'll be thar, waiting fer yers."

As the launch pulled away, Jeremy thrust his dial plate in front of me. "I've been promoted to the foretop. No more ship's boy for me." He was positively giddy with glee. "Where are Mary and Fíona?"

"In the launch."

Jeremy looked at me quizzically and then seemed to make up his mind. "Mr. Mounce wants t'see yers."

With that, he whisked me to the quarterdeck, where Mounce was in heated conversation with a top-hatted man who had inspected the passengers. By and by, Mounce finished haranguing the man, and they parted frostily.

Jeremy tugged at his sleeve. Mounce turned with an irritated look that quickly vanished.

"Oh, aye. The Irish lad. What's yer name, lad?"

"Gogan, Sir. Billy Gogan." I doffed my cap.

"Got some manners, now, don't yers." Mounce looked pointedly at Jeremy, who smiled even more broadly.

"Ye showed some fine hustle, there, durin' the storm. Ye'd make a fine packet rat."

Mounce considered me for a moment. "So how's about it? Want to run away to sea?"

So, there it was. Despite all of my bluster with Jeremy to the contrary and the memories of our recent privations banished from my mind, I was suddenly seized with the notion of becoming a packet rat. Probably the only one on the Western Ocean with a working knowledge of Latin, mind you. And even better, I could squirrel away the chink and return to Ireland with a grubstake.

"Now that the missus' has gone ashore, ye may be able t'consider it a little more gentleman-like," Mounce was observing.

And there was the rub. I did have to consult with Mary. I owed it to her. Not as Mounce thought, but as a friend—one whom I'd promised to meet on the pier, and the only person who had called me "family." That crystalized the matter, and I made the only decision I could.

I was going to America.

⌒

PART THREE

Gotham:
The Promised Land

JANUARY–AUGUST 1845

CHAPTER 8

I'm So Cold I Could Die

DUSK WAS PASSING QUICKLY INTO NIGHT when the steam launch finally returned, and we remaining passengers boarded. The launch rocked a bit as it made its way to the wharves. There were about a hundred of us on board, and we hardly spoke as we peered through the deepening gloom at the city. Finally, the launch pulled up to the pier, and we were allowed to disembark. As I waited my turn, I craned around, looking for Mary and Fíona. But I didn't see them. I had expected the pier to be a veritable madhouse. Instead, it was virtually deserted. The two ships tied up on the opposite side of the pier were dark and quiet, and the pier itself was just as dark and empty.

We passengers trudged in disconsolate little groups to the head of the pier. Most walked without stopping past a night watchman, who was looking at us curiously.

I stopped and asked him, "Could you tell us where the Irish Emigrant Society representative is?"

"Not here, pal," the watchman replied.

"He's gone already?" I asked in surprise. "He was supposed to meet the people from the *Maryann* as they disembarked."

"Yeah, well, he waren't coming here t'day, 'cuz them micks waren't s'posed t'be coming here," the watchman said. "Nobody's coming ashore through Bulgers Slip. Not today, leastways. We waren't 'spectin' you micks."

"This isn't Pike Slip?" I asked.

"Nope," came the laconic reply.

"Well, sir, then where is Pike Slip?"

The night watchman swung his lantern vaguely in the direction of some other piers. "Go down about three piers, and that be Pike Slip."

"Thanks." I gestured to the few of my fellow travelers who were still within earshot, and told them what had happened. They all shrugged, and continued on their way. They weren't looking for anyone, and they were anxious to be going. I trudged along the mostly deserted street lined with low-looking lusheries and chandleries and countless other businesses, all closed for the evening. Except for the lusheries, that is.

Pike Slip was utterly deserted except for a man wearing a bright green necktie. He was plodding down the pier like the last guest leaving a raucous party. When he saw me, his face positively lit up.

"*Mo fear maith*," he said in the thickest Irish accent I had ever heard.

I must have looked at him quite blankly because he immediately switched to a relatively clear English—though with much of his Irish accent still remaining, "Ye look a mite bit lost, there, pal."

I put on my best American drawl, courtesy of Jeremy. "I'm looking for my cousin," I lied casually, conscious of not wanting to appear the simkin. "I'm meeting her fresh off that barky yonder, the *Maryann*." I gestured out into the East River.

The man in the green necktie's Irish accent faded dramatically. "Oh, they're long gone now, pal. We sent most of 'em to the 'Points. Them coves was all as poor as Job's turkey. Waren't two nickels to rub together among the lot of 'em. I couldn't 'a sold nothing to them church mice," he finished in disgust.

"Thanks," I said, not wanting to ask this runner directions to the 'Points, the only place I knew of to begin searching for Mary and Fíona. The Irish Emigrant Society circular I had read back in Cork had warned of these runners, dangerous fellows who would as soon sell you something worthless or send you to a rum boarding-house to be fleeced or robbed at knifepoint as look at you.

The runner wandered off into the dark.

There was a pier watchman on Pike Slip as well. He looked like a better source of information.

"The 'Points?" The watchman scratched his head. "Tough place, there, friend. You watch out fer yerself. You hear?" He paused. "Lemme see." He scratched his head. "Go down South Street thataways, and take a right on Oliver. Head up there, and ye'll be running into Chatham Square. Head over to Mott, and then to Cross, and then ye'll be in the middle of it."

I memorized the directions.

"Oh, and stay away from that Old Brewery, friend. It be a pow-erful bad bit of hell's half-acre."

"Thanks," I replied. "By the way, was there a young lady and a small child here, waiting for someone?"

"I don't rightly recollect, pal. But we made 'em all skedad-dle an hour or so ago. Cain't have 'em hanging 'round after candle-lighting."

I waved my thanks and departed down South Street, in search of the Five Points and Mary and Fíona, and very conscious that I had only a single gold sovereign secreted in my wallet and that Mary had everything else I owned (including all of the rest of our—my—money).

⌒

I followed the night watchman's directions impeccably, and just as it began to snow I arrived at Paradise Square—which was anything but paradisiacal. No one was about other than a single drunken woman, bare-shouldered and bare-breasted in the falling snow, standing under a single gaslight that illuminated the center of the square, where an unpainted fence in an advanced state of disrepair defined a triangular plot of land containing three or four sickly-looking trees. The shadows cast by the flickering gaslamp created a scene as spectral as it was forlorn.

The woman proposed to me what I took to be a most indecent act—for a shilling to buy food for her *wain*, no less. I declined her offer as best I could, and she disappeared into the gloom. I shivered, not entirely from the cold, and did not linger.

I moved out of the square and up a street. I walked up and down it and many other streets for many hours, in and out of occasional pools of light from other gaslamps, until I could walk no more. I stumbled up a narrow, deserted alley, half blind with fatigue. I thankfully found no footpads. But I did find a doorway in the side of a brick building well up the alley that was recessed deep enough for me to escape most of the snow. I shivered violently for a while as I huddled in the doorway, until sleep mercifully overtook my last conscious thought, which was that I was so cold I thought I might just die.

I awoke with a start to a narrow slice of piercingly blue sky arced above the alley, the opposite side of which was an unpainted two-and-a-half story frame building that leaned drunkenly into the alley, threatening imminent collapse. About six inches of snow had fallen during the night, and had covered virtually every exposed surface. I had never seen so much snow—it being a rare event in Ireland, and snow does not collect at sea. I was thankful that the doorway had been deep enough to shelter me from the worst of it, and I was even more thankful for the pile of rags that someone must have thrown on me during the night as I slept, for they had provided at least a little additional warmth. But I was nonetheless as stiff and cold as I'd ever been.

I finally roused myself and began wandering the streets, partly to warm myself, and partly to try to find the Irish Emigrant Society office at No. 18 Spruce Street, where I was sure Mary would be waiting for me, and all would be well. I refused to think about the alternative. As I wandered, I caught a glimpse of my reflection in the filthy store window (the hand-lettered sign over the door and window proclaimed "Second-Hand Dry Goods") on Baxter Street and did a double take, not recognizing the long, lank hair and filthy face of a street urchin. I looked at my fingernails critically and was equally appalled, for the lowest cadger idling on St. Patrick's Bridge over the River Lee would have been ashamed of them. My clothing was in a sad state of disrepair, having seen neither brushing nor cleaning in many weeks—ever since it had become too cold for Mary, bless her heart, to go topside in the waist of the ship and hang them over the lee gunwale and beat them until the dust flew.

I resolved to make myself as presentable as possible, given my slender resources. I could not have my hair cut, for that took money. But I could do something about my face and fingernails, which I cleaned with my small penknife and then chewed and pared to a relatively acceptable length. I scrubbed my hands and face with a rag I had providentially taken with me from where I had slept. Finally, I slicked my hair back with my newly cleaned fingernails (which unfortunately necessitated another cleaning) and restored my cloth school cap (well beaten against the corner of the brick building, along with my coat and waistcoat. There was naught I could do with my shirt or trousers—which hung loosely with all the weight I had lost since leaving Ireland).

I returned to the shop window, and was moderately satisfied with the improvements. I had done what I could to restore some modicum of respectability to my person, and I presented myself at No. 18 Spruce Street at eleven o'clock by my pocket watch.

A brass bell tinkled faintly as I closed the door behind me, and I luxuriated in the sudden warmth, there being a large fireplace on the far side of the room, oblivious to anything else.

"May I help you, sir?" I heard a polite voice in the faintest of Irish accents.

I gaped at a gentleman at the enquiries desk peering at me owlishly through a pair of wire-rimmed glasses perched precariously on the bridge of his nose. I remembered my manners and hurriedly removed my battered cloth cap. "My name is Billy Gogan, sir. I landed last night from the good barky *Maryann*, and I must find my travelling companions. We were separated yesterday as we came ashore."

"The good barky *Maryann* ..." he said to himself. He smiled slightly and said, "That may be a little generous given what we heard yesterday from cabin passenger and steerage alike."

He snapped from his momentary reverie, and continued briskly, "Did you see our representative, Mr. Byrne, yesterday? He was able to assist a number of your erstwhile companions in avoiding some of the worst of the runners and touts—you know," he said to my questioning look, "thieves' lookouts and such-like riff-raff."

"No sir," I replied. "I did not see Mr. Byrne. By the time I came ashore, late last evening to the wrong quay, there was no one there. By the time I found Pike Slip, there was only the night watchman ... and a tout of the type you just identified. I paid him no mind."

"Very wise," he said equably. "It is unfortunate, though, that you did not meet your companions. Do you know where they were to be travelling to?"

I replied in my best public school accent, "We had not had the opportunity to make specific arrangements, sir." I smiled faintly at him in explanation. "We were travelling in steerage, and so we had little guidance other than your circular."

"Well, that is unfortunate. If you knew where they were to go, I could assist you in making further inquiries. But further than that, I cannot help, for the Society does not maintain any registry that would assist us in such an endeavor. But you may leave a note. Perhaps your travelling companion will call here, looking for you as you are looking for her."

My heart sank. But I refused to consider the full implication of Mary and Fíona having gone missing. To do so would be to stare into the abyss. And I felt my spirit far too weak for such a trial.

The gentleman looked at me sharply, "Where did you spend last evening?"

I didn't know how to reply for the shame of it.

"You spent it rough?" he asked, not unkindly. "No money?"

"My travelling companion has all of it, save a sovereign. And I wasn't going to spend that last evening."

"No. I wouldn't think so. You sound educated. Can you read and write?"

"Of course," I began haughtily. The gentleman stiffened slightly, and I remembered the Quality knight of the barrow pigs. "My apologies, sir." I modulated my tone, "I can indeed read and write."

"Very good." The gentleman seemed somewhat mollified by my change in tack. "Unfortunately, I cannot direct you to employment that would, shall we say, take full advantage of your abilities …" He abruptly shifted tack, himself. "When did you last eat?"

I had to think. "It's been a couple of days, sir."

"Ours is not an eleemosynary society," he said, and I thought he must have had to recite that proposition any number of times each day to poor Irish immigrants desperate for help.

"But," he continued, "I am hungry myself, and I would be most honored if I could oblige you to lunch with me."

I agreed thankfully, and we left the Society's offices to the faint tinkle of the brass bell and the turning of a sign in the door so that it stated that the Society would be closed until 2:00 p.m. We walked hardly a few yards before we were assaulted by the cries from men—and women—selling food from carts that resembled nothing so much as oversized wheelbarrows. The cries came thick and fast. A colored woman with great hooped brass earrings sang:

Hot corn, hot corn—
Here's your lily-white corn;
All you that's got money
(Poor me that's got none)
Come buy my lily hot corn,
And let me go home.

A clam seller competed with her, claiming that his clams "lately came from Rockaway." We presently came to a pushcart vendor under a gas lamp—Jewish, from Poland, the gentleman told me—who gave us a lunch of buttered hot corn, warm bread and steaming oysters. All of it washed down by a generous draught of ginger beer. It was food and drink as good as any I had ever had in my life—notwithstanding the lack of bone china, tablecloths, or even tables, for that matter.

When we were done, we walked some blocks to Mott Street where a building was being erected, and the gentleman introduced me to the foreman, Mr. Jimmy Verdon, late of Dublin and sporting a fading Irish accent that was hardening into that nasal Yankee speech I had first heard on the *Maryann*. Within a few minutes, I had acquired a job carrying bricks at eight shillings a day and the address of a "clean and respectable" boardinghouse where I could stay for ten shillings a week with breakfasts and dinners included. The gentleman from the Irish Emigrant Society then shook my hand, and bid me adieu most elegantly. He departed, and I never saw him again, even on the several occasions when I returned to the Irish Emigrant Society, first to leave a note for Mary should she present herself there, and then after that to see if she had left any word. Stranger still, when I enquired after him on more than one of those visits, the two or three different gentlemen who occupied the same desk with the same sign at No. 18 Spruce Street seemed not to know him. There were, apparently, only four or five gentlemen who regularly volunteered their time once a week or so at the desk at No. 18 Spruce Street to entertain enquiries from Irish immigrants such as myself. But the gentleman who had peered so owlishly through his glasses at me on that very first visit was not among them.

I would have liked at the very least to have thanked him once again, and perhaps taken him to a stand for buttered hot corn, bread and oysters, for I believe to this day that he saved me from slow starvation or worse on those mean streets of the Five Points. And as I thought about it much later, I did find it a trifle strange that the gentleman had never introduced himself.

During those next few weeks I don't think that I ever was entirely warm, even in my boardinghouse bunk, wrapped in that very fine blanket that I bought for myself after receiving my second day's pay. I certainly was never warm while I was working. It either snowed or rained without any particular rhyme as to which occurred when (it could snow the day after it rained—and vice versa, so perverse is the weather in the New World). When sun did shine, it was entirely without warmth. Carrying hods of brick for a living meant being outside eleven hours a day, from 7:00 a.m. by my newly regulated pocket watch until 6:00 p.m., with a single one-half hour break at high noon—so the Jonathans called mid-day.

There were about three dozen fine details involved in carrying sixty or seventy pounds of brick up scaffolding two to four stories high several score times a day. And the bricklayers' appetites for bricks to lay were insatiable. There were a dozen of them at work throughout the day, and each one laid some 1,500 bricks. But there were only a few of us hod carriers. So I can assure you that it is hardly the unskilled labor that the average native American thinks the Irish are only fit for. I would challenge any man-jack of them—Gotham's teetotaling, paddy-baiting Mayor Jimmy Harper included—to spend a day carrying the bricks in icy or wet weather and not promptly break his neck (a turn of events that, were it to happen to most of the miserable, Catholic-hating natives, would have redounded quite measurably to the benefit of all mankind). I was blessed with having Mr. Verdon as my foreman, because I could count on five or six days of work each week that winter and spring—work I was lucky to get as I followed him through three different jobsites (as did a number of his other paddy and dutchy ruffians, as he liked to call us).

Each one of these buildings was a tenement, the very latest new-fangled method of cramming two hundred or so Irish, dutchies and darkies—which is what polite Gothamites generally called the Negroes—into tiny, dark rooms for a so-called landlord (who seems little removed in type or temperament from the worst rack-renting Irish land agent) to extract as many shillings as humanly possible from the poorest of the poor. One of the buildings—five stories high when it was finished—was so slightly built that it remained standing only by the grace of its neighbors on either side, neither of which looked long for this world. Worse, it stood over a former privy that I believe smelled as strongly on the day we completed the building as the day we started, which unfortunately was not the last day that the privy was used as such.

I can only record my distaste for these practices, because I didn't shun the work of helping build these tenements. One can salve one's conscience only so much, and I had the entirely practical concern of being able to feed myself and put a few shillings a week into the Bowery Savings Bank. In any case, jobs were very hard to come by in the late winter and spring of 1845—there was a depression on—and I was most fortunate to be working only because Mr. Verdon seemed to set store by my ability to carry bricks and mortar from morning until night. So I worked those five or six days a week, and as I mentioned before, I followed him from one jobsite to the next.

Mr. Verdon had little regard for the rest of his fellow country-men unless they were followers of the good Father Mathew (only then did they earn the sobriquet "paddy ruffian"), for the rest were in his mind slow, stupid and drunk. I suppose that, since I was so young and had not ever gone "liquor," I escaped this opprobrium. I never did want to get him started on the darkies, so poorly did he think of them. So Mr. Verdon hired dutchies when he could. They worked the hardest, Mr. Verdon said, and learned the fastest.

Every other Irish laborer in the Five Points was lucky to earn his dollar—eight shillings—a day three days out of six, which meant that if he were a family man, he couldn't think of meeting his obligations to his wife and children—which meant his wife had to find work as well, just so that the family could make ends meet. I cannot tell you how many times I saw women working 12 and 15 hours a day as seamstresses or the lowest of washerwomen for a few pennies. Their children—often hardly old enough to walk—ran free in the streets, begging for rags to wear and gathering scraps of wood for fuel where they could. When they were lucky enough to collect some of these treasures, the older children like as not robbed the little ones with dire threats of instant beatings.

Worse for those poor women were the other eight or ten hours each day that they worked in their homes obtaining the bare necessities of life—water, wood for fires and food. Moreover, every respectable woman, no matter how poor, took great pride in keeping a neatly swept hearth and a bit of carpet on the well-scoured floor in front of the fireplace. Such tasks involved a myriad of errands and evolutions—and an intricate web of cooperation among neighbors and children. The men, of course, as was the case onboard *Maryann*, were remarkable by their absence from such endeavors, which were far beneath them.

I cannot begin to tell you how much better off I was than these poor folks. I was employed, and better, I was getting paid a decent wage, so I was able to eat well enough to gradually put some weight back on and tighten the waist of my now threadbare trousers to something like what it had been so many months ago in Ireland. This welcome development was greatly aided by my landlord, a man who was most definitely not a rackrent, and his wife.

The esteemed gentleman from the Society had put me in contact with the most generous of boardinghouse proprietors, a German named Otto Schreiber, who catered to a finer class of German Catholic immigrant at a warm and dry boardinghouse on Walker Street, hardly more than two blocks from Broadway itself. Once Mr. Schreiber had decided that he liked the cut of my jib, my eight shillings a week (payable in advance) procured me a clean, if small, room with a bed that I never had to share and two meals a day, seven days a week. The meals prepared by Mrs. Schreiber each morning and evening were truly prodigious: beefsteak, pork or mutton chops, bread and butter, sausages, German dill pickles (I became a convert for life) and buckwheat cakes (which also became a staple for life)—plus that great Yankee addiction, coffee (which I love to this day). Mr. Schreiber and his wife were assisted by two of the prettiest lasses on whom I had ever had the pleasure to lay my eyes. (They looked so much alike with their blond tresses and crystalline blue eyes that they could have been twins. But they were not related, if I understood their fractured English properly.) They paid me scant attention, however, as within a couple of weeks of my arriving they became engaged to two Jewish-German brothers who were glaziers—an uncommonly well-paying job.

So my immediate creature comforts were met. But I had seen neither hide nor hair of Mary and Fíona. Moreover, I feared for their safety, alone, in the Five Points, or worse, up by Corlears Hook, prey to the sailors, Bowery toughs and the Good Lord knows who else. I was honor-bound to find them, and find them I would. So every Sunday, and at least three or four nights a week, I wandered the Five Points. As I came to know the alleys of the 'Points as well as the back of my hand—and my face and my task became known to many of the women and children of the district—I widened my search into the Bowery and up South and Water Streets, into Sailortown. I learned to navigate around the muck and offal that covered the streets several inches deep in places and smelled worse than you might think. There were wooden sidewalks rising just above the filth. But many of them were too rotten to safely pass over, and if you were too cavalier about walking down them you might end up face first in the street. I also developed a keen instinct for identifying and avoiding potential footpads and other good-for-nothings who seemed to infest all of these neighborhoods, particularly in the darker alleys.

I checked every few days at the Irish Emigrant Society to see whether there had been any reply to my missive left there with the gentleman whose name I never knew. I also asked whether any letters had arrived from Evelyn. I heard nothing from either of them.

This silence from Mary haunted me, as did her absence from the streets and alleys—even down in that hellhole of Donovan Street, one of the Five Points' many pretenders to the title of Murderer's Alley, where I ventured only in the broadest of daylight. I tried to rationalize why I should have been indifferent to her fate—and that of poor, little Fíona. I had bunked with them in steerage on the *Maryann* only as a practical matter of survival. My infatuation with Mary could never have borne fruit. That last magical night on board with our whispered fantasies had been no more than passing fancy, chiefly remarkable, I told myself, for creating the fiery scenes I dwelt upon only in my own sanctum sanctorum, as infrequently as I could manage, and then only far from the madding crowds. Mary had also taken all of my money, leaving me nearly destitute on Pike Slip on that cold January night. Worse, she hadn't left word with the Irish Emigrant Society—a simple task for her, so obvious. So why should I search for her and Fíona, risking life and limb?

In a year, I reckoned, I would have a budget swelled rhino-fat with chink. I could do whatever I wanted. Go west to the mountains. Return to Ireland to claim Evelyn as my own. But that thought remained fanciful, for Evelyn had been as silent as Mary. I rationalized that silence away by the width of the Western Ocean, reckoning that I would one precious day see a letter from that fetching girl with the golden ringlets and infinitely superior ways and knowledge, who was so very often the protagonist in those perfervid dreams that so often enflamed my nights.

Yet, search I did, restlessly, driven by a nameless animus of unknown origin to venture deep into some of the grimmest haunts to be found in Gotham: the deepest and farthest caverns of the Old Brewery, the most infamous slum in the Five Points, and the frightful misery of the Gates of Hell, a tenement in Cow Bay, where the Negroes lived (a slum even more godforsaken than the Old Brewery, which was entirely unsurprising, as the only people who lived there other than the Negroes were the occasional Irish or native American women who stayed loyal to their Negro mates, much to the everlasting disgust of their white-skinned brethren), a smaller five-story tenement, wooden-framed, jerry-built and sagging from the rot, named the Knife to the Throat and yet another, the Bucket of Blood, distinguished in name only from all the other ghastly tenements I visited. I went to places in those slums where, it was said, children who were born to their destitute, depraved inhabitants were known to have ventured into the light of day only when they were taken, clad in their winding sheets, by open wagon to the boats, from whence they were transported to their final resting place in the Potter's Field on Ward Island, in the middle of the East River.

One evening, an hour or two after dark, I ventured into the Old Brewery, which loomed over Paradise Square from the far side of Cross Street. Until a decade ago, I had been told, it had been a working brewery that produced the most poisonous malt liquor in Gotham until (depending upon whose story you believed) it was either converted into a giant tenement by the owner because he could make far more rhino exploiting the misery of destitute Irish immigrants without prospect and equally desperate Negroes seeking to escape the Gates of Hell, or it was merely abandoned, whereupon it evolved naturally into the disaster it had become. The Old Brewery was, without doubt, the largest building I had ever seen. It did not rival the height of City Hall, whose cupola rose majestically above the trees of City Hall Park to dominate the skyline to the southwest of the Five Points. But its sprawl dwarfed that of our city's finest building, and its dirty yellow stucco and brick main building rose as high as five full stories to dominate one side of Paradise Square. The main building was topped by a steeply pitched roof notable mainly for its many penetrations, which cast light into the vast interior of the building, along with snow and rain, and served as impromptu chimneys for the innumerable cooking fires lit each day.

In one corner of the Old Brewery stood Brennan's Store, another place I ventured into only in daylight, so vile were it and its denizens. One day, I saw a five-year-old girl walk into Brennan's with a rusty coffee pot. When she came out a few minutes later, it was full of poteen for her mother. Milk and decent food were not to be found there.

Brennan's faced perhaps the filthiest alley in all of Gotham. The alley stretched back into the block, along the entire length of the Old Brewery, mounded with trash and filth and beggars huddling in the shadows. Many a time I passed through Paradise Square only to see two or three men carrying a body out of the alley—the real Murderer's Alley, some said—and pile it unceremoniously onto the undertaker's cart for transport to the Potter's Field. But the Old Brewery was not restricted merely to its principal building. It stretched over an acre or more, running deep into the block on its far side, almost to Pearl Street, in a jumble of inter-connecting wood and brick outbuildings, each in a worse state of disrepair than all the rest.

I stood before a gaping entrance where there must at one time have been a wooden double-door for deliveries. The door was gone now, and the entrance led into a void blacker than the night outside. I stood there, uncertainly, as my eyes slowly adjusted to a dim, flickering light of unseen torches that seemed to illuminate figures scurrying about the very edges of the inconstant shadows. After a few moments listening to the unnerving sounds of people living their lives (and worse, whispers seemingly directed at my having intruded), I spied a small exit from the void, and I headed for it, moving at hardly more than a shuffle.

"'Ello, dearie." An English accent of the lowest sort, and she suggested an act even more indecent than the naked woman in Paradise Alley had offered that first, awful night in the snow. "Two bits," she said lewdly. "I'd normally charge double, but you're an 'andsome one, ain't yers."

I demurred almost inaudibly, and she called after me, "a liberty head, then, and you can…"

I fled from a shout of, "a liberty dime, then, ye worthless cur," skittering through an opening into the flickering torchlight, which lit walls of deal and all other manner of wood, obviously put in higglety-pigglety to divide a large chamber into a veritable rabbit warren fetid with the smell of humanity. It brought back steerage on the *Maryann*, except here there seemed to be a modicum of privacy. I sensed people rather than saw them, although I caught myself staring through a torn sheet serving as a door to a little, dimly lit room as it dawned on me that they were, as we put it in school, having a tumble. I gawked in salacious wonder for a moment and then turned away, ashamed at knowing the red-hot image to have been indelibly burned in my brain. I ventured further, round a bend and a corner and up some rotting steps into yet another chamber, where I could see a pair of care-worn women peeling their spuds next to a small cooking fire built on the dirt floor, which illuminated the faces of their *wains* staring longingly at the potatoes. I was lost in a demimonde straight from Hell, and the sounds of its unseen inhabitants echoed spectrally in my ear.

I realized with a sinking heart that I couldn't hope to explore all of the tenement's nooks and crannies in one expedition. Mary and Fíona could be in any one of the ten-score little rooms and warrens I had passed by, dirty blankets and all manner of other cloth covering them. I would need to fling back every one of them if I were to have even a prayer of finding Mary and Fíona.

"A large cent, mister," a voice lisped.

I stopped and stared down to a small girl, Fíona's age. I fumbled in my pocket and saw in horror there were half a score more small children swarming from every aperture, pickpockets and cutpurses every one of them. I congratulated myself on my foresight of having left my purse with Mrs. Schreiber, shoved my coins back into my pocket and cut my way through the suddenly clamorous mob and ran blindly until I could hear them no more. I was brought up short by a pretty girl about my age standing in front of me, amused eyes and the ghost of a smile.

"Are you looking for someone?" she asked in that hard accent of the native Gothamite. "Or have you just lost your way?"

I nodded mutely.

"You don't want to be here. You need to find Mr. Burke. He can save you," she said, taking my hand to lead me away, to where only God and she knew.

"Mr. Burke?" I found my voice.

"Old Man of the Brewery and the Father of Temperance. The only sane man in this Hell." She chuckled drily. "A chairmaker who reformed his drunken ways to become our only source of succor. That is, besides the good Reverend Pease."

"Ye devilkins!" exclaimed an outraged bass voice. The girl froze as the voice continued. "Where the divil d'yer think ye be goin'? Filthy bit o' mutton, ye be, breakin' the leg of every little faggot tha' ye be stumblin' over."

Taking my hand, the girl whirled about to confront the voice, which came from a huge shadow behind us.

The shadow said derisively, "Off t'grind the little bastard, are yers?"

She turned my hand loose and blazed back, "Leave him be. He ain't done nothin' to yers, ye catamite. And leave me be. I be goin' where I please with what I please."

The shadow ignored her and loomed large in front of me, a giant, broken-down Irishman of indeterminate age, wearing a top hat that must have put him well above six and a half feet. A Plug Ugly. Mr. Verdon had told me of the gang and their terrible ways, their lug hats stuffed with wool and leather, which were pulled down tight over their ears to serve as a helmet when they fought. I must have stumbled onto their turf. I shivered.

He bellowed at me, "Ye na' be no homeboy o' mine, yer wee gabbey, and ye na' be honeyfuggling me over me g'hal. I be after rippin' yer ..." His cudgel was out and he made to swing at me, and I knew that I would be a dead man if he caught me clean. I stood rooted to the spot in a bemused horror, wondering what I had done to deserve such an ending in this squalid, fetid tenement.

The girl caught his arm and saved me, for the moment. She pressed herself against him, her head craned so that she could softly talk to him. I couldn't tell what she was saying, nor see what her hands were doing, but the anger remained in the Plug Ugly's eyes, and they remained locked with mine. I remained rooted to my spot and time seemed to pass very slowly, indeed. I could sense eyes peering from every angle at our contretemps. The hum of conversation and human movement seemed to have ceased as the Plug Ugly and I continued to stare at each other.

"Críostóir, my lad." A man's mild voice came from over my shoulder. "You know that you are being most unchristian. We do not tolerate such behavior in this part of the Brewery. This is God's country."

I whipped around in amazement at the voice.

The Plug Ugly mumbled behind me, "I be beggin' yer pardon, Mr. Burke. I be thinkin' tha' the gabbey ..."

"Críostóir." There was sternness beneath the mild tone.

I looked back at the Plug Ugly as he removed his hat, revealing long, lank, black hair above his pale, wrecked face, "I be beggin' yer pardon. Truly, Mr. Burke."

"Thank you, Críostóir."

The Plug Ugly vanished, girl in tow. They were giggling at each other as they left.

I opened my mouth to thank Mr. Burke, who waved it off, saying, "I hear that you're looking for a woman and her kiddeen."

I looked at him in amazement.

"They come to me, you know." He waved his arms at the eyes I could feel rather than see peering at me. "And they tell me everything, for as sweet Evelyn says," he gestured to the now-vanished girl as I gawked at him in wonder over the use of her name—and all that had just transpired. "They call me Old Man of the Brewery. A rather exalted name, I fear. But I do lend my ear and I give a good lecture now-and-again to a mother seeking to lose her way and her misery in a bottle of the devil's poteen. But," he said with a deprecating smile, "the good Reverend Pease does far more than I to attend to the corporeal wants of this godforsaken populace, with schools for the *wains* and jobs as seamstresses for their mothers, giving them all some hope and purpose in this life. He is truly doing the Lord's work."

With that, Mr. Burke led me to his quarters in a far less parlous part of the Old Brewery—for even I could see that the Old Brewery had its own districts and neighborhoods just like any city, some worse than others and more than a few actually seemingly bearable to live in. He ushered me to a stool, took his place upon another and said, "Tell me of the woman and kideen you seek."

And so I did.

When I was finished, he said to me, "This sweet young lady and her *wain*, as you Irish are wont to call them, are lucky to have you looking to save them. I shall do all in my power to aid you. When I know more, I shall send word to you."

⌒

True to his word, Mr. Burke did send word to me one Friday evening, and on the following Sunday morning, I passed through Paradise Square, down an alley to an entrance close to Mr. Burke's apartments. A pious-looking old man dressed in a flat minister's hat, black frock coat and silk bow tie arrived at the entrance at the same time as I. He was trailed at the subservient distance of a pace and a half by a very pretty Negro girl burdened with a huge basket filled with religious tracts.

I nodded to him politely and he lifted his hat to me, saying, "How do, sir. What brings a fine lad as yourself to this den of iniquity? You can only find sin and misery here. You'll lose your soul here, lad."

I resented his implication and replied in no more than a civil tone, "I'm looking for my friend and companion and her daughter—to rescue them, sir. Their names are Mary and Fíona Skiddy. Do you know them?"

"I am sorry to say that I have never made their acquaintance. But perhaps that is for the best, for if they are here, then they are already lost to a God-fearing soul such as yourself, son. You cannot hope to rescue them without endangering your own immortal soul."

I looked at him without replying.

He said, "I am the Reverend Simpson. I am here to save souls, sir, one soul at a time, for the glory of God."

"Do you work with the good Reverend Pease?" I enquired innocently.

"Mr. Pease," Reverend Simpson scoffed. "He thinks nothing of the souls of these poor and damned. He thinks that he can improve their corporeal bodies when their flesh has already been irredeemably corrupted by sin and sloth." He snorted. "All you can do is save their souls for everlasting salvation. There is nothing to be done for them here in this life." With this, Reverend Simpson looked to the sky and invoked his Lord God to save my soul.

I said, "Good day," and made to pass inside. The colored girl looked at me, glanced deliberately back at the praying minister and then looked me directly in the eye. She asked, "Good sir, could you take a tract?"

I hesitated. She looked at the praying minister, and once more looked me directly in the eye. "Please, Mister, it won't cost you nothing."

I took the tract and was rewarded by a flash of brilliant smile that immediately vanished underneath her stoic exterior. Taking one last deep breath of clear air, I entered the fetid building, leaving the minister muttering his imprecations, with his loyal Negress servant standing in attendance, burdened by her heavy basket of tracts. I traversed several antechambers as empty this Sunday morning as they had been full last evening, serving as impromptu lusheries for the Old Brewery's tenants, and quickly found Mr. Burke's apartment.

When I told him of Reverend Simpson, Mr. Burke waved his hand, saying mildly, "I do wish he would lead a service now and again in a church. It is Sunday, after all." Then he said, "I have someone you should see."

We walked past the clean, if threadbare apartments where Mr. Burke's temperance folks lived. We eventually passed into the darker and meaner parts of the tenement, in a stretch I had not visited before. As we picked our way through the gloom, I could hear drunken laughter—even at 10:00 o'clock on a Sunday morning—and crying babies.

"Watch the stairs," Mr. Burke said to me. I stepped carefully around the broken stair and looked down. I could see clean through into an apartment below me where a Negro man slept on a dirty straw mattress as his woman, Irish by the look of her red hair, moved about with a mulatto baby stuck to her breast.

An old man appeared before us from the gloom and quavered, "Smallpox ... the *leanbh bocht* be dead."

Mr. Burke said gently, "Swaddle her in a winding sheet, and when I return, we'll put her to rest."

A few steps farther, and Mr. Burke swept aside a dirty curtain, exposing a filthy and fetid room hardly the size of a decent dog kennel, and asked, "Is this your friend and her daughter?"

My heart pounded for a moment as I peered through the gloom at a woman and her bedraggled child cowering at the back of the filthy nook. Both of them were clothed in rags that hardly covered them at all. I met the woman's dark eyes for a moment before she looked away—in shame, I thought. I could see why Mr. Burke had brought me. If the woman's hair had been clean, she and Mary could have been twins.

But the woman and child were not Mary and Fíona. I didn't know whether to be relieved or disappointed.

⌒

CHAPTER 9

Right in Front of Me

I GUESS IT WOULDN'T DO ANY GOOD TO JAW about it much. But I have found that the Good Lord may give with one hand, but He is just as likely to take away with the other. I was lucky that winter of 1845. Many Irishmen and their families were starving on Gotham's streets. I had a good job hodding bricks, paying eight shillings a day, forty-eight shillings a week, and I was piling away the brass and building my grubstake in order to head points west to the *Limes Americanus*. (Ain't that a nice bit of Latin? A fat lot of good it was doing me in Gotham.) That is, assuming that I didn't find Mary and Fíona, my hopes for which were growing dim.

Then the scaffolding gave way, three stories up on the tenement where we bricklayers were putting the last of the walls up. The wood splintered under me, I slipped and my hod of bricks pulled me down. I followed the bricks helplessly as they smashed through the lower layer of the scaffolding to the ground. Then I got lucky. Something broke my fall, and I bounced onto an unbroken bit of scaffolding, away from the bricks and their mad, smashing descent. I scrambled to my feet in a horrified rush, thinking of a hod-carrier I'd once seen fall from some rotten scaffolding. He had ended on the ground, under a pile of broken bricks.

Verdon had been right next to me when I fell, and he was kindly enough to steady me instead of kicking me over to the ground for having broken two or three dozen bricks. Bricks were expensive to replace, and hod carriers and bricklayers were not. But Jimmy Verdon was a decent man.

I winced as I stood. My right arm would hardly move. I was hurt, and one look at Verdon confirmed that he knew it, and that look confirmed that I was out of work. That was the risk: if you were hurt on the job and couldn't work, you were out of the job that minute, to be replaced by some other hungry mick or dutchy.

As I said, though, Jimmy Verdon was a decent man, and he paid me my entire day's wages plus the rest of the wages he owed me. Most foremen would have robbed me and then laughed about it, knowing that a banged-up kid couldn't have done anything about it.

So when I pocketed my money with a smile of thanks, Verdon told me to come back when I was fit, and he'd see what he could do to fix me up with something. The tenement building boom was just about over, he said, so he didn't have any more jobs lined up. But he promised that, when I was mended, he'd do his best to send me somewhere I could find some work. I thanked him again, and made my way to my boardinghouse, my shoulder and arm throbbing each step of the way.

I didn't break my arm or do any other serious damage. But a lot of bruises developed in the most amazing locations. One of the serving girls took mercy on me those first few days and made sure I didn't starve before I could move about without being in agony. For all that, I was thankful. But it was well over a week before I could get around easily and pretend to the outside world that I was perfectly healthy. So with a shadow of the former jaunt to my step and some whispered thanks to my Maker, I made my way back to the tenement. True to Verdon's prediction, the tenement was finished—at least the brickwork was. The rest of the building lay unfinished and open to the weather, as if the owner had abruptly run out of money.

It wasn't the only half-built tenement in the 'Points. In fact, it was just one of several score in the 'Points and throughout the city where construction had simply stopped midstream and the builder had walked away. Somebody told me that many of the tenements, particularly the more poorly-built of them, were worth less than what it would cost to finish them. So derelict they would stay until property values returned, making it worthwhile to complete the buildings or, more likely, simply tear them down in order for some freshly conceived project to be built.

It took me a couple of days to run Verdon down. I found him alone at a table at the back of a small, empty coffee and cake saloon, nursing a now-cold cup of coffee. He smiled broadly when he saw me, "Billy, how are yer, lad?"

I flexed myself and said, "Ready to hod bricks, Mr. Verdon."

"You're a bad liar, Billy."

I shrugged and sat down across the table from him.

"But I'd take you on in heartbeat if there was work. Even if you are looking a mite poorly. You know that."

I nodded.

"But look at me." He spread his arms in a dramatic flourish. "I sure ain't building tenements this week." He shook his head. "Nope. Them days is gone. The market's gone bust. Nobody's building 'cuz they ain't got no money, and they can't borrow none, neither. Banks ain't lending."

I leaned across the table to listen better to his story.

"And here I can't even buy you a decent cup of coffee. Not 'til I get paid for that last job—you know, the one where you got hurt. But that Bleecker Street scrimp, he's pretending he's bankrupt, and he's gone to earth. No one can find him. That's just plain dishonest, doggaun it. But I knew you'd be coming round eventual-like, looking for work. And y'always was my best paddy ruffian." He scratched his head. "So when I was 'round to see my pal, Magee, 'bout another matter, I put a good word in for you with him, told him ye might be stopping by once you was up and about. He runs a saloon over on Mulberry Street."

I thanked him with a fresh cup of coffee.

Magee's saloon was on the ground floor of a three-story brick board-inghouse with a fine wide porch opening onto Mulberry Street, just a couple of blocks from the Old Brewery. The boardinghouse was remarkable for the fact that, unlike most other buildings in the 'Points, it didn't look like it was about to fall down at any second. And, if the windows were any indication, it was as clean on the inside as Mr. Schreiber's place.

I walked through the door, which was propped open even though it was hardly eleven o'clock, and down a short flight of stairs into a long and narrow and gloomy—the gas lamps were not lit—front room with a great polished oak bar to one side. The floors were rough sawn pine, covered with fresh sawdust ready to soak up the coming night's spilled beer. Fresh sawdust was a sign of a well-run Gotham establishment, I had learned. Many propri-etors simply threw fresh sawdust over the old until the place stank to high heavens of stale beer. Others, particularly in the 'Points, didn't even do that much.

At the back of the front room was another door, at which stood a hulking Irishman with a great black beard and swarthy skin—as fine an example of the Black Irish as I'd ever seen.

"Whaddya want, laddie?"

So thick was his accent that I couldn't imagine this prodigious lump of humanity had been off the boat from Eirinn any longer than I had. I decided that, however tempting, it would have been

cheeky to have replied in Irish (which I viewed as a missed opportunity to show off my improved fluency).

"I'm here to see Mr. Magee. Mr. Verdon sent me."

The blackbearded guard laughed. "There ain't no Mister
Magee here. Just Magee. And yers in luck as himsel' be holdin'
court, yonder. Let me see if himsel' be receiving visitors t'day.
What be yer moniker, *bouchal*?"

I told him.

A voice boomed through the door from the back room, "Who
d'ya got there, Blackie? Has that bastard by-blow Cassidy come by
yet? We're s'posed to go see Con Donoho together."

Blackie shook his head, and said, "It be a *wee wain* t'see yers,
Magee. Says that Jimmy Verdon sent him."

"Well, send him in. Send him in. We can na' be keeping a
friend o' Jimmy Verdon's waitin' on the doorstep," the voice
boomed back.

Blackie ushered me into a larger room with a cramped stage
at the far end, illuminated by a couple of gas lamps turned down
to a guttering flame. In the center of the room, six or seven men
sitting at a table were almost lost in the flickering shadows cast by
two smoky oil lanterns.

The voice boomed out again, "Well, sit yersel' down, lad. And
who might yers be?"

"Billy Gogan, sir. Mr. Verdon suggested that I come see you …
about a job."

Everyone at the table erupted in laughter.

"A job, ye be after?"

"Yes sir." I stood my ground. "I was working for Mr. Verdon as
a bricklayer, but the work has dried up."

"Well, first things first, lad," the voice boomed. "As Blackie
said, I'm Magee. Not Mister Magee. Just Magee. And we na' be
standin' on such *Sassenagh* sensibilities such as "siree" this and

siree that. No sir." The voice paused for a second, collecting itself. "But we do call ladies, ma'am. Don't we lads?"

Amid the general assent I identified the speaker as he leaned forward into the light to knock the ash from his cigar and pick up a glass of what I presumed to be whiskey—the earliness of the hour notwithstanding. He was a large man, with an imposing black beard and great shock of black hair, wearing perhaps the loudest brown-and-yellow, checkered suit ever sewn. It emphasized his bulk, every bit of it as hard as iron. And tall, I thought, as he stood up. He clearly was the man in charge, and his tablemates were his knights errant.

Magee shook my hand and grinned. "Glad to know yers, Billy Gogan." He then looked at me thoughtfully and murmured, "We're gonna get along famously, I think."

He ushered me to an empty chair. "Tell me about yersel'. From the old country, are yers? Ye don't sound like ye be hailin' from Skibbereen or some other hellish bog. In fact," he mused, "I'd reckon yer one o' them high falutin' public school sorts ... Ye can read and write, can't yers?"

"Of course," I replied, and instantly regretted it.

"Of course," Magee mocked. "That's powerful high and mighty, ain't it, lads? Why, Billy Gogan, half of these esteemed gentlemen prob'ly can barely read that greasy bastard Harper's Protestant Bible."

I looked a little blankly at Magee before I realized who he was talking about. Magee explained anyway, "Hell ... you know, Hizzoner Jimmy Harper. That bastard Harper never met an Irishman—honest or not—what he didn't hate on sight. You could be Washington Irving hissel', and if you was Irish, Harper wouldn't publish your book on a bet. That no-account nativist fice." Magee fell silent for a moment. "I digress," he said finally. "Ye wants a job, eh?"

"I would." I stifled the "sir."

"Well," he replied. "Let's be seein' what yer made of. Ever sweep streets?"

I replied that I had not, to general laughter.

⌒

I presented myself at six o'clock the next morning at No. 17 Orange Street, at Con Donoho's grocery, yawning from having stayed out most of the night, prowling aimlessly and restlessly up and down the alleys and through some of the lesser basement tenements, looking for Mary and Fíona. In front were twenty or so boys and young men being issued brooms and shovels. A bored and extremely scruffy-looking Irishman led me to a mean-looking alley just across from Cow Bay and told me to sweep the alley clean, dump the filth into the barrow and unload the barrow into the night cart when it came by.

I looked at the alley with dismay. In front of me, the street's broken down brick paving blocks gave away to mud at the alley's entrance, which was blocked by a compacted, yard-high ridge of trash and God knows what else. A pig was contentedly rooting about on top of the ridge. At the far end of the alley, which abutted an unpainted wooden framed house, a dead horse lay atop another, much higher pile of trash, its bloated belly split open to the world. I sighed, suppressed a gag and got to digging for the rest of the day and for many days thereafter.

⌒

About two weeks or so later, I showed up at the duly appointed hour of six o'clock in the morning. There was a cold March drizzle falling. I was soaked to the bone and thoroughly miserable, once again missing my oilskin, which led me to think of the last time I saw Mary looking back disconsolately at me as the steam launch bore her to the pier. I had been equally cold and wet many times while I was hodding bricks, but I had always been warmed by the thought of eight shillings at the end of the day. Today, I'd earn two bits—just a shilling—for my twelve hours of labor—if I was lucky, and when I got back to the boardinghouse, Mrs. Schreiber would be wrinkling her nose at me until I changed my clothes and scrubbed the worst of the smell from myself.

As usual, Donoho's grocery was locked and dark at this early hour. But today, unlike every other morning except for Sundays, there was no one there to hand out brooms and shovels. So I waited, huddling out of the rain as best I could in the shallow entrance way to the grocery, watching the sullen dawn reveal the filthy streets that never seemed to get any cleaner, despite the best efforts of Con Donoho's private legion of street-sweepers, a legion as I had come to learn that was an integral part of Con Donoho's little empire in the Sixth Ward, otherwise known as the Five Points. Con's view was that one of the benefits of his rule should be clean streets and alleys—or at least as clean as they could be.

As it became light, Mrs. Donoho came to the front door and unlocked it. She said in a kindly but strong cockney accent—which surprised me because Con Donoho was as Irish a Gothamite as ever strode through the 'Points—"Well, the good Lord bless me, but you are here early. Con don't usually have the guards come 'til later on a rainy day. He says it's only right that they sleep a little later when they're so giving of their time to him." She gestured, "Come in, come in, lad. Have a toddy to ward off the chill. 'Tis a foul day to be abroad."

I warmed myself before the stove, dozing a bit, as Mrs. Donoho bustled about, the toddy apparently forgotten.

"Why, Mrs. Mulrooney, top o' the morning to ye," Mrs. Donoho said as the bell over the door tinkled quietly. "We haven't seen you for days. How be Colm and the boys?"

Mrs. Mulrooney said that Colm was back at work now, and that they'd not been into Donoho's grocery because they had been watching their pennies because, until yesterday, only Mrs. Mulrooney had been working. Doing the laundry at night at Astor House over on Broadway, across from City Hall, don't you know. A grand palace, it was, with all them marble columns, not that she ever saw much else from the alleyway entrance to the laundry. But the night work was all right. It allowed her to keep her house, mind her *childer* during the day and keep them from running loose about the 'Points. There were, Mrs. Mulrooney allowed, far too many distractions for the *childer* in the 'Points. It isn't like back in Ireland, she said, where folks were all decent, God-fearing Catholics. With that, Mrs. Mulrooney crossed herself and finished her soliloquy by observing that she was much happier now that it was so much quieter on account of Colm not getting drunk as much anymore.

"And the boys?"

Mrs. Mulrooney commenced a fresh soliloquy: "Oh, they're fine. Jimmy was sweeping the streets, and he planned to be by to stand guard today. So he'll be saying hello to you, Mrs. Donoho. Patrick's been selling newspapers, and making good money, too— three or four bits a day for selling Horace Greeley's *Tribune*. Mr. Greeley's papers do sell so, and Patrick has a wonderful spot up on Broadway to sell them, and nobody's been trying to take it away from him since that last set-to. So he doesn't want to be giving that up."

Mrs. Donoho nodded and smiled as she poured the gin into Mrs. Mulrooney's dented pewter milk pitcher and wrapped a pair of herring for Mr. Mulrooney's dinner today (along with a third herring—on Mr. Donoho—on account of Mr. Mulrooney having found employment). Mrs. Mulrooney counted out her pennies and handed them over. Mrs. Donoho gave her the milk pitcher full of gin and the herring wrapped in yesterday's edition of Mr. Greeley's *Tribune* and asked, "And I take it that Mr. Mulrooney and Jimmy've paid their five dollars at Tammany Hall and are ready to vote, Mrs. Mulrooney?"

"Oh, of course, Mrs. Donoho," Mrs. Mulrooney gushed. "They're so proud to be *Meiriceánaigh* now, with that ..." Mrs. Mulrooney hesitated, bringing the word fully to her lips before saying it, "dispensation ... from Mr. Donoho so they could vote now, after just a year here in *Meiriceá*, instead of the reg'lar five."

"I'm sure," Mrs. Donoho said, "they'll be looking to Magee as the assistant alderman in June's election? He's such a good lad, Magee is. So hardworking, and with him keeping the young 'uns out o' his saloon. He is such a good neighbor. I do worry about him, though, what with that upstart, Cassidy, and that silly prize-fight that they're fixing to have."

Mrs. Mulrooney replied that, of course, her menfolk'd be voting for Magee this time around. They were so very happy to be living in Magee's boardinghouse right there on Mulberry Street. Magee kept it clean, and the ground-floor saloon was never that noisy. Anyway, she sniffed, that good-for-nothing *bastún dall*, Cassidy, he's naught but a *reathaí* what turns good young men bad.

Mrs. Donoho smiled knowingly as Mrs. Mulrooney bade her good day, and I thought it time that I should see if there were someone about to direct me to my day's work. As I stepped out the front door, I saw a young man not much older than I had taken up my position in the rain.

We nodded to each other, and shook hands.

"Bill Tweed."

"Bill Gogan," I replied, eschewing the familiar diminutive.

Tweed went to the other side of the door, and we both stood, huddled in the rain for some time. Then Tweed said, "I was expecting to be by myself, today. The guard duty, that is. Looking after

Mrs. Donoho while Con is gone up to Bleecker Street and all. Nice to have company, though. Can't do any harm to have two of us."

To cover my ignorance, I replied, not untruthfully, "I thought I'd be by myself today, too. But I agree with you, company's nice."

Tweed looked thoughtful. "Magee sent you around, didn't he?"

"A couple of weeks ago."

"I remember. You're the fellow who can read and write."

"Of course," I said lightly.

"Of course," Tweed replied. "Who doesn't?"

We stood quietly for a while longer. Tweed appeared completely absorbed by his thoughts, and I thought it best not to disturb him. I let my mind wander again, from the slow but steady diminution of shillings in my pocket to the prospect of having to give up my warm room at Mr. Schreiber's boardinghouse and inevitably to my completely unsuccessful efforts finding Mary and Fíona. It was as if they had ceased to exist. I ignored the odd twinge I felt at the prospect of not seeing them again, and concentrated on fulfilling my dream of wanting to go west to the frontier. But that was impossible without a sufficient grubstake, which brought me full circle to the steady extraction of shillings from my pocket. Worse, I was mired in this place, the 'Points, where I was effectively friendless and which I did not yet fully understand, although I knew enough to appreciate its dangers and my inadequacy in protecting myself from those dangers. The 'Points was not somewhere I wanted to pass my life.

"You haven't been here in Gotham very long, have you?" Tweed seemed to read my thoughts.

"No, I haven't. Only since the new year."

"Jimmy Verdon says you're a good paddy ruffian, and that you've a smart head on your shoulders. That's fine praise from him." Tweed stared off at a point far beyond the houses across the street. After a while, he said to me, "Hell of a difference from the old country, ain't it, the Big Onion?"

"Overwhelming. Even Dublin pales in comparison. The sheer size of it. And the people. Herds of them. Although, I must say, the misery I've seen—and escaped, God knows I've been lucky not to end up in some basement tenement, starving to death or knifed to death."

"Hmmph," Tweed grunted. "There are those who don't make it or don't have the native wit to make it. It's a damned shame."

"Yet, sir, there are good-hearted people who care. Reverend Pease and Mr. Burke, for example. Not enough of them, though."

"How do you know those two?" Tweed looked at me with genuine curiosity.

I shrugged. "I get around. An awful fascination with what I've escaped, I suppose."

I didn't know why, but I stayed silent on my real reason for prowling about the tenements of the 'Points. Was I afraid of being ridiculed for sentiment? Was Mary even real? I wondered, sometimes. I mean, the man from the Irish Emigrant Society, the one who fed me hot corn and oysters that first day in the 'Points, when the bright sun was melting the snow, didn't seem to be real. So I was reticent to speak to anyone about either him or Mary and Fíona—or about Father O'Muirhily and his murderer, the man in funereal black. Not to Jimmy Verdon, Mr. and Mrs. Schreiber or their two busty lasses who served the meals did I breathe a word. And Magee and his compatriots were the last people on earth to whom I would unburden myself, particularly about Father O'Muirhily and the man in black. Despite the best of intentions, I had not rid myself of the fantastical paranoia I had experienced that terrible day *Maryann* left Cork, as I watched Father O'Muirhily pitch into the dirty water lapping against Lavitt's Quay and disappear forever, his murder unseen by anyone other than myself, Fíona, and maybe a packet rat who had turned a blind eye—even though *Maryann* and her twelve-score passengers and crew had been hardly fifty feet away.

Falling in with Magee and all the other Irish denizens of the Sixth Ward and listening to them rail on about armed revolution against the *Sassenagh* and how the Young Irelanders were Ireland's best hope of liberation only reinforced my vow to remain silent. I would never know whether one of them just happened to be a clandestine Young Irelander fled from the *Sassenagh*, and thus more than amenable to exacting revenge upon the scion of the man who betrayed O'Connell and destroyed the Repeal Year. Or even worse, such a Young Irelander turned out to be some *comhbhrathair*, or companion, of Magee's—or Magee's father—from the old country. In any case, the whole story was all so preposterous that I was convinced that I'd be manacled to the wall of the nearest booby hatch if I said anything to anyone—ever. It was easier to say simply that I left Ireland when I was orphaned, and that was how I'd always left it.

"You are an odd fellow, aren't you," Tweed mused. "You've got some feeling for the downtrodden. The lower tendom, as it were."

"There, but for the grace of God, go I. Particularly if the chink were to completely vanish."

"I hardly think so …" Tweed responded drily. "You speak English like an Englishman and you can read and write."

"I suppose."

"But those poor paddy peasants …"

I forgave him both the slur and the excessive alliteration.

"That fellow, Pease, he does give those folks some hope with the jobs and the schooling, though," Tweed said. "Most other preachers don't. They're too busy with their own humbug to give a good goddamn about those poor. Particularly those Yankee bible-bangers who come down from places like Croton, where they've never seen a mick or a nigger in all their born days." Tweed went quiet for a moment, and then said, "It's different down here than it is up there in the country. Almost like two different worlds. 'Specially at night. Dark and formless out in the country. All you can do is sleep or fornicate."

"Sounds like my cousin's farm in Ireland—except for the fornicating, of course," I said loftily.

"Of course. Can't be fornicating in the old country, can we?" Tweed smirked. "It's different in Gotham. The city lives by gaslight. My father and me? We make chairs by day, and I live with my lovely wife by day. But at night? That's when I make my way in the world. With the likes of Con Donoho, Magee, Rynders and all the rest. That's New York."

"Yep," I agreed.

"There is only one Gotham."

I thought about what I'd said earlier about Dublin, swallowed my Irish pride and said, "Well, there is London."

All I earned was a derisive snort.

"You're right, though," I said softly. "You can't make your way in London like you can here."

"You learn quick."

I nodded.

"Magee's right. You 'n' he will get along famously." Tweed looked up at the sky. The rain had eased. "Do you know who Magee is?"

"Next assistant alderman?"

"Hmm. Yep. You do learn quick," Tweed replied. "Yeah, well, he'll be the next assistant alderman if Cassidy doesn't get in his way."

"Cassidy?" I asked. "I've heard of him a couple of times. Seems to be something between him and Magee."

"Oh, yeah, there's a story for you. Magee and Cassidy go back a long way. Magee's an old prizefighter. Except he isn't soft in the head from one too many haymakers. And he still likes to give a good gouging every now and then, although Blackie does most of that sort of thing for him these days. Con likes Magee. Magee's paying his dues. Runs a respectable business. Hell, he's actually got a liquor license—why, Donoho himself don't even have one.

So Magee can sell his anti-fogmatics and beer reg'lar-like. I mean, Magee's place isn't like most groggeries. You've seen it. It isn't any old basement dancehall with rotten joists. And it doesn't stink. He changes his sawdust every morning."

"So what about him—Cassidy, I mean?"

"Oh, yeah. See, Cassidy's a newcomer. Came from somewhere upstate, and won himself a following on account of his own prize-fighting skills—and other skullduggery, hear tell, anyways. Stiff-necked cove, as well. Won't genuflect before Con. Con runs the Sixth Ward. It's his personal fiefdom, and he's the kingmaker. Or at least he'll crown the aldermen and assistant aldermen from the 'ould bloody Sixth. Cassidy and Magee both want to be the next assistant alderman. Con hates waking snakes, unless he's doing the waking."

"Waking snakes?"

"Yeah. Con hates having a ruckus raised unless he's raising it. So he wants Cassidy and Magee to make nice together with him, and figure out gentleman-like, between themselves, who's going to be the next assistant alderman. I mean, if Cassidy had been assistant alderman first, Magee would have been next in two years. Or vice versa. Magee accepts that. Hell, he understands how it is here in Gotham. But Cassidy's got a thing with Magee—even more so than his being stiff-necked with Con. And he's in much too much of a hurry. So, anyways, Con had told the two of them to make nice and come see him together, friendly-like, and Cassidy stood on etiquette just like some high and mighty lord something or other, and wouldn't go. Funny enough, I think that was the day you showed up. Magee was as mad as a March hare on account of Cassidy not showing him respect and, worse, not showing his fealty to Donoho."

Tweed looked at me slantendicular-like, but I waited patiently to hear more about etiquette in the 'Points. He finally added, "So, there's to be a duel. Scheduled for this very evening, as it happens."

"Swords or pistols?"

Tweed smirked and said, "No need to be so wise."

"But a duel?"

"Well, perhaps more of an old-fashioned prize fight. Bare knuckles. No mittens. And no London Prize Ring rules or any such foolishness." Tweed looked thoughtful. "But it was arranged through seconds—the principals cannot even be in the same room without one of them trying to kill the other, at this point."

"Well, prize-fights can end up with one party dead or maimed beyond recognition, I'm told, even today, let alone a few years ago, when they could go a hundred rounds or more—and that's what this sounds like."

"Yep," Tweed said. "I haven't any time for Cassidy. But I don't want to see Magee killed or maimed." We fell silent for a moment, then Tweed continued, "As I said, fight's tonight." He looked morosely at the drizzle. "Rain or shine … or high water, for that matter. Want to go?"

"I wouldn't miss it for the world." Then I asked, "So how'd Con get to be so powerful?"

"Oh, that's easy. You heard of Tammany Hall, haven't you?"

"No."

Tweed looked at me. He must have been considering the extent of my ignorance.

"Well, Tammany Hall—the Wigwam—that's how we Democrats get things done here in Gotham. The Sons of St. Tammany've been around forever. They call Tammany Hall the 'Wigwam' on account of their having adopted the red man's traditions. That doesn't make any noise with me. But Tammany is the way to get things done here in Gotham. They used to be right anti-Irish, like everybody, but now they're as Irish as paddy Murphy's pig, so Magee told me once. That's because these days you've got to control the Irish vote to win in Gotham."

I nodded, waiting for Tweed to continue, which he did.

"Con's been a rising star at Tammany for a while. He made his chops last year in the presidential election. Surely you must know that Polk won, right?" I shrugged non-committally. "Captain Isaiah Rynders over in the Third Ward was the face of Tammany in the election—that's who everybody thinks won the election for Polk." Tweed shook his head as if he believed otherwise.

Tweed told me that Rynders was a real character. So the story went, Rynders had been a gambler in New Orleans, and apparently a very dangerous man with an Arkansas toothpick—a huge knife supposedly invented by Jim Bowie, the Texas hero who died at the Alamo a few years back defending the native Americans' right to live God-fearing American lives in Texas without those brown Mexican monkeys lording it over them.

I'd never heard of Texas, but I didn't betray my ignorance.

Tweed said that Rynders was a vicious fighter, having once driven a boxer six inches taller and two stone heavier than he from the saloon on a riverboat simply because Rynders had been losing at faro to the boxer, and wanted to kill him for it. Rynders was also a thief, having successfully stolen a large sum in Treasury notes. He had been arrested, but was let go because nobody could prove he had been involved in the robbery. After that, Rynders showed up in Gotham, well-heeled and politically ambitious.

"Well, just before the presidential election, Rynders had held a big parade, led by his Empire Club—a select group," Tweed said, "of 'a choice variety of picked worthies who could argue a mooted point to a finish with knuckles', as some wag told me a while back. Well there were a thousand people in that parade, with himself, as Magee would say, on his white charger. That's what Rynders likes to call it. Really some nag he hired at the nearest stable. Anyway, they had this big parade, and those who don't know say that Rynders won Polk the city on account of the parade, and then on account of showing up to a Third Ward polling station to chase off a whole passel of Whig voters who'd been sent up from Philadelphia to stuff the ballot boxes. They were, so the story goes, making the rounds to vote in every ward.

"So Captain Rynders gets up on a soapbox, and after the crowd at the polling station quietens down—that quietening being done by Rynders's Empire Club toughs—he roars to the crowd in that booming voice of his, 'I am Isaiah Rynders! My club is here, scattered among you! We know you! Five hundred of you are from Philadelphia—brought here to vote the Whig ticket! Damn you! If you don't leave these polls in five minutes, we will dirk every mother's son of you'."

Tweed chuckled. "I heard that, within four or five minutes, every one of those five hundred Philadelphians had skedaddled, lickety-split … gone home without voting, for fear of assassination. But Rynders didn't win Gotham for Polk—he was all theatrics, and no substance. Con Donoho did. He stuffed those ballot boxes right smart-like—he went those damned Whigs one better. He used local Irishmen and dutchies—and got them to vote four and five times each (paying them two bits apiece for their pains), and here's the killing thing: There were 45,000 voters in Gotham in last year's election, but they counted 55,000 votes for Polk alone. And Rynders had nothing to do with that. Con Donoho did," Tweed said admiringly. "And he ensured that Gotham went for Polk—which everybody knows. Even those who don't know—they know that, without Gotham, Polk loses the election, and then we don't take Texas into the Union.

"That's how vital Con was, and it's why I'm here. To learn from Con. Because I want to run Tammany one day. Me. A Seventh Ward chair-maker. I'm going to run Tammany—and the whole damned city of Gotham one day—me, William Marcy Tweed. So that's why you're finding me standing guard in the rain at Con Donoho's grocery, paying my dues to him."

At that moment, a great commotion in the middle of Orange Street down towards the 'Points got our attention. Tweed and I straightened—Tweed because he recognized something, and I because, well, it seemed the thing to do.

A short, red-faced and clean-shaven (below an enormous set of black whiskers) man with an unlit cheroot gripped in his teeth, followed by half-a-dozen minions in formation, swept towards the grocery, stopped and said to Tweed, "Why, Mr. William Marcy Tweed. What a great honor it is to have ye coming out on such a terrible day to be guarding the Missus fer me."

Tweed mumbled something or other.

"So, how's Magee been treating yers?"

"Fine. Fine, Mr. Donoho. I'm learning a lot," Tweed said.

"Well, I do wish Magee would buy more of my fine, aged Binghamton whiskey." Donoho gestured through the window at several barrels embossed with the "Binghamton" label burned into the wooden staves. "We be manufacturing quite a bit of that mountain dew, and Magee keeps wanting the real thing at double the price. Not as profitable for him—or for me, for that matter. Unaccountable, really. Quite unaccountable."

"I'll mention that to Magee when I'm over there this afternoon, Mr. Donoho," Tweed said drily.

"Nah. Don't worry. He be comin' here. We've important electoral business to be conducting 'afore tonight's little shindig." Donoho drew out "electoral," and swept aside his dark overcoat to stuff his hands in his trouser pockets, thereby revealing a yellow worsted waistcoat violently checked with scarlet.

As Donoho prepared—minions in tow—to enter his grocery, Tweed stopped him. "I'd like to introduce my friend, Billy Gogan. He's one of your street-sweepers, and he's been good enough to help me stand guard today." Tweed gestured up to the sky, which was now beginning to emit occasional raindrops once again.

Donoho turned to me, and said, "Well, nice ta meet yers, son. Many thanks to yers fer standing guard wi' the Missus and the good Mr. Tweed. I do like me street-sweepers t'keep themselves occupied on a rainy day. Hard to sweep the horse shit when it's wet, and we do want the good citizens to see that I'm gettin' them their money's worth in clean streets." Donoho flashed a politician's smile. "You should come up to the Clinton Street docks to see the match. Best entertainment to be found in Gotham." With that, Donoho led his hangers-on into the grocery and loudly greeted the Missus.

⌒

I walked with Bill Tweed up to the Clinton Street docks just as it got dark, stopping with him at several lusheries along the way, where Bill would glad-hand, introduce me to various dubious-looking characters, pretend to drink a beer and move on. The touts and bookies were doing a land office business taking bets on the coming fight, and each time Bill and I made to exit an establishment, we were waylaid by sporting men of every stripe, asking us our thoughts. All told, we probably took a solid two-and-a-half hours to get there, going well past Pike Street and its dock, where I had missed Mary and Fíona ten long weeks earlier.

There were several hundred gawks there when we arrived, hailing from all walks of life and milling about Front Street and the cobbled verge falling away to the East River, with eyes shining with lust for the blood that was to come. There were more bookies and touts swarming among them, shouting, arguing odds and taking bets, than we had seen combined in the various saloons and groggeries we'd passed through on the way there. Even the upper tendom were in attendance, by the score, it seemed, and the bloodlust was as bright in their eyes as in those of any Bowery b'hoy—or g'hal, for that matter. Upper customers all, they were, palavering loudly and knowledgeably about the forthcoming fight, crystal stemware and cigars in hand—the swells, that is. All of them, coves and Corinthians (it seemed that women of virtue—or reps—were likely thin on the ground in such a venue) alike, were dressed for an evening on the town, and almost all of them were ensconced in an array of carriages, some of which were truly magnificent, gleaming four-in-hands, complete with liveried smacking coves fit for the finest *Sassenagh* nobleman, and some of which had clearly been hired for the occasion, harnessed to knackers ready for the boneyard.

A tout approached one swell, only to be shooed away like a pesky fly. Undeterred, the tout approached another, elegant in his black cloak and top hat and as cool as you like in a wreath of cigar smoke. Discussion ensued and a wallet appeared from within the cloak and gold coins flashed. The tout tugged at his forelock, just like a tradesman would to a gentleman in the better parts of Dublin. That is, except the tout had a huge smile on his face. I wondered who had gotten the better of whom in that exchange.

Tweed tugged at my sleeve. "The odds were damned near even earlier this evening. But they're slipping pretty heavily in Cassidy's favor."

"If Magee's such a huge milling cove, then why are the odds shifting?"

Tweed looked at me with a blank face and said, "Cassidy's younger, fitter and has a longer reach. Anyway, Con's not one to waste an opportunity. See that little cove over there?" Tweed pointed at a little gnome of a man with wisps of white hair sticking out haphazardly from underneath an enormous—and enormously battered—top hat.

"What of him?" As I asked the question, the answer became obvious. For as much as the touts and bookies were swirling through the crowd, they did so with a north eye to the little gnome, who seemed to guide them almost telepathically.

"He's Con's man. More importantly, he's Magee's man. They make monetary magic together. Just watch."

With that, Tweed took off towards a small crowd growing more and more restive as a burnished black four-in-hand from one of the finer livery stables clattered towards them. They began clapping and cheering, "Huzzah!"

"It's Cassidy," Tweed called to me. I hurried to catch up with him.

The door to the carriage swung open and Cassidy alighted, stripped to his waist in the bitter early March air, his skin glistening as if oiled. He raised his hands in triumph, and the crowd went wild.

"Watch the betting," Tweed whispered.

Shouting and taking coin and paper at every turn, the touts and bookies dove into the crowd as it surged around Cassidy, whom a few enthusiasts had hoisted to their shoulders. A little premature, don't you think? Tweed murmured to me *sotto voce*. I nodded, watching the little gnome. He had a small, enigmatic smile as he watched the commotion.

The moments passed and the crowd's cheers for Cassidy subsided, and were overtaken by feverish murmurs: "Magee's gonna show the white feather, boys! He ain't got the bottom." Another voice cried, "A chicken heart, he is." The betting surged again, and the little gnome's smile grew even more inscrutable.

"A boat," someone cried over the hubbub. "A boat's coming."

The crowd surged to the dock, and I thought that surely five score would be cast into the dark, chilly water of the East River. Bill and I picked our way through the crowd. A boat scraped onto the cobblestoned verge. Magee was standing in the boat's peak, stripped to the waist, just like Cassidy. An elegantly dressed woman, her face obscured by a bonnet, pulled at his arm and he leaned over and seemingly whispered something to her. There seemed something familiar about the woman and how she held herself, but I couldn't place it. Then Magee bounded from the boat, which shoved off and was quickly lost to sight. The crowd's greeting for him was noticeably more tempered than it had been for Cassidy, and I took it to reflect the odds, which as I'd learned to understand from the odd snatches from the nearby bookies, were running almost 3-1 in Cassidy's favor, with a nice 3-2 on Cassidy delivering a floorer in the first five minutes.

The crowd parted, and a passage double the width of a man's shoulders formed. At one end, at the top of the verge, where it met Front Street, was Cassidy, a minion by his side. At the other was Magee, with Blackie towering over his shoulder, a leather-wrapped iron drumstick dwarfed in his enormous hand. He slapped it into the palm of his other hand and the crowd cowered before him, creating a much larger, albeit still restively pulsing, circle around Magee.

There was a loud shout from somewhere near Cassidy. I couldn't see who. The crowd quieted, and a voice boomed out, "So yers be needin' yer nanny today, Magee?"

"Merely *liom comhbrathair*. Not that you'd know what that was, Cassidy," Magee roared. "You friendless cur."

"Them's brave words, boyo. Ye be ready fer a right comprehensive trimming, me cully?"

"Ready to thrash you, Cassidy."

"Not fucking likely."

The two men had edged closer and now circled each other, a mere couple of arms' lengths from one another. Magee was a gorgeous specimen, lean, muscled, with the coiled menace of a big cat. But he was half a head shorter than Cassidy, had a shorter reach by at least a couple of inches, and gave up perhaps as much as a stone or more to his adversary, who was an equally imposing specimen, himself.

Perhaps the punters weren't all that wrong. I didn't know Magee, having met him just the once. But I nonetheless felt a pang at the prospect of what damage this shake-up was going to do to him.

"No mittens?" Cassidy asked in a roar.

"No mittens, Cassidy," Magee confirmed. "And no London Prize Ring rules. No rounds or time. All we be needin' is a scratch."

As if on cue, Con Donoho bounded out from the crowd and landed between the two milling coves. He raised his hand. The crowd once more quietened. He said, "I'll be drawin' the scratch now." Donoho scraped a rough line in the muddied cobblestones. "Come close, the both o' yers. Don't ye be shy, now. Shake yer dandles now. Like the foin swells you is."

The two men went toe-to-toe at the scratch, each barely touching the other's hand, almost as if they both suspected the other of wanting to do mischief as they shook hands. The crowd went berserk. Cassidy towered over Magee, staring down ominously at the smaller man. Magee was poker-faced. Con leaned up to both of them and spoke so that only they could hear him.

Then he stepped back and faced the crowd with a big grin on his face. "Come out milling, me boyos, when I drops me fogle," whereupon he drew an immense scarlet silk handkerchief from under his cloak. He raised his hand and let the handkerchief flutter slowly to the muddy cobblestones. He whisked it out of harm's way just before it landed, and the crowd went berserk yet again.

The two sloggers circled each other, feinting this way and that, each seeming to take the measure of the other. Cassidy shot a hard rib-ender to Magee, who danced just beyond range, beckoning Cassidy to follow him. Twice more, Cassidy advanced. Each time he threw a swift combination of punches. Each time, Magee danced just beyond range, taunting Cassidy to come at him again.

There was a lull in the noise, and a tough-looking palooka next to me screamed in frustration, "Lend the pam a polt in the muns, Cassidy. Fer the love o' Christ. Put him on his beam-end, will yers?"

The two men circled some more, each jollying the other. I couldn't hear what was being said over the roar of the crowd. Magee backed up once more, into a space newly cleared of the crowd by Blackie and a couple of what appeared to be his mates, who had spread their arms and pushed at the crowd, where Tweed and I stood. The two fighters were now very close. I hopped up to see over Blackie's shoulder. I heard Magee say, "Come and get me, you ponce. Come on, you old catamite." And come Cassidy did as Magee made to once again dance away. Except this time, he didn't. Cassidy threw a punch, slower than his last several, and Magee danced underneath the haymaker, and engaged in a little fibbing against Cassidy's exposed ribs. Both men broke apart, their chests heaving with the effort. Sweat poured from them, and steam rose in the frigid air.

The crowd murmured as the two men once again circled each other. Magee was bleeding a little from his nose, and the side of his forehead was reddened and beginning to swell. So he had not been quite as quick to dance beyond Cassidy's range as I'd thought. He dropped his hands just a little, as if fatigued and Cassidy pounced, with a chopper right to Magee's potato trap. So severe was the blow that I expected to see teeth explode from Magee's mouth. But Magee once again danced away and the blow slid harmlessly down his shoulder. As the momentum took Cassidy past him, Magee grabbed Cassidy's extended arm and threw Cassidy across his hip, sending him sprawling into the mud.

"Sweet Jesus, what a cross-buttock!" exclaimed Tweed.

Cassidy started to spring to his feet, his hands and elbows raw from the fall. But before he could fully right himself, Magee smashed a chopper to his beak, and it exploded in a gout of claret, and Cassidy sank to his knees. Magee made to back away to allow his opponent to rise to his feet. But as soon as Cassidy made a move, Magee pounced with a flurry of blows and a hard kick or two, which put Cassidy face down in the mud, inert and insensate. The crowd exploded, half in delight, half in fury. Fistfights broke out everywhere. Several shots from a repeating pistol rang out, and the crowd stopped cold at the shocking noise.

Magee had vanished, as had Blackie and his minions. Cassidy was being pulled away by his allies, and stuffed unceremoniously into the four-in-hand he had so proudly arrived in hardly fifteen minutes before. Tweed was nowhere to be found. I walked back to the 'Points alone, quite bemused at how alien the Jonathans and their blood lust were from my sheltered upbringing. Then again, I thought, perhaps they aren't so different from the Irishman in the street. Growing up in Dublin, I had seen any number of fights, and worse.

On a rainy March day a couple of weeks later, one of Donoho's minions asked me to stand guard at the grocery because Donoho was away on business, and so I found myself trying to stay dry under the narrow eave over the front door, once again missing my father's oilskin coat. I must have looked quite pathetic, because after an hour or two Mrs. Donoho invited me inside to stand at the coal stove glowing in the middle of the store. I say stand advisedly. There was quite literally nowhere to sit, not even behind the bar that Mrs. Donoho patrolled, a great oak and brass affair, incongruous in the relatively humble half-basement which the store occupied. That is, there was nowhere but a half-pipe of "Swan" gin lying on its side near the bar or one of the Binghamton whiskey barrels stacked against the walls and, more precariously, on the steps leading down to the main floor from the front door.

Donoho's grocery was called such, not because it boasted comestibles of every sort, but because it was an unlicensed saloon that served as a waystation to other groggeries for homemade whiskey and gin, and it had to be called something other than a saloon. In its defense, Donoho's grocery did have a number of open barrels that did not contain liquor of one sort or another. In one there were a few brooms. Another was half full of the herring that Mrs. Donoho occasionally sold, and one was always full of charcoal, which was fed steadily into the pot-bellied stove that was slowly baking me dry.

After a few minutes of thawing my hands and feet while Mrs. Donoho bustled about, I thanked her and made to go outside again before I outstayed my welcome.

"Oh, don't be so daft. It's cold out there, and wet, and I'd just as soon have someone to talk to. There's been hardly anyone in all morning."

I thanked her again.

"So how did you come to land here in the 'Points? You don't seem like the usual mick fresh off the boat," she said archly. Tweed had told me that, although she was married to a fine Irish ward boss, Mrs. Donoho was a Londoner, and she was not at all shy about her views on the worth of the average Irish denizen of the Five Points. Apparently, Anglo-Irish marriages were not unknown here in the New World, although I wondered at them, sometimes, given the sort of conventional *Sassenagh* prejudice with which Mrs. Donoho seemed to have been infected.

I told Mrs. Donoho my story—suitably edited to preserve a story that provoked her to gasp in shocked outrage that I, a poor orphan, had been tossed so cruelly from the bosom of my only remaining family (with another arch aside about Irish savagery). She also complimented me on being a smart, educated boy who was sure to go far in this world. When I mentioned my expeditions into the Old Brewery—I declined to elaborate as to why and she did not enquire, Mrs. Donoho sympathized with me about the wretched state of its denizens, and agreed with me that Mr. Pease and the Temperance Man, John Burke, were truly doing the Lord's work over at the Old Brewery. It was such a good thing that they were keeping the menfolk from liquoring too much. Although, she observed, if they did too good a job, they'd put her man, Mr. Donoho himself, out of business right quick. "But," she sighed, "that don't stop Mr. Donoho from making sure those wretched folk stay safe from those bloody Bowery gangs what get riled up over the Irish every once in a while. And then there's those Shouting Methodies." She shook her head in exasperation. "All they care about is how many souls Mr. Pease has converted. Mr. Pease, bless his heart. He don't set store by those Shouting Methodies, and he tells 'em that the souls should be kept with the body as long as possible, and it don't matter whether any of those poor folks are ever converted."

Mrs. Donoho then fed me a cup of strong hot tea, and asked me to run an errand for her, which I did. After a while, the sun broke through, and I left to return to my street-sweeping.

A few days later, I was unsuccessfully trying to chase off a couple of pigs rooting about on Mott Street so that I could attack a moderately sized pile of filth blocking the wooden sidewalk. I stopped to catch my breath and felt someone tap my shoulder.

It was Blackie, his face expressionless. "Da boss wants t'see yers."

I wondered how long he had been standing there.

When Blackie ushered me into Magee's saloon, Magee wrinkled his nose, and I noted that the signs of the fight had almost vanished from his face.

"Sweet Jaysus, Gogan. Go get yersel' cleaned up, for God's sake. You too, Blackie. What shit hole did you drag him out of? Clean him up, fer the love of … something. Jaysus."

Needless to say, I "got cleaned up" and duly presented myself back at Magee's about an hour later.

"Better," Magee said dubiously. "Have a drink."

He put a good Irish whiskey in front of me. It brought home to me the smell of the fireplace in the parlor—and the last time I'd had a whiskey—that last Christmas with my father.

"Well don't go getting lost on me." Magee brought me back. "*Seo do shláinte.*"

"*Do shláinte.*" We touched glasses.

"So yer not too *Sassenagh* in yer ways, are yers?"

"I s'pose those'd be fighting words," I drawled self-consciously. "But I don't want to be dueling with you like Cassidy did."

"No chance o' that, kid." Magee chuckled. "No chance o' that."

He leaned against the bar. I mimicked him.

"Had enough o' that street-sweeping yet, kid?"

"It's good 'til something else comes along."

"Well, perhaps something has. Mrs. Donoho's taken a shine to yers. Thinks yer Quality." He looked at me and smiled. "No, not like that. Yer no high n' mighty swell."

We leaned against the bar some more.

"I've got a bit o' something for yers. Interested?"

No more sweeping shit? Oh, frabjous day. Well, I would have said that if Carroll hadn't waited another twenty-five years to invent the damned word.

"I want to try yers out here in the lushery. Actually, in the ten-pin saloon. Settin' pins." Magee looked up and called to someone skulking in the gloom. "Cian, come on over here."

The figure materialized out of the gloom into the very picture of a Bowery b'hoy: a battered black silk hat tipped well forward above a sly, calculating look and a cheroot in the corner of his mouth, a long black frock coat over a flowered silk vest partially concealing a fiery red serge shirt tucked carelessly into tight, black pantaloons, and heavy black boots more suited to stomping someone's face in than for ballet.

"Cian," Magee said in a mock pretentious tone, "This is Billy Gogan."

"Cian Dineen," he said though his cheroot. "Nice to meet you."

He reached to shake my hand, and I glimpsed a knife stuck through his heavy leather belt.

Magee explained to me, "Cian may look and sound the part of a Seventh Ward swell, but he ain't no Nativist 'know nothing.' He's as Irish as yer and me and Paddy Murphy's pig." He added affectionately, "And a good kid. Ain't cha?"

Cian gave Magee a long-suffering look.

Magee said, "Take care o' Billy here, kid. He's been paying his dues. Time for him to set a few pins in the ten-pin saloon." Magee gestured through the gloom at a curtain, and left the bar without another word.

Cian replied to his back, "Sure thing, boss."

That night, Magee's ten-pin saloon was crawling with uptown swells and pigeons from Poughkeepsie (so Cian called the befuddled rural merchants with money to lose), every last one of them ready to be plucked. I was setting pins for some punter who claimed to all who would listen that he owned 100 slaves and a thousand acres of cotton in the Carolinas. "Up here in Gotham to meet with my banker and my English shipping agent, don't you know," he drawled to me at one point, as he tipped me a shilling for a cigar and a brandy well diluted (by his request) with water.

The Carolina planter had been bowling with an increasingly drunken Yankee merchant for several games, and the merchant had just won two straight, with the Carolina planter seemingly gracious in defeat. They bantered over the stakes at the end of each game as I fed them waters and brandy (heavy on the cheap brandy—and no water—for the merchant). Just before they began their fifth game, the Carolina planter leaned over to the merchant while I lit their fresh cigars.

"You're getting the better of me," he drawled. "But I think I might make it up." He paused to consider his words. "Why don't we double down?"

The merchant beamed at the prospect, and he and the Carolina planter each clattered their gold coins onto the table. The Carolina planter fell steadily behind through the first eight frames. On the penultimate frame, the Carolina planter sent a particularly wild ball crashing improbably down the lane to miss an easy spare.

As I skedaddled to reset the pins, the Carolina planter said to the Yankee merchant, "You make this next strike or spare, I can't win, even if I hit three perfect strikes."

The merchant again beamed his approval, asking the Carolina planter if he wanted to once again double the stakes. The Carolina planter agreed in a seeming haze of gracious inebriation, although I thought I may have seen the merest hint of a spark in his eye.

I felt Cian's hot, sour breath in my ear, "Give that pigeon a split. Like I showed yers. His lordship's gonna tip us real good." Cian gestured to the Carolina planter. I glared at the pins for a moment, and then resolutely thrust all thoughts of cricket and fair play from my mind as a luxury I couldn't afford.

With my back to the Carolina planter and the merchant, I set all but two of the pins in their triangle, each equally placed from the other on top of faint marks painted on the polished wood. I then placed the corner pins some inches away from their respective marks on the floor, on top of two stained and slightly sticky spots. Even if the merchant bowled perfectly, he'd leave the two back corner pins—seven and ten—standing, and too far apart to get them both on the spare—just as Cian had carefully instructed me that afternoon, when my conscience had panged even more strongly at the mere prospect of cheating.

So it came to pass. The merchant cleared his head of the brandy fumes long enough to roll what should have been a perfect strike, sending pins scattering all about, but the seven and ten pins remained upright. The merchant rolled again and missed, badly, swearing at his "infernal bad luck." I quickly reset the pins—properly this time, and the Carolina planter rolled three quick strikes, to the merchant's mounting frustration.

As the pins clattered from the last strike, the Carolina planter laughed and gathered the money stacked on the table, gesturing to me to bring him a celebratory "seegar." The merchant let out an anguished cry. It was clear that the Carolina planter had tapped him dry.

"You cheated." The merchant's voice shook with fury.

"Watch it, sonny," the Carolina planter drawled slowly, suddenly very sober.

The merchant lunged at the smirking Carolina planter, but he never made it. Blackie and another equally large and dark Irish ruffian grabbed him firmly, without undue cruelty, and unceremoniously dumped him—with a couple of swift parting kicks—into the alley behind Magee's saloon. Two or three hours later, when Cian and I emptied the slop buckets into the alley, we saw that the merchant was still lying there in a heap in the filth. Cian stooped over the merchant, and felt through his pockets.

Cian swore and said, "Some scalawag's already been at him. Should'a checked him earlier. Never mind. We made a half eagle between us off'n that Carolina swell. That's a good night."

I ignored my conscience and agreed with Cian. I'd made as much from my share of that single tip, twenty shillings, as I would have in half-a-week's work hodding bricks. And it was a damned sight better than sweeping shit.

We left the merchant to sleep off his brandy.

⌒

The next day, I was head down and a bit out of sorts over the Poughkeepsie sucker, when I arrived at Magee's Saloon to begin my second day setting ten pins and plucking pigeons.

"Well, hello there, Billy Gogan. Fancy your oilskin back?"

It was Mary. Standing there in front of me, twirling a parasol, a broad smile on her face and a twinkle in her eye.

⌒

CHAPTER 10

Building the Grubstake

MARY WAS DIFFERENT. SHE WASN'T THE LOST WAIF on the quay anymore. She was a regular prim. Fetching, and beautiful even, she was absently twirling her parasol above her modest—but not quite a coal scuttle—bonnet and delicately avoiding the muck in Mulberry Street. She outshone the prettiest Bowery g'hal and rivaled the most elegant debutante waltzing into Astor House for tea.

I stared at her. "I thought you were dead."

Mary folded me into her arms, and whispered softly into my ear as if I were her younger brother, "No, *a chuid*. Me 'n' Fíona be just fine. Don't ye be worryin' yersel' on our account. You come upstairs now, and I'll make you a cup of tea and give you a thick slice of cakebread. God knows you could use some meat on your bones. You look like a scarecrow." Mary assessed me for a moment. "Taller, though. That's good."

"You live upstairs?" I pointed at Magee's boardinghouse.

"Since the day we arrived."

"I work down there." I pointed down to Magee's Saloon. "Since yesterday."

"I know."

I stared at her again.

She gave me a knowing smile. "It's all right, now. We're together once more."

With that, we went upstairs to her two rooms. Fíona squealed with joy, and I finally cried for the first time since I learned that my father had died.

⌒

Magee smiled at me a little crookedly and said nothing when I clattered into the saloon an hour later, flinging apologies at every turn for being late.

Mary was off to work up in Gramercy Park, at one of those brand new mansions, where she was a domestic during the evenings. She said she'd see me in the morning as she'd be back late, and Fíona was to be spending the night with Mrs. Shipley, the widow next door with a pair of *wains* of her own who took in children to help make ends meet. I was to spend the night, on a *réleaba* that Mary put together in the corner of the main room. She and Fíona shared the other room. I was not to spend any more nights at Schreiber's. I was instead to move in with Mary and Fíona. All the better to keep my promise to teach Fíona to read and write, Mary said. She was bound and determined that Fíona was going to become an *ardollamh*—just like Margery Meanwell in *Goody Two Shoes*, which was still Fíona's favorite book. So Mary wanted me to start reading with Fíona again, particularly as next year she was going to be attending St. Peter's Free School over on Barclay Street at Church, just across from City Hall.

The school was eight blocks farther away than the Public School Society's brand new school at the corner of Mott and Cross Streets. But that was of no consequence, Mary declared emphatically. Hell would freeze over, she said (this from a proper Irish Catholic square moll!), before she would send her good Irish Catholic girl to the public school (a public school in the truest sense of the word, so unlike a *Sassenagh* or Irish public school)—even though she'd have to find the money for tuition for St. Peter's—because that Methodist Mayor Jimmy Harper would make her poor Fíona read that *Sassenagh* Bible at the public school, and she was not going to have her Fíona being seduced by the *Sassenagh* Antichrist just because those Methodists want to convert every *gach leanbh Éireannach gan choir*—every innocent Irish child—away from the one true religion. But that was next year, and, Mary told me, this coming Sunday morning, I was to go to church with her and Fíona, even if we did both work late Saturday night. She said that I needed a thorough confession as antidote—yes, she used just that word—to all the malign influences of the 'Points. There'd be time enough to sleep on other nights. St. Peter's is so beautiful, she said, with those six marble columns. She'd never been to such a grand church before in all her life, and the good Father Williams treated her, a poor little Irish servant girl, just as nicely as he treated those nice ladies from Gramercy Park.

Mary handed me my cup of tea, and I asked her why she didn't wait for me the day we arrived. A regretful smile flashed over her face, and she replied that they'd told her that no one else would be coming from *Maryann* that night. She was told that she'd have to find me in the morning and that she and Fíona could not stay on the pier all night to wait for me. The Irish Emigrant Society's runner—she couldn't remember the man's name, but he had been so very nice—had directed her to Magee's boardinghouse as a clean and safe place to stay—and he hadn't been wrong about that. She and Fíona had been here ever since. Why, Mary said, Magee had even fixed her up with her job in Gramercy Park. But anyway, she'd gone back to Pike Slip early the next morning, only to find *Maryann* departed. I was nowhere to be found. She looked at me a bit blankly when I remonstrated that she should have gone up to the Irish Emigrant Society that very morning, where I'd left word and where I'd gone so many times since then in the vain hope of hearing from her. Her eyes were large and liquid as she apologized to me for having been so thoughtless.

We hugged once more. Mary pulled away as we heard the church bell ring and appraised me for a moment, much as a sister might. Then she said that I had to be going to work, and so had she. I saw Magee's crooked smile just a few minutes thereafter.

Magee sought me out again a few days later. I hadn't seen him around much except for an hour here or there when he held court in the gloomy dancing hall in the afternoons before Gothamites of all stripes began flooding by the score into the 'Points, many of them crowding into Magee's saloon and bowling alley. Magee's place seemed to attract a broad crowd with the bowling, decent liquor and nightly shows of an ever-changing "orchestra." Some nights, the "orchestra" was just a wizened, old colored fiddler who knew how to match the mood of the place perfectly. Sometimes as he played, I closed my eyes and swore that I was in Dublin or Cork, listening to the mournful Gaelic wails drifting out of the public houses in the damp fog as I passed by. Papa John (that's all anyone knew him by) also knew how to turn the place on its head in an instant, burning up his fiddle with scorching melodies that galvanized everybody—Magee and Blackie included, if they were there.

Saturday nights were an entirely different matter. The stage, if you could call it that—it was little more than a rickety, deal platform—sagged under the combined weight of Papa John and a constantly changing cast of other musicians. I remember one of them was a huge colored man. A true *dead ráibéad*, not like the hulking Roach Guards who sometimes plagued Paradise Square or the giant Irish Plug Uglies. This giant, bald, colored man had arms the size of small trees, and he beat his bass drum like a rented mule in complete violation of every law of rhythm known to man and God. A colored trumpet player frequently joined him, playing in counterpoint to the fiddle and keeping time with the wildly syncopated beat of the drum—all the while spitting red-hot knitting needles of energy from his horn into the crowd. The tambourine man would dance a jig, moving his feet like a blur, while banging his tambourine (which could hardly ever be heard) in time—first to the trumpet player, then the fiddler, and finally to the colored man thrashing his drums. It was music unlike anything I'd ever heard. It brought a *teas*—only the Irish will do to describe it, so Magee said. There was, Magee declared, and I believe him to be right, no *Sassenagh* word to describe the music and how it drove every cove and mort (punks and proper prims alike) into a blind, unseeing lust as they danced until dawn in the spiffest stepping ken in the 'Points.

Uptown swells and country simkins alike patronized Magee's, mingling with the micks as hail fellow and well met as you please. Even the nativist Bowery b'hoys and g'hals from over in the Seventh Ward, Tweed's stomping grounds, laid aside their enmity with the micks for the moment and allowed themselves to find Magee's to be a sociable place. About the only Gothamites who didn't venture into Magee's were the coloreds—aside from the occasional beautiful dell looking for a cully. Nobody said why, but I didn't need telling. Nobody did.

After I'd been setting pins and helping fleece the simkins for a week, Magee told me that I'd been "doing well." Cian and Blackie liked the cut of my jib and my willingness to rough it, serving even the most ill-tempered customers and cleaning up at the end of the night. I tried not to kiss Magee's ring too much when I told him I liked the job—and the pay—right fine. Magee grunted and said that he wanted to make better use of me. There was someone he knew who could use a longheaded fellow like me. He asked me if Cian had told me about Charlie, the policy man. He grunted again when I said no, and then told me that Charlie ran a highly lucrative policy game (and made book on a host of sporting and other events) with his and Con Donoho's backing—which meant that no Irish gang would touch him, or the chink. The nativist gangs wouldn't either, if those galoots knew what was good for them.

Magee told me that he liked the numbers because everybody played them, especially the coloreds, who mixed in the policy bucket shops right along with the buckras, all of them picking numbers with gleeful abandon, as if there were not a whit o' difference between them. He said with a serious look that there was a lot of money to be made running a square policy game. So many games were crooked, and came and went as punters realized they were being jostled. Charlie played straight—Magee said this with a bit of a shrug—and paid out square to the winners. Although, Magee allowed, the games weren't too square, not if he, Magee, had anything to say about it. As Magee spoke to me mellifluously of his real livelihood, I could hear the rumblings from my father and Father O'Muirhily. But I turned a deaf ear. I was in a different world now, and the alternative was to shovel shit in the streets. The simkins be damned.

At Magee's behest, Cian took me to Charlie's "offices," which were behind a cheap pine door on the second floor of Magee's boardinghouse. It was just like every other door in the place—unlocked and unguarded when we arrived.

"Who's that?" An irascible voice emerged from behind several stacks of ledgers piled high on a table in the middle of the room.

"Just me, Charlie." Cian ventured in.

"Well, knock. Fer Chrissakes. You'll gimme conniption fits one day, you will."

"I got that kid Magee was telling ya 'bout."

"Send 'im in. Send 'im in. Where is 'e?"

With that, the same gnome with the enormous, battered top hat I'd seen at the fight between Magee and Cassidy scuttled around the table. He'd been the one to whom the touts and bookies had deferred as they made their killings.

"'Oo're you?" The gnome blinked at me through a pair of decrepit spectacles.

"This is—" Cian began.

"Didn't ask you. Asked 'im."

"Billy Gogan, sir." I extended my hand.

The gnome ignored it. "Name's Charlie Backwell. Late o' London town. Iff'n yers got a problem wiv 'at, then fuck you, mick." He skittered back behind his books. "Call me Charlie."

"Charlie, the policy man," Cian said ingratiatingly.

Charlie cleared his throat. "Take 'im 'round the shops, Dineen, and show 'im the ropes."

"Sure thing, boss."

Charlie held sway over a dozen or more bucket shops scattered throughout the Sixth and Seventh Wards, clear up to Corlears Hook, where the sailors flung away their brass on dells, ragwater, faro and the numbers until they were dead broke and ready to be shanghaied back onto the nearest barky bound for God knows where. Cian and I went from shop to shop, collecting money from the policy men. The exact relationship between them and Charlie was a little unclear. But I got the sense that Charlie owned the shops—or more accurately, Magee or Donoho did. In any case, it was clear that the policy men worked for Charlie. Some of the shops—the ones in the 'Points—were crowded with Irish and coloreds, most of them virtually destitute, although I did see the occasional well-dressed punter, almost always deep in his cups. Shops farther over in the Bowery and up towards Corlears Hook were full of dutchies, natives and sailors, depending on the block, the side of the street and the particular gang controlling that side of the street. But the routine in each shop was invariable: every player had a sheet of paper, and he (or she, there were as many morts as coves playing the policy) was busy marking numbers and then handing the sheet to the shopkeeper with his brass and receiving in return a ticket imprinted with the selected three numbers, all of which were between 1 and 78. Illiterates were helped by their fellows to mark the numbers on their tickets. They then read the numbers to the illiterates afterwards so that the poor devils wouldn't be cheated when their tickets won.

In the second shop Cian and I visited, I overheard one colored woman talking to another, saying that she had dreamed of a dead man laid out in a bed in his winding sheet. She didn't know who had died. But she had been very surprised to find the man there, as she realized that the man was lying in her bed. Later in the dream, she said, she'd told her mother about the dead man. Funny thing about it was, though, the woman said, shaking her head, her mother had passed over many years ago. She told her companion that she had confided to the policy man about her dream. He'd counseled her that the dream was a good omen to bet heavily today, before the next drawing, on her own age and the age of the corpse in her dream. She'd told the policy man that she didn't know who the dead person was, so she couldn't possibly know his age. The policy man had replied that she should then just pick 56 as her fourth number. I later heard the same sort of folderol after that in any number of policy shops as I collected the punters' offerings.

Cian and I returned several times to Charlie's room to deposit the rhino. Cian explained that we didn't want to carry too much brass, because we'd be marks for muggers and other miscreants ready to relieve us of it. Only the stupid ones, of course. But, Cian said, it was the stupid floorers and footpads you had to be worried about. We'd be eased of our brass, and probably croaked in the bargain. Of course, Donoho's and Magee's gangs would stifle our assailants 'afore they'd even counted their ill-gotten lucre. Cian gestured casually across the street, where one of Magee's minions was keeping a watchful eye on us. But, Cian said, we would not benefit from it. We would be pegtantrum and thus beyond caring.

"Pegtantrum?"

"Yeah, ya slubber. Pegtantrum. Croaked. Slated. Toes up."

On our second or third trip, Cian said, "Let's beef it."

We repaired to an oyster cellar. You could always spot an oyster cellar by the gigantic painted lamps—usually candlelit in an unearthly red color—marking the door. Tonight, the oyster cellar was filled with sporting men—nary a square moll among them—tucking into plates of raw oysters on the half shell, oyster stew, oyster fritters, poached oysters, stuffed oysters and just about any other conceivable way human beings can consume oysters. Some sat at the bar, others at a few tables in the center of the room. The rest of the punters sat in booths with curtains you could pull closed to conduct confidential meetings with business associates and pursue assignations with bleak morts. I noticed with some delight that the curtains were often open just enough for one to catch an occasional glimpse of goings-on as the supper hour approached.

Cian and I sat in one of the booths, which had apparently been reserved for him (all the others being occupied) and he pulled the curtain closed.

He nudged me and winked, "Sorry to interrupt the show, me cully." He grinned mischievously, "Met Cassidy in one of these places a while back, wi' me brother."

"Yeah?"

Before Cian could say more, the curtain flung open, and Cian's spitting image—but for the maniacal eyes—stood there with a huge grin on his face.

"Buddy!" Cian embraced him. "Lúcás, Billy … Billy, Lúcás."

Lúcás slid in next to Cian and studied me. I did my best to meet his gaze while I studied him in turn. Lúcás was every inch as much the Bowery b'hoy as his brother, right down to the oiled hair, flowered silk vest and tight black panties stuffed into heavy boots.

Cian explained, "Billy's that greenhorn I was telling y'about. Magee's taken him on. He knows his figuring."

"That so?"

I nodded.

"Lúcás is a tout up on the docks. He works for Cassidy, steering all them simkins fresh off the boat to Cassidy's. Don'cha, Lúcás?"

Lúcás looked at Cian, who shut pan.

We sat there in uncompanionable silence for a few moments.

The curtain was flung open again, and three large plates of raw oysters appeared. The oysters were huge, bigger than anything I'd ever seen in Ireland, where they'd been eaten since time immemorial, and exported to England ever since the *Sassenagh* clapped out their own oyster beds. A couple of them were as big as a small wheel of cheese.

Lúcás reached behind his shoulders, under his coat, and yanked out an enormous knife and began spearing the meat of his oysters with it. When he pulled his knife out, I caught a glimpse of the battered brass butt plate of a decrepit-looking percussion pistol stuffed into his belt. Lúcás adjusted his coat, and the barking iron disappeared.

Cian grinned at my reaction to the knife. "Ya like that? It's Lúcás's Arkansas toothpick. He won it from some simkin wearing a deerskin coat and claiming to be a mountain man, whatever that is. He's a reg'lar Cap'n Hackum with it." He chuckled again. "Ain't that right, Lúcás?"

Lúcás grunted, and we lapsed into silence again as we systematically cleared our plates. I studied the knife, fascinated. This must be a Bowie knife, like the one Rynders had used in New Orleans, according to the stories.

Hardly had we finished our raw oysters when the curtain was once again flung open and enormous bowls of oyster stew were deposited in front of us. When we finished eating, Lúcás wordlessly licked his blade clean of gravy and then wiped it dry on the leg of his fancy black panties. His eyes were no longer maniacal. They were now merely dead black buttons.

"You like to frolic?" He was playing with the gleaming blade.

"I suppose," I extemporized. I'd seen enough gang fights in Paradise Square and in the streets of the 'ould, bloody Sixth to suspect that schoolboy scuffles were not what he was talking about.

"Ye suppose." He leaned close to me, his hot, sour breath assailing me. "I loves it."

With that, he slid his toothpick back into the scabbard under his coat and left. Cian and I sat for a few minutes, wordlessly looking at each other.

Finally, Cian said, "We oughta liquor up with him some night. Mebbe we'll go up to Cassidy's."

"Sure."

"Cassidy's gonna give Lúcás something real good, real soon. Lúcás is a good guy. He don't say much, but he's a real good guy."

Cian and I didn't talk a lot as we visited the last of the bucket shops, and I felt a little cold despite the warmth of the early spring afternoon.

⌒

"Charlie, how do the numbers work?"

I'd spent days traipsing from one bucket shop to the next, collecting five dollars here and ten dollars there, nervously looking over my shoulder, afraid that some stupid, strong-arm cove was looking to wrest a few simoleons from me. But I had no real understanding of what these poor people were doing picking numbers— nor did I understand how Charlie and Magee were making their brass running the game. So I asked him.

"Eh?" Charlie stopped moving the beads on his abacus.

"How do the numbers work?" I repeated.

"I 'eard yers the first time," Charlie snapped.

I shut pan.

"It's like this," he began after a minute or two. "Numbers is nothing more than a lottery. Randomly chosen numbers—randomly chosen by me." He grinned.

"By you?"

"Well, I could, if I wanted to. But I don't. We play straight games—all kinds of 'em. And we mint the brass doin' it. The other policy men? They rig their games. So they don't last. We got something different."

He lit a cheroot, and I waited.

"So," he grinned again through a wreath of choking smoke, "what we do is use lotteries from different places for our numbers—in addition to the wheel we use every day at Magee's. We use Baltimore, Philadelphia. Hell, I'd use Paris, France, if it didn't take six weeks to get the numbers—and that's iff'n the barky don't sink. So we jes' use Baltimore and Philadelphia. Once a week. All I gotta do is close out the punters before the lottery is drawn— even if it is in Philadelphia. No way I can guarantee being the first to know the numbers. We use the best pony express to get the numbers up here. But things happen, and I don't want no shaver placing a big bet and then 'ave 'im spicin' me. I'd hate that, an' Magee'd hate it worse.

"So it's the punters knowing they'll know the numbers jes' like me—jes' a little later than I will—that's wot gives us a straight game, an' the straight game is wot brings the punters to us. But that don't mean that we gotta be suckers. No sir. There's knowing how to sell lottery tickets—any two-year-old mick fresh from the bog an' his mother's teat could do that, for heaven's sake," he said mildly. "An' then there's makin' money doin' it." He grinned again.

"What we do is take the odds of the lottery, and I fix 'em so the big prize don't ever pay—leastways, the odds of it paying are worse than you or some other mick becoming King of England. And all this … we do it without getting cross with the punters."

I looked at him quizzically.

"Well," he explained. "Let's say you got numbers one through 78, and 3 of the numbers are drawn randomly. The punter needs to have all three numbers on his ticket to win. Three numbers out of 78. Odds are pretty high you'll win, right?"

I nodded non-committally.

"Ye'd be wrong to think that, though, boyo," he said. "Here's why. Remember, we print scheme books that contain 1,560 three-number tickets, and we can print as many of them as we want so's we can sell 'em at every bucket shop you collect from. So, you says to me, jes' buy all 1,560 tickets, and one of 'em'll pay off, right?"

I blurted, "There are more than 1,560 three-number combinations, right?"

He looked at me. "You know 'ow many?"

"Good Lord," I muttered as I tried to calculate the number. "Thousands."

Charlie laughed. "There are exactly 76,076 three number combinations of the numbers one through 78 where no three number combination is duplicated. Work it out."

"So, if a punter were to buy all 1,560 tickets, he'd still only have a one in what, fifty or so, chance of winning the big prize?"

Charlie looked at me with a satisfied look. "That, pal, is why we don't need to run a cross game."

⌒

Within the week, I was no longer working the bucket shops, and I was happy to leave such collection work to Cian and others like him. Charlie pulled me into his office to work as his bookkeeper several hours each day. The work was easy—as long as I had good candles to work by—and Charlie paid me a bonus every time I caught up to one of his bucket shop proprietors—it turned out that Charlie and Magee employed them as "independent contractors," as Charlie called them—jostling him out of his brass.

Nobody talked about what happened to them, and I tried not to think about their fate.

Charlie showed me all the swindles they—and others, including the punters themselves—would try to get off without Charlie knowing about it. Eternal vigilance, he counseled me. Eternal vigilance. "The only way to keep yer brass," he grumbled. It was at Charlie's knee that I received my advanced education in gambling, and in gamblers and their flash ways. I not only learned about policy, but also about faro, perhaps the most popular card game ever. Only simkins play faro today, of course, and that's because there hasn't been a square faro game since before Hoyle was born, 200 years ago—notwithstanding Mr. Hoyle's pious treatment of how to play a square faro game. Only a fool would be the dealer in a square game of faro, and only a greater fool would play against a faro dealer—cross or square.

Neither Charlie nor Magee would countenance faro anywhere in Magee's saloon, let alone in the back room where the private games of poker (known as bluff) were played by the likes of Donoho, Rynders, Matt Brennan and other Sixth Ward luminaries. Charlie told me to steer clear of those games, and I did. They may have been square, and Charlie had taught me how to play—and play well—but I would have been a mere sucker in that crowd.

⌒

That wonderful and ancient game of "prick the garter" was another matter. The poor had all seen the game one too many times. Indeed, many was the time as a child at some fair or another with my father when I had seen the nob-pitchers hard at work separating the credulous from their coppers. Charlie had confided in me one night that nob-pitching was how he got his start as a boy in England. But the game wasn't familiar to the upper tendom nobs and their molls who came 'a touring the 'Points. But the salacious naughtiness titillated them, and therein lay yet one more money-making opportunity.

That's right. The upper tendom (and others of a not quite so socially lofty status, such as touring rubes from Croton and points north and east) would come toddling over in groups to stare in wonder at the squalor and misery and unnaturalness of the Five Points. Slumming, they called it, and it was all the rage. Paradise Square was only three blocks from Broadway and all of its splendor and wealth and hotels, and the wealthy coves and punters and their ladies who inhabited that world, all of them all too willing to be separated from their rhino if it brought them a sense of surprise and adventure.

So it wasn't shocking that Charlie and Magee organized tours of their fine establishment, using touts with some modicum of polish to guide the suckers from the safety of Astor House into the 'Points and its myriad dens of iniquity—they'd been using Cian Dineen and others of similar ilk since the beginning of time. I had occasionally been pressed into service acting as a tout, where I used my most highfalutin' accent to jolly along the more nervous of our customers. Other nights, Charlie taught me the finer points of "prick the garter" and "fast and loose," an even more ancient variant.

On one such evening, the crowd was pressing into the saloon. Papa John was playing a slow, almost mournful jig in the background. Tom the trumpet player was in the alley, cigar in hand and nice young thing tucked in the crook of his elbow, having just killed the punters and molls with a bravura set. Charlie had set me up with my garter—which in truth was little more than a longish, narrow, thin piece of leather more suited to be a tourniquet or a belt than a lady's garter—carefully folded to conceal what Charlie called with a concupiscent grin, "the one true fold." When I looked at him blankly, he retorted in a tone he generally reserved for the particularly dull, "the quim that we all seek." I nodded more to shut him up than in understanding.

A group of upper tendom punters we had been expecting hove into view, eyes glittering at the thought of slumming at so notorious a watering place as Magee's saloon. On cue, Papa John picked up his pace, and Charlie cried, "Come one, come all. Try 'er Mope-Eyed Ladyship, Lady Luck, 'ersel'. Play 'prick the garter'. Find the one true fold. 'Oo knows," he said with a quick, devilish grin, "ye might just finds 'er. She gets 'appy an' you get rich." He spied Cian, who was loafing about, apparently indifferent to the sudden hoopla. "You, sir, my fine man. Over there. Ye're ready to try 'er Ladyship's one true fold, ain't cha?"

"Ya say what, bub?" Cian looked almost too surprised, but none of the upper tendom flats and their fine and tawdry Corinthians noticed him overplay his role. They were too engrossed by Charlie's pattering the flash and a few of them, no doubt, were bent by the prospect of besting Charlie, a creature clearly fallen from the grace of God and the ranks of mankind merely by his being a denizen of the Five Points.

Charlie almost grinned at Cian's impudence, which another time would have earned him a swift kick. "Play 'er Ladyship," Charlie said, thrusting a large, blunt needle into Cian's seemingly unwilling hand. "Prick her in her one true fold."

"What do I do?" Cian gave a hoosier's grin.

"Prick the garter, me cully," bellowed Charlie. "Prick the garter in its true fold, ye daft bastard." Charlie muttered this last bit under his breath. He then leered knowingly and one or two upper tendom culls guffawed and a nearly bare-breasted Corinthian tittered appreciatively at the double-entendre.

I let the garter come unfolded and flourished it to our now-curious audience. I quickly doubled it, raised it once more to show the audience where the one true fold lay. The nearly bare-breasted Corinthian winked at me salaciously as her cully fondled her. I then folded the garter up to hide the true fold and presented it for the pricking, taking care to hold each of the ends tightly.

"All right, me bucko," Charlie said conversationally to Cian, "you bet a shilling that you can prick 'er Mope-Eyed Ladyship's garter in the true fold. Ye do that, ye'll get yersel' a liberty head. If ye can prick 'er three times in a row, Lady Luck'll be 'appy an' ye'll be winning a full quarter eagle." Charlie stared at the Corinthian's milkshop and murmured, "an' iffen ye does that, 'er Mope-Eyed Ladyship might take yers home to keep. Money and bottom. What's not to like?"

Cian flipped a shilling to Charlie, waved the pin about and gently thrust it home. I unfolded it to the true fold, which had been pierced by the needle. There was applause and guffaws from the men and knowing giggles from the molls.

"Again," cried Charlie. I refolded the garter. Once again, Cian found the true fold. "'Er Ladyship's one happy nectarine, she is. Jes' listen to 'er. Now, me bucko, prick it deep once more an' ye'll be havin' yer quarter eagle. What are the odds?"

Cian found the true fold lickety-liner. The crowd reacted, and Cian played the excited nocky boy to the hilt as I paid over the quarter eagle to him with the grimace of a man who'd been fleeced.

"Now who'll try 'er Mope-Eyed Ladyship?"

The men in the crowd dithered.

Charlie was having none of it, proclaiming, "Now, my bene culls, don't none o' yers be a muck-worm by bettin' only yer eyes. Show them bleak morts wots 'angin' on yer arm wot ye be made of. Come on, boys, let's place yer wagers." Charlie plunged into the group of touring punters and grabbed a young fellow with no more whiskers than I had. He pulled the young cully forward and I made a great show of folding the garter to show the one true fold and then covered it over. My conscience did not prick me at all when I moved the fold. The cully stabbed eagerly at the garter and damned near ran my finger through, though, which I played for a quick laugh from the crowd and a flush of embarrassment from him. He flushed even more deeply and the crowd laughed louder when I opened the garter and they saw that he'd missed completely. We made quick work of him on his next two tries—at a liberty head per try for a half eagle.

Another cove fell almost as quickly, this time for a full dollar a try. The moll he was with gave him a playful shove when he returned to her side, chagrined. She whispered in his ear, and his face went bright red, to the amusement of his friends and their escorts.

As a third cove made his way up to me, I caught sight of coal-black hair under a silk top hat moving through the crowd. My heart lurched, for I knew in my bones who it must be—the man in funereal black who had murdered Father O'Muirhily. I looked up again, and the man had vanished. I quickly dismissed the surge of panic filling my chest as absurd, rationalizing that there must be a thousand men in the 'Points who sported the black hair of the Irish. For the love of Moses, I screamed to myself, there must be two thousand of them in the 'Points alone. I couldn't look for him again, as I had to set about the task of burning the chink from one more insensate tom-coney with my disappearing true fold.

Much later that night, when we were fifty or seventy dollars the richer for having fleeced noddles from three different groups of upper-tendom tourists, I sat in the now-quiet saloon, nursing a glass of lemonade before heading upstairs to my bed and brooding upon who the black-haired man with a top hat could possibly have been—surely, I wasn't followed the better part of 2,500 miles from Cork to Gotham, was I?

Magee loomed over me, smiling. "What's eatin' yers, Billy-boy? Ye've been as quiet as a church mouse all night."

I opened my mouth to spill all to Magee and then shut pan, too tired to contemplate having to patiently explain my fears at two o'clock in the morning, thinking them at once foolish, even imaginary and yet all too real. And even more, I realized that I didn't want to upset the cart and end up back on the streets, hodding bricks at best, or worse, sweeping the streets clear of shit. I rationalized to myself that I would be gone soon enough. Off to the frontier where there would be no shenanigans like the ones I found myself caught up in, and where I believed men would be honorable and upstanding and reliable, like Hawkeye. I swallowed my newly-awakened sense of candor, and contented myself with waving my hand and saying, "I think I've got a way to bring in more chink from these visiting swells."

Magee looked delighted, replying, "That's good, my friend. I'm always looking for a new way to separate a man from his money."

⌒

I had put the letter I wrote to my old headmaster from Galway out of my mind for so many months, particularly as I hadn't heard from him—not that I would have, for I had left no forwarding address. But the shock of seeing that man in black had brought home to me the certainty of what I saw happen to Father O'Muirhily on Lavitt's Quay. So that night, I set about writing another careful letter to the headmaster, inquiring about Father O'Muirhily. This time, I asked him to respond to me care of the Irish Emigrant Society. I contemplated writing a second letter to Cousin Séamas to ask after Evelyn, but I dismissed the thought. He'd made it plain he wanted never to hear of me again. It was then that I wrote a short letter to Oonagh, his housekeeper, ostensibly to thank her for giving me my father's oilskins, with as casual an aside as I could asking after Evelyn.

⌒

"Four plus three is seven," lisped Fíona proudly.

We were sitting under the trees in Battery Park on a beautiful April afternoon. It was a wonderful spot to take Fíona when Mary was working, many blocks clear of the filthy streets and tumult of the 'Points. I thought it fitting that the park and its calm were clear across Manhattan from the rough-and-tumble of South Street and its quays, ships and sailors and all that attended them. Over our shoulders was Castle Garden, and in front of us was the bay, stretching south past Governors Island and the forts.

"Can you count the boats on the water?"

"There's too many."

"Well count as high as you can."

Fíona began to lick a finger for each five boats she counted. As she got to fifteen, I looked back over at Castle Garden, looming hugely out in the bay at the end of a narrow causeway connecting it to the Battery Gardens. It was an old fort that had been given over as a venue for all kinds of orchestras and singers. There was to be a new show there next month, and I wanted to take Mary. I was calculating how much money I could spare for this surprise. I wasn't quite sure whether she would be thrilled at the prospect or if she would call me a silly galoot for my pains, because I'd wasted precious brass. But if I asked her first, then I'd run the risk of being a silly galoot for ruining a wonderful surprise. No matter, I'd take her to a show before the summer was over.

Fíona was tugging at my sleeve. "I counted 36!"

I smiled. There must have been twenty score or more watercraft of every manner of description between here and Jersey City, let alone the two score or more farther down the bay, towards the Narrows, including what appeared to be a small squadron of packet ships scudding at full chisel towards Gotham and Brooklyn and a like-sized squadron of packet ships headed south, bound for God knows where. Jersey City, as everyone called it, was another world, a gateway to the west once I—Mary, Fíona, and I—had escaped Gotham. It seemed as far away as China, even though it was hardly more than a mile from us. As close as it was, nobody I'd ever met in Gotham had ventured over there and returned to tell me about it. But I'd met plenty of Irishmen who had decamped from the 'Points and crossed by ferry to Jersey City and vanished, presumably for the *Limes Americanus* (or maybe a job on the railroad up in the Mohawk River Valley somewhere in the wilds of upstate New York), never to be seen in Gotham again.

Fíona was tugging at my sleeve again. "Billy," she asked, "are you my brother? My older brother?"

"Well," I paused for a moment and thought. "I suppose I am. In my way."

Mary and I had fallen into an easy, if entirely chaste camaraderie in these past weeks, which mystified me. I had expected more, what more, I wasn't sure. But I somehow knew not to press matters. Mary had also been a little close-mouthed with me about what she thought about our future, other than to say she was putting a pretty penny away for us—and she was making sure that I did the same. I still wool-gathered about becoming a mountain man, living deep in the wilderness, but I was conscious that the vision had begun to seem remote and perhaps even fanciful. I even saw the three of us staying in the Big Onion, although that fleeting glimpse of what appeared to have been the man in black still shook me. I looked at Fíona and smiled.

Fíona leaned her head against my arm and clung to it, as we sat on the wooden bench, looking at the seagulls, the boats and all of the people strolling along the promenade between us and Castle Garden.

"Momma says you have to be my older brother."

"Why's that?"

"Well," she said matter-of-factly, "Momma says that we're a family, and we don't have a daddy. My daddy be dead, and so is your'n. What else could you be?"

I could hear Mary's voice in Fíona.

"What's an 'older brother'?"

⌒

225

I checked my numbers again from the day before. There was $30 missing, and there was only one place it could have come from. Cian had collected all of the day's bucket shop offertories, and the tickets didn't lie. Charlie was out, and I was alone in the counting room when Cian burst in with a fresh collection of brass. He stopped cold as I looked at him.

He recovered. "Hi there, pal."

"Hi."

He put his money bag on the table. "Twenty-seven dollars. Went to every bucket shop in the Bowery this afternoon."

"I've got a problem."

"What do you mean?"

"I'm short $30 from yesterday's collections."

"Yeah. So?"

"You were the only one collecting from the shops yesterday. Where's the money?"

"I didn't take it." Cian looked at me threateningly. "So you're coming to the wrong shop, my bucko."

I ignored his implied threat. "Look. If I can't find it, I've got to tell Charlie, and then he's going to tell Magee."

Cian said nothing.

"Charlie'll be back in a few minutes. Cian." We locked eyes, and then he looked away. "The tickets don't lie."

He still didn't say anything.

"Charlie told me that the last bookkeeper had been skimming ... and someone had been helping him. That was you, wasn't it?" Charlie had never told me what happened to the man, a real long-headed dutchy named Schmidt who was right smart with figures, and I hadn't asked.

Cian moved uncomfortably.

"Look. I'm going to have to do something."

I thought of Lúcas, and shivered. I wouldn't want to have to deal with him if I were to blow Cian to Charlie and Magee. But in any case, even if Cian wasn't the squarest cove in the 'Points, he had been pretty decent to me, so I wasn't inclined to blow the bloke if I didn't have to. But if I didn't make sure the books were square, then I likewise wouldn't want to deal with Charlie and Magee, who had been little short of positively generous to me in the past few weeks—particularly since I had found Mary. Funny that—how things had really been looking up since then. I was seized by the urge to talk this over with Mary, and listen to her soft voice as she mulled over the problem. She was still the same solid, decent person she had been the day I met her on the quay in Cork—a square moll with the reps. But she was also so much more now ... worldly wise ... and beautiful in a way I'd not seen before.

"Let me square it," Cian said.

Thank God.

"When?"

"Today. I can square it today."

"All $30?"

"Yeah."

"I can cover for you today. No more."

"Thanks." With that, Cian disappeared.

Square it, Cian did. I was very happy not to have to tell Charlie about it or about who the cove was who had been helping the crooked bookkeeper I had replaced.

⌒

Church. I hated it and everything about it. The priest droning on, sanctimonious in his certitude. The tight collar to the new white shirt Mary bought for me for Sunday mornings was pinching my neck. And the fact that I had hardly slept on Saturday night. I'd work the various games with Charlie, counting the rhino and squaring the accounts until the wee hours. Then there'd almost always be an hour or two—or more—of idle chit chat with Magee, Bill Tweed, Charlie and whoever else showed up.

One Sunday in church I was wool-gathering about the night before, when Donoho had visited Magee's and the two of them had held court together. Donoho was grousing about that damned Shouting Methody mayor, Jimmy Harper, and some outrage committed by his police against an Irishman in the 'Points. Worse, Donoho declared, was that Harper was ruining the city for decent Irishmen who simply wanted to make a square (or cross, if the truth be known, Donoho guffawed) dollar. Harper and his buddies wanted to clear every lushery and every cavaulting house right out of the 'Points, the Bowery and every other part of Gotham—except Church Street and Park Row, where the high-pike strumpets serviced the city fathers. Donoho laughed harshly when he said he was sure that Harper, a faithful autum-cove if there ever was one, didn't frequent the goosing slums. (Although only the good Lord himself knew why Harper didn't stray. Mrs. Harper apparently dreaded the mirror as much as any catamaran in Gotham.) But Harper's American Republican and Whig cronies surely did, right along with their Democratic brethren. Harper's minions were thus as hypocritical as any Shouting Methody, on account of having gotten themselves elected on a reform ticket. Funny, Donoho declared, how reform is precisely what Gotham had gotten this past year or so since Harper became hizzoner. *Bastúns dall.*

Donoho complained that Harper banned the sale of mountain dew on the Fourth of July last year. Then he'd had the cheek to try to entice everyone to drink iced Croton water in City Hall Park. How the devil was a God-fearing saloon-keeper to make his chink? Worse, Harper and his pigs had started enforcing Sunday tavern laws, even to the point of the sons-of-bitches shutting down Con's grocery one Sunday. Donoho chuckled that Magee had been smart that weekend to make himself scarce, right along with Charlie Backwell. Magee had told Donoho that the crackdown was coming, and he (Donoho) didn't really believe him. Lesson learned. The pigs wouldn't even let the coloreds and the hot corn girls ply their trades as street vendors. That wasn't a total loss for the hot corn girls, because they could still sell themselves in every alley and boardinghouse in Gotham. Harper didn't have enough pigs to police that. But worse than that was the prospect of not being able to find a decent lunch. Hell, Donoho said, nobody, not even Hizzoner himself, can afford to dine at Delmonico's for lunch every day, and he, Donoho, was not going to subject himself to Mrs. Donoho's *Sassenagh* cooking every noontide. Not when there are oysters and fresh hot corn to be had at every street corner. "Lord knows," he smiled, "I'd starve to death if I ate her *Sassenagh* cooking."

What was really the worst, though, according to Donoho, was the unholy alliance between Harper and his reformers and the damned nativists, who hated everyone whose grandmother wasn't getting it from Uncle Sam way back in 1776. "Well, to hell with them," Donoho declared, "the paddies are here now, and there's many more coming. I've heard that things are getting bad back in old Eirinn," he said sadly. "The pitaties are rotting in the ground, and the harvest's gone bust. Worse than ever before, what with the clearances and stories of poor *papul* starving along the roadsides. It be a terrible thing what the *Sassenagh* have done to our poor homeland. And now we have the blight on the pitaties, for pity's sake. *An Gorta Mór*, the 'Great Hunger,' is what they be callin' it. An' ye know the worst of it?" Donoho gave a heartfelt if somewhat theatrical sigh, for the whiskey had clearly let him pipe his eye in a way you'd've never seen on a Monday morning. "It be killin' the music. Imagine that. Eirinn silent, wi'out no pipes, no harp an' no singin,' jes' the feeble an' despairin' wail fer the dead."

He recovered himself and continued his diatribe. "The dutch-ies're also here to stay and them Jews down on Orange Street ain't about to go back to Poland. Of course, the niggers ... well, they're a different story, entirely." Donoho stopped, and then looked Magee in the eye, saying that he was very sorry to have been impolite, having meant to have said "coloreds" and not "niggers." But, he concluded, "whatever anyone calls 'em, they can't vote, and so they don't count.

"But this *bastún dall*, Cassidy. He could really upset the apple cart. He won't wait his turn, and now he's ready to jump on the American Republican bandwagon. Cassidy's such a fraud," Donoho said in disgust. "He's as Irish as the day is long and he's throwing in with them damned nativists—to the point of signing on with their Excelsior Engine Company. Worse, the *bastún dall* thinks that he's popular here in the 'ould, bloody Sixth, all because he believes what them what drinks for free in his tavern say to him. Funny what a bloke will say for a free drink. There's naught for me or Matt Rynders to do, 'ceptin' beat him in the election." Donoho grinned. "We'll vote faster and harder than them nativist know-nothings—just like we did for Polk last year."

Later, after Donoho had left and as I was looking to slip away for an hour or two of sleep before Mary dragged me to church for three hours, Magee put his arm around my shoulder and said to me in a fine, whiskey-soaked confidence, "Yer a game lad, Gogan, a right fine chisler. A bit scrawny, perhaps. But a gamer. We're going to have to learn you some fightin' manners, though. They're a bad business, some o' these gangs. Particularly them True Blue American Guards, although them mick Roach Guards ain't a damn sight better. And ye gotta be able to protect yersel', lad."

Magee then said to me just as I was making off to a stifled yawn, "An' we'll be after getting's yers round to a militia meeting. An' ye'll be after bein' a fire laddie, as well. Ye've got a bit o' meat back on yer bones now, so ye can work a brake as well as any."

I smiled and said good night, pleased at the thought of being invited into Gotham's two most important social institutions. Magee waved his hand, and I was abruptly brought from my reverie straight back to church by a sharp elbow in my ribs and Mary hissing in my ear, "Don't you be driving your pigs to market in the House of God. Show some respect for Himself, and stay awake."

Eventually we escaped St. Peter's, but only after Mary had exchanged pleasantries with a couple of ladies wearing coal scuttle bonnets, who nodded civilly (if coolly) to us, their husbands frozen ornaments at their sides. The priest, Father Williams, was a kindly old man, and he greeted Mary warmly, urging her to visit him in the rectory during the coming week to discuss Fíona's attending St. Peter's in the summer term. He shook my hand, saying that Mary had told him so many wonderful things about me and how I had helped her on that terrible passage across the Great Western Ocean after her husband died. It was terrible that we had been separated for all those weeks, but wasn't everything fine now that we had been reunited. He hoped that I was finding good work because it was so hard for a God-fearing Irishman to find work in Gotham during these terrible times.

Mary and I walked on this beautiful Sunday noon down towards Battery Park. We bought a couple of lemonades, and sat on a park bench overlooking Castle Garden.

"When we're better off …" her voice trailed off, and she sat there, parasol on her shoulder, looking at the boats plying the river behind the garden.

I touched her shoulder.

She started, and said, "Oh, it be nothing."

I liked it when she forgot herself and slipped from proper English back into her Irish patois. Her face softened when she did, and she became even more fetching than she usually was. Less forbidding, which was how she looked so much these days.

"You thinking about what it's like over there?" I pointed to Jersey City and the marshlands and woods beyond the village. "The west?"

Mary contemplated me for a moment. "Yes," she finally replied. But she didn't elaborate.

"We'll be there soon enough. I'm saving loads of rhino these days."

Mary smiled at me for a while, before she spoke. "You really want to see those tall mountains, don't you?"

"Yep." I stared at the far side of the river.

"I sometimes wonder …"

"What?"

"I don't know." She seemed to prevaricate. "Oh, it's nothing. You're right, Billy, we'll be headed west soon enough. Together. I'm putting away the rhino just like you are. It'll be good to get Fíona out of this wicked city, to somewhere people are …" She stopped again.

"Are what?"

She considered her answer for a moment. "Honest," she said. "Honest, and just who they are, instead of always pretending to be someone else."

CHAPTER 11

Dells, Swells and Fires

⌒

"LET'S LIQUOR." CIAN DINEEN BEAMED AT ME.

It was late on a Saturday night, and I knew Mary would be looking for me in the morning, starched white shirt in hand. I groaned.

"Oh, don't be such a molley."

I looked at him. Those were fighting words, but Cian was laughing. There was nothing for it.

"Where?"

"Patsy O'Hearn's."

"Rat fighting?"

"Yeah, Dusty Dustmoor's got a fresh load o' rats tonight, and Patsy's got some fresh dogs."

He leaned over the bar and grabbed a bottle of cheap whiskey, saying, "Magee won't mind about this mountain dew."

Blackie walked into the bar from a back room and then out the front door. He eyed us tossing back our drinks, but said nothing.

Patsy O'Hearn's was located in the basement of a most disreputable boardinghouse—one of those ghastly places to which the runners sent truly credulous Irish and dutchies fresh from tumbling off the latest boat from the old country. The stench in Patsy's was almost unbearable. I could only imagine what the boardinghouse's poor inmates must have thought of it.

The basement was perhaps forty feet by forty, and twenty feet to a scabrous ceiling of the greasy pine planks of the floor that lay above. In the center was a pit perhaps 15 feet on each side, surrounded by several rows of rickety plank benches. Two bookmakers were taking bets. Two rat terriers were let into the pit with one rat, and bets were taken on which terrier killed the rat, and how long it would take—and whether the terriers would fight over the carcass once the rat was dead. It was a grisly business, and the place was brimming with sporting men, prostitutes and members of the Patsy Conroy's gang, under whose protection Patsy O'Hearn operated. Bowery b'hoys were allowed, but only on their best behavior (no knives or barking irons permitted). Bowery g'hals were very welcome of course, as were gals of any stripe—not that a square moll with the reps would even think of crossing the threshold. Only shakes looking to tickle a cully's toby for a bit of brass. Some of them were desperate enough to service their cullies on the upper benches or even underneath the stands as beer, roasted peanut shells and God knows what else pelted them from above, the terriers and rats going at each other all the while.

After a few nips of Magee's bottle of mountain dew and a couple of grisly rat fights, I'd had enough. Cian sensed it, and we moved along.

"Black Muireann's is where we're headed." Cian pronounced it as "Mirren," like a native American would. But I'd always thought it a pretty name when pronounced properly—with a long "u" in the first syllable.

I nodded. I'd heard of the place. Very exclusive. Over on Church Street, clear on the other side of New York Hospital. Magee had some sort of pecuniary interest in the place, as did Donoho. Not that they were brothers of the gusset, misusing the poor dells and taking all their earnings. They were merely silent investors in a high-falutin' coupling ken who took an occasional interest in the strumpets. The morts were to a girl, so the story went, *les belles petite*, as befit the Church Street address and the high tax assessments that came along with it. I knew that neither Magee nor Donoho were particularly worried about the taxes (or any other of the myriad expenses, such as silk dresses for the girls, endless rounds of laundry and fine liquor), because Black Muireann's was a favorite location of the swells and punters staying at Astor House and the American Hotel, or so Blackie had told me one night, confidential-like, although he allowed as he'd only been over there once or twice. The mabs were so fine that they made him nervous, Blackie confessed, and so he preferred his haunts over here in the 'Points instead of over there where only the high-falutin' punters played. I'd asked Blackie why they called the madam "Black Muireann," and he had only shrugged indifferently.

At the door was a *dead ráibéad* who eclipsed even Blackie in stature. Probably just another of Magee's or Donoho's minions, to be called upon for a frolic when the occasion demanded. The *ráibéad* was blocking the way of an ill-dressed cove whom he was trying to direct to a goosing slum back over in the 'Points, which the *ráibéad* was telling the cove, was quite certain to be far more to the cove's taste than this place—and perhaps, the *ráibéad* said, a little more affordable.

Cian muttered under his breath as he walked by the cove, who was retreating disconsolately. Whatever it was Cian said, the cove started angrily. Cian turned to him again and said, ingratiatingly, "*Dead ráibéad*, ain't he?" motioning to the doorman.

"What's a dead rabbit?" The cove's jaw moved above his filthy, fly-away collar. "Him? The door man? He ain't no rabbit. Fucking huge son of a bitch, more like." He tugged his forelock at the *dead ráibéad*, who glowered at him menacingly and then greeted Cian as a long-lost brother.

Behind the *ráibéad*, a window looked out onto the front porch, and sitting on a stool in the window, lit from behind by a soft red light, was a beautiful young woman—in truth, hardly more than a young girl by the look of her—with golden ringlets, posing like a marbled statue. I stared. She was a dead ringer for Evelyn. But what a difference. A rosy nipple peeked out from under Ringlet's silken toga—I supposed it to be rather like what Roman women wore at the time of Christ. She looked just like I imagined in my most unguarded moments how Evelyn might look on our wedding night. I was turgid in an instant. Ringlets must have seen my consternation, because she giggled when she met my eyes.

I'd never seen a woman—a girl—like this, in such an erotic state of dishabille. I'd seen my share of whores grappling with blokes in every conceivable way in every conceivable corner of the 'Points. *Dia Uas!* I'd seen that cow on her knees servicing a bloke under the wood-planked stands at Patsy O'Hearn's not twenty minutes earlier, and there'd been that bare-breasted slattern who'd propositioned me my very first night in the 'Points, as I wandered about, alone in the snow and cold. You couldn't avoid such tawdriness in the 'Points. It was simply a fact of life that many women were so reduced—I won't say debased, although most would be so damning—by their circumstances that they had to earn their livings on their backs. Otherwise, they'd starve, or worse, their children would starve. This, though, was so different … even from the fine Corinthians escorted by the upper tendom swells as they slummed their way through the 'Points.

"Quite the cavaulting house, ain't it?" Cian ripped me from my reverie with bad breath and a slack-faced leer at Ringlets. "Nice bit o' kid leather there for the stretching."

I had stumbled into the front parlor without having been conscious of it, and we were immediately surrounded by six or eight beautiful women, most at second glance no more than young girls, each of whom greeted Cian with great familiarity.

"Shoo, girls, shoo." A commanding voice scattered them hither and yon. "Master Dineen isn't a paying customer. So don't you be paying him any mind."

The voice belonged to a woman who cut through her girls like the finest *Sassenagh* frigate cutting through the fishing boats in Cobh harbor. She stood as tall as I did, with hennaed hair and milky white skin framed against an exquisite black silk gown that would have done a duchess at the *Sassenagh* Queen's court proud.

"Why Cian Dineen, my old pal," she exclaimed in a broad Irish accent. "How are you this evening? It's been a coon's age since I've seen you."

"Why, Mrs. O'Marran, my favorite Irish madam." Cian bowed deeply, removing his hat as he did. It wouldn't have occurred to me until that instant that Cian would have ever seen a man bow or a woman curtsy.

Mrs. O'Marran curtsied just deeply enough to acknowledge Cian. Then she curtsied to me—properly—and held out her hand, which I took in mine as I returned her bow, once again giving thanks to St. Patrick's dancing master—who would have rapped my knuckles had I attempted a maneuver as grandiloquent as Cian's.

Mrs. O'Marran's eyes locked on mine, and she made me feel as if I were the only man in all of existence.

"William Gogan, ma'am," I introduced myself, as proper etiquette required. Cian certainly wasn't going to introduce me. He was too busy ogling the girls, who were returning to the parlor despite Mrs. O'Marran's admonishment.

"My, you are a fine swell," she murmured, looking down at my newly acquired worsted burgundy waistcoat (I hadn't yet ventured to red and yellow plaid like Con Donoho, but I had taken my first steps in not looking as if I had just fallen off the last famine ship from Liverpool) and then to my boots, which were wet with spring mud and sadly in need of brushing. "Although you do look as if you just left the Bowery."

"Just the 'Points, ma'am. I only make it over to the Seventh Ward on business."

"Please call me Muireann. All my friends do, even Mr. Dineen." She glanced at Cian. He was busy groping a young girl, who was giggling. Muireann looped her arm through mine and led me through some velvet curtains at the far end of the parlor into a smaller chamber.

"Sherry or tea?" When talking to me, Muireann's Irish brogue had vanished, and had been replaced by an accent I could not quite place, but which sounded remarkably like Mary's newly cultured tone (when Mary remembered to adopt it).

"Tea, please." Of all the cavaulting house goings-on I could imagine, sipping tea with a brothel madam was not one of them. Muireann waved her hand and what appeared to be a maid standing in the shadows disappeared through a curtain.

"I suppose Cian's a little like a supper customer, isn't he," Muireann sighed in the direction of the parlor. I must have looked at her questioningly, because she explained, "You know, one of those sham swells who'll dine at a gambling house for free but never gamble. But I suppose he's not even really a supper customer, because he does want to partake of the wares on offer. So I let him. The good Lord knows that the only reason I do is because he and that creepy brother of his are the best cadets out in the 'Hook. They bring in only the freshest cherry-ripes from the boats."

There was nothing I could say.

"So …" Muireann looked at me expectantly.

"I work for Magee and Charlie Backwell. I'm the bookkeeper," I said as matter-of-factly as possible.

"The bookkeeper."

"Yes, ma'am."

"I see."

"I haven't been here in Gotham for very long. Came last winter on a terrible coffin ship." The new term seemed to roll off my tongue. Good ship *Maryann* had been nowhere near as bad as some of the more recent arrivals. Why, on one ship alone, the penny-dreadfuls had blared in their headlines one morning not long after Con Donoho's diatribe about the "*An Gorta Mór*," 78 had died of ship fever on the voyage, and 104 had been sick when they arrived. That by itself was bad enough. To everyone's horror, the refugees had been naught but walking skeletons when they spilled from the quays into the 'Points. Why they hadn't been quarantined like the gaunt man and his family, nobody could say. The Lord only knows how many must have died here in the 'Points or up in some boardinghouse in Corlears Hook itself after having survived the crossing from Ireland.

"You're that kid Mary Skiddy lost track of when she first arrived in Gotham, aren't you?"

Recognition seemed to dawn in her eyes.

"Yes, ma'am. You know Mary?"

"Of course. Magee and I are old friends and …"

The tea arrived. Lemon instead of milk—an odd American custom that ruins the tea, in my view. The tea and the china and the pouring prevented me from asking any more questions.

"I apologize," Muireann said finally. "But I do have to tend to my young wards. It's the end of the evening, and they can get a bit restless. Will you be all right here? I shouldn't think you'll be needing … any company?"

I assured her that I would not. Muireann made her apologies and departed the chamber just as I'd first seen her—like a proud *Sassenagh* man o' war slicing imperiously past everything in her path.

I sat quietly, and thought about what Cian had said of Muireann O'Marran as we had left Patsy O'Hearn's. "Them accommodation beauties are reserved for them huckleberries what believe they're above the rest of us persimmons. And Black Muireann is always needin' fresh ones. So she pays me 'n' Lúcás right handsomely to … procure … the sweetest little dimber morts off n' them coffin ships." Cian had seemed to almost want to give me a particular example. But he instead contented himself with observing that he and Lúcás procured only the most scrumptious young Irish dells— and sometimes a few equally young and scrumptious things from Connecticut or New Jersey who had come to seek their fortunes in Gotham—all of them pure cherry pie, don't you know, he winked.

Cian had chuckled salaciously when he confided to me that Muireann advertised the virginal state of her stable to her rather exclusive and demanding clientele. Apparently they favored such great luxuries. "An' she has coloreds as well. There's a lot o' sportin' men who'll pay a pretty penny for a bit of Ethiopian mollygash if it ain't diseased and the cove don't have to wear no French letter." He looked at me and sniggered. "You know, a sheath for …"

I shrugged to tell him that I knew what a sheath was used for.

"Ya' may not know this, but Black Muireann has a real inside track on acquiring real fine colored blowens."

Light dawned. "Hence, 'Black Muireann'?"

Cian sniggered and leaned closer to explain. "See, there's this colored fellow she knows. Name's Big Jim, I think. He come round every so often to see her. I asked her about it, thinkin' that me 'n' Lúcás could expand our business lines, so to speak. But she shut me down real fast. Too bad. Although, them gals are a mite dusty for my tastes. Anyways, even if they're gentle as lambs, some of them niggers are runaways, with rewards out for 'em. paddyrollers ain't inclined to ask before snatching them, and God help what gets between a bounty hunter and his prey."

I thought of what my father and Daniel O'Connell would have said when Cian casually continued, explaining to me that runaways were slaves who had escaped tobacco and cotton plantations in Virginia and the Carolinas. It was the law, Cian declared, that fugitive slaves were to be returned to their masters, and lots of poor whites, including Irish immigrants, saw slave-catching as a way to a quick bit of chink. Muireann was different, Cian declared. She had an amalgamatin' (Cian's word) predilection (not Cian's word) for bull niggers (Cian's words) such as her dead husband. Cian chuckled when he told me that Black Muireann was a widow on account of her husband having gotten himself shot a while back—which was likely on account of his being too damned uppity for his own good. And, Cian said with a salacious grin, "Black Muireann's got a nigger daughter to boot. What a magnificent milk shop that young dange-broad has. Brannagh's her name."

I asked Cian, "Isn't her daughter a mulatta, though? You know, half white and half colored?"

"I dunno. She's still a darky, just like her old man, ain't she?" I didn't react, so he continued. "Anyways, them Ethiopian molly-gashers all look the same to me. Although," he confided, "I gotta tell ya, I ain't above forking that little Negress out if for no other reason than to raid that bodacious milk shop o' hers. But she ain't no easy game. Way too much botheration for me—from both her an' from Black Muireann. Muireann'll kill any cove what puts a paw on that young bit o' dange. An' it's not as if a white man can ever be seen with a colored moll outside a banging shop. Not if ye've any front to yers. So I'd be right malletheaded to try. Give me a fresh Irish cherry-ripe any day."

The high, tinkling laugh of a young dell and the lower guffaw of her cully brought me back from thinking about the finer points of what types of molleys a high-falutin' knocking shop should have on its string, and I wondered whether I should simply leave now and get some sleep before my penance at church with Mary. Something compelled me to stay, though, and so I sank back, thinking about how many coloreds I'd seen and talked to since arriving in Gotham, and how I'd never seen a colored—man or woman—until I saw the young colored steward on Maryann. The colored were free here in the Big Onion—New York had long since abolished slavery—but they were anything but equal to native Americans. And as Cian had said, they were always at risk from unscrupulous slave catchers.

My father had reflected to me one day about the incongruity of America's promise as a great republic and the stain of slavery. O'Connell had come to Boston a few years earlier and challenged Americans to treat colored people as equals. It had not gone over well at all. My father had also reflected during one of our talks about the American west that Irishmen emigrating to America were republicans by choice, and they bore a special responsibility to help bring about the abolition of slavery. He told me that I was to remember that responsibility if we ever got to America. Yet, here, actually in America, it was all just a bit different than he'd thought …

I felt a hand running through my hair as a voice purred, "You are so cute. I want you all to myself." Ringlets, now (somewhat) more decently clad, dropped into my lap. "You were so funny, stopping like that to look at me, and so sweet," she repeated herself. "I'd a' thought you'd never seen a woman's nipple before."

I stared at her, completely flabbergasted, but intensely enjoying the sensation of this girl squirming in my lap, all curves, softness and the promise of untold delight.

"I'm Jessie," she purred.

"Billy," I stammered.

"I thought you might be back here, an' I was hoping that you'd be wanting a bit of company, seeing as how you are waiting for Dineen. Not that you'll have to wait long for him. He don't have much in the way of bottom. Two pumps, and he's down the Swanny river."

I was speechless, and she didn't seem inclined to say more. So we sat quietly for a few minutes, and my thoughts ran wild.

Jessie slid off my lap and sat beside me and sank into the sofa's deep cushions, her soft and yielding flesh and intoxicating scent cuddling against me.

"You've never been with a girl, have you?" She giggled a little bit. "We don't get many virgin boys in here. Just old blokes with bad breath and soft ..." She looked at me and giggled again. "You're blushing."

We sat in silence awhile longer.

Finally, she said, "The old goats will pay more if they think that I'm still a cherry pie ... Silly buggers."

I looked at her uncomprehendingly.

"A virgin. Like you. But I'm just a cloven, acting the article of virtue every night, right down to a little blood on the sheets." She explained. "Black Muireann kills a chicken almost every day. A little blood for me and a couple of the other girls for our old goats, and the chicken for her dinner—an' whoever she's invited for the evening. She likes her poultry as fresh as her molleys. They pay extra, you know—the old geezers. I cry, too, sometimes," she said matter-of-factly, her eyes hardening. "I get a much bigger tip if I do."

I found my voice. "Why do you do it?"

She laughed derisively. "What else am I going to do? Clean outhouses for six or eight bits a week? I can make that as a tip from just one of these damned old goats after he's already paid the cavaulting house fee—like I said, that's if I wriggle my hips for him and then weep well enough afterwards." She thought for a moment. "I suppose I could sell hot corn on Mott Street. But then I'd just end up doing the same thing, except I'd be doing it in some cheap boardinghouse and giving my earnings to some brother of the gusset with rotten teeth."

Jessie ran her fingers through her ringlets. I thought of Evelyn. She purred again, "I really don't see many nice boys like you."

Funny, even the fourteen- or fifteen-year-old girls thought I was a boy—they were just like Mary. I wondered what Mary would think of my sitting here with a molley, even one as young as Jessie. I was mighty curious about Jessie. Hell, I was mighty curious about what any woman was like, and what it would be like to be with a woman, that one night with Mary notwithstanding.

I heard a rustling in the curtains and a girlish giggle.

Jessie said in an irritated voice, "Brannagh."

I saw a beautiful mulatta standing in the shadow of the curtains. I was dumbfounded. Jessie, for all her allure and proximity— I could feel her soft breasts crushing against my arm and her sweet breath in my ear—an assault I was responding to with a reeling mind and a turgid member—instantly paled in comparison to this almost spectral mulatta shadow. Black Muireann's voice came from somewhere. "Brannagh, get along, and don't be bothering Jessie when she's with a customer."

I looked sharply at Jessie as she pulled away from me, and I saw her hardened eyes once again. I realized that she may have been Evelyn's double, but she wasn't Evelyn.

"I have to go."

Jessie pouted, "Why?"

"I don't feel well."

"Why, Billy boy, you're giving me the mitten." She laughed in mock disappointment. "That's for the lady to do. T'ain't right for you to do it."

"I … I do have to go. I'm sorry."

I got up, embarrassed, and went straight home to Mary and Fíona. When I awoke the next morning, I was struck by the fact that I'd dreamt of Brannagh and not of Evelyn—or Mary, for that matter.

⌒

Within a day of having made his whiskey-laden promise to make me a fire laddie, Magee had made good on it. (The militia was to come in good time, he said.) I learned quickly that there was nothing quite like a good fire to stir the blood. In the wake of Magee's promise, I'd become a runner and brake man (a brake man worked the engine's pumps to supply water to the hoses—I only wished that *Maryann* could have had pumps anywhere near as good as a fire engine's) with Phoenix Engine Company No. 21, where Magee was the assistant foreman. Their engine was kept in an old stable converted into a firehouse, right on Chambers Street, next to the Mutual Hook and Ladder Company No. 1.

They and the Hope Hose Company, which was just over on Mott Street, all worked together to cover all the fires in the 'Points—and as far beyond that as they could. We were the best in the city. The Phoenix's engine—a brand-new Philadelphia pattern double-decker fresh from James Smith, the best engine builder in New York, and known as the "Haywagon" on account of her peculiar look—was the best engine in all of Gotham, because we could have twice as many men operating brakes as the standard gooseneck then in common use by other engine companies.

The Chief, who was a famous nativist and a great friend of Mayor Jimmy Harper and our growing nemesis, Cassidy, was as mad as a March hare about Matt Brennan having gone behind his back to have our newfangled engine built at the astronomical cost of $1,195. The Chief had designed a patented capstan for the old-fashioned gooseneck engines—so-called because it had a swivel joint atop the riser, which allowed the jet pipe to rotate in a complete circle. Naturally he didn't want anyone coming along and improving on his design. That, and as Bill Tweed said, the Chief got a cut on every engine built with his patented capstan for Gotham volunteer engine companies.

Matt was a sharp fellow, as befit his reputation as a political comer in not only the Sixth Ward, but more broadly across the city as well. And he wanted the Phoenix to be the best engine company in the city. So the Chief's desire to line his own pockets notwithstanding, Matt commissioned James Smith to build the Haywagon. Now, according to Tweed, there was going to be a big frolic over who paid for it. The Chief was bound and determined that the city would not pay for it. That would either force Matt Brennan to find the rhino to pay James Smith himself, or force James Smith to come, hat in hand, to the Chief for more orders of good old-fashioned goosenecks so that he could afford to eat the cost of the Haywagon—which the Chief would cause to disappear forever in favor of his beloved goosenecks—if he could. At least that's what Bill Tweed told me.

No matter. Regardless of the type of engine, whether gooseneck, haywagon or otherwise, one had to have a strong back for pumping, far more than was required on the fair barky *Maryann*, where the trick was to maintain slow but steady effort to keep the water in the bilges from rising (or better, to pump them dry). Fighting fires is entirely different from pumping a bilge dry. It requires an immense amount of water—which requires pumping as hard as you can as part of a team for as long as the entire team can go, a period measured in minutes. So we went at it in shifts, with quaffs of beer in between shifts to restore our strength.

I was getting better at it all the time as I got stronger, which I reckoned stemmed from the regular exercise of being a brakeman, along with having grown some inches since arriving in Gotham. I was one of the men on the top brakes, and when we clambered up topside, we looked for all the world like grasshoppers. We could pump for a clean ten minutes before we needed spelling, and there was no engine company that could rival us. But we engine companies could not, and did not try to, do it alone. The hook and ladder companies were needed to get onto the second floors, and the hose companies? Well, they were the ones whose hose teams charged bravely into blazing wooden boardinghouses, lusheries, tanneries and all manner of other wooden buildings, so many of which caught fire far too often in this jerry-built part of old Gotham, hoses streaming water and stiff leather helmets and leather jerkins steaming from the heat of the fire as they went.

The three companies, Mutual, Hope and Phoenix, shared runners, and all the volunteers threw themselves into fighting the fires in whatever way they needed to. At one blaze, I'd been part of the hose team that charged into a blazing building. I'd only had my regular coat and a firefighting helmet I'd grabbed from an exhausted Hope Hose Company volunteer to protect me. As we fought our way into the burning boardinghouse, the water, steamed by the blaze, ran off my helmet and underneath my tweed wool coat, burning down the back of my neck as it went. My coat had been smoking when we emerged triumphant—we'd saved a couple of *wee wains* cut off by the flames from their mother and all hope of escape until we bullied our way to them. I loved fighting fires, even if Mary did complain about my stinking clothing after I came home. She even cried if I was scraped up or a little burned—and plain got angry the night I ruined my tweed coat.

We fought fires anywhere, even clear over on the other side of Broadway and all the way uptown at Washington Square and points north. We brawled with competing fire companies for the privilege of fighting the blaze, partly for the honor of it, but mostly it was a tribal affair. There was no such thing as a city fire department. Instead, the Chief commissioned volunteer hose, engine and hook and ladder companies of like-minded volunteers—the Hopes, Phoenixes and Mutuals being Irish and Excelsior being nativist. Each company ostensibly had its own district. But the fire laddies honored that rule more in the breach than they did in the observance as a matter of honor and dominance over their hated rivals—the Bowery b'hoys would be damned before they'd see paddy ruffians from the 'Points fight a fire and we paddy ruffians felt quite the same way about the nativist Bowery b'hoys. So runners would alert their company to a fire, and hold their ground at the fire as best they could until their company arrived with its ally companies and fought their rivals. More than once during my time in Gotham a building burned to the ground while rival companies brawled over who was to fight the fire.

We three companies of Phoenixes, Mutuals and Hopes were a sturdy, single gang drawn heavily from Magee's and Donoho's toughs and fleshed out with like-minded Irishmen and dutchies from the 'Points—as well as the occasional native American who understood and liked his Irish compatriots. We even had a *Sassenagh* who had deserted from one of Her Majesty's regiments of foot in Upper Canada and had come south in search of a better life.

We reckoned we could lick all comers. One night, we'd been over in the Bowery, and gotten to the fire before the Excelsior Engine A Company and its Bowery compatriots hove onto the scene. We chased away their runners and jeered loudly when Excelsior finally showed up. They glowered and threatened a brawl until one of their fellows pointed out that one of their assistant foremen lived there in the house that was on fire, and so we all needed to save his missus. They shut pan immediately and pitched in, helping us douse the blaze before anyone died. But there were hard feelings afterwards, and we of the Phoenix Engine Company knew that we'd not heard the last of it. It only made matters worse that Cassidy and the most nativist of the Bowery toughs ran Excelsior, and the Chief accordingly had a soft spot for them.

One day, not long after my introduction to Black Muireann and her daughter, Tweed hove into sight as Magee was holding court in the dance hall with Blackie and half-a-score more, fulminating yet again about Cassidy and other Democrats who had defected to the American Republicans. Cian was there, and he was scowling a bit, I thought, as Magee was carrying on. Tweed thought nothing of interrupting Magee's story to report loudly, "I think there's going to be a bit of firefighting adventure today."

Magee good-naturedly waved him down and resumed telling his story with nary a missed beat. Tweed had kept his ear to
ground, because sure enough, just as Magee delivered the clincher
to his story to the lewd guffaws of appreciation from his audience,
a runner came in, panting, crying that Excelsior had just gotten
their new fire engine, and they was testing it down at Riley's Pole.
If there ever was a glove chucked down, this was it. It had been
rumored for weeks that the Chief had ordered up a gooseneck to
outdo the Haywagon—and was going to give it to Excelsior Engine
Company. So down to Riley's Pole we went, fifty sturdy Irishmen
and friends pulling the Haywagon down Broadway as fast as we
could, bells ringing, crowds cheering and omnibuses and carriages
scattering before us. It was a grand journey of twelve full blocks to
West Broadway and Franklin.

On the way, another runner found Brennan and Magee as
they led us north on Broadway, and breathlessly told them that
Excelsior's new gooseneck was throwing water up 150 feet, clear
over Riley's Pole. That was something. Riley's Pole stood 137 feet
high, and to throw water anywhere near the top of it was the *ne plus
ultra* for an engine company. It was a city landmark, and a gathering place for Democratic (which meant Tammany Irish more and
more of late) politicians to pass the time of day and cut political
deals when they weren't at Dooley's Long Room nominating the
next mayor (or so they hoped). We had yet to take the Haywagon
down there on account of we'd had her for hardly a week.

When we arrived, the Excelsiors were waiting—and so were
a growing crowd of fire laddies from other companies who'd heard
about Excelsior chucking down the glove. They were not alone, for
throngs of coves were flooding in, anxious to see the excitement,
bet on the outcome (whatever form it might take) and generally
pine to be fire laddies right alongside us. Best of all, there were a
couple score or more uptown ladies present, many of them affecting
to swoon at the mere sight of volunteer fire laddies (not that any

of these uptown ladies, much to my adolescent dismay, had ever so much as cooed in my direction, let alone swooned over me), as well as a welter of Bowery g'hals deserting their shops to watch their Excelsior heroes vanquish their hated Irish Phoenix rivals.

As we arrived, the Excelsior engine stopped pumping, and Cassidy and the Chief stood defiantly in front of it and the glowering Excelsiors. The two men looked rather like the ancient Greek champions standing in front of their phalanx, challenging the enemy's king or champion to a duel to the death. We quickly set up. Brennan and Magee walked over to the Chief, as cool as you like, and congratulated him on his fine new engine, all the while ostentatiously ignoring Cassidy. Brennan then allowed in a loud voice that all in the now-hushed crowd could hear—his grammar deteriorating and his Irish accent thickening as he went—that it waren't near half the engine the Haywagon was, and well, a company of honest paddy ruffians was always better than them jumped up b'hoys (said as exaggerated as you please), who was just that— b'hoys sent to do a man's job, jes' like last week when we had to save their assistant foreman's *autum cackler* and her *wee wains*.

The crowd roared (approval or disdain, depending upon outlook) until the chief raised his hand for calm, which eventually if reluctantly returned. Cassidy spoke. We accept your glove, he said, thrown down in such a pretty fashion—a slight bow to Magee in acknowledgement of the last time the glove had been thrown down between them.

"We the Excelsior men," Cassidy's oratory started to soar now. He took particular pride in his public speaking on account of his drinking buddies at his saloon having proclaimed him a finer speaker than Daniel Webster himself. "We dedicate ourselves to the return of the reform Mayor, Jimmy Harper (the crowd roared, again split as to approbation or opprobrium), who has been indefatigable in both cleaning up the streets and sweeping from our fair city of Gotham those foreigners who dare sully it."

Half the crowd—nary an Irishman among them—cheered. The other half, the Irish half, stuck their hands in pockets and stared ostentatiously at the cobblestones.

Brennan waited for the cheers to die down, and then asked Cassidy, "Care to make a gentleman's wager on our engines, Jimmy?" Brennan mimed thinking for a longish moment. Then his look brightened, and he asked with an air of mock innocence, "How's about the longest to keep shooting water?"

Cassidy glared at him, as did the Chief.

"Say, $500?" Brennan looked around and inquired innocently, "Is there someone to make book?"

Charlie Backwell appeared precisely on cue. I could feel Magee beaming inwardly.

Charlie looked around myopically, and said to no one in particular, "I've got $500 from Mr. Brennan here. Anyone care to cover? Even odds."

The crowd buzzed. The chief and Cassidy conferred. Brennan and Magee stood like statues. Finally, Cassidy spoke. I thought I heard a quaver in his voice, "I'll meet it, and double it on shooting water over Riley's Pole." Cassidy gave the crowd a satisfied look. "Which is to say, a thousand dollars!"

The crowd roared—everyone this time. Brennan raised his hand for quiet—which eventually came. You could hear the flag snapping at the top of Riley's Pole. Brennan waited for just a few seconds more. The tension built.

"Done."

Charlie raised his hand and piped up (as best he could), "Pay it over to me, boys—iff'n yer betting t'day."

The crowd overwhelmed Charlie's speech, and Cassidy looked a little dismayed as he dug deep into his wallet. Brennan nonchalantly handed Charlie a packet, which presumably contained the magnificent sum of $1,000—more than a scullery maid might make in a lifetime at $2 a week plus room and board. Cassidy looked slightly flustered. The Chief was inscrutable. Finally, Brennan raised his hand for quiet again—which came quickly because everyone was eager to hear what he had to say.

"Jimmy, *mo cuallaidhe*," Brennan said in as broad an accent as he could muster. "I knows yer good fer it."

The crowd roared its appreciation of Brennan's double entendre, for *mo cuallaidhe*, which was pronounced "my cully," meant "my friend" or "my companion" in Irish. But in Gotham's argot, of course, a cully was a molley's customer or, worse, a mere simpleton.

Ignoring Brennan's jibe, the Chief raised his hand again, this time holding his violet silk handkerchief, and we readied ourselves. The handkerchief dropped and we Phoenixes pushed down on our brakes for all they were worth. The Excelsiors strained mightily as well, and two streams of water shot up, ten, twenty, thirty feet and more as each engine and her crew strained to build up the pressure. None of us enginemen could see how high the streams shot. Our heads were down as we flung ourselves to the task. But Bill Tweed said later that both streams shot near to the top of Riley's Pole and collided, water splashing all over the crowd. Then, to the Chief's horror, the Excelsior engine just quit pumping. The bellows had sprung a leak, and had to be repaired. We Phoenixes continued pumping for a clean five minutes to the cheers of the crowd (those favoring the Excelsiors having wisely changed sides or simply shut pan), and we even managed to get the stream up well over Riley's Pole when we really put our backs into it. Poor Excelsiors: their engine did not pump again that day. But pay up Cassidy did—long before the sun set that afternoon, thus once again establishing that a gentleman is only as good as his word.

Tweed told me later that the Chief left in disgust while we were still pumping. But before he left, he told Brennan there was no way in creation that the Board of Aldermen would approve paying James Smith for building the Haywagon. Neither Brennan nor Magee said a word—and neither did Con Donoho or Matt Rynders, who were standing with them after having both rushed over from the 'Points to see the hated Excelsiors utterly exfluncticated.

Tweed later reported to Blackie and me—over glasses of lemonade and beer—what happened at the weekly meeting down at City Hall of the Board of Aldermen. The meeting, which included all seven aldermen plus the mayor himself, happened to have been the very next night, and Brennan, Magee, Donoho and Rynders went down to see the proceedings. They sat as calm as could be on the benches, uttering nary a word to each other. The Chief and Cassidy were there too, sitting equally as calmly across the aisle. But their calm façades shattered when a resolution came up to pay for the Haywagon. When the resolution passed 4 votes to 3, the Chief and Cassidy strode from the room only to run into Brennan and Magee, who had moved into the hallway so they could chat quietly. Rynders and Donoho had left already, mentioning something about wanting to look in on Black Muireann.

The Chief said in a furious whisper to Brennan and Magee— he couldn't shout like he wanted to on account of the ongoing Aldermanic meeting—by God, you may have gotten four aldermanic votes, but you've got to get the resolution past the Assistant Aldermen, and there are seventeen of them, and there's no way you'll find nine votes—why, they're all American Republicans and loyal to a fault. He had hardly finished speaking when a boy tugged at Brennan's sleeve and whispered in his ear. Brennan thanked the boy, handed him a shilling and sent him on his way. Brennan then calmly announced to the Chief and Cassidy that the resolution had passed the committee of Assistant Aldermen, ten votes to seven.

CHAPTER 12

Free Mulattas and Texas Slaves

MAY IN GOTHAM IS BEAUTIFUL — WHEN IT'S NOT RAINING. Mary had disappeared one Tuesday afternoon, leaving Fíona in my charge. We were down at City Hall Park, where the Croton fountain had just been turned on, shooting water 50 feet into the air. We sat companionably on the freshly painted park benches, enjoying the sun and the emptiness—the queens and streetwalkers who liked to congregate in the park as evening rolled in were thankfully not yet about. I had met a queen one night to my immense horror and his (her?) equally immense amusement when he (she?) pawed me and offered himself (herself?) to me for a quarter eagle. I told her (him?) to skedaddle, and she courteously bade me good night in the deepest bass voice. I didn't dare ask Mary what she knew about such matters, nor was I inclined to ask Blackie and display my ignorance. I did, however, swallow my pride and ask Magee one night in private. He laughed so hard that tears came to his eyes. He eventually took mercy upon me and explained, admonishing me that I should stick to chasing all the sweet prims running around Gotham and not fash myself with such molleys.

Fíona was reading her book to me—a word here and there, and in between the words she regaled me with plenty of made-up soliloquies interpreting the characters. She asked me questions about everything passing through her rather vivid imagination. In between her questions, I thought about my wavering resolve to go west. Life was pretty good. I was earning good money. Mary seemed happy—well, certainly happier than when we'd met on the quay back in Cork, if more forbidding and concerned about being "proper." Fíona was happy as only a well-loved, well-fed and safe child is. Magee thought I was okay. Better still, Charlie Backwell trusted me, even if he wouldn't listen to me about the risk he was running having all that money in the counting room on the second floor of Magee's boardinghouse without a decent door and lock, or even so much as a single one of Magee's many *ráibéads* to protect him. I'd not thought about it until Cian brought it up one day with a smirking and idle observation about robbing the place, what with all the rhino lying there for the asking. I wasted no time in cornering Charlie about it, but I was careful not to mention Cian's bit of patter.

"The *ráibéads* is too stupid," Charlie said querulously. "They're always getting in the way. An' a door ain't gonna do no good, neither."

"Better that than a pistol to your head or a Cap'n Hackum settling you," I retorted.

"Yer naught but an old lady, Gogan. Ye needn't worry yer rosary on my account," he snapped.

A couple of days later, I went to Magee and told him of my concern. Magee laughed and said that there wasn't a soul in Gotham with the balls to do a job on Charlie's counting-room. I live just above it, he said—which indeed he did, in a large, airy apartment—all the better to keep an eye on his prized investment. (An investment made, by all accounts, with Con Donoho as a silent partner. Bill Tweed had said once that Magee was convinced that a decent, clean boardinghouse and a well-run saloon would make more money than the typical diving bells and boarding-houses found in the 'Points—let alone such horrors as the Old Brewery and the Gates of Hell. By all indications, he was dead right.) Anyway, he said with a superior air, he was keeping all of his brass in a couple of different banks, now, the Bowery Savings Bank chief among them, so what did it matter? Blackie, who'd been listening to us, didn't say a word and wandered off to find a lemonade. Nobody ever mentioned it again, and the door stayed as it was.

Cian no longer worked for Charlie—or Magee, for that matter. He had quit both jobs, airily announcing something about working more with Lúcás down at the quays. Until the day he left, Cian had been good to his word. He'd not diddled with his collections—not even once, and not even for a half cent. I was confident he hadn't hidden anything from me, because I had taken great pains to verify that what he took from the shopkeepers he delivered to me or to Charlie (which I counted later, anyway). So I was a little sorry to see him go, even though I was secretly happy that I didn't have to worry anymore about him diddling with the lottery shop offertories. But I made no bones about being happy about not having as much chance of running into Lúcás again. As Muireann had said that one night, Lúcás was creepy—and dinner with him had not been any great shakes either, thank you very much. I and everyone else I knew was happy that Lúcás didn't come around anymore with his trinkets.

Nontheless, Cian and I did meet fairly regularly to catch up on the gossip (without Lúcás, thankfully. And, come to think of it, without Magee really being aware of our meetings, or so I thought). Cian told me as we sat one day gorging ourselves in an oyster cellar that the cherry pies coming off those coffin ships were thicker on the ground than ever before, all of them bearing terrible tales of this Great Hunger back in the old country. Potatoes rotting in the ground and not a damned finger being lifted to feed the starving. Instead, Ireland's bounty—just as Mary and Fíona and I'd seen it on the quays of Galway, was still being shipped to England to feed the *Sassenagh* overlords. And what made those little cherry pies valuable were all those goosing slums where he could send his wares for more brass than Black Muireann was willing to pay. He also confidentially allowed to me that he was taking as great a pleasure as ever in sampling his wares—but only after they'd been properly broken in. No tears, fake or otherwise, from articles of virtue (fake or otherwise) for him. Just a good hard gallop was all he wanted, he said in a satisfied tone.

Sunshine fell on Fíona and me as a cloud passed, she stopped chattering and chirped, "Hello, Miss Brannagh."

"Why, hello, my little pet."

I could not take my eyes off the luminous mulatta from Black Muireann's cavaulting house standing in front of us, smiling.

"Brannagh O'Marran," I said involuntarily.

Brannagh sat down next to Fíona, who said to her, "Billy and I are reading and watching the clouds. They make funny shapes … we've seen a ship, an angel and two fairies."

"Well," Brannagh said without acknowledging my presence, "why don't you and I look and see what shapes are up in the sky now?"

Fíona looked up, and Brannagh looked over at me and winked. I damn near melted into my boots. Her eyes were fashioned solely for a man (I decided then and there that I had joined that exalted fellowship) to lose himself in. I sat quietly, watching the two of them talking, their heads close together. I couldn't quite hear what they were saying, as they were girls communicating in that way that only girls do—to the utter exclusion of the male race—man or boy.

Finally, Brannagh looked up. "Fíona, my pet, can you and Billy walk me home?"

"Please?" Fíona looked up at me earnestly. "Brannagh is my bestest older cousin." She beamed.

"The cat have your tongue?" Brannagh was smiling at me, it seemed affectionately, or so I prayed.

"I'm Billy Gogan." My voice felt as if I hadn't used it in a millennium.

"I know."

We all got up, and started walking across the park, with Fíona skipping between us as we walked on either side of her, holding her hands. Every so often, Fíona would stop walking or skipping and, laughing heartily, she would swing from our hands as we lifted her up.

"Where do you live?" I asked.

"On Church Street."

The same street as Black Muireann's cavaulting house. It made sense, actually. Virtually every shopkeeper and saloon-keeper in existence lived over the premises.

"We're going the wrong way."

Brannagh laughed. "Only if we're not dropping Fíona off at home."

"Mary's not there, and I took Fíona for the afternoon."

"Mary'll be there," she said with certain knowledge. How would she know? "Or," Brannagh quickly added, "we can drop her off with Mrs. Shipley."

"You know Mrs. Shipley?"

"You don't know much, do you?" Brannagh laughed again. "Momma and Magee are great friends, you know, and Momma knows all of Magee's friends, including Mrs. Shipley … and sweet little Fíona and her momma." Brannagh lightly pinched Fíona's cheek. Fíona smiled in delight and looked at the both of us in turn.

Mary wasn't home, and so we left Fíona with Mrs. Shipley.

⌒

We walked wordlessly for a while, Brannagh and I. We skirted Paradise Square, and walked the long way to her house. I said something gentlemanly about not wanting her to see all the horrors of the 'Points. Brannagh giggled, and I blushed. Then we were wordless once again. I'd never felt like this before, walking with a girl—not even with Evelyn. And I was now carrying Brannagh's bag, full of books from her day's lessons with her tutor, Mr. Graham, who lived uptown on Bond Street, near Washington Square, where most of his students lived.

It was the only respectable way for her to get an education, Brannagh said when I asked her about it. Muireann didn't want her attending the school for colored girls. Only the commonest sort attended the school, and many of the teachers there, most of whom were colored (only the most desperate—or idealistic—of native Americans would stoop to such work), could themselves hardly read or write, let alone properly teach their students to do so. Nobody figured that the coloreds needed anything better, particularly as there weren't many coloreds who got to be huckleberries above the persimmon, Brannagh observed.

She had passed from primary school when she was eleven, knowing how to draw—and to read—some. "Of course," she said breezily, "Momma can hardly read or write either, having been just a poor *spalpeen's* daughter back in Eirinn. But," she said proudly, "Mother's awfully long-headed about her figuring. She sure knows how to choke the last shilling from even the most miserly of those cullies." Brannagh giggled at using such a naughty word. "Anyway," she continued, "when I passed from primary school, my figuring wasn't very good, and I'd never read any of the classics.

"Momma wanted better than that for me. So she started sending me to Mr. Graham for private tutoring. He is such a gentleman. He went to Columbia College and everything. He can construe Latin and Greek—which I find so very hard to learn. He speaks the finest French, and he knows both his classics and his modern literature. Not only that, he also teaches deportment, drawing and dancing. A *pas de deux* only, though, Mr. Graham says. That's because I can't be seen dancing a quadrille with his other pupils on account of I'm his only colored student. The finest colored girl he's ever known, he always assures me. He simply cannot risk invoking the rage—so he says— of the mothers of his other pupils, whether they be young ladies or young gentlemen—even if I am the most polite and well-mannered young mulatta miss. But that's okay—Mr. Graham detests that word 'okay'—it is so common a word, he says, so louche."

Brannagh changed the subject, and told me that she loved reading ... Jane Austen, Mary Shelley ... "Think of it, women writing books. Do you know what Mr. Graham just gave me?" Brannagh was positively conspiratorial once again.

I shrugged.

"Margaret Fuller's *Woman in the Nineteenth Century*. It was published just this year. Miss Fuller works for Horace Greeley at the *Tribune*," Brannagh said with authority. "She says that women should be the equal of men ... can you imagine? She also says that the Indians and the coloreds should be treated as equals to the white man ... Momma says that such notions are foolish. She says that the Irish—and they're white—are treated hardly better than the coloreds or the red man. Oh, Lord," Brannagh sighed. "I do so want to go to college and be like Margaret Fuller. But Momma wants me to be able to go to a finishing school when I turn sixteen. That's so I can be admitted to society where I can meet a respectable young man ... if there's one who would have me as I am."

She stopped for a moment, but I didn't dare ask her whether I was a respectable young man. I knew the answer without asking. Respectable, I was not. Far from it. I was the bookkeeper for one the most notorious bookies in the 'Points. I was also a quondam member of the Phoenix Engine Company. Worse, I was one of Magee's minions and an occasional, if still virginal, frequenter of Black Muireann's cavaulting house. Once upon a time, perhaps, I had been respectable. That is, during those halcyon days when I was junior prefect at my house at St. Patrick's, starting eleven for the house cricket side, son of a respected Irish patriot and prospective scholar at Dublin College. I could feel the judgment of my father and Father O'Muirhily ready to fall upon me over it all ... I shook off the sudden shadow on this beautiful afternoon ... and banished the sudden intrusion of Evelyn's golden ringlets, although not before regretting the fact that it had been many weeks since I had taken pen to paper to write a letter to her. A defect I resolved to remedy post-haste.

"You are a dreamer, aren't you?"

I reverted to the reality of Broadway as Brannagh gently grasped my arm, stopping me from blithely stepping in front of the hooves of the lead horses of a matched set of six, which were hauling an enormous omnibus at a more than respectable clip down the smooth and unbroken cobblestones of the busiest street in all of Christendom, as that fellow Dickens once wrote.

Brannagh was smiling at my sudden discomfiture.

"Sorry." I wasn't really, because I could feel her closeness. The universe seemed to once more fold in on us.

Brannagh giggled again. "Magee says you walk around with your head in the clouds."

"Really?" I didn't believe that. Me? The young kid on the make?

"Sure. But he says you're the best bookkeeper Charlie's ever had. A real long-headed fellow, Charlie says. Square, too."

"How do you know Charlie?" I asked.

"You mean, how does a proper young lady know about punting shops and the coves who make them profitable?"

"Well ..." I dithered as we dodged our way across Broadway.

"Billy ..." she seemed exasperated, although not really. "We met in a cavaulting house. My mother's a madam. A buttock broker." This last with just a hint of savage satisfaction.

Even if I'd had a witty response—actually, I'd've settled for mere coherence—I couldn't have answered her for love or money, because we were avoiding yet another omnibus in the middle of Broadway. It had been thundering along right behind the first one. There was now a hansom cab on our left as well, overtaking the omnibus at a furious pace, the horse's ears laid back with the effort. In front of us, to our right, was another hack, right behind a dray cart that was directly in front of us. It had stopped cold in the middle of the street on account of a collision between two other dray carts, barrels spilled onto the cobblestones and split open, their contents just beginning to blend with the muck from the day's traffic. The two draymen were screaming at each other, to the delight of a gathering crowd. When we reached the relative safety of the porticos in front of Astor House, we still couldn't talk. We were dancing—a *pas de deux*, to my immense delight—out of the way of a bevy of uptown ladies going to tea at the magnificent hotel and the swells who were seeking to attend them. We were just a little breathless—and Brannagh was glowing in the most fetching way—when we stopped running.

She grabbed my elbow, and said to me emphatically, "I'm serious, you know. Momma is a buttock broker. And I am no Jane Austen heroine."

She looked directly at me as she said that, and once more, I was convinced that there was not another person there on the crowded sidewalk besides the two of us.

"But you're ..."

"A what?"

"A nice girl ..."

"You mean I'm not some high-priced, exotic *belle petite* in my own mother's brothel?" An arch tone with equally arched eyebrows.

This was not a conversation I ever imagined happening—not even with Jessie.

"You can talk to me straight, Billy Gogan."

"Okay."

"Okay what?" she demanded.

"Okay, I'll say it plain," I said. "It doesn't matter that we met in a cavaulting house. It doesn't mean anything about you that you were there." I drew a breath before going further. "And it sure doesn't amount to a row of pins that your father was colored. I don't know you, and I'm not going to treat you differently than I would otherwise simply because of who your mother is or the hue of your skin. And if someone does treat you differently, then God damn him to hell." I finished fiercely, not quite sure of the import of what I'd just said.

She smiled at me. "You're a sweet boy, Billy Gogan." And yet again I felt as if I were the only man—notwithstanding her referring to me as a boy—on all of Manhattan Island.

We were on Murray Street now, and it was quiet compared to the pandemonium on Broadway.

"So, how do you know Charlie?" I asked again, conscious that she had changed the subject when I asked before.

This time, she said, "I know Magee."

It was all she'd say on that subject. We walked for a while longer, quietly, eventually turning onto Church Street. Presently, we were opposite Black Muireann's brothel, which, I could now see in the daylight, was hidden away in a most respectable, three-story brick house that was indistinguishable from any other house on the street. The window through which I'd seen Jessie was decorously curtained.

"I live right there." She pointed to the equally respectable three-story brick house just next door to the brothel.

We stood on the sidewalk for a moment, each of us unsure of what to do next. Then I screwed my courage to its sticking place.

"Can I walk you home tomorrow?"

"Yes." Her answer was so quick that it almost tumbled over my question. "Yes," she said again. "I'd like that. I'd like it very much."

⌒

At three o'clock the next afternoon, I made sure that I was sitting on the same bench in City Park. Except this time Fíona wasn't with me, and I'd made an extra effort to brush my shoes and comb my hair. I had briefly considered getting a haircut, but then I feared not having enough to pay for some ices at the stall at the foot of the park. As I said earlier, Mary had me on the short leash with the brass. Remember the mountains and Jim Bridger, young Billy Gogan, she had admonished me on many more than one occasion, several such admonitions occurring in rapid succession after I had brought home my new waistcoat—the one I wore the night I first saw Brannagh. Although Mary did allow on that occasion, after a bit, that I didn't look quite like a decrepit schoolboy anymore. I wasn't yet the paddy incarnation of an uptown swell—or of a Bowery b'hoy, for that matter, but I was looking a little more as if I belonged. Then Mary had cautioned me that I shouldn't enjoy too much of a good thing.

Thus I had only a few coppers in my pocket.

"Hi."

I bolted to my feet, hoping that I hadn't been slouching too much.

"H-hi, can I take your bag?"

Bag in hand, I asked in a tumble of words, "Would you like an ice, or," impulsively, "an ice cream?"

Not, of course, that I knew where an ice creamery was, except back up in the 'Points, and I was not going to drag Brannagh back there. Then I remembered—there was a wonderful ice creamery down on State Street, just across from Battery Park. Then ... did I have enough brass in my pocket? I thought so. Damn! I bitterly regretted my half-baked planning.

"Oh, it's been so long since I've had an ice cream. Momma doesn't allow that—too high falutin', she says."

Muireann was well known for her delicate confectionaries, which were served with a sherry to the prospective cullies who waited, some nervously or impatiently, for their turns upstairs with the dells. Unlike most riding academies, Muireann did not allow anything stronger than sherry in the parlor, thank you very much—even if there was a rosy-nippled academician in the window late at night.

"I love chocolate," Brannagh positively sighed.

"Chocolate it is," I said gallantly. Sweet Jesus. A penny more per ice cream for the chocolate.

Presently, we were sitting on a park bench under the shade of a willow tree, overlooking the promenade, the river and Jersey City, eating our ice creams. I had hardly a half-cent left in my pocket.

"Have you ever heard of Louisa Missouri Miller?" Brannagh whispered with a suppressed giggle.

"Who is she?"

"How could you not know?" Brannagh uttered in disbelief. "It was in all the flash press. Not that Momma lets me read such wicked stuff. That terrible Mr. Snelling was the first one to report the story in that absolutely scandalous sheet, the *Polyanthos*. Jessie showed it to me one day." She put her hand to her mouth to stifle a naughty giggle. "Oh, you couldn't have. You weren't even here then. How could you have known?"

I was very happy that Brannagh had restored me to her good graces from that purgatory she apparently reserved for the insensate.

Without taking a breath, Brannagh began her story. "Louisa was the beautiful daughter of a madam with a cavaulting house on Church Street, just a few doors up from Momma's. The finest in Gotham—just like Momma's, really. Well, maybe Mrs. Miller had a couple of more chandeliers than Momma.

"But never mind. When she was a little girl, Louisa wanted to be an actress. Her mother, wanting better for Louisa, groomed her to be married off to a nice respectable young man from an uptown family, or better, to an even more respectable young man in a town very far away from Gotham—you can understand why. So, when Louisa turned twelve, Mrs. Miller spent a pretty penny sending her up the Hudson on a fancy steam packet, to Emma Willard's academy in Troy, where Mrs. Willard also boarded and taught 300 other young ladies from all over the country, some from as far away as Charleston, South Carolina, even. Every one of those young ladies was from a rich, respectable family, or so the *Polyanthos* said.

"You do know where Troy is, don't you?" Brannagh asked, suspicious of some new defect she thought she had discovered in me.

I didn't know where Troy was—in America. Homeric Troy was in Anatolia, wasn't it? That was in the middle of the Ottoman Empire nowadays, right? But I didn't say anything, and resolved to go sneak a peek at the display atlas at a bookseller I knew of up on Broadway, Wiley & Putnam's, near Eleventh Street. I had visited Putnam's quite a number of times since I had discovered the place a few weeks ago, and had fallen in love with it. Once I had discovered the bookseller, I was surprised by my latent hunger for reading just about anything other than my now dog-eared copy of *The Last of the Mohicans*. There simply were no books to be found in the 'Points—unless you counted Charlie's account books. I had bought a couple of books at Putnam's to assuage my hunger. Nothing expensive, both used. But it meant that the proprietor at least tolerated my presence, particularly when it wasn't busy, letting me pass an hour or two solemnly browsing his endless bookstacks.

Brannagh continued her story, having now hooked her arm through mine as we sat enjoying the breeze, the boats and the people parading up and down the promenade.

"Louisa loved her time up at Mrs. Willard's academy, learning her deportment, her dancing and her drawing—you know, all the things that Mr. Graham is teaching me—plus, Louisa apparently could tinkle a tune on the piano. Momma tells me that respectable young men swoon over pretty young ladies who can play the piano. So all of the girls at Mrs. Willard's academy learned how to play the piano.

"I can't play, though," Brannagh sighed, "on account of Mr. Graham not knowing how (a shortcoming he related to Momma quite apologetically), and Momma hasn't been able to find anybody 'respectable' to teach me. Momma gave Magee a very firm 'no' when he offered her the services of that colored piano player who sometimes plays on Saturday nights up at his saloon. The piano player didn't drink much, Magee told Momma, and he could be trusted with a nice young lady such as myself." Brannagh gave me a mock arch look. "I didn't hear that from Momma, of course, but from Mary. We were gossiping one day, when Momma and I were visiting Magee. Momma is always keen to make sure that Magee is a happy investor, so we visit him all the time, and Mary was passing the afternoon with him there one day. They are such great friends. Fíona was there, as well," she quickly added, "reading that wonderful book you got her in Ireland. You are so sweet …"

Brannagh drifted back to her story. "Everything was going so well for Louisa at Mrs. Willard's that Mrs. Miller thought that Louisa had forgotten all about wanting to be a stage actress. Mrs. Miller was so thankful for that, because her oldest daughter, Josephine, had become a stage actress and, worse, had become involved with a notorious rake named Thomas Hamblin. Now you have heard of him, haven't you?" Brannagh looked at me defiantly.

This definitely was another test of my sentience. One, fortunately, that I could pass. Hamblin was a *Sassenagh* thespian turned impresario. He owned the Bowery Theatre, which used to be down on Chatham Street, right in the heart of the Bowery. It had been the biggest theater in Gotham before it burned down last month—what a great fire that had been. Every company from lower Manhattan, hook and ladder, hose and engine alike, had shown up, and there hadn't been a single fight on account of the Chief himself being there and threatening the fire company of any fire laddie caught fighting with instant and permanent dissolution. I had enjoyed the excitement that night, even though all I did was work my brake on the Haywagon until I thought my arms would fall off.

Anyway, the Bowery Theatre had been magnificent—a Greek-style portico supported by five Corinthian columns. It was as splendiferous as the Astor Hotel, and could hold 3,000 people. Hamblin had staged all kinds of shows there: circus shows, blackface minstrel shows, animal acts and the most debased form of Shakespeare, all of which the Bowery b'hoys and g'hals loved, as did the Irish and Germans from the 'Points, not to mention the respectable uptown denizens with a sense of adventure. The Bowery Theatre was similar to Magee's saloon in that it was a place where enmities were laid aside for the duration of the show, and everyone could mix without fear of unrest. (And one was always assured of safe conduct out of the Bowery, of course, if you were Irish or dutchy. The coloreds, well they were another story.)

I nodded confidently to Brannagh, and she continued her tale.

"Josephine was Hamblin's protégé, and so the story goes, his lover." Brannagh blushed ever so slightly as our eyes met involuntarily, but she recovered with a mischievous smile. "But she wasn't his only lover. He had a wife back in England, and he lived with yet another fine Corinthian." She cast a conspiratorial glance my way. "I can't remember her name for the life of me, though." She whispered this last bit as if, were she to say it louder, Judgment Day would come early. "No matter."

"Whoa, bust me!" I interrupted. "How many lovers?"

"Well," Brannagh spread her fingers, which were beautifully encased in kid leather gloves. She caught me gazing at her hand, mesmerized. "A gift from Momma for my birthday, last month. Aren't they beautiful?"

She held her gloved hands up for me to admire, and we both looked at them for a moment.

I finally replied, "Lovely." Except I was thinking of her hands, and not the gloves encasing them.

Brannagh's hands disappeared, and her spell over me was broken for the moment.

"There was his wife. She divorced him and went back to England. Quite the scandal, apparently. I was just a little girl then. Don't recall anything about it."

"Okay, who else?"

"The lover he lives with."

"Dissolute."

"Isn't he? Then there's Josephine."

I sniggered. "Now that you explain it, there don't seem to be that many."

Brannagh ignored me and continued her story. Hamblin made Josephine a star and his new lover—all the while still living with his old lover. Louisa was up at school. But that came to an end when the flash press—not Snelling, but someone else—published a story about how Mrs. Miller was the most stylish madam in all of Gotham. The story also contained salacious details about Josephine, who was then starring opposite Hamblin at the Bowery Theatre in some new production.

"And do you know what was even worse?" Brannagh looked at me, and I realized with a start that I was supposed to shake my head in the negative. "All the gossip about Hamblin's rather questionable domestic practices—two lovers residing with him at his house and the good Lord knows what else. That would have been all right for Louisa if the story hadn't also named Louisa herself, and related how she was attending that most respectable of finishing schools, Mrs. Willard's academy. Well, Mrs. Willard had a conniption fit when she found out who Louisa really was."

I wondered mildly how a respectable woman such as Mrs. Willard would have found out about Louisa, as she did not seem the sort to partake of the flash press.

Brannagh glared at me for interrupting her story, "However Mrs. Willard found out, it didn't matter, because she put Louisa on the first steam packet back to Gotham. Of course, Mrs. Willard protested to anyone who'd listen that Louisa had been sent to her school under false pretences, because she had been given to understand that Louisa had been an orphan with a rich and philanthropic aunt." Brannagh turned and looked at me knowingly.

"So, what happened?"

Brannagh snuggled a little closer to me. "Well, Louisa arrived back in Gotham bound and determined to be a stage actress, just like her sister. It turned out that, contrary to what Mrs. Miller may have thought, Louisa had never given up her dream of treading the stage. Louisa had known all about her sister and Hamblin on account of her and her sister having been writing to each other the entire time that Louisa had been at Mrs. Willard's academy. Louisa was sixteen when she left Mrs. Willard's. Just a year older than I am now," Brannagh mused. "Louisa went home to Mrs. Miller. But within the week, Josephine had introduced Louisa to Hamblin, and Hamblin promptly fell in love with her.

"Hamblin made Louisa a star in her very first role, giving her the lead opposite himself. Mrs. Miller was beside herself, and tried to stop the production. But Louisa moved out of her mother's house and straight into Hamblin's, on account of Josephine apparently having recently decamped, forgotten by Hamblin, the Bowery's audiences and Louisa herself, by all accounts, the minute that Louisa hove onto the scene. Hamblin had a judge appointed as Louisa's guardian to protect her from Mrs. Miller, who was widely known to be the wickedest buttock broker in all of Gotham." Brannagh gave me a fetchingly naughty look.

"Well, Snelling got ahold of this part of the story—about Louisa and Hamblin—and published it. Nobody knows where he learned about it, and he wouldn't say. Maybe Mrs. Miller gave him the story in an attempt to ruin Hamblin and prevent her daughter from becoming a fallen woman. Who knows? But the story's publication seemed to have precipitated a tragic turn of events, because within the week Louisa Missouri Miller was dead, nursed until the very end by Hamblin's lover. They say that Louisa died from the shame and embarrassment brought upon her by the story, which ruined her stage debut. But nobody really knows."

"What happened to Josephine?"

"You know, I haven't the faintest idea."

"Terrible story."

"Well, I told it to you because it's so naughty: an older man seducing a young lady—and a virgin, to boot." Brannagh giggled wickedly. "You look so shocked."

"I'm not shocked."

"Yes you are. Just admit it. How could an innocent little girl like me know about such scandalous matters?" She grinned. "Even if my mother is a buttock broker."

"Seems to me all you have to do is breathe the air in Gotham and you get to know these kinds of stories," I replied as drily as I could.

Dear, loving God, I thought. What would my father and Father O'Muirhily have thought of this wicked story? What must Mary think of it? It was inconceivable to me that she wouldn't know about it. But from whom? I couldn't imagine Brannagh—even though she did have the most confounding sense of playful naughtiness—telling Mary. Who else would have told her? Something told me that I probably would be well advised not to bring it up with Mary.

"Do you know why else I told you the story?"

I shook my head.

"I'm Momma's only family." Brannagh disengaged her arm from mine and turned and looked me directly in the eye. "And she does not want to have happen to me what happened to Louisa Missouri Miller."

⌒

Magee was also good to his word in sponsoring me to join the volunteer militia company. It was a lot like joining the Phoenixes. Not just any mother's son could join. You had to get invited, first off. Very exclusive. But a good way to avoid ordinary militia duties. Even better was its usefulness in making one's way in the community, so Bill Tweed told me when I asked him about it. Everybody was supposed to join the militia, he explained. It was a state law.

But nobody paid any attention to it anymore on account of the law having been left over from the American Revolution.

You know, Tweed needled me, the war where the English let us Americans get away. I drily reminded Bill that every honest, God-fearing Irishman would bow down and praise the Lord three times over if Ireland were to be delivered from under the heel of the *Sassenagh* jackboot by a Declaration of Independence. The self-evident truths for native Americans held equally as true for God-fearing (or in my case, somewhat more agnostic) Irishmen. Bill slapped me on the back after that little speech and told me I needed a beer 'afore I found a fight to get into.

Well, Magee invited me to join him as a member in good standing of the volunteer company, announcing to the afternoon crowd in the saloon escaping the chilly May drizzle that the company needed a drummer boy, and that I'd fit the uniform. The colored man, Joe, who played the drums on Saturday nights at the saloon (he also worked for Magee as a general handyman, and was Magee's preferred source of gossip concerning the goings-on among the 'Points' colored denizens), just happened to be there on one errand or another as Magee was inviting me to rap out a tattoo, and I was trying to decline on account of my ignorance of that particular term—and my more general ignorance of drums. Joe was trying to slip through the dance hall unnoticed, as was his wont, despite his knowing of Magee's outright tolerance for colored folk, it being safer to adopt a low profile in even this friendly confine. Some *reathaí* noticed Joe, and it was decided instantly by general acclaim that he should be detailed to teach me how to play the drum so they'd all know when to quit drinking at night if the company were to ever venture out of Gotham on maneuvers. It was also agreed by all present that such maneuvers would be extremely unlikely, "even if," as one stalwart put it, "them Mexicans was trying to get back Texas—let them try it now that Texas is going to become part of the Union."

Someone else snarled martially that "It waren't them Mexicans what was the problem. It's them blasted *Sassenagh* what's tryin' to unlawfully grab what's rightfully American soil. So we might have to pop them a chopper to the knowledge box, just like we did back in '76." Nobody quite knew where the disputed lands were—Oregon, somebody thought, but he wasn't sure. Nobody seemed very clear on where Oregon was. Somewhere by the Pacific Ocean, but nobody quite knew where the Pacific Ocean was, nor why either the *Sassenagh* or the Yankees wanted Oregon in the first place. It was just that "them *Sassenagh* got no right to the place," they knew it and that was the end of it. I made a mental note to find out what part of the world they were talking about the next time I ventured up to Putnam's.

The volunteer company's monthly meeting was at Warren's Sixth Ward Hotel, over on Duane Street. By the general consent of all concerned, the hotel was neutral territory, and no one was allowed to fight there on account of the public business taking place there of nominating (for Tammany on one night and the American Republicans and Whigs on another) or electioneering (when everyone showed up—no fighting allowed inside … although Katy bar the door outside). No one violated that precept for fear of general retribution from, and ostracism by, all known (I'd say polite as well, but it was not) society. The Roach Guards, the Patsy Conroys, the Plug Uglies, the True Blue American Republicans and all the other gangs thus stayed clear of the place during the rest of the year, when it quietly went about its business of housing merchants and other simkins visiting from the countryside.

Just two weeks earlier, the Tammany slates for the upcoming elections had been set at a big meeting at Warren's. Magee's saloon had been abuzz all week about the nomination for assistant alderman, which was between Magee on one hand, backed by Donoho and the Irish, and Cassidy on the other, backed by the nativists who still fought (their steadily losing) battle for control of Tammany. Magee had told me to hold the fort back at the saloon. But the prospect of missing all the action had been too much for me to bear. I also suspected that Mary may have had a hand in the matter, on account of her and Magee having become such great friends. But I wasn't going to let her sideline me like that. So I disregarded Magee's orders and slipped out the back of the saloon, through the alley and then over the couple of blocks to Warren's, where I skittered through the kitchen, a miserable affair chiefly known for its filth and bad food, and up to the balcony above the ballroom (so-called by some, but it was entirely too grand a name for so prosaic a space; most called it Dooley's Long Room), where I perched with a magnificent view of the floor below.

The room was virtually empty when I got there. The Irishmen arrived first like a Roman legion occupying a city, gloves and hard bowlers only, for no weapons were allowed in neutral territory on nominating and election days—there were standards of decorum, don't you know. Con Donoho swept in at the tail end like a triumphant petty potentate, hand raised in self-deprecation to acknowledge the rousing cheers that swept the suddenly crowded room.

He took the podium and gaveled the nominating meeting to order. He began with a joke. Then he got down to business, and after the other nominations had been made, he nominated Magee as assistant alderman and asked for a second, which was thunderously given. He asked for a voice vote to approve the nomination, an approval he would have had very peacably and quite unanimously if he'd asked just 30 seconds earlier. For no sooner had he asked for the voice vote than the doors to Dooley's Long Room crashed open, and everybody looked back to see what the commotion was all about. Cassidy strode in, his minions at his side, with Lúcás Dineen chief among them, standing at Cassidy's shoulder.

I looked again, and sure enough, there was Cian, standing in his brother's shadow. I wondered if Lúcás was carrying his barking iron and toothpick—such trinkets, as I said, being generally banned at Ward's Hotel on occasions such as these.

There was a dead silence for just a moment, and then Con continued, with merely a nod to Cassidy's entrance and a brief, "gents, thanks fer attending, but nominations fer assistant alderman be closed now, and we be voting. Yer welcome to stay ..." He got no further.

Cassidy said to him, "I place myself in nomination."

Con remonstrated mildly with him, "That's mighty forward of yers, Jimmy. Have yer a friend to do the honors?"

Lúcás piped in with a surly grunt that I suppose constituted Cassidy's nomination. Another of Cassidy's other minions, a boxer, lisped through smashed lips, "I second."

"Highly irregular of yers, Cassidy. Yer too late."

"The hell I am."

Magee sat respectfully, allowing Con to fight the verbal battle. But after a moment or two I saw Magee reach under his chair and pick up his cudgel—a politician in those days had to be seen leading the charge to defend what was rightfully his (even if he was not permitted to bring such weapons into Dooley's Long Room).

"Jimmy, me lad." Con put one last, knowingly futile effort in. Cassidy ignored Con's entreaty, whereupon Con winked at Magee, who let out a bloodcurdling scream in Gaelic that was probably along the lines of, "Boys, let's throw the bastards out."

With that, the festivities began. Magee's cudgel was one of the few weapons, and he used it to great effect, slashing a path to Cassidy, who seemed content to wait for him. Three or four unfortunate Cassidy supporters collapsed under Magee's cudgel before he and Cassidy were face to face. Nobody touched either of them. In fact, the fighting gradually died down as everyone began to relish an impromptu rematch between the two men.

Too bad Charlie wasn't here to make book. Then again, it would've been unseemly to take odds on Cassidy, the bastard, and all the punters would have bet on Magee.

A circle formed gradually around the two combatants. Magee saluted Cassidy with his cudgel and then tossed it to Blackie. Cassidy acknowledged Magee's gallantry. They removed their coats and tossed them to their respective minions. Each then rolled up his shirt sleeves and spit in his hands. With these preliminaries completed, Magee and Cassidy began to circle each other. There was hardly a sound in the place as the two men, each well over six foot tall and in fine fettle, sized each other up.

I quickly realized that this time there was to be no sudden foray by Magee to end the affair with a cross-buttock throw before it had hardly begun. Cassidy was patiently awaiting such an attack, and Magee had no intention of making it and leaving himself open to a lethal counterpunch. So they circled some more.

Finally, Magee backed up just a step and signaled to Cassidy, "Come get me." Cassidy did not react. Magee then said in a voice that seemed to rock the nearly silent room, "Oh you poor, poxed Fenian turncoat, whoring for them know-nothings, come over here and finish it if you can, yer yellow *dallachán*."

"Fuck you, Magee. You come here, and I'll take the shine right out o' yers, or are ye gettin' a little funky?"

They sounded like a pair of schoolboys as they jollied each other—each looking for the small advantage of having angered the other with the jollying more than he had been angered. Unaccountably, it did seem that Cassidy's calling Magee a coward had stung Magee more than Magee's having called Cassidy the same thing. With a small snort of rage, Magee moved in to engage Cassidy, his left mitten jabbing, finding the range. As Cassidy gave ground, there was a faint whistle of derision. After a couple of backward paces, he was bracing up against the crowd. As he stopped, Magee attacked. Two quick jabs and an uppercut—which missed badly. Cassidy saw his opening and counterpunched with a terrific rib-ender that staggered Magee. Cassidy followed it up with a pair of facers, one of which landed cleanly on Magee's conk. Magee's head snapped back and blood instantly gushed forth from both nostrils, caking his beard and mouth.

Cassidy, sensing the kill, moved in, looking to level Magee and end it. But he dropped his guard, and Magee was able to sting him with a blow to the masher, splitting Cassidy's lip.

The two of them backed away after another vicious little exchange, and began to circle each other yet again—far more warily than before. Each had drawn the claret from the other, and neither was prepared to throw all in to finish it.

The two of them fought on, exchanging quick flurries of blows, some of which landed, some of which did not. Magee's left eye was weeping blood, which flowed down his face to join the bloody mess in his moustache and beard. Blood flowed from Cassidy's nose and lip as well. Both showed fearsomely bloodstained teeth as each strained to breathe and focus on his opponent.

The battle riveted every cove in the ballroom. Normally, you'd think that the place would have been going mad. There were above a hundred brawlers, Irish and native alike, who were crowded into the stifling hot room. Yet there was hardly a word uttered as these two valiant knights dueled. (Yes, that is precisely what they were doing that night. And each fighting for ... what? Honor? Place? I won't dare speculate except to say that it was now about so much more than who was going to have Tammany's nomination that night for assistant alderman.)

But end it had to, and end it did, when Con Donoho, perhaps sensing that this was not Magee's night, jumped to the center and cried, "Lads, lads, this is magnificent. Two more stalwart warriors, I couldna' imagine. Such bottom ... the both of them ..."

Con slowly insinuated himself in between the two bloodied combatants. Each was tired and battered enough to take Con's lead and quietly withdraw to his respective corner and the sympathetic arms of his supporters. It was funny how the two sides had naturally coalesced with nary a blow landed or a shove made—Magee's minions and assorted Roach Guards and Patsy Conroys on one side, and the American Guards on the other. Both sides were quiet. No taunts or challenges thrown. It seemed that somehow the steam had petered out of the evening.

Con said something about there being an eventual rematch, and the ballroom emptied out quietly. Everyone there had been dispirited by the inconclusive nature of the affair. At least that's what Bill Tweed said later that night as Magee was tended to in the saloon's dancehall—Papa John having been sent on his way for the evening. The suckers, the swells and the b'hoys somehow all knew to stay away that night as well, so only Magee's regulars were in attendance. Yet it surprised me how crowded the room was, even so, and how quiet everyone was. I thought I saw Mary for an instant, wide eyes and pale, strained face framed in the doorway. But when I looked again, she wasn't there, and I put it down to fatigue or distraction.

I thought that Tweed had it wrong in arguing that the ballroom had been dispirited by the draw—not that I said anything. Blackie agreed with me, though, in an unnaturally long speech for him, declaring that no one wanted to disturb the natural order of things, and that was why the fight ended in a draw. The whole scrimmage between Magee and Cassidy, and who was to get the militia captaincy and who was to become the new assistant alderman, was not going to be decided by their respective pugilistic skills and courage. No, Blackie said, their futures, and those of the City Council and the militia company, were going to be decided by the likes of Rynders and Donoho and other like-minded Tammany barons, well away from public view, like as not in some room at the top of the Wigwam filled with cigar smoke and the titter of pretty young dells.

That had been two weeks ago, and now tonight the volunteer company's monthly meeting was being held at Dooley's Long Room. Magee and Cassidy had not seen each other since nominating night. Magee's bruises had faded, although, as Mary groused to me a couple of days later, his conk would never be quite the same, and a tooth or two had been loosened and would eventually fall out. Presumably Cassidy's wounds had similarly faded—or failed to heal. Nobody in the 'Points really knew, and no one had been inclined to wander up to Cassidy's saloon for a reconnoitre. Despite the temporary nature of the marks inflicted on Magee in the aborted match, there had been an undercurrent to events over the intervening couple of weeks. Nothing overt. Nothing said about it. But palpable none the less—notwithstanding Magee's bonhomie the night he invited me to be the volunteer company drummer.

I began to understand a little better as the company's volunteers trickled in. Volunteer company nights were another of the observed armed truces in Gotham's deadly little war between nativists and Irish and dutchy *arrivistes*. Cassidy and his lads, Cian and Lúcás in prominent form, came in one door, and Magee and his minions—with me in the middle of the scrum—came in the other. Unaffiliated or neutral volunteers slouched into the room in groups of two or three through either entrance—or through the filthy kitchen, as I had done on nominating night.

Tonight's business, just a couple of weeks before the election, was the matter of electing a new captain. By (perhaps not so curious) coincidence, both Magee and Cassidy had been elected lieutenants earlier this year, and it was widely expected that one of them would succeed to the post of captain for the term of a year. Tonight was not the night for this to occur, though, because the outcome of the aldermanic election would determine who became captain—presumably as part of a deal, or not, depending on how events unfolded. At least, that's what Tweed had told me as we made our way to Ward's from the saloon.

So we gathered in two distinct groups, with the neutrals milling about in between. It was a little unclear to me who was supposed to open the ball. The company's old captain, a Mayor Harper protégé, was no longer a Gothamite, apparently having struck out for the frontier for some obscure reason or another. Unusual, I thought, that there wasn't some colonel or general taking charge—and Con Donoho wasn't there either—but then again he wasn't involved, which was odd to me because he seemed to have his finger in just about everything else I had seen happening in Gotham.

Thus it was all a little hazy for me, which I put down to my only having lately been invited to join. Yet I had the distinct impression that no one else really knew who was going to open the festivities, either. Neither Magee, who was standing just to my side with an unreadable expression on his face, nor seemingly Cassidy, whom I glimpsed across the room with what appeared to be a vaguely amused expression on his face, seemed inclined to be the one to commence matters.

Then from Cassidy's side of the room came a sudden roar, "Rynders! Rynders!"

In through the side door, the same one through which Cassidy and his supporters had entered, came a man of medium height and a knowing smile. He strode to the podium, flanked on either side by a set of toughs—if they were Irish, I'd have said they were *ráibéads*. But these were not Irishmen, nor were they quite Bowery b'hoys, either. They were just toughs who towered over their leader.

Bill Tweed was whispering into my ear, "This is Captain Rynders."

"Oh."

"Con Donoho's rival. The man on horseback."

Then I remembered. Rynders had famously said that he'd dirk every mother's son of a Philadelphian who dared stuff the ballot box for the Whigs on that damp November day in 1844 when he and Con Donoho, each in his own way, helped win the Presidency for James K. Polk. A day when I had been lost somewhere in the trackless wastes of the Great Western Ocean—or had we still been stuck in Galway? I couldn't remember, and anyway, Rynders was about to begin.

As Rynders settled in at the podium, I noticed that the toughs who had come in with him had spread out around the perimeter of the room. There must have been thirty or forty of them, not one of them a member of the volunteer company. Magee's expression was as unreadable as ever. Tweed had fallen quiet and Cassidy's vaguely amused expression had perhaps just a whiff of expect-ant satisfaction.

"Lads!" Rynders began. He had a hard, projecting voice, the voice of a man who was not to be trifled with. Everyone paid rapt attention.

"We've a couple of pieces of business this fine evenin'. Then we can get down to the real business of the evenin'—drinking and gambling ..."

Cheers and huzzahs for "Good ol' Cap'n Rynders" rang out from almost every corner. Magee and his few stalwarts remained silent.

Rynders lifted his hand for quiet, the room hushed and he con-tinued, "Not, mind you, that I'm slighting the mabs, now lads."

The room erupted with laughter—even Magee and his stalwarts cracked a smile or two—and a fresh round of cheers and huzzahs.

"But first, lads," Rynders continued, once more raising his hands for silence. "First, we're going to talk a little about Texas."

"Annex Texas," someone shouted from the crowd.

"No," somebody else cried. "Abolish slavery. Don't give the slavers Texas as well. T'ain't Christian."

I felt like cheering to that. But Magee remained motionless, and so did I.

"Lads," Rynders raised his hands. "Slavery ain't the issue with Texas. So don't listen to that God-damned barnburner. He don't know what he's talking about. I don't care whether you're a hunker or a God-damned barnburner who'd as soon let the niggers run free over the South—Hell, all them damned niggers'll come north here to Gotham and take jobs away from God-fearing Irishmen if they was ever to be freed. And we can't be havin' that, now can we?" There were cheers that soon died away. Rynders continued. "Jobs in Gotham are for Americans—and Irishmen. They ain't for the niggers. But, as I was saying, that ain't the issue with Texas."

"Yes it is!" the same voice shouted. I noticed Rynders's toughs beginning to crane their necks, looking for the man.

Rynders ignored him. "The issue with Texas is freedom. Freedom from the Mexican empire that slaughtered all those fine lads at Goliad and the Alamo. Freedom from perfidious Albion, whose whore of a queen also seeks to rule Texas."

This last raised a roar from every man-jack in the room, yelling and screaming every manner of invective about England.

Rynders raised his hand. "That's right, lads. England wants to rule Texas. Just like they want to rule the Oregon territories. We cannot allow England ..." he paused and then said, "*Sassena!*"

The crowd roared again, heaping still more abuse on the very thought of England.

"... We cannot allow perfidious Albion to rule Texas. We Americans ... all of us ... Democrats and Whigs, Gothamites and Virginians, Boston abolitionists and Mississippi cotton planters ... We all know—or we should know—that the United States of America has a God-given right to rule America from the frozen wastes of Hudson's Bay south as far as America goes and as far west as the Pacific Ocean. We cannot allow any foreign empire a foothold from which to trammel American freedoms. So, I say to you, Mr. President: Go ahead. Annex Texas. Annex California. Annex the Oregon Territories. Spread Old Glory from the Atlantic to the Pacific Ocean—and the map will have your name—James K. Polk—on it for all eternity."

Rynders paused for every man in the crowd to roar his approbation. Any man disinclined to do so was not to be found in Dooley's Long Room on this night.

"I'll conclude by saying that we freedom-loving Americans will dirk every mother's son of an Englishman and a traitor who would dare oppose annexation of Texas."

The roaring reached a crescendo.

Rynders quietened the crowd one more time. "So, I ask you lads, if one of you will kindly second a motion to resolve that this glorious company of American volunteers should support the immediate annexation of Texas."

The motion was seconded.

"Then lads," Rynders said after the cheers had once again subsided. "I take it that the resolution is passed unanimously."

He glanced about in total command of the crowd, making eye contact here and there and fixing on Cassidy and Magee in turn, with everyone waiting for what he had to say next. They didn't have to wait long. "Now lads, let's see about electing a new captain for this illustrious company of volunteers ... I have a suggestion for yers ... Jimmy Cassidy ... how about it?"

The roar coming from Cassidy's supporters and from each of the Empire Club toughs left little doubt as to who the company's next captain would be. Magee's expression was as inscrutable as it had been since we arrived.

CHAPTER 13

Brannagh's Story

THE VERY NEXT AFTERNOON, I WAS SITTING with Brannagh in Battery Park. She and I had been spending more and more time together over the past few weeks, sitting in the park—or in City Hall Park as the fancy took us, talking sometimes, and at other times just sitting quietly. There were few other places we could go. I couldn't afford tea at Astor House or lunch at Delmonico's. Frequently, I had Fíona in tow, particularly when Mary was working, which she seemed to be doing more and more these days. This ruled out just about every other public place we could go, even if I'd been inclined to court Brannagh at any of them. But I didn't resent Fíona's presence. Very much the opposite. I loved her as the sister I had never had. In any case, Fíona and Brannagh loved to talk and play games. On such occasions, I liked watching them. I could not take my eyes off Brannagh, and her being engaged with Fíona gave me ample opportunity to get my fill of gazing at her without having to worry about being too forward.

Today, though, Fíona was with Mary, who had asked me where I was off to as I skittered from our rooms, late for my rendezvous with Brannagh. Mary's reaction was quite muted and not the least bit cautionary when I told her about Brannagh and the fact that I liked her, and also about having come to know her through Fíona. (I obviously elided some of the more sensitive facts—such as my knowledge of Black Muireann's brothel—and about brothels in general, not of course that I was a true sporting man. But Mary was a lady, and one simply should not talk of such matters with a lady—unless that lady were Brannagh, whom I'd met in her own mother's brothel ...) Even so, I had to fairly fly to Battery Park after leaving the boardinghouse, first to secure an ice cream for Brannagh, and then to secure our special park bench, which thankfully was unoccupied.

I had made it just in time, hardly a minute before Brannagh was standing in front of me, blocking my squinting view of the Jersey shore. She was silhouetted beautifully in the sun streaming through the dark broken clouds, which were threatening to perhaps storm in an hour or two. Brannagh was smiling tenderly at me, instantly transporting me to that special universe which existed only when I was with her.

She sat next to me, and I handed her the ice cream—chocolate, of course. She kissed me quickly on the cheek in thanks, and immediately set about demolishing it. After she finished, we sat companionably, watching the gathering storm clouds.

After a while, Brannagh said, "I heard about the militia meeting last night."

"What did you hear?" I was all ears.

"That man Rynders said that abolitionists are not patriotic Americans because they're questioning the spread of slavery to Texas."

"He sure did. But some barnburner spoke up against Rynders, and asked him why slavery should be allowed to spread to Texas when it's annexed. But he was shouted down pretty quickly. A lot of hunkers and Locofocos, pro-slavers, in the crowd, I guess. They were all screaming about the proper place for the colored man—in bondage on a cotton plantation." I sneaked a quick glance at Brannagh. She did not react. "Magee and the boys didn't say anything, though, which was a little odd, because I've always figured that Magee's pretty much a barnburner himself, an anti-slaver, and doesn't have much truck with the hunkers and Locofocos. I think it—Magee's being quiet—had to do with Rynders being there with his Empire Club toughs, and Con not being there to back him up."

I chuckled sardonically, adding, "I've got to say that those Empire Club toughs looked none too happy about that barnburner speaking up about Texas being admitted to the Union as a slave state, solely to benefit slaveowners. Although I don't think they knew who he was, or even if they did, I don't think anything happened to the cove. Pretty brave of him in that crowd. I guess everybody was more focused on Cassidy's stealing a march on Magee on account of his—Cassidy's—being elected the new captain of the volunteer company."

As I thought about it, Magee hadn't seemed too broken up about Cassidy's election as captain. In fact, he had been outright indifferent, which seemed a little odd given his and Cassidy's history. So I figured that Donoho and Rynders had brokered a deal, and Magee knew all about it. Otherwise, the surprise election would have degenerated into a vicious brawl. I resolved to ask Tweed about it the next time I saw him. He'd know. I was sure of that.

Brannagh broke into my train of thought. "Well I heard that you piped up afterwards and said that the barnburner fellow was right. That slavery was immoral, and that the colored man and the white man should be equal."

"Who told you that?" I had said it only to Tweed and a couple of others—Blackie and a couple of other *ráibéads* whom I could trust—or so I thought. I'd regretted saying it at the time, because almost everyone in those days (even more so than today), including the abolitionists, figured otherwise—that the colored man was of a race inferior to the white man.

Brannagh laughed, "I have my ways."

"It wasn't anything."

"Yes it was. Not many white men will say that out loud. Not here in Gotham. Especially not since the election."

"Why not? Abolitionism is respectable—you yourself said that the other day ... the woman whose book you read. Who was it? Oh, yeah, Margaret Fuller."

"That's different."

"Why?"

"She's not here in Gotham, where men such as Rynders run free. And that was you and me talking—in private. Not you to Bill Tweed. Anyway ..." Brannagh looked thoughtful for a moment.

At the time, I didn't think anything about her look. I merely charged ahead with my proposition like the boy I was, "Well, Daniel O'Connell has seen worse from the *Sassenagh*, and he's not afraid to say that slavery should end."

"Well that's because the *Sassenagh*, as you call them, have already abolished slavery."

"True enough."

"You didn't have to say you were an abolitionist. You could have been beaten for that. For the other thing you said ... well, somebody could have killed you over that."

I dismissed her concern, saying that Magee would have protected me.

"I'm not so sure."

"Well, I wasn't being heroic."

She snorted derisively. "What would you call saying out loud at a minstrelsy show that whites and coloreds ought to be equal?"

A reckless bit of bravado. But I didn't say that.

"I'm not proud of having gone to the show," I said instead.

I was actually quite indifferent to the show itself. There were two or three minstrelsy shows running in different theaters around the city on any given evening. It was hard to miss them, and they were wildly popular that year as the new thing—white men parading about on stage in black face, singing faux-Negro songs written by white men about such perennial favorites as Zip Coon and Jim Crow. What had made me feel guilty was discovering that some of it was pretty funny—if you ignored what they said about the coloreds. I hadn't liked the fact that I had laughed, and my father would not have been proud of me for having been there in the first place, let alone finding some of the show funny. So I guess that's why I had piped up to Bill and to Blackie like I did. But I wasn't going to say that to Brannagh.

"Had you ever been to one of those shows before?"

"No."

"Well, you left before it ended, didn't you?" Brannagh looked at me seriously. "You're the first white boy I've ever met who treated me as if I were white."

I thought about Mary's question to me about mulattas all those months ago, as we talked that night about *The Last of the Mohicans* and she told me that the idea that white men and colored women couldn't be together was "stupid." I hadn't said anything then, but now, knowing Brannagh, I knew in my soul that it was a stupid notion. The only problem was that I was almost alone in thinking so. I started to say something to Brannagh about it, but she said, "Shhh. Let me finish."

I sat back on the bench, no longer squinting at the Jersey shore, because the sun was now shadowed by a looming bank of grayish-black clouds.

Brannagh began to talk. "I don't have any real friends … no girls … and certainly no boys. Nobody I can call a friend. Shhh." I closed my mouth again. "White girls can't be my friends—even if they wanted to be—because their mothers won't let them. I'm colored …" she said with more than a trace of bitterness.

I wanted to break in again, but I didn't.

"I can't go talk to the colored girls. What is there to talk about? They can't read … let alone read *Jane Eyre*. And the boys?" She snorted. "All they want to do is play at push-pin with me. I don't know whether the uptown swells want me because I'm an exotic mulatta who can speak proper English … or because my mother's a strumpet, which means that I'm a notch moll as well, and all too ready to play at lift leg with the first boy with a double eagle."

I really kept my mouth shut now.

"The colored boys are just as bad as the white boys because I'm half Irish, and they want that light-skinned mulatta ... as a sort of prize ... I don't know what kind ... Jessie could tell me ... but I don't want to know."

We sat for a moment, both of us silent. I studied the shoreline by Jersey City with particular interest, not daring to look at her. But I could feel her gaze on me.

Brannagh then said, fiercely, scatalogically, like a man, "What the devil am I?"

I was glad to know a rhetorical question when I heard one, though I did sneak a look at her. Brannagh's head was down now, and she was studying her kidskin gloves as she talked.

"I want to be like everyone else, to belong somewhere ... and to marry a nice boy and have babies ..." She looked at me with the merest hint of a smile, "... someday ..."

I smiled back at her, tentatively.

"Momma wants the best for me, but I'm not going to get it on account of this." She touched her face.

I finally spoke, "You're beautiful. You'll be happy ..."

"Not that, you silly boy. You're right. I am beautiful. Every man who sees me tells me so." She touched her face again. "But none of that matters. I'm still nothing but a colored girl with woolly hair," she said brutally. "And I always will be."

Brannagh did not have the woolly hair I had seen on most coloreds—not, I declared to myself, that it would have made a tinker's damn of a difference. Her hair instead flowed beautifully in great waves, just like I imagined Cora Munro's would have, "tresses shining like the black plumage of a raven" that fell luxuriantly past her shoulders when unpinned and not daintily stowed beneath her bonnet. I had seen Brannagh like that only once—that first night when she spied upon me from the shadows. And now I saw her hair again as she impulsively ripped her bonnet off and pulled the pins from her hair, shaking it free. It was beautiful, no doubt, but whether her hair was long and flowing, I decided in that instant, or "woolly," as Brannagh so derisively described it, she was—and always would be—beautiful.

"No white man will ever let me forget the color of my skin— even with this." She grabbed her hair and thrust it towards me. "I will always be a ..." She could not bring herself to say the word. "... to any white man." She practically spat the words at me.

I touched her hair involuntarily. She gently removed my hand and kissed it. We locked eyes.

Finally, I said, "Stop it. Just stop it."

She said nothing.

Our faces were close now. Just a few inches apart. She still gently held my hand, waiting for me to speak.

I hesitated for a moment or two, thinking about what I wanted to say, needed to say, to Brannagh—but had hardly even articulated to myself until this instant, and certainly had never breathed a word of to another human being. Then I plunged in, headfirst and headlong, with a delightful frisson of pure terror, "I've never been with a woman ... or a girl. I've never even kissed a girl." I resolutely thrust my one night with Mary from my mind, telling myself that it had not really happened. "Not Jessie, not anyone. So I won't tell you that I know much about what happens between a man and a woman. But I do believe that you can be happy. And I believe that people can fall in love, even if they are of different colors. Your mother and your father did."

I thought it wise not to say—yet—that she and I could fall in love as well, although I'd long since made my own peace with the color of Brannagh's skin. I thought it even wiser not to delve into Fenimore Cooper and his tragic mulatta heroine, Cora Munro— even if her hair was like Brannagh's. Cora died at the end, because nobody would've bought the book if she'd married a white man (or even a red man, for that matter) and lived happily ever after.

"One more thing, though," I added. "You don't have to be long-headed to see how coloreds are treated here in America. It's despicable. Slavery is despicable." I figured that a further disquisition on Daniel O'Connell's views on the heinous nature of slavery in America was probably out of place at this point. "I never saw a colored man—or woman, for that matter—until I was on the ship coming to America. He was a steward. He worked himself to the bone for two couples and their daughters, none of whom gave him the time of day, even though he, they, and we were all on the same wooden ship in the middle of the ocean when she nearly sank. The worst of it was, those people held themselves out to be better than they were, socially."

I explained to Brannagh the incident on the *Maryann* with the "knight of the barrow pigs" who pretended that he had been a public school boy. She smiled her appreciation of how I had insulted the man without him ever knowing it.

I continued, "Near as I can tell, the Irish're hardly half a step above the coloreds here in Gotham, anyway—public school, bog-trotters or otherwise. If Magee, Tweed and Con Donoho have taught me anything in these last few months, it's that the native Americans loathe us Catholic Irishmen almost as much as they hate the …" I smiled, and said, "I won't use that word you hate so much."

Brannagh didn't say anything, and she wasn't looking at me. She was looking at the ground, her face shadowed by her beautiful hair. I lost sight of where I was going with my speech, and so I stopped, seized by the sudden impulse to kiss her. But I didn't—and was later very glad of it.

Brannagh began to pin her hair back, and in less than a minute, her beautiful tresses were once again thoroughly skewered and covered primly by her bonnet. Then she sat and seemed to think. I let her be.

After a minute or so, she said, "Let me tell you a story."

Brannagh began quietly, in a low voice that reminded me of Mary telling me her story in the dark in that Galway boarding-house so many months ago. I violently thrust that image from my mind and focused on Brannagh and what she had to say.

Brannagh's daddy had run a saloon on Orange Street, right in the heart of the 'Points, just above Paradise Square. His daddy— her grandpa, she said proudly (adding that she never met him, because he'd died long before she was born)—had been a free-jack—a freed slave, she explained—and as coal-black a Negro who ever lived, Brannagh said proudly, standing 6' 4" in his bare feet. So Daddy and his older brother, Uncle Jack, had been born free men, and had been free when slavery ended in New York, not long before Brannagh was born. About that time, Daddy met Momma.

"Momma was just a poor Irish girl." A small, bittersweet smile played on Brannagh's lips. Momma's first husband and her baby were dead from the bloody flux or some other incurable ailment, and Momma was left destitute, forced to the sidewalks of the 'Points, where she hunted cullies late at night, like a bat, to keep body and soul together. Daddy didn't care about any of that, not about what she'd done to survive, where she came from, the color of her skin or her Irish patois. He always said he fell in love with her the first time he saw her traipsing across Paradise Square one night under the gas lamp and into the shadows. He caught her before she disappeared. Brannagh smiled, and said that Momma didn't care about Daddy's skin color, neither. So Daddy swept Momma off her feet, and the preacher at St. Philip's, over on Centre Street, married them. Brannagh remembered what a grand church St. Philip's had been when she was a little girl.

Daddy and Momma lived above Daddy's saloon—and Brannagh was born there.

"Daddy was a real swell," Brannagh said proudly. "He wore a silk waistcoat and a top hat and carried a gold fob watch. His saloon was a pretty flash place." Then Brannagh turned fierce again, just like a man, "'Til that ..." she paused, as if she were skipping a word "... Jim Crow mobocracy—each one of 'em a ... hunker—burned it down in '34. I was just a little pickanniny, as Daddy used to call me, back then." Brannagh smiled in recollection.

As she told the story, the mob, driven into a frenzy by groups of abolitionists meeting in colored churches, had broken into the Chatham Street Chapel and St. Philip's and all the colored stores and saloons on Centre Street, and demolished them for no reason other than they were owned by colored folks. Brannagh's Uncle Jack was singing in the choir at the Chatham Street Chapel when the mobocracy broke in, smashing windows and breaking down the door. Uncle Jack and a couple of others had tried to stop the mob, but they were beaten to within an inch of their lives. Worse, the police took six of them away—including Uncle Jack—all of them accused on the most dubious of grounds of being maroon-ers who had escaped from bondage down in the Old Dominion. Uncle Jack always said afterwards that he had been lucky that he hadn't been sent south and sold into bondage as an escaped slave. Brannagh explained that many free coloreds—and even swarthy whites—were sold down south into slavery every year—even though they were free-born.

"Can you imagine?" she asked.

I could not, and we sat. I was struck quiet at the thought of a white person—or a freejack, for that matter—being sold into slavery.

After a while, Brannagh began talking again. Her uncle, per-haps spurred by the horror of being arrested and almost sold into slavery, moved to Canada, where they hate coloreds less, "and at least you aren't called ... that word," she said disconsolately. "I can't tell you how many times as I was growing up that Momma told me that Uncle Jack's moving to Canada was the best thing for him, because it was getting harder all the time for a colored person to live a good life in Gotham. Momma says that it was so much easier to be colored in the old days, before the big riot.

"But Daddy was a stubborn cuss, and he wouldn't leave Gotham, no matter how difficult life became. He rebuilt his saloon, and it became the biggest, and best-known lushery in the 'Points. He had the best musicians—and dancers. Even that *Sassenagh* writer, Charles Dickens, came to visit."

"*Sassenagh?*" I mocked. "You've never even been to *Eirinn*."

"Well, I'm at least as Irish as I am colored," she retorted. "Even if everyone sees me as nothing more than a smoked Irish moll."

A new one on me, except that the epithet really fit Brannagh … and added immeasurably to her allure.

"So, as I was saying before you so rudely interrupted me." Brannagh positively flounced, even though we remained perched on the park bench. "They say that Mr. Dickens was mighty impressed with Master Juba, who was dancing at Daddy's the night that Mr. Dickens came in."

"Who's Juba?"

"Only the greatest dancer who ever lived. He's in England now, making a fortune tap dancing with the Virginia Minstrels."

"Who are they?"

"This from the boy who went to the blackface minstrelsy show last night?" She giggled. "The Virginia Minstrels—who aren't from Virginia, by the way—are just the best known minstrelsy show ever—and the ones who started the whole craze. Just a couple of years ago, they were out of work. Then they put their show on, faces daubed with charcoal and greasepaint, playing the banjo, the violin, banging on the tambourine and singing songs such as *Happy Are We, Darkies So Gay*." Brannagh snorted derisively. "And then, swimming in the brass already, they're off to *Sassana* to play for Queen Victoria. Amazing. Of course, none of them can dance, so they hired Master Juba to come to England with them to star in their minstrelsy show. I guess I can't blame Juba. It's the rhino … and lots of it."

"So why is Master Juba so famous?"

"Oh you've never seen anyone dance like that." Brannagh's eyes sparkled. "Everybody came to see him, especially after Mr. Dickens wrote about him and Daddy. Daddy's place was even more popular than before. Everyone wanted to have fun and enjoy himself—or herself. All sorts of women went to Daddy's place, even reps more than a couple of huckleberries above the persimmon. Suitably escorted, of course." Brannagh tossed her head just like the finest nob's rep. "When I was just a little kid, I sneaked into Daddy's saloon and watched Juba dance."

"Your Momma didn't catch you?" I sniggered. "And send you to bed without supper?"

She ignored me.

"Momma didn't catch me that night on account of Master Juba coming out to dance just as Momma was making her rounds. Instead of dancing by himself, as he usually did, Juba grabbed Momma's hand, and twirled her about as if he were the most aristocratical, uptown swell around. They danced a *pas de deux* as just the violin played. Daddy was beaming, because Momma looked so lovely and danced so elegantly, flashing the merest hint of ankle above her brocade ankle boots."

The crowd hushed as they danced, Brannagh said. "You could hear Juba's—and even Momma's—shoes on the floorboards. But Juba's shoes were so much louder. That's when I realized that Master Juba had something on the bottom of his shoes. He showed me later what it was—thin, little iron plates on the heels and toes of his shoes that went tap, tap, tap as he danced. Well, Juba gradually began to dance a little faster, and then faster still, until the taps began to sound like a drumroll. Momma started laughing when she realized what he was doing, and went along. He was swinging her around as if she were a rag doll, all in time to the banging drum and the fiddle—and the trumpet, which broke in over the top of the other instruments, spitting hot needles of *teas*, as Momma called it. Juba'd leave Momma twirling in the middle of the floor—everybody had shuffled out of the way to give them plenty of room to dance. After she stood aside, he danced by himself, his fingers snapping, his feet tap, tap, tapping all the time.

"Then back he went to Momma, sweeping her around for another *pas de deux*, except this one was at breakneck speed, as fast as a galloping horse. Momma was done for after that, and she retired to Daddy—with everyone shouting huzzah!

"But Juba wasn't done. Not by a long shot. With a big grin on his face, Juba started to spin on his toes. First one, then the other, then from heel to toe and toe to heel, one foot at a time, then both. His legs seemed to change as he moved. They were made of wood at one point, then of wire in the next instant. Then he was dancing as if he had two left legs and then two right legs. Sometimes, it was as if there were three or four legs all going at once—wire in one instant, wooden in the next. The music had stopped almost immediately when Juba began to dance by himself, except for an occasional flourish from the drummer or the fiddler, just to let Juba know that they were there, with him, appreciating him. All the while, you could hear the tap, tap, tapping of Juba's shoes—even over the noise of the crowd, as they whistled and whooped their praise.

"Juba was sweating like a madman. So out he popped the brightest purple handkerchief, wiping his head and hair down, all the while tap, tap, tapping away. Finally, Juba looked like he was beginning to tire. He slowed down. Some of the coves were whistling, telling him to keep dancing. One ignoramus even called Juba a dumb ..." Brannagh shrugged instead of mouthing the word, "for wearing himself out. But that *bastún* was hushed right up by a glare from Daddy. Anyhow, Juba wasn't done. He was just playing with us, because all of a sudden he leaped on top of the bar—drinks flying everywhere, whether into rescuing hands or otherwise—and he began to dance up there to the renewed whoops and whistles and hollers of his enraptured audience. Juba finally finished with a spectacular slide down the entire length of the bar that ended by where Daddy was standing. Daddy coolly handed him a cold beer, which he drained off in a single quaff. The crowd went wild."

"That must've been something."

"Where do you think Magee got his ideas from about the music and the *teas* of it? He was there. He saw it. And Momma told him that the music and dancing was the smartest thing he could do if he wanted his place to be successful. They were always close, Momma and Magee, particularly after Daddy died."

Her face, which had been so radiant with the telling of Juba's dancing, became graven stone as she softly returned to Charles Dickens. "Everything changed after Mr. Dickens's book was published. You know, the one where he made Master Juba famous. Daddy's place was crowded every night. Lots of outsiders came now that it was famous all over the world, and there was plenty of brass coming in. Momma and Daddy were so happy, and that was a good thing. They moved out from over the saloon, and bought a house farther up on Orange Street, in the Fourteenth Ward. It was nicer up there, and nobody bothered us, even though Daddy and I were the only coloreds on the block. Momma pulled me from the school for colored children and started sending me uptown to see Mr. Graham so that I could become a proper young lady with all the social graces.

"Daddy even bought a Colt revolving pistol off some Texas gambler named Walker, who was tapped out and wanted to play another few rounds of faro before retiring for the evening. Daddy always liked the stories the gambler told him: that he was a captain in some outfit called the Texas Rangers, and that he and fourteen other Texas Rangers had used these revolvers in a nasty little scrape with 75 or a hundred Comanche warriors out on the frontier some-where and won a great victory, purely because the Colt revolving pistols held five shots and the Indians only had bows and arrows."

"What a fantastical weapon," I exclaimed. "How did it work?"

"I don't know," she replied, making me feel quite stupid for asking. Her Daddy said that the gambler had called the pistol a Colt Paterson revolver, and he told Daddy confidentially that he was on a trip to New York to meet with Mr. Colt regarding some improvements to the pistol that would make it an even better kill-ing machine. Brannagh shivered a little and said that her daddy had used those very words when he told her the story. "In any case," she continued, "Daddy kept this revolving pistol behind the bar with Magee, who was his most trusted bartender—along with two extra cylinders already loaded with bullets, just in case.

"But sometimes there was trouble. Daddy didn't brook any horseplay from anyone—unless it was Juba and the band cutting up. So he started keeping a horsewhip behind the bar right along-side his revolving pistol, and all his bartenders—white or col-ored—carried cudgels, knives and brickbats of one sort or another. But they were almost never used. Most times, trouble ended with a mere threat." Brannagh smiled wryly. "That's on account of Daddy being a foot taller than most men. But Daddy's temper gave him particular fits when some cove would call any colored man—even one of the colored bartenders—a bad name."

Brannagh paused, her face twisted in pain. When she spoke again, her voice rose. I thought she was going to burst into tears. But she didn't. Her voice hardened. "But it wasn't his temper that did Daddy in. It was his pride that led to the death of him. Momma told him that it would happen eventually if he didn't watch him-self. So did Con Donoho—Con was such a great friend of Daddy's back then."

I nodded, remembering that Magee had told me that once, when it was just him and me at one of his afternoon levees, that he and Donoho and Brannagh's daddy had all known each other back then, and had been the very best of friends—and Magee had gotten his start in life working for Brannagh's daddy. Magee smiled sadly, noting that it was unaccountable that a white man would work for a colored. But there it was, and he didn't regret a single moment of it.

Brannagh continued talking to me softly, saying that one night, in the middle of the saloon, some rednecked cove had proclaimed to the crowd that he was a slave trader come to pick up some runaways. He had said that in a saloon owned by a colored man—right in front of a colored bartender, who tried to buy him off with a free whiskey. To keep the peace, don't you know. Brannagh ended in a tone that mixed outrage and pain. She also said something else under her breath. I didn't ask what.

"It got worse," Brannagh whispered. Her daddy came over to settle the situation down, just like he did a dozen times a night with some cove or another who got a little out of hand. Except this time, this benighted redneck called him a "damned field ..." who belonged down on the plantation, and maybe he, the redneck blackbirder, was just the man to send her daddy back down there, where he came from, and where all them ... darkies (Brannagh's word) ... belonged, on the plantation, picking cotton. Nobody knew why the man said that other than to make trouble. She noted that it had been Magee who had told her that he thought her daddy was going to explode over the insult made to his very face. But her daddy didn't. He just stood there and stared coolly at the man for a moment, as if taking his measure—which he found thoroughly inadequate.

Only then did her daddy nod to Magee. Magee pulled his cudgel out from under the bar—a barrel stave strengthened by an iron pipe and wrapped in leather—leaped over the bar, and hit the redneck with it, once, hard. Then Magee said as loud as can be that this blackbirder was nothing more than a sluiced redneck sodomite who should just be thrown out of the joint. So Magee and several coves in the crowd grabbed the man and threw him out the door, into the hands of the local night watchman. Everybody jeered as the redneck was frogmarched out of the place, bleeding from his head, which he was holding in his hands. Once he was gone, the band struck up again and Juba began to dance. Brannagh's daddy ordered a round of drinks for the coves who helped throw the redneck blackbirder out, and everybody promptly forgot about the son of a bitch.

Brannagh snorted that it was too bad Blackie hadn't been around in those days, for he "would've taken care of that bastard forever, and then he could have been forgotten for good."

Brannagh stopped, and looked shocked at herself for having used such a word.

Then she said defiantly, "Well, he was. He was a goddamned bastard."

She put her head on my shoulder, I hugged her close and we sat quietly for a minute.

That wasn't the end of it, though, she continued. The redneck came back a couple of days later. This time, he had a couple of confederates. When he came in, the music had just stopped, and there was a lull in the place, Magee said, where you could hear a pin drop, even though it was a Saturday night and there were 300 coves and morts there, every one of them sweating with the *teas* of the place.

The redneck had a pistol with him. He was waving it around, yelling loudly for that "… field … that Dickens loves so much" to show himself, Brannagh again pausing where the words she hated so much belonged in her story. His two confederates looked like they wanted to melt into the crowd or into the walls themselves, if they could have, instead of in the middle of Brannagh's daddy's place, side by side with a crazy man who was waving a barking iron and seeking a showdown with Brannagh's daddy.

"Nobody moved except for Daddy and Magee. Daddy grabbed his horsewhip and Magee grabbed Daddy's revolver. Daddy walked over to the redneck, who was still waving his gun around, and said something quietly to him. Magee said that Daddy had been 'exquisitely polite.'

"The redneck stepped back," Brannagh said in a whisper, "and without saying another word, simply shot my daddy dead, declaring 'take that, you damned …'" Brannagh finally said the word, spitting out its foul taste. It was as if I could hear Magee's harsh language echoing through Brannagh's telling of this part of her story. Brannagh finished quickly, "Magee shot the redneck. Not that it mattered, of course, because Daddy was dead. The crowd tore the wounded redneck apart, and nobody quite knows what happened to his two confederates.

"Momma ran the saloon after that. But running a saloon as a woman was tough. So she sold out to a fellow named Pete Williams—a colored man, just like Brannagh's daddy. And Pete Williams's place continues to this day to be one of the most popular spots in all of the 'Points, and perhaps in all of Gotham."

Brannagh's mother started over again with what she knew best: prostitution. Except this time, neither she nor anybody she worked with was going to be a bat flitting about the sidewalks late at night, looking for cullies. Instead, Muireann took the profit from selling out to Pete Williams, and with a little help from Magee and Con Donoho, went over to Church Street, where she is now.

Brannagh laughed acidly after she finished her story. "Here I am. Three more damned peoples I could not imagine."

"Three?" I asked. "The coloreds and the Irish are damned as surely as the sun will rise tomorrow. But who's the third?"

"Don't forget women," she answered. "I'm thus triply damned."

Not long after that, the wind picked up and a few drops of rain fell. Brannagh and I hurried from Battery Park, and I walked her back to Church Street. We slipped through the gate to the side door, which was under a porch, just as the rain started to pour down. We stood there for a while, neither of us saying much. It was then that I kissed Brannagh for the first time. I asked her politely before I did so. She said I was a silly goose, because I didn't have to ask.

CHAPTER 14

Election Day

⌒

"WAKE UP, SLEEPYHEAD."

I opened my eyes to Mary smiling at me indulgently, her eyes hollow with fatigue. She had been getting home later and later over the past few weeks—with muttered explanations of too much work to do cleaning the house up in Gramercy Park.

Not that I'd passed much of last night abed. It had only been a couple of hours since Charlie and I had finished plotting the final odds on today's election: who had placed what bets with which bookies. Charlie had also once again reviewed with me how he had strategically laid off on some of our fellow bookies a number of huge bets that he had taken from uptown punters. Betting on the election had been heavy on both the Democrat and American Republican sides—with just a little money going to the Whigs, who had been left for dead in the 1844 city election, when Hizzoner Jimmy Harper had been elected.

The papers—Horace Greeley's *Tribune* chief among them—were saying that Gothamites were wearying mightily of Hizzoner's vain attempts to wean them from their evil drinking, gambling and whoring ways, epitomized in the minds of many when on the Fourth of July he offered them iced Croton water instead of good, honest whiskey! Perhaps Gothamites were also wearying of the nativist baiting of the newly awakening Irish strength in some of the wards—Irish strength that now also supported annexing

Texas. But everybody was saying that it was likely Hizzoner was going to be reelected because the opposition—the Democrats and the Whigs—were so badly split. Charlie didn't spend much time thinking about such political folderol, as he put it, and he wasn't interested in the knowing of why Gothamites were perhaps turning against Hizzoner. Nor was he interested in why Hizzoner might be able to return to office. He just knew what his numbers were telling him.

You see, the way Charlie had it figured—as best as I could follow—just about every sucker in Gotham—the sort of fellows who thought they understood the science of wagering, whether at poker or gambling on elections—had spent the days and weeks running up to the election watching the odds slowly shift so much in Hizzoner's favor that he was likely going to return to office in style, and would just as likely drag minions such as that Scotch-Irish *bastún*, Cassidy, right along with him for a big Common Council majority. That's because every punter in Gotham knew that election returns always followed the betting odds—that is, Charlie had noted drily on a couple of occasions, except when they don't.

So much money had gone on Hizzoner in the last few days that, by the time betting had closed in the wee hours of the morning of election day (by general, if unspoken, consensus amongst the city's bookies), Harper had become a 3-1 favorite to win re-election against the Democratic candidate, William T. Havemeyer—helped in no small part, Charlie had noted to Magee and Donoho earlier that evening, by a very large bet placed by Cassidy himself (along with several other bets placed by his friends and backers), at midnight last night with a bookie whom Charlie knew well. Charlie said that Cassidy must have gone all-in because he had given the bookie the title to his saloon as collateral for his bet.

But that wasn't the whole story, Charlie had said with a smile, repeating what he had told me several days earlier. "Think about what coves is bettin' their brass on the American Republicans. It ain't the insiders, on account o' the fix bein' in and they're bein' in the know. No sir. It's every other dumb flat what thinks he's in the know 'oo's bettin' on 'Izzoner."

Rynders, Donoho and the other Democratic power brokers, along with a few key Whigs who could not abide the thought of another term with Hizzoner, had worked a deal—arranging who would win up and down the ticket, from the mayoral contest to the least of the elections this year (but the most important of them all to Magee, and to me, as I was to find out—who would win the Sixth Ward's assistant alderman's seat). Cassidy's election as captain of the militia company had been merely a small sideshow—a bit of subterfuge designed to lull Cassidy and his American Republican bettors into thinking that Rynders was now in the American Republican camp, supporting Cassidy, the breakaway Democrat, running against Magee, the Sixth Ward Tammany candidate.

But the flats didn't know this, and so they were following the odds. The beauty of it was, Con had observed with a sly grin a few days earlier as we passed yet another afternoon in Magee's saloon, that Hizzoner would have just as soon shut down gambling and whoring forever and drinking whiskey on Sundays and the Fourth of July (and every other one of Gotham's favored recreations) as he would have gone to church on Sunday. A perfect Morton's Fork, I thought to myself—two equally insalubrious tines. If these noddles were to win their bets on election day, Hizzoner's reforming ways would forevermore put paid to gambling as a way of life in Gotham, thus ruining all that they treasured. But if Harper were to be cast from office? Well, that particular tine would have its own pain to impart to those punters who were so foolish as to have backed Hizzoner with their chink.

Conversely, it was an equally perfect opportunity for the insiders—as long as nothing unexpected happened. So Magee and Donoho, as fully paid-up insiders, decided to go all-in themselves, betting on Havemeyer to replace Hizzoner—as well as on Magee himself. In fact, they had gone much more than all-in, and had bet on time—as they called it in the gambling hells in those days. That is, they were being good for their word to the dozen or so bookies across the city who were making a big book for the cash they would owe if they lost. But with the fix in … I'd placed a pretty penny all of my own with Charlie on the strength of being in the know.

"Wake up," Mary repeated.

I must have nodded off again.

"A lot to do today." Mary sat down in one of our two chairs and gathered her robe around herself, having shed as she did every dawn her worn, almost disreputably worn, work clothes the instant she walked in the door. She closed her eyes and luxuriated in the warm June sun that was just beginning to peek through the freshly scrubbed window—Mary, as ever, remained fanatical about cleanliness and order, although now that we were no longer on the ship, she was rather insistent—and rightly so—that I do my share of the housework. Even Fíona did her share of the chores—with a little gentle guidance.

"Yep," I grunted as I sat in the other chair. I took a sip of coffee and felt more like talking. "Bill Tweed and I are to patrol the polls and make sure that the lads are out to man them and guard them. Then we're off for our voting prisoners. So we've got to get going early."

"Voting prisoners?" Mary asked.

"Oh yeah. I didn't tell you about them. We're bringing in fifty prisoners from Blackwell's Island to visit every polling place between Corlears Hook and Paradise Square. That'll be hundreds of votes."

"Donoho's imagination …"

"Oh that wasn't Con," I replied proudly. "Bill and I dreamed it up." Then I admitted, "Really, it was Bill who came up with the idea when we were talking with Con. Like I said, those prisoners're going to be worth hundreds of votes."

"What about Cassidy and his boys stuffing the boxes?" Before I could reply, Mary demanded, "What about them running Magee's boys off? Lúcás and some of them are right dangerous."

"Without Rynders?" I replied confidently. "Cassidy can't run us off or hurt us today. He doesn't have the backing."

"You really think that Rynders and his Empire Club toughs'll stay home on Park Place today and not help Cassidy?"

"Yep."

"Does Cassidy know that?"

"Not yet." I explained that keeping Rynders's double-cross of Cassidy a secret until today was all about lulling Cassidy into betting his bottom dollar—which he had done at the very last moment on election eve." I grinned with the pride of being privy to the trick being turned on Cassidy.

"You see," I continued seriously, "Magee and Donoho mean to ruin Cassidy. Not just win the election."

"You're in a dangerous game, Billy."

I shook my head. "Con and Magee say it's in the bag. So, there's naught to worry about. Anyway, how do you know what's dangerous?" I almost said, "All you are is a housemaid in Gramercy Square, and I'm going to reap a fortune today, because I am in the know." But I didn't. Instead, I said, "You hardly even know who Con Donoho is."

"Billy," she replied patiently. "I'm alive. I live in the 'Points. I live in Magee's boardinghouse. I know Magee. I know Donoho. I know every mother's son of them. I know what they do. It's no secret."

"So?" I said, perhaps a little more truculently than I wanted to.

Mary shook her head in frustration. "You're … what's the word … impulsive." Every so often, Mary's English deserted her. Nothing like back in Galway and on the *Maryann*. But occasionally as now it did, and I loved her for it. Her proper English was back in place instantly, though. "You're still a boy. And this is no game—at least not for a boy such as yourself."

"I can take care of myself."

"Well, you won't be taking care of yourself if you go looking for trouble like you did on nominating night. Magee told you to stay away …"

"He was happy to have me there afterwards."

"He hardly noticed you were there until Blackie told him— the next day. And it was still foolish."

"But nothing happened."

"Nothing happened? Magee half beaten to death?" There was a note of anguish in her voice that surprised me, although, as I thought about it, perhaps I did see her just briefly that night in the saloon, just after Magee and Cassidy's bruising fight.

"You like Magee. A lot." I surprised myself with the sudden insight.

"None of your business. And don't change the subject."

Her look told me not to press, so I said, "Yeah, well, nothing happened to me. I was in the balcony. Spectating. Nothing more."

"But next time …"

"I'm taking boxing lessons. From Blackie … and from Magee, too. When he's there."

And I had, too. I was a skinny young *ponach*, as Magee (and everyone else, it seemed) liked to remind me of from time to time. A *ponach*—a word that Tweed had simplified to "punk"— who needed toughening up, a task which Blackie was only too happy to undertake. The testimonials to Blackie's enjoyment of it were numbered in the many slaps, pats and light punches he landed on my jaw, my nose and just about every other part of my body.

"A fat lot o' good that'll do you."

I also loved Mary for her combativeness, which every so often peeked through her newly acquired (and still maturing) gentility. She was the toughest woman I'd ever known—not that I'd known very many.

"'Specially if some *bastún* like Lúcás were ever to come at you with that ridiculous knife of his—it looks like a sword. *Dia Uas!*"

"His Arkansas toothpick?" I asked innocently. I didn't mention Lúcás's barking iron. Let Mary bring that up, if she knew.

"And that silly gun of his, too." Mary sniffed contemptuously. "Thank the good Lord it'll probably explode and kill him when he pulls the trigger. But that isn't the point. He'd kill you for no reason at all, if he had the chance."

"Like Brannagh's father was killed?" I didn't know why I said that, bringing Brannagh out there between Mary and me. Perhaps I was being defensive because Mary had in essence voiced to me my own very real—if inchoate—fear of Lúcás, a fear which I wouldn't share with her, just as I hadn't shared with her my fear of the murdered *cábóg* on the *Maryann*, a bumptious bully who had been positively harmless compared to the seemingly homicidal menace of Lúcás.

Mary stared at me before replying, "Yes. Just like Brannagh's father."

"She told me the story."

Mary looked at me directly. "You and Brannagh ... you're getting to be friends?"

I smiled, "Yes."

Mary didn't answer for a moment. Then she said, "Watch yourself ... and Brannagh."

"Why?"

"You're both young ... and impetuous."

I returned her gaze. "I am a gentleman, you know."

"I know you are, Billy Gogan. More than you can possibly imagine, I know. You are a rare man in this wicked city for being a gentleman. Billy ..." She seemed to think the better of what she had been just about to say. Instead, she said at barely more than a whisper, "Just be careful. That's all."

I didn't reply, and we sat in silence.

Finally, I asked, "You really think that Gotham is that wicked?"

"Yes," she said. "Yes, it is."

"Then we should leave. Go west. Like we used to talk about."

"We should," Mary said wistfully. "You and I could have a great adventure. Go on a canal boat as far as we can go. Then strike west. See the Rocky Mountains your father told you about. Between us, we've got enough money put away. Anyway, you'd be safer out there."

I looked at her quizzically.

Mary opened her mouth to say something, but she seemed to reconsider, contenting herself with saying, "You know, you 'n' me 'n' Fíona. We'll be away from all this terrible wickedness."

She sighed and we once more sat quietly. I let pass the oddness of what she'd said, and I instead thought about how much brass we'd have in just a day or so, and what that would do for our prospects once we were shot of Gotham.

Then she asked, "But what about Fíona?"

"What about her?" I replied, not quite understanding her. "She comes west with us. It's her adventure, too."

"Of course, she would." Mary sounded shocked that an alternative to Fíona coming west with us could be imagined. "Oh, yer such an eejit. Such a dense b— ... man, sometimes. What I meant was that we've got her in a wonderful school over at St. Peter's. She'll be an *ardollamh* if she stays at school. I don't want to lose that."

"We can both teach her."

"You can," she said flatly. "I can't. I can barely read. This accent ... my English ... it's all a veneer. It's what I've picked up at the big house ..." Her eyes flickered almost imperceptibly. "Both in Ireland and here," she finished quickly. "I don't want her to grow up like me—not being able to read or write or to be able to do her sums."

"I'll be her tutor."

Mary sighed again, and looked at me. "That's a lot to ask …"

"I've told you I'm going to do it."

"I know."

We sat for a while longer and Mary told me about the growing frustration among our fellow Irish denizens of the 'Points about Hizzoner's new police force—Harper's Police, a handpicked (by Harper himself) force of native-born—and nativist—bullies. They were every bit as corrupt as the complaisant watchmen—who were still about, protecting us—and utterly vicious to Irishmen, Jews, dutchies and coloreds outside of the 'Points, and too afraid to venture into the 'Points except in squads of a dozen or more. I replied that, after today, with any luck, that threat would be over when all good Irish and dutchy Democrats had voted to give Hizzoner his marching orders.

With that, I gave Mary a hug, and she blessed me as she always did now that she had become a regular churchgoing woman.

I met Tweed at Magee's saloon. We were on our way out to our first poll when Magee strolled in, looking every bit as tired as Mary had. Of course, this was the first time I'd ever seen Magee up at 6:30 in the morning—unless I'd been up with him and Charlie all night, counting the brass or some such thing. He barely acknowledged us as he went to the bar to pour himself a whiskey. As we left, we heard Magee call after us, "Bring home them votes, boys. Bring home them votes."

Tweed gave him an airy farewell wave, and we went off to find some votes. We had hardly gone around the corner when we ran into Lúcás Dineen and half a dozen Cassidy stalwarts.

Tweed was nonchalant, "Top o' the morning to you, lads. Didn't think I'd see the likes o' you down here in the 'ould bloody Sixth, even if your boyo is trying to win here." His tone turned slightly mocking. "Everybody's voting square down here in the Sixth, today, lads. You'll be lucky to get a score of votes in this Irish ward."

Lúcás made to go around Tweed without a word when Bill reached out and touched him on the lapel, saying, "You're working for the wrong side, you know. They hate the Irish. And they're going to lose today."

"What do you care? Ya jockie *bastún*. What do yer know 'bout it? Yer no more Irish than the Pope, ya' fucking kiltie."

"Scots, Irish … Cassidy's no more Irish than I am—he's a Presbyterian Scotsman, just like me—except, I like the Irish. Cassidy doesn't. He's nothing more than a two-bit bootlicker who's kissing Hizzoner's ring just because Con Donoho favored Magee for this election. All he had to do was wait his turn—but he couldn't. Anyhow, to an Irishman, a Scotsman, a German— does it really matter where you're from when Harper and his American Republicans hate anyone who's not a Methody native- born *Sassenagh*?"

"How can you even say that word? You don't even know what it means."

"I know well enough."

I interjected, "Lúcás, Cassidy's just using you …"

"Go fuck yersel', Gogan," Lúcás sneered. "Ye're naught but a pouffe what diddles little nigger kinchen …"

"Fuck you, Dineen," I said involuntarily.

"We'll see who's going to fuck who …"

"Whom," I said. "You ignorant …"

"I'll gut you …"

Lúcás's toughs crowded behind him, muttering. Tweed stepped between Lúcás and me, palms up.

Lúcás pulled back and said to Tweed and me both, "One night, very late, boyo. You and the pouffe, and it's this …" He pulled his enormous knife partly from its scabbard. As he did, I saw his decrepit little barking iron, stuffed into his belt. "Me 'n' Cap'n Hackum."

With that, he and his toughs were gone.

~

Tweed and I said nothing to each other for the next ten minutes as we walked to the first poll. There was a watchman outside and two election board officials inside—two men whom I had met in my street-sweeping days and who were constant companions of Con Donoho. They gave us a hearty halloa and a big wink to the watchman, who had followed us in.

"How's business been, boys?" Tweed asked.

"Slow so far. No repeaters as yet." One of them replied with another elaborate wink to the complaisant watchman.

"We'll be back in a while," Tweed replied, and we left for Corlears Hook, stopping at several other polling stations along the way.

In those days, Gotham was an amazingly small city when you got right down to it. Neighborhoods were measured in numbers of streets and blocks that often could be counted on one hand with fingers to spare. We skirted around the edge of the Bowery— no sense in running into any more of Cassidy's thugs, particularly when we wouldn't have been on our own home turf like we had been when we saw Lúcás. Then we plunged down to Madison Street, where we went into a tumbledown boardinghouse.

Blackie was there with several disreputable-looking blokes, some of them obviously drunk.

"These the coves?"

Blackie nodded. "Some. There's another two score or more upstairs with a bailiff. They all spent the night here—on a field day from Blackwell's Island, they are." He chuckled. "They've eaten— and got peloothered. They've had a regular *clabhsúr* these past few hours ... of course, the good Lord knows they needed it after being in limbo." He shivered. Then he guffawed and gestured to a slattern of uncertain sobriety. "And they all had a right bit o' *flah*. They was all right happy, even if some o' them cows warn't quite up to Black Muireann's standards."

On cue, the slattern, pushed along by half a dozen others in varying states of dishabille and sobriety crowded by us and out the front door, driven by a man who must have been the bailiff, dressed as he was. As the last of the slatterns was ushered from the boardinghouse, the bailiff turned to Blackie and said, "Forty-nine of them. All of them ready to go. Where to first, Blackie?"

Blackie looked at Tweed and me. I answered, "We're going to work our way down Broadway and then over into the Tenth Ward, and then down into the Sixth at the end of the day. We've a dozen polling places to visit before dark. Then ..."

"Then, sir," the bailiff interceded. "I believe that there may be a number of escapes."

We spent the next several hours leading these worthy voters from one polling station to another. Each time, they all lined up and gave different names than at the last polling station. Every one of them voted a straight Democratic ticket, and thus steadily added to W. T. Havemeyer's totals. By the time we reached the Sixth Ward, we had attracted some additional followers as Bill and I were seen to be handing a shilling apiece to our blokes as they left each polling station. There must have been seventy-five or more men straggling for half a block behind us, with Tweed leading them along, looking for all the world like the Pied Piper of Hamlin.

As we approached the last polling station, which was a particularly disreputable lushery up on Bayard Street, I had moved ahead of Tweed's parade to prepare the election board officials for the onslaught. At the entrance, I bumped into the good Reverend Simpson, who was being trailed by the same colored girl I had seen him with the day I had searched the Old Brewery for Mary and Fíona.

"Good day, Reverend." I tipped my hat to him.

He looked at me blankly, clearly not remembering me. "Good day, sir." With a small bow, he swept in front of me into the lushery. The colored girl settled down to patiently wait for her master. I followed him in, where a rather befuddled looking fellow, a battered hat in hand, was attempting to vote.

"Your first name, sir?" The election board clerk blinked at a prospective voter, who was swaying, clearly the worse for drink. The clerk looked familiar, but I couldn't quite place him.

"Aah ..." The prospective voter scratched his head in thought and swayed a little more. Finally, he focused on Simpson, and said, "Why, hello, Reverend Simpson!"

With a wink to the watchman and then to me, the election clerk said to the drunk voter, his face transformed into a mask of unctuous solicitude for the legal niceties of voting, "You're the Reverend Simpson, aren't you?"

The drunk gave the clerk a mystified look, and then as comprehension dawned, he snarled, "Why of course, ya louse. Who the devil did ye think I was? The good Lord himself?"

Simpson opened his mouth to say something and then shut pan as the watchman standing behind the clerk snorted.

The clerk wordlessly handed the drunk a ballot and pointed to a name on the page, presumably that of W.T. Havemeyer. The drunk shakily carved his "X" on the ballot, which the clerk scooped up and deposited in the ballot box.

As the drunk lurched away, the clerk looked up. "Hello, Reverend."

"Good afternoon, Mr. Freely. Who was that man?"

"Why, Reverend," the clerk replied, "that was Reverend Simpson."

"But I'm Reverend Simpson."

"Of course you are, Reverend. Here's your ballot."

The clerk and the watchman both started to laugh at the consternation on Simpson's face as he once again opened his mouth and then said nothing, this time resigning himself to voting without further ado.

While Simpson filled out his ballot, I beckoned to the clerk and whispered to him quietly, "Got about seventy-five more votes for you. Got enough ballots?"

Freely smiled at me. "For any friend of Con Donoho's and Magee's, I'll always find enough names."

"Thanks very much," I replied, finally remembering where I knew Freely from—he was most often found passing the day as yet another stalwart member of Con Donoho's retinue, lighting Con's cigar and fetching a whiskey whenever Con looked a little parched.

As I left the lushery, Simpson was standing at the curb, his back to me and to his colored girl. I reckoned that he probably was wondering about whom he could complain to about rampant voter fraud. The colored girl looked up at me as solemnly as she had at the Old Brewery, her tract in hand. She seemed to recognize me, though, as I held my finger to my lips.

I turned to Simpson and said, "Reverend, do you recompense your colored girl for the tracts she hands out?"

Simpson spun around with an irritated look, "Eh?" He recovered himself quickly, "Why, my good man, she does it out of love for the Good Shepherd, Himself." He crossed himself quickly. "No recompense needed."

"My dear Reverend, then how does she survive?"

"Why, I keep her, of course ... Why do you ask?"

"Well, Reverend," I drawled as best I could. "That sure sounds a lot like slavery, don't it?"

Simpson spluttered, "How dare you."

"You don't pay her. You keep her?" Rage flared—why it arose, I didn't understand. "That, sir, is slavery."

The colored girl's eyes widened—whether in fear or surprise, I couldn't tell.

Simpson protested. "I, sir, proudly support abolishing that cursed abomination of slavery." Then he looked at the girl with what likely passed for affection in his mind. "Jemma is free to come and go as she pleases."

"Well," I drawled again, my rage somewhat back under control. "That makes you a right hypocrite, don't it? Keeping a colored girl and not even paying her a wage. Well, I'll bet you ..." I pointedly looked at the girl and said, "There is a lady present, so I'll go no further."

Simpson said nothing, not even to protest the implication, and we glared at each other. He finally lowered his eyes and flushed slightly—which pleased me to no end and firmed my resolve to continue bullying him.

"Bill," I said to Tweed, who had just sauntered up alongside me, "the good Reverend here has decided that he wants to give Methody tracts to the boyos here." I gestured to Tweed's straggling mob. "He's so happy to have his colored girl hand out so many tracts all at one go that he's going to be giving her a bonus." I glanced at Simpson with a savage pleasure.

"Sir ..." Simpson's protest died stillborn.

"That bonus'll be two bits a tract. There's eighty or so boyos here, each of them eager to have a tract of his own. That's what?" I paused. "Say, a double eagle for the girl?"

Tweed and I stayed until Simpson fumbled in his pocket and produced his double eagle—a bright golden double eagle, the likes of which the colored girl had likely never seen, and almost certainly never had to call her own.

I asked Jemma what her last name was. She said didn't have one on account of her momma having passed. I briefly glanced at Simpson, who was already distancing himself, and then asked Jemma whether she wanted to come with me or stay with the good Reverend. Jemma left with Bill and me, and as we departed, I reflected that I hadn't a clue what I was going to do with my new-found responsibility.

⌒

After I deposited Jemma with Mary, I ambled along to my next assignment—counting Sixth Ward votes at Dooley's Long Room. Mary had given me a very long look indeed when she pulled me aside before I could escape, and asked in a furious whisper, "What … are you doing?" I explained and she relented, saying that she'd "sort something out." I then hurried out, muttering that I was late, and skittered over to Dooley's Long Room. I burst through the door to the ballroom to a dour look from Donoho—I really was late—and I gave Jemma and Mary no further mind, although I did later recall that Fíona had stared wide-eyed at Mary and me, soaking in our little contretemps.

I sat there, sedulously counting ballots for the next couple of hours with Donoho, Tweed and Freely, who poured Con a whiskey and lit Con's cigar before sitting down. There was no one else in the ballroom. Just the four of us, grouped around a table, counting ballots. Occasionally, a poll worker came in with a fresh bushel for us to count by the flickering gaslight. It must have been about 9:00 that night when the outside door burst open with a bang and an angry shout, and Cassidy stormed into the ballroom, followed by Lúcas and a score of angry-looking toughs. I didn't see Cian, but I was sure he was there, lurking somewhere behind Lúcas.

Cassidy stomped to the table where we were sitting and said to us, as civil as you please, "Good evening."

Donoho looked up and broke into a wide grin. "Why Cassidy, what a pleasure to see you. Unexpected, I'm sure. But you will excuse us, won't you? We're so busy, and the vote counts are due at City Hall in an hour. We have so much to do." Donoho gestured sadly to the three bushels of ballots remaining to be counted. "So, if you'll excuse us …"

320

Cassidy leaned on the table and said, "Con, me lad." You could have sworn that Cassidy had just left Dublin, so thick was his accent ... funny that, considering that Tweed had called him a Scotsman earlier in the day. But then again, Magee had called him a Fenian turncoat ... "There's been a development."

"Oh?"

"An entirely unexpected result."

"Really."

"Yes." Cassidy straightened himself. "You see, Con, Hizzoner's carried the 'ould bloody Sixth."

"How's that?" Tweed interceded, looking mystified. "We haven't finished counting the votes yet."

"Oh," Cassidy said in a silky tone. "I think you have. Ain't that right, Dineen?"

With that, Lúcás extracted his disreputable-looking barking iron from his coat and smirked. I thought about what Mary had said about Lúcás's gun and figured that she probably had it right: the damned thing would blow up in his face if he ever pulled the trigger. Donoho and Tweed affected not to notice the gun. I couldn't see Freely. But there were anticipatory grins aplenty on the mugs of Cassidy's toughs.

Tweed said mildly, "You know, Cassidy, it's a crime to be interruptin' the countin' of the ballots like this."

"We're not interrupting," Lúcás replied rudely. "We'll be doing the counting for the rest of the evening. You can all ... absquatulate ... now."

Cassidy chimed in, "In fact, Con, I think we're done with the counting, and Hizzoner carried the ward. Oh, and Magee lost. Convincingly." He smirked. "I won."

Donoho stopped counting ballots, and with a slightly impatient look at Cassidy, said, "Yes, boyo, ye be done here, tonight, an' ye'll na be countin' any votes. So ye best be leaving 'afore there be any trouble."

Cassidy laughed and leaned on the table again. "Rynders's boys are out there, Con. They'll stave yer head in if you don't clear out now."

"Really?" Donoho smirked. "Ye better be checkin' again, yer *bastún dall*."

Cassidy's head jerked spasmodically, and Cian—I had finally seen him standing behind his brother—ran to the door. He came back in and said, "Boss, there ain't no one out there ..."

"Cassidy, you are a right daft bastard."

Cassidy jerked around and looked up at the balcony where I'd hidden myself on nominating night. Magee and Blackie and two others were standing there, each armed with a pair of flintlock shotguns. Ancient beasts, but effective at the range. I wondered whether I should duck beneath the table.

"Did you really think I'd leave *mo chomhbrathair* down there alone, did you?" Magee gestured with one of his shotguns.

Cassidy looked back at Donoho, who was smiling broadly now.

"The good Captain Rynders sends his regards." Donoho waved his hand at a half dozen Empire Club toughs who had quietly slipped into the room. "And I did want to pass along that the good captain kindly asks you ... to fuck off."

Cassidy said nothing, and began to turn away.

Magee called out, with just a hint of laughter in his voice, "Oh, Cassidy, I trust ye'll be vacating yer saloon? I be holding yer title to it. You know, on account o' yer gambling losses and all."

⌐

Greeley's *Tribune* reported the next morning that W. T. Havemeyer had won the mayoral election, and Tammany had secured a majority of 26 votes on the Common Council. Among them was Magee, who had thoroughly trounced Cassidy in the Sixth Ward. Hizzoner, Jimmy Harper, went back to publishing Methody bibles and tracts, and thankfully never held office again.

⌐

CHAPTER 15

Citizen Gogan

I BECAME AN AMERICAN CITIZEN ON JULY 5, 1845, hardly more than six months after I arrived at Bulgers Slip. Some of you may protest that one has to have lived in America for five years before becoming a citizen. Well, it just so happens that it is recorded somewhere in the bowels of New York City's Marine Court over on Broad Street that, as of July 5, 1845, I had been resident in the United States for at least five years—attested to by one William Marcy Tweed under threat of perjury. One might also belabor the fact that I was just sixteen—and not eighteen, as the law then required an immigrant to be before he could be naturalized. Well, those same records show that I was indeed eighteen on that particular day. But all of this, I submit, is utterly beside the point. For the certificate proclaiming one a citizen of the United States of America merely recognized officially a much more profound fact—one that in my experience is nearly universal—one can hardly remain in the United States without becoming in some way an American, with every bit of a right to be an American as any born-and-bred nativist.

For several hours on that hot and humid Monday morning, I had been helping Charlie count the rhino and balance the books. Apparently, not quite everyone in Gotham had been watching the volunteer companies' parade, because betting on the various numbers games that Charlie and I had set up the previous week had been very heavy on Sunday. Charlie had been pretty happy about the profits—which was to say that he had not grumbled at me very much that morning as we piled the counted money into bags for Blackie and his mates to take over to the Bowery Savings Bank. When Charlie finally released me from my abacus, I was parched, and I made a beeline to Magee's saloon, where Blackie kept a jug of lemonade—often on ice (when he could afford it). Magee occasionally teased Blackie about it, claiming that Blackie was the only teetotaling Irishman he'd ever met. Blackie never rose to Magee's bait, and was happy to quaff his lemonade on a hot afternoon while everyone else drank whiskey and beer. I was happy to join him.

"Billy, my lad." Magee was smoking a cigar and had a glass of whiskey in his hand. He had been little short of ebullient since Election Day, now that he was the Sixth Ward assistant alderman. Even better, his arch rival, Cassidy, had virtually disappeared after his election night humiliation, which had cost the *dallachán* everything he owned. Several of Magee's cronies were there as well, including Bill Tweed and the ever-present Blackie quietly sliding about in the background.

I waved hello.

Magee said, "Ye know, lad, it's about time we made a fine upstanding citizen of yers."

I grunted.

Tweed interjected, clearly egging Magee on, "We have to make an American of you, Bill." Tweed was about the only one who did not call me "Billy," and I appreciated the sentiment.

"Why?"

"Well, ye're a proper volunteer these days, ain't you?" Magee asked.

"Sure," I replied noncommittally, not sure whether he meant the engine company or the volunteer militia company.

"Well, we can't be having a loyal subject of the *Sassenagh* Queen being a member of our company, now, can we lads?"

"A loyal subject?" I was ready to yell "Sweet Jesus." But then again, that was precisely what Magee wanted, so I shut pan.

"Well," Magee said, his Irish suddenly surfacing in a stagy sort of way, "you was born in Eirinn. An' the *Sassenagh* Queen be after claimin' the country for her own."

"Oh, aye." I dismissed Magee and asked one of Magee's loyal hangers on to pass the coffee pot. Somebody had thoughtfully placed some dubiously clean mugs on the table, and I had decided that, in view of Magee's present mood, drinking the coffee was safer than asking Blackie—who had disappeared for the moment, anyway—for a cup of his ice-cold lemonade. I wasn't in the mood to tolerate the chaffing.

"Seeing as how the company's going to be needing a new captain now that bastard Cassidy has gone to ground." Magee almost chortled with glee.

"With his lushery under new management," Tweed added.

"A much cleaner place now, ain't it? Now that a proper Irishman owns it." Heads nodded in approval.

"Anyways. The new captain, whoever he is." Magee looked around for further approbation and received it. "He's going to need a new orderly, seeing as how the old one has disappeared along with his fallen master."

Magee had been talking about Cian, who had told me with some satisfaction a few days before the election—the last time I had seen him—that Cassidy had made him his orderly, a position that brought with it a quite grandiloquent uniform, complete with a sash. I wondered briefly where Cian had disappeared to. He wasn't a half bad cove, when you got right down to it, even if he was socially a bit rough around the edges. Who wouldn't be, after Cian's childhood? Orphaned at the age of ten, raised by his murderous brother, Lúcás, on the streets of the 'Points and the Bowery, penniless, homeless and half-starved. The two of them weren't unique. There were far too many children, Irish, German, Polish and colored alike, who were left to roam the streets like that, scavenging precarious existences. With such an upbringing, it was any wonder that Cian was even alive, let alone having turned into a half-decent cove. Although with Cian having thrown his lot in with Cassidy, I wasn't about to give two bits for his surviving much longer if he was still here in Gotham. If anyone needed to depart for greener pastures …

Magee continued. "The captain's orderly has to be a citizen, don't you know."

I remained unmoved.

"Yes, you, lad." Magee smiled, finally conceding his effort to bait me. "You'll make a fine orderly."

I smiled, not knowing what to say.

"What Magee's trying to say," Tweed added, "is that we're going to make an American out of you this afternoon."

"An American?"

"Yep," Tweed replied. "Every bit as American as young Magee over here."

Magee raised his whiskey glass and drained it.

"Well, how can I do that?"

"Simple," Tweed said. "You're eighteen, right? And you've been here in America, what, five and half years?"

I looked at Tweed blankly, and he said patiently to me, "The Marine Court, Bill. The judges over there can make you a citizen as long as you're eighteen and you've been in the country for five years and you aren't a nigger, a bastard or a criminal."

"Bill …" Magee said.

"Sorry, boss," Tweed flushed. "Forgot … you're about the only white man in New York who feels that way about the coloreds." Tweed shook his head. "Unaccountable, really."

Magee ignored the gibe. I cleared my throat.

"Well … perhaps there are two of you," Tweed said, "seeing as how young Bill here does like that young colored girl."

A couple of Magee's minions chuckled. I had no idea that my friendships were of such interest.

"So," Tweed continued, "we're going to take you down to Tammany Hall. You got a half eagle?"

Five dollars? This was going to be a bloody expensive business, this getting naturalized. What was Mary going to say? How was I going to have any rhino for ice cream and what-not for the next week or so?

Tweed explained why. "Legal fee for naturalization."

I opened my mouth to protest.

Magee said, "Doesn't Charlie pay you enough? Bloody cheap john, he is. D'ye need a raise, Billy?"

This brought general laughter.

"Yes, as a matter of fact, I could use a raise," I said. "Charlie isn't half hauling in the rhino."

"He is, is he?" Magee looked at me in what I took to be mock concern. "Next, ye'll be askin' for a bloody bonus because yer honest."

"Now that you mention it," I said, playing to the crowd a bit.

"Ye're the best paid fifteen-year-old whelp in Gotham." Magee sounded positively outraged.

I shrugged. He was absolutely correct. I had a sinecure that few men, let alone boys such as myself, could dream about. So I wasn't complaining. But then again, I was as avaricious as the next cove.

Someone called out, "Not giving him the Tammany discount, Magee?"

"Eh?" I asked.

Tweed answered, "The poor Irishman getting naturalized through the good offices of the Wigwam usually get a discount—just a simoleon instead of half an eagle."

This was four dollars I might not have to spend. Worth humbling myself for. So I said, "You know, Magee, Mary does have me on a monkey's allowance."

I endured the inevitable laughter. Somebody called out, "He ain't even an autum cove yet, and he's already a bloody henpeck."

Magee said, "You've got the best of all worlds with that lady, Billy. An older sister, she is." Laughter. "With control over your purse." More laughter. "And ... with free live-in help with her *chuidín*, her little dear." Still more laughter. "And a damned fine woman, she is ..."

There was silence, which Tweed promptly filled, "Bill, go and say good-bye to Charlie for now, and we'll be off to Tammany. Your days as an Irish subject of that *Sassanagh* bitch, Queen Victoria, are over."

Tweed and I ambled down to Tammany Hall, over on the corner of Nassau and Frankfort, just south of City Hall Park, where a complaisant clerk filled out two sheets of paper, took a dollar from me and stamped one of the papers with a smudge of ink signifying .... Well, I wasn't sure what it signified. But it looked official enough. We then ambled over to the Marine Court down on Broad Street, near the Battery, for the afternoon session.

A half-eagle—out of my own pocket, mind you—surreptitiously passed to the clerk earned me the right to appear before his Honor before any of the other half-dozen or so parties in the dusty courtroom. I had never been in a courtroom before, and I quite frankly expected more grandeur. Well, I had at least expected the bailiff to be wearing a clean uniform and the clerk to be sober and dressed neatly, and not disheveled and half drunk.

"All rise," the bailiff commanded.

The judge was neither remote nor magnificent, as judges always seemed to be described in books. He wore neither robes nor wig and there was nary an ermine hair to be found adorning him. To boot, he apparently hadn't shaved in several days, and probably was two or three whiskies into the day. With an off-handed wave that everyone took for a signal to be seated, he sat on a low, roughly built dais of unfinished deal, which was at about the same height of eye as a tall man.

The judge peered at the papers handed to him by the clerk, who pointed to me as he did so. After a moment of close study, he put the papers down and pulled out a pair of spectacles, which he polished assiduously. He peered at the papers again and cleared his throat.

"In the matter of the naturalization of William Patrick Gogan." The judge gestured to me.

"Come forward."

I complied.

"You are William Patrick Gogan?"

"Yes, your honor."

"Do you have a witness?"

"Yes your honor." I gestured to Tweed, who had come forward as well, and now stood next to me.

"Name?"

"William M. Tweed, your honor."

"Tammany?"

"Yes, your honor."

"Hmm. Mr. Gogan, place your hand on the bible."

The judge thrust the bible in front of me, and I placed my hand on it.

"Do you swear to tell the truth, the whole truth and nothing but the truth, so help you God?"

"I do."

"Hmm." The judge glanced at the Tammany-produced papers again. "Mr. Gogan, your place of residence?"

I told him.

"How long have you resided there?"

"Seven months."

"Before that?"

I gave him the address of Schreiber's boardinghouse.

"How long have you resided in New York?"

"Five and a half years, your honor."

"Hmm. Age?"

"Eighteen, your honor."

"No beard yet," the judge observed.

"No, your honor."

"Who's the president?"

"The President of the United States, your honor?"

"Yes, son."

"James Polk."

Seemingly satisfied, the judge turned to Tweed and asked, "Is Mr. Gogan of sound moral character?"

"Yes, your honor."

"Do you have personal knowledge of Mr. Gogan's answers?"

"Yes, your honor."

"Hmm." The judge then scribbled something. "Mr. Gogan, you are now a citizen of New York and of the United States. Congratulations. Next matter."

⌒

Tweed and I walked back to Magee's saloon.

"Magee and I figured that you ought be an American," Tweed said. "You brought in the votes on election day with the best of them."

"No different than you."

"Yeah, well, I had the advantage of having seen an election before and having known Donoho for a very long time. Like we've talked about, I realized last November, after watching what Donoho did in the presidential election, that there's a fortune to be made in politics and controlling who gets elected. And I've decided that's what I'm going to do. But you, Bill, you're a natural genius, coming up with how best to use the Blackwell's prisoners by marching them all day from one polling station to the next, and collecting the beached and the public building inspectors and the like to add to our numbers. Of course, we should have figured that the prospect of a shilling a vote—which is more than what Cassidy or anyone else was paying—would bring out every Paddie in Gotham. But that was real long-headed of you."

I felt like saying, "Aw shucks," but I didn't. In truth, I was proud of that little innovation, taking advantage of the longstanding traditions of prisoners voting once or twice in elections and then "escaping" from custody and of paying the bums a bit to vote and combining those traditions to produce a lot of votes in a lot of different polling stations—even though I had always been quick to give Tweed the credit. That had seemed the right thing to do, whether with Magee and Donoho or with Mary. I wasn't sure why, but nonetheless ...

Tweed was talking again. "That whole bit from Magee about your needing to be a citizen to be his orderly is about as bogus as paper money."

"Then why go to the trouble? I can't vote."

"True, but Magee and I figured that it seemed the right thing to do."

"Why? Who cares whether I'm Irish or American? I'm still just a kid."

"True enough. But Tammany is getting pretty particular about bringing the Irish on. They're the key to running this city for the next generation. And if those rumors about this Great Hunger and everything else going on in Ireland are true, then there'll be more paddies in Gotham in a year or two than we know what to do with. Think of it. What a base to build an empire on." Tweed's eyes positively shone with ambition.

"Okay," I said. "We've all heard more of those stories of the blackened potatoes and people going hungry earlier this year than ever before. That doesn't explain ..."

"Stop being such a bottle-head."

I didn't say anything.

"You're a longheaded kid. You've got a future. Anyway," he added, "we can't have a longheaded cove like you not able to vote.

There'd be nothing separating you from a common n— ... sorry ... colored fellow. The Irish can vote—if they're citizens—and the coloreds can't, at least they can't unless they own a lot of property. Of course," he flashed a grin. "None of them do."

"I suppose," I said slowly. "There doesn't seem to be much separating the poorest of the paddies from the poorest of the coloreds here in Gotham. They all do the same kind of work. Hell, they even live together ... over in the Old Brewery, at least."

"And have kids together," Tweed said.

"Yep," I replied.

"But they're different. A different race."

"Yeah, but ..."

"You and Magee. You're about the only folks I know—Irish or native American—who'd put a kind word in for the coloreds." Tweed looked at me out of the corner of his eye. "Magee? I understand him. He's thick with Muireann—and with her husband 'afore he was killed. In fact, her husband gave Magee his start. But you ... you were born a huckleberry above the proverbial persimmon, weren't you? Your sort think that ... coloreds ... should be slaves or servants. I've got to tell you ... well, you are dallying with fire with that young vixen of Muireann's."

"How do you know about her?"

"Sweet Jesus, as you paddies say. There isn't one of us who hasn't seen you and her mooning about with each other."

"I like her."

"Don't get too attached."

"Why not?"

Tweed looked at me like I was a bit slow. "She ain't white." Tweed scuffed at something on the cobblestones. "Anyway, what're you going to do with her? Marry her? Or is it just a case of your cock in your eye? Either way ..."

I took Tweed's question to be rhetorical.

"Just watch yourself. That's all ... and maybe you should be a little more discreet. A white kid like you and a colored girl ... 'Specially after you rescued that other colored girl from that stiff-necked preacher." Tweed chuckled in remembrance. Then he turned serious, "You don't want to be seen as a nigger lover ... It ain't healthy ... Too many coves out there who'd as soon kill you as look at you for that."

We walked quietly for a while.

As we approached Paradise Square, Tweed turned to me and said, "I'm off home. The brushmaking business and the wife. If I don't get home, I'll get a regular rib-roast from her, and my old man'll have a piece of me because I've not been around enough to attend to business." He smiled, and then shook my hand, saying, "So—and I mean this, all joshing aside—congratulations on becoming a citizen, even if it didn't happen quite as square as it could have."

"Thanks. But I've got to say, I'm not sure I've earned it just yet, this being an American citizen."

"You will," Tweed gravely predicted. "And it'll grow on you."

Tweed was the second person to have warned me about having become friends with Brannagh. Mary, of course, was Brannagh's friend—and mine. My conversation with Tweed was an entirely different matter. Worse, Tweed was right. I did have a cock in my eye for Brannagh—not that I'd really admitted it up until then, even to myself. I nonetheless had felt a bit of a cold shiver when Bill and I were talking about her.

But I was just a boy—still—and I had forgotten all about Tweed's admonition by the next afternoon. I had a date with Brannagh I'd been looking forward to for days. This date was different, though. For two months or more, Brannagh and I had passed many an afternoon in Battery Park or at City Hall Park, sometimes just sitting quietly with ice creams in hand. Other times, we often talked about whatever struck us—and those topics could be far-ranging indeed.

One day, a couple of weeks earlier, Brannagh had been extolling her mother's superior treatment of her dells as compared to other brothel madams. Muireann apparently was more enlightened, and perhaps even more savvy, than just about any other madam in Gotham—even Mrs. Miller—so Brannagh had told me once, confirming similar observations which Magee had made to me in boozy confidence late one night. Unlike most other madams, Muireann didn't force her dells to live at the brothel. Most madams insisted on their dells living in the brothel, the better to control them and prevent them from, shall we say, going into business for themselves.

Muireann instead let her girls, as she called them, by and large live in their own homes—whether they were in boardinghouses in the 'Points or elsewhere—with exceptions such as Jessie, who chose to live at the brothel, simply because she had no family and nobody other than Brannagh to call her friend. But Jessie didn't mind. She had told me one day—a sentiment which Brannagh subsequently confirmed—that she found whoring a much more palatable alternative to living a hardscrabble existence up in Dutchess County with her widowed father, an unpleasant man who, I had gathered, was bereft of prospects.

Muireann avoided the threat of her girls competing with her by achieving deals with them (which all varied, depending upon the individual dell, according to Magee in a sniggering aside at one of his afternoon levees at the saloon) that motivated the girls to work as hard as they could—whether as a matter of quantity or quality, the latter being a means by which a dell could limit the number of her cullies by, as Magee smirked, enhancing the act—or acting the cloven, as Jessie routinely did.

Moreover, Brannagh whispered one day, Muireann did not like her girls having to visit Madame Restell.

"Who's Madame Restell?" I felt like a comedian's feeder at a vaudeville act.

Brannagh looked at me to see whether I was entirely sentient. "You know how babies are made?"

A question that, like so many others, I took to be rhetorical.

"Well," she explained patiently. "Getting apron up is, shall we say, a risk that every woman has faced since the dawn of time. Momma doesn't want to lose her girls, so she makes them use French letters." Brannagh looked quite amused. "You've never seen one, have you?"

"No. Heard about them, though." I remembered Cian's sneering disregard for them—and presumably for the dells he snoozed with.

"I'll show you one, sometime." She snuggled against me. After a bit, she continued. "Momma charges the cullies double if they want to … well, you know …"

In principle, I did know what Brannagh meant. In practice, though, my knowledge of such affairs was more than a little deficient.

"If the cully insists on being such a beast, Momma will make her girl use a syringe to clean herself."

I didn't ask how the syringe was to be used.

"But sometimes a girl can get pregnant anyway. That's when Momma will call Madame Restell in …"

"To do what?" Her ellipsis finally lost me.

Brannagh looked at me impatiently, and said, "She'll abort the fetus. That way, the poor girl isn't burdened."

"Christ."

As I recall, neither of us said much after that.

~

Today, though, that conversation and the concerns of concupiscent (and hungry) women were very far from my mind. As I said, today was different than all my other dates with Brannagh. Storm clouds were lowering, and Brannagh and I were wandering about restlessly. She had said that she didn't want to risk ruining her new dress—a sentiment I had wholeheartedly agreed with, as she was very fetching in it. So we walked. By unspoken, mutual consent, we eventually ended up in front of Black Muireann's brothel on Church Street.

"I've got an idea," Brannagh whispered.

"What?"

She didn't answer me, but instead grabbed my hand (my heart instantly melting) and led me through the side gate to the back entrance. We slipped in and up the back stairs. The place was deserted—which was not surprising since it was only 2:00 p.m., and business didn't start until 9:00 or 10:00 p.m. each evening. Up to the upstairs parlor we went, the same parlor where Brannagh had spied on my discomfort with Jessie. Brannagh led the way, holding my hand in the silkiness of her kid leather glove. The room was as dimly lit as that first night, and seemed all the more remote from the brightness of the outside world, where the sun was shining through the storm clouds.

We sank into the love seat, our shoulders, hips and thighs touching as the cushions enveloped us. We sat quietly, holding hands, and later we kissed, our hands roaming farther than they had ever before. Brannagh led the way, sliding her hands inside my coat, loosening my waistcoat so that I felt the warmth of her fingers through the thin, worn linen of my shirt.

Almost involuntarily, I began to unbutton her dress. She helped me, and her dress fell open. I gazed upon her breasts, nipples hard, pressing against a thin, silk shift.

"I haven't worn very much today," she whispered.

I could feel some sort of impending crisis. I had felt such crises before, but they always subsided—eventually. Today, though, the crisis was not subsiding. I was lost as Brannagh fumbled with buttons to my trousers. After an eternity, she reached into my trousers and grasped me, at which point the crisis was impending no longer.

Brannagh pulled her hand away and we both stared at it bemusedly. Then I remembered myself and wiped her hand with my none-too-clean handkerchief.

We cuddled, lost in the cushions of the loveseat. "Now I understand ..." she said some time later.

"What?"

"Well, what Jessie and the other girls have been talking about. I never really understood," she whispered.

"I didn't either," I replied.

Presently, we both understood so much more.

CHAPTER 16

Saving Her Flesh and Blood

⌒

BEFORE I LEFT, BRANNAGH PRESSED A KEY to the side door to my hand, and we made plans for my return the very next afternoon. When I unlocked the side door at the stroke of 2:00 p.m., heart pounding and palms sweating, it felt as if two or three eternities had passed since I had taken my—quite protracted—leave of Brannagh, which had been punctuated by our mutual protestations of love. But Brannagh wasn't there. Instead, Muireann O'Marran was standing in the foyer, hands on her hips, a formidable duchess protecting her domain.

"Good afternoon, Mrs. O'Marran."

"Oh, aye, a good afternoon, it is, Mr. Gogan." Her suddenly Irish-inflected tone was arch. "Won't you come in? We can go through to the parlor."

We did not go to the upstairs parlor where Brannagh and I had retreated yesterday, but instead went through to the front parlor where I had first met Muireann the night Cian had brought me here.

"Why don't you sit. I'll ring for some tea."

"Thank you."

We sat quietly in the cool shadows, remote from the summer heat and humidity, until the tea came. I was deep in the shit—and I knew it. One did not cross Muireann O'Marren, and yesterday I had done just that. So there was nothing for it but to keep my hair on and wait patiently for what was to come—no matter my impulse to do otherwise. A maid appeared noiselessly from the gloom over Muireann's shoulder and deposited a silver tray with a gleaming silver tea service and two of the finest bone china tea cups I had ever seen before vanishing again into the gloom.

Muireann busied herself with the ceremony of serving me tea, pouring the boiling water from a silver kettle into the teapot, along with teaspoons of black tea … no green gunpowder for Muireann. I wondered briefly whether it was Chinese, which was then far more common than it is today, or the newfangled Assam tea that was all the rage among the upper tendom.

"One lump or two?"

"Just a bit of milk, please."

"Cream?"

"Please." I hadn't had cream in my tea since I left Ireland.

"So rare to find an American who takes cream in his tea. Very English of you," she said deliberately.

"Yes, ma'am."

I took the proffered cup of tea, and we both sipped politely.

"I don't want a scene," Muireann said at last.

"No, ma'am."

"She's not here."

"Ma'am?"

"I've sent Brannagh to Canada—with that young colored girl you rescued … what was her name?" Muireann affected an air of disinterest, but I remembered the look of approbation she'd had when she heard the story and promptly thereafter taken Jemma in, no further questions asked. "Oh yes … Jemma. Poor thing. Such a sweet girl. But you won't be seeing her again—Brannagh, that is, or Jemma, for that matter."

There was nothing to say, and so I said nothing.

"I suppose," Muireann sighed. "It's really my fault. You two were seeing each other virtually every day. *Dia Uas*! I was a fool. I run a bloody goosing slum and I refused to see where human nature would take the two of you."

We both sipped our tea again. It was exquisite. A mad thought crossed my mind to ask her whether it was indeed from Assam. But I kept my peace.

"I'd have sent her away even if she were white and you and she were both from good, established families. You're both far too young. And you ... well, you are anything but a suitable catch. An orphan tossed from his cousin's home in Ireland. Manners of the hoity-toity aristocracy." Muireann sniffed as if she were a noble lady herself. "But living in the 'Points with one of my girls."

What did she mean by that?

She finished with a disdainful sneer, "You're more hair about the heels than most of my girls when they get here."

I suppressed a smile at that last jab—Muireann worked wonders with her girls. They escaped from dirt farms in the Catskills, like Jessie, or were ejected from Irish landed estates or taken in, orphaned, from the streets and given a stiff dose of gentility—along with the requisite other skills—for which the well-heeled cullies were happy to pay handsomely.

"You're a mother's worst nightmare, you are. Now I understand how Adeline Miller must have felt." Muireann turned and glared at me with hard eyes, as flat and cruel as those of Aloysius Quincy Urquehar when he'd beaten the packet rat for ruining his fawn greatcoat. "Well, at least she's not with child. What were you thinking?" She stared at me again. "I asked her the same question." She smiled mirthlessly. "And I received the same answer from her ... nothing."

She looked me directly in the eye and asked, "So what do you have to say for yourself?"

I took a breath. "I can't apologize."

I thought Muireann was going to come out of her chair and beat me to death. But she didn't move even a hair.

"Brannagh and I … we like each other."

"Are you going to marry her?" Muireann demanded. "When you sleep with a girl … a good girl … and God only knows she's a good girl … you marry her."

I looked Muireann in the eye as hard as she'd looked at me. "Yes. I'll marry her."

"How?" Muireann sounded doubtful.

"I've a job." I tried to keep the truculence out of my voice.

"Doing what? A mere clerk for a bookie. You're a numbers runner. You're …"

"What, Mrs. O'Marran?" I blazed hot with indignation, not hearing what more she said. I had done what I had to do in terms of making a living. As Magee once said to me in one of his boozy confidences late one night, "Nothing's certain in life. Live it for all it's worth, grab your opportunities while ye can, boyo, an' don't get too comfortable, because ye never know when some bastard's going to upend yer apple cart." I had agreed with Magee heartily then, and I agreed with him now. I was curiously proud of having taken full advantage of the luck that had come my way. Otherwise, I'd still have been sweeping shit in the streets, or worse. I had nothing whatsoever to be ashamed of in being a bookie's clerk. Although, truth be told, I wasn't sure in my innermost thoughts what Evelyn (let alone my father and Father O'Muirhily) might say were she to know what kinds of scams and angles I had come to know in this past year. In fact, I was unfortunately growing more confident that I had fully fallen from the ranks of the worthy in her eyes.

Muireann was looking at me curiously. I must have been quiet for a while, so I said to her conversationally and with a certain amount pride, "I'm a young man with an education. And long-headed, so I've been told. I'm ambitious, too. I'm going to make my way in this world. I'll make a good husband."

"What about Mary? You don't think I don't know about her? Are you going to leave her and Fíona behind?" Muireann laughed sardonically again. "Are you and she lovers?" she demanded. Before I could answer, she said, "Young man, that's hardly a fair question. I already know the answer." Then her tone became almost kindly. "You might not think it, Billy Gogan, but I do know about star-crossed lovers. And you and Brannagh were primed to be thwarted by a most malign star."

"Why?" I thought it best not to ask Black Muireann how on God's little green earth she had become so literate. "I have the best of intentions."

"Young man, your intentions, however admirable—and Mary and Brannagh have both told me that you are the perfect gentle-man—will get you nowhere."

"Why not?" I persisted.

"Brannagh has told me a lot of what you and she have talked about," her tone becoming gentler. "She is my only flesh and blood, and I love her so … but she's cursed, and I want to save her from at least some of the consequences of that curse. She can never have a decent life here in America. She has little enough in common with most colored people. I raised her to be white, and look what that has gotten her. If she marries you, where do you go? Where can you live without being in constant danger—both of you?"

"You and her father married."

"It was a different time. There wasn't the same hatred. We thought it would last—that is, until the riots in '34. It didn't." Muireann gave me a brittle smile. "My husband paid the price for it. I can't allow Brannagh to go through that same kind of hell. And even if I were to allow it, you're far too young to protect her … to really protect her."

We sat and drank some more tea. Muireann offered me a fresh cup, and I accepted. Muireann concentrated once again on the ceremony of straining the tea and preparing my cup. We sat for a while longer before she spoke again.

"That's why I sent her away, to be with her Uncle Jack—her father's brother ... He's the only other family I have. Maybe she can find some happiness up there, with him. She can attend that finishing school we found, and perhaps she can dance a proper quadrille there."

"Where'd you send her?"

"I'm not going to tell you, son."

I opened my mouth to protest. She raised her hand to silence me.

"It's for the best ... for the both of you."

I didn't need to ask why. I'd already said what I had to say— what proper manners had compelled me to say—and to resolve to do what I said I'd do. So I said nothing.

"There'll be other girls for you, Billy Gogan. Perhaps this pretty girl with golden ringlets ... what's her name? Oh, yes. Evelyn O'Creagh. Your cousin. Brannagh told me that you still write to her."

I looked at Muireann with a bit of surprise, although I probably shouldn't have.

"Yes, dear." She smiled indulgently at me. "If I've made a success of one thing, it's that my daughter talks to me ... even if not about quite everything. God only knows there's many a mother and daughter who don't talk at all." Muireann concluded by saying, "Evelyn ... yes ... it's the mere existence of her in your mind— and Brannagh's knowing of her—which explains when all's said and done why I sent her away. Neither of you are ready."

We finished our tea, and I made to leave. As we arose from our chairs, Muireann said with an amused twinkle in her eye, "Don't make a stranger of yourself here. I know you men, and I won't think any the less of you for paying me a visit now and again now that you've tasted it. You'll thirst for it again after a while, and quite frankly I'd rather you found your women here than anywhere else."

Thanking Muireann for this bit of generosity didn't seem quite right. But I did have one question. "Mrs. O'Marran …"

"Now that this is all over," she gave me the sort of sugary smile that many a cully had seen over the years, "call me Muireann."

"Muireann, how do you know Mary?"

She looked at me speculatively. "You don't know, do you?"

"What?"

"You really don't, do you? Bless Mary's heart." Muireann smiled. "Mary works for me. She's my best girl. And she's my friend, my very, very dear friend—and my future business partner," she said with an odd expression on her face.

CHAPTER 17

Taking a Round Turn

"WAKE UP, YER PELOOTHERED BASTÚN."

My head pounded, and I was ready to be physically sick.

"Wake up." It was Mary. I had never heard her quite so angry before.

I groaned, opened my eyes and then wished I hadn't. "You're going to have to face the day."

"Okay." I finally found my voice, scratchy as it was.

"Here, drink this."

The tea was wonderfully restorative, even if it wasn't Assam black.

"We've got to talk." Mary's tone was urgent. "What happened yesterday? I talked to Muireann. I know what you and she spoke about, and we can discuss that later. What I want to know is—what happened afterwards?"

What did happen? That was a good question, and it was one that I could not easily answer. First things first: I had drunk more than one whiskey for the first time in my life. I didn't drink any of it at Magee's saloon, where I would've been lucky to get even that single glass, unless Magee had given the bartender the high sign. I remember working my way around Paradise Square through some of the less desirable lusheries and then wandering over into the Bowery for some reason that was now entirely lost to me. After that, my memories were, to say the least, somewhat jumbled, although …

"I think I ran into Cian Dineen last night … somewhere …" I trailed off, remembering in fragments what it was Cian had had to say to me.

I'd been in some lushery up in some godforsaken bit of the Bowery, already well on my way to being three sheets to the wind, when he'd spied me, greeting me all hail fellow and well met. The sight of him momentarily sobered me.

He cried jovially at me, "Look like you're seein' a ghost, there, Gogan."

"How …" The words were beyond me.

Cian filled in the silence (if you call it that at a table along the far wall from the bar in a lushery big enough for thirty, with sixty of its finest customers imbibing as much as they could as quickly as they could with all the hilarity and violence attendant thereto). "How ya doin'?"

We shook hands and embraced, but I said nothing, for I didn't know what to say.

"What? You're not happy to see me?"

A foaming beer found its way to his hand to an airy "cheers," he quaffed deeply from it, and said, "You're surprised to still see me here, aren't ya?"

I shrugged.

"Well, we got plans, Mr. Cassidy 'n' Lúcás 'n' me." He noted my ill-concealed look of skepticism, "Honest Injun!"

I raised an eyebrow.

"Well," Cian exclaimed. "We're all headed west. We're just putting a grubstake together." He looked at me conspiratorially. "You should join us. It'll be a 'high adventure', as you'd say." I must have looked at him a oddly for he exclaimed, "On the square, my bene cove!"

I ignored his entreaty, saying, "We're going west, ourselves, Mary and I are. One day, when our own grubstake's big enough."

"Hah, you'll play the devil breaking Mary loose from the Big Onion. She'll be rolling in the chink in a year or two, and that's far too good a rosy to give away."

348

I grunted dyspeptically. It was a subject I wasn't inclined to discuss with anyone, particularly as I had figured out in the intervening hours since I'd decamped from Black Muireann's that I had likely been the only sentient cull in all of Gotham not to know that Mary had been enjoying a good long innings as Black Muireann's finest *belle petite*, the joke at my expense having become all the richer the longer my ignorance had lasted. I suppose the joke had lasted as long as it did, simply because the thought of Mary doing what she did for a living shook me to my core.

Cian turned serious for a moment, drawing close to me. "You need to get out of Gotham, my bene cove."

I tried as best I could to focus on Cian.

"You're in more trouble than Cassidy is with Donoho and Magee."

I laughed at him.

"Seriously, me bucko. Cassidy met this fellow. Dunno what his name is. Wears all black. Creepy bastard, he was." Cian paused to quaff more beer. "Anyhows, he was askin' around about yers."

A sudden cold chill gripped me. I had not been imagining seeing the man in funeral black in Magee's saloon that night.

Cian's next words turned my blood even colder. "The cove was blethering all gammon and pickles about yer Da'. You never said much about him to me," Cian hiccupped accusingly. He then murmured, "Did you really nigh on croake a kid at that high-falutin' school o' yers?"

I shrugged.

Cian then mumbled something about having heard about the sins of the father being visited upon me. God knows what else he said to me, whether about my father, this mysterious fellow that he and Cassidy talked to or anything else, for my memory of the remainder of the evening was far too jumbled to make sense of.

I must have fallen asleep again, because I was suddenly conscious of Mary shaking me as she said, "You're lucky you're not dead."

I stared at her, conscious of what Cian had told me and equally aware of never having said a word to her—or Magee—about my father or the Irishman who had murdered Father O'Muirhily. But I didn't explain. I contented myself with a terse, "Why?"

"You were apparently quite the rowdy-dow with all your carrying on and wanting to fight whoever got near you."

"*Dia Uas.*" I held my head in my hands, partly from the mortification of it all and partly from the viciously pounding headache announcing that I had a righteous case of the jim-jims.

Mary continued, unsympathetic to my plight, "Cian Dineen did you a good turn when he didn't have to. He dropped you at the entrance to Magee's saloon and obtained a pass to safety from Blackie on account of his not having left you in the gutter to die."

I swore again, and Mary looked at me reprovingly. I looked up at her, and asked as so many a peloothered man has done before me, "To whom should I make amends?"

"Hard to say. You were out cold by the time Cian left you in a heap on Magee's stairs."

Mercifully, Mary didn't fash me any further, and I slept some hours more. It wasn't until the next day that Mary repeated an old Irish proverb to me, "A man takes a drink, the drink takes a drink, the drink takes the man," adding that she could not cope with yet another man in her life being a drunkard. I'll give Mary this. She shed no tears that day, and she did not raise her voice to me. She merely made me swear on a bible (which she had gone to the trouble of finding for this precise purpose), as a wide-eyed Fíona looked on, that I would never get peloothered like that ever again.

In the days that followed, a little at a time, we talked of what Muireann had told me, each of us taking great care not to broach the subject when Fíona or anyone else was around. At first, Mary tried to insist that she was not a prostitute. But I lost my patience and asked her whether she had confessed her sins to God at St. Peter's last Sunday morning, and if so, which ones.

Mary looked at me as if I'd physically attacked her, and I instantly lost all the wind from my sails. So I changed tack and told her what I really thought, "Here, in Gotham, now, there's no dishonor in a poor woman earning her keep on her back. What else were you going to do? Earn two dollars a week scrubbing floors six days a week? You'd've still ended up on your back."

I had few illusions left, and I'd gotten over the shock of Mary, dear sweet Mary having succumbed to a harsh economic calculus that was hard to miss. It was her only option. Thus, young women—and girls—had an economic advantage that older women did not. They could—and very often did, especially the pretty ones—turn to prostitution when they were out of work, and they often supplemented their incomes by walking the streets late at night when they did have jobs. Some of the more fortunate were able to rent rooms in brothels or cheap boardinghouses to entertain their cullies.

I finished by saying, "You've done nothing wrong."

Mary looked at me and burst into tears. I held her for a very long time, until her convulsing sobs died away. Later, after she had regained her composure, Mary and I began to talk. She began by telling me what she had not dared tell me in Galway—that men other than her dead husband had systematically abused her since she had been a young girl.

Mary was first despoiled just after she went into service at the big house. A footman had found her cleaning one day in a remote bedroom, and had threatened to kill her if she made a sound or if she ever told anyone about what had happened. She never did, and he kept coming back to her for the entire year that she stayed in service. Had Mary said anything to the butler, she would have been sacked instantly and nothing would have happened to the footman. That would have left her homeless and without any prospect other than imminent starvation. She also never breathed a word to either her mother or to Liam, who believed until his dying day that Mary had been a virgin when they married.

In truth, Mary told me, Fíona likely was not Liam's daughter. She had probably already been pregnant when she and Liam wed. Mary had always felt afterwards that God had punished her by not allowing her and Liam to have any more children after Fíona was born—all because she had acquiesced to the footman's transgressions—however unwillingly. But when Liam died, Mary had thanked God for not burdening her with more than one little *wain*, because she wasn't sure that she could have taken care of more than just Fíona.

Worse, the land agent's man who had accompanied Liam and Mary and all the other ejected tenants to their ship in Cork also had put the boot to Mary—hardly more than an hour or two after Liam had died, and with Fíona sleeping not five feet away. Mary loathed herself for having given in without a struggle to the land agent's man in exchange for him having paid for her room and her new passage. I didn't tell Mary, and it certainly did not justify the bastard's assault on her, but I did consider Mary to have been lucky that she had not been left stranded on the quays in Cork, destitute and with no one to turn to and nowhere to go.

But Mary's sense of self-loathing as she submitted to these assaults had not become so great that she failed to take advantage of the opportunity, when a Galway shopkeeper propositioned her one day as she was buying food for us. Indeed, Mary had earned enough from her assignations with the Galway shopkeeper that, unbeknownst to me until the day before we arrived in Gotham, she had enough chink to have gone a long way to replenishing my wallet, which she had intended to do the night we left Galway. She stopped talking then, the tears rolling down her face as she sobbed and sobbed.

"I don't care about any of that," I said. "You did what you had to. I wish you'd leveled with me then. But that's over and done with now."

She said convulsively, "It's not … that."

"Then what?"

"You remember that *cábóg*, that's what you called him, who was murdered in Galway?"

Dear God. I'd put that suspicion from my mind before it had even entered on that morning when we passengers filed past the dead man propped up in his coffin. "The bruises on your face …"

"I …"

"Don't say it." I cradled her close. "Don't hurt yourself like that. He deserved it."

"You don't even …"

"Yes, I do, and I didn't protect you."

She stared at me, nose running and tears streaming. "How …?"

"Do I know?" I replied heavily. "He threatened to have his way with you. I couldn't bring myself to tell you."

"That day you came back from manning the pumps."

"Yeah," I said tightly. "I forgot what he said to me, because I wanted to forget it."

"He'd have torn you apart."

"Like he did to you?"

"He never had the chance," she replied bleakly. "I knew the *bastún*'d come for me, eventually. So when he did, I protected myself."

"He was killed with a knife, I remember the constable, or somebody, saying."

She nodded. "The shopkeeper gave it to me. For services rendered."

"Jesus."

"I never let him touch me."

"He deserved it."

"Yes, he did. And you couldn't have done it. I knew what had to be done, and I did it."

She was right. But it didn't feel good to know that I couldn't have protected her.

"I made it look like a robbery. Of course, he had only a few coins on him. Stolen, most likely. God knows where."

"That chink you took from him and all the rest … from the shopkeeper … it kept your body and soul together those first weeks in Gotham? You and Fíona?"

Mary nodded.

"So then you've nothing to feel guilty about."

With that, we said no more about what happened in Galway, and Mary told me the rest of her story of the weeks before we found each other. She hadn't been able to find a job—any job, even though she had spent many days traipsing from one shop to another, looking for a position as a shopkeeper's assistant. She had also spent equally as many days looking for a position as a servant or chambermaid, also to no avail—all because there was a depression on. Worse, Mary learned the economics of being a poor woman and the seeming inevitability of her having to once more sell herself.

Mary told me that during her futile search for a job, she had been propositioned by a bewildering variety of touts and every other manner of loathsome knights of the gusset to join this brothel or that accommodation house. But she had been determined to earn her keep some other way as long as she had the cushion of my wallet and her earnings to fall back on, particularly as I had vanished without a trace. Eventually, though, money began to run short, and Mary began to panic. That was when she met Magee. At first, Magee was little more than a cully who visited her once or twice when Fíona wasn't around. Magee introduced her to Muireann, and Mary resigned herself to becoming a prostitute, earning far more than she could have imagined—and working for perhaps the squarest brothel madam in the city, a point that Brannagh had long since made clear to me.

And then, Mary sighed, I showed up on the doorstep. She'd spent several days after our arrival in Gotham searching for me. But she eventually gave up because she had to take care of herself and

Fiona. She was mortified that I would find out about how she was earning her keep. So, with Muireann's and Magee's connivance, Mary strove to keep her livelihood a secret from me. It went on long enough that some, particularly Tweed and Blackie, regarded my obliviousness to the situation as the best sort of joke—and one they were determined to keep running as long as possible. Brannagh was equally determined to keep me from knowing as well—purely out of regard for Mary and Mary's wishes. Mary's lie thus worked to keep me in the dark for a long time—that is, until Muireann confronted me. So, Mary said, here we are, the two of us, a prostitute and a numbers runner. What a pretty pair we are, she sighed, and fine examples for Fíona.

At some point during her story, I asked Mary, "What are you going to do about Muireann's offer?"

"You mean, am I going to take her place on Church Street so that she can join her daughter?" She added, "Wherever she is."

"You know where she is, don't you."

"Yes. And I swore not to tell you."

"Another secret? Haven't there been enough?"

"Billy …"

"Do you trust me?"

"Yes."

"Then tell me."

"Promise me you won't do anything stupid."

"Such as?" I was enjoying the dragging out of this little contretemps.

"You're not going to go after her, are you?"

"I told Muireann that I would marry her. It's the proper thing to do."

"But you don't want to, do you …"

I considered the implications of her proposition. Before I could answer, Mary said, "Muireann was right, you know, this isn't entirely about you being white and Brannagh being a colored girl. You two are both far too young—and would be even if you were both white and truly wealthy."

I didn't disagree with her.

Later we talked more about Muireann's offer.

"She wants me to be her partner and gradually buy her out," Mary said. "I'd be a rich woman in ten years." She laughed. "I could expand the business by doing what Adeline Miller and others are doing: I could hold balls for the upper tendom—the uptown swells and sporting men, anyway—in fancy hotels, with orchestras and the latest dances with the fairest dells—you've heard of the polka, haven't you? It's the latest thing. I'd end up a well-known lady about town, featured in the sporting press, and riding about in a coach and four with a colored maid and a sporting man to escort me."

Mary wasn't joking—not much, at least. There were disreputable newspapers which virtually dedicated themselves to publishing evermore lurid stories of Gotham's sexual peccadilloes, and naturally the city's finest brothel madams figured prominently in such stories. One recent article had noted that if Adeline Miller had rented Park Theater to tell her tale, she could have sold out at a half eagle a head and retired on the proceeds. The story went on to note that the more notorious a brothel madam was, the richer she became. Being featured in an article on the front page of the *Whip* was free advertising of the sort that most businesses nowadays can only dream of.

"But," Mary said, referring to another story lambasting Adeline Miller, "I don't want *Whip* calling me 'a gray-haired hag'—at least not before my hair really does turn gray, and I really don't want to be known as 'the wickedest procuress in Gotham'. And I do not want to visit on Fíona what happened to Adeline Miller's daughter, God rest her poor soul."

"So what are you going to do?"

"I could marry, I suppose."

This was unexpected, and I felt an unanticipated stab of jealousy at the thought of losing her—and Fíona—the only sister and niece I would ever have.

"A gentleman took me to Delmonico's last week and proposed marriage to me. He's been one of my most faithful cullies. He was so sweet. When he proposed, he swore an oath that he had been with no other woman since he had first had his way with me."

That was even more unexpected.

"I said no." Mary smiled at me, and I felt relieved. "I have even less desire to marry now than I did in Galway. I have Fíona, my daughter, and I have you, my dear, dear friend and ..." she paused for a moment, and then added, "You are my brother, my dearest brother, and we belong together."

I met her eye for a moment before we embraced fiercely, albeit chastely, for some time. I did not allow myself to be disappointed that Mary did not see more in me.

Later, Mary said, "We've enough money to do what we want now. We don't have to stay in the 'Points any longer. We can leave New York within the week and strike west for a new life."

She continued her daydream, saying that she didn't want to farm, and she was obviously through with earning her living on her back—this last bit said with a mordant glance at me. But she had an idea, she said. There are cities out west where we—she, Fíona and I—could make a fresh start where no one knew us. We had a big enough grubstake—Mary was right about that. We could go anywhere: St. Louis, a jumping off spot for pioneers striking west for Oregon and California; Cincinnati, which was an important river port on the Ohio River. There was also a little place called Chicago on the shores of a huge lake in the middle of the country, somewhere, and, if we really wanted to be adventurous, there was a town in California called Yerba Buena, near a Spanish mission called San Francisco. "I read about California in a book," Mary said proudly. "We'd have to cross the Rocky Mountains to get there, though," she exclaimed. "Or cross the ocean." She didn't appear enthusiastic about the prospect.

I knew enough from the militia meetings and many discussions with the likes of Magee and others to realize that California was not in America. Owned by Mexico, wasn't it? The same Spanish-speaking coves we were on the threshold of getting into a tussle with over Texas. So why go to California? That is, unless someone discovers an El Dorado. And how often does that happen? Anyway, I thought, whatever childhood fantasies I'd had about the forests and being a self-reliant mountain man, whether born of Fenimore Cooper's *The Last of the Mohicans* or my father's stories of Jim Bridger, they seemed perhaps even more unreal than ever. But those were the wool-gatherings of a boy who knew nothing of America. This going to California was every bit as fantastical—except that California was real, and not the figment of a novelist's imagination of a war in a bygone century.

"We can run a restaurant," Mary interrupted my thoughts.

"I know nothing about that."

"I've got an idea, and I've been talking to people who do know how to run restaurants." She explained that Delmonico's was a French restaurant—the first of its kind in Gotham.

"I can cook the food," she said. "Delmonico's uses all kinds of fresh vegetables—they grow them on their own farm. We wouldn't need to do that right away. It would be enough at first to have a nice restaurant with good, French food—and confectionaries. I can do all of that. But we'll need more than that. We need the service to be French as well. You speak French, don't you?"

I spluttered that I did, but … I worried about the audacity—and completely foreign nature—of the idea. But Mary was making sense. We could go into business for ourselves.

"We could have a good life for all of us—for Fíona, for you and for me." Mary sighed contentedly.

CHAPTER 18

The Waste of It All

⌒

LATE JULY IN GOTHAM IS ENERVATING. But the thought that Mary, Fíona and I would soon be embarking on our great journey west energized me to traipse over to the Irish Emigrant Society one last time on the forlorn hope that there would be a letter from Evelyn. It had been a few weeks since I had last checked. My desire to make the short trip had flagged in the face of the increasingly difficult task of meeting the looks of well-meaning from the various gentlemen who manned the enquiries desk. But this day was different.

To my surprise, the gentleman at the enquiries desk said to me, "Yes, Mr. Gogan. I believe that we do have a letter for you. I trust that it will bring the news you have been waiting for these long months."

My hands shook a little as I took the letter from the gentleman and thanked him. I dared not look at it until I reached the door. I closed my eyes for a moment, and then turned the letter over and read the return address, written by a man's hand: "St. Patrick's College for Young Men, Dublin, Ireland." I swore softly to myself in disappointment. Then, my heart lurched with a shudder of disquiet. I tore the envelope open as carefully as I could, and stared at the letter from my former Headmaster:

June 14, 1845

Dear Master Gogan:

Thank you for writing to me late last year and again earlier this year. I was quite pleasantly surprised that you took the time to do so. I regret the circumstances under which you left St. Patrick's. There was a highly unfortunate confluence of events that led to your departure, and I can say now that it was highly untoward of me to have sent you down as I did. I owe you an apology, and I humbly request that you see your way to accepting it once you have read this letter.

It took some courage for you to write of the unfortunate and tragic news concerning Father O'Muirhily. You may not know, but Father O'Muirhily was your greatest supporter at school. On the day after you left, he and I had an unfortunate quarrel. Father O'Muirhily then left to find you, and I am sorry to say, I never saw him again. I never had the opportunity to tell him in how high an esteem I had always held him, and I confess to you that I bitterly regret the unassailable fact that my last words to Father O'Muirhily were ones of recrimination and anger.

I was thus deeply distressed some weeks later when the Bishop wrote to me, enquiring about Father O'Muirhily's whereabouts. Father O'Muirhily had missed an appointment with the Bishop, and the Bishop had become concerned, as this had never happened before. I had not known it before, but the Bishop wrote that he and Father O'Muirhily were life-long friends who had met and talked regularly for many years. I also did not know the extent to which Father O'Muirhily had been an instrumental supporter of the Great Liberator, nor did I quite appreciate how he had worked assiduously to gain the Church's support during the Repeal Year. Father O'Muirhily and your father were close collaborators in that task, and I am happy to report that they were quite successful.

Father O'Muirhily also counseled your father to advise Daniel O'Connell to surrender in the wake of the Clontarf Monster Meeting, and further counseled your father to surrender himself as well, as the Lord Lieutenant's men saw stopping your father as a key to stopping the Liberator from capitalizing on the momentum gained for Irish independence during the Repeal Year.

I learned further of these matters when the Bishop came to visit me in response to my letter back to him. As a matter of coincidence, his visit came the day after I received your first letter, sent from Galway, and which I note took many months to reach me.

Now that the Bishop and I have pieced the story together, I fear that it is a distressing one. As we speak, the Chief Constable in Dublin has undertaken a manhunt to locate Father O'Muirhily. On the strength of your letter, inquiry was also made in Cork.

It was during the course of this inquiry that it came to the Chief Constable's attention that a catastrophe

overtook your cousin, Mr. Séamas O'Creagh. I
have enclosed a newspaper article that explains
the particular circumstances, but suffice it to say
that Mr. O'Creagh and two others of his house-
hold tragically perished in a fire set under suspicious circumstances.

Mr. O'Creagh's daughter, Miss Eibhlin O'Creagh,
and you, yourself, were both reported to be missing,
and a search was undertaken to find you both. The
Bishop and I have informed the Chief Constable
that, based upon your letters to me, it is clear you
had embarked on the good ship Maryann for the
New World some days prior to the fire. We further
informed him that Miss O'Creagh is not with you,
and that we remain unaware of her whereabouts.

Finally, my dear boy, I must make a pair of additional observations about the events that led to your
being sent down from school. Just before you and I
met, and I gave you the tragic news of your father's
death, I had occasion to meet with a gentleman
who gave his name as "MacGowan." He came to
inform me of your father's passing and to prevail
upon me to send you down, into Mr. O'Creagh's
protection. You may have actually seen him in my
antechamber that ghastly day when I informed you
of your father's passing.

As I recall, I mentioned to you that he had passed
himself off as poor Murray's uncle, and as a doctor.
In my discussions with the Bishop and in commu-
nication with the Chief Constable, it turns out that
Mr. "MacGowan" may have had a history with
your father, but they are not sure of the depth or

the complexity of the matter. Indeed, they tell me, they may never know. Mr. "MacGowan" is not to be found. Your father has, of course, passed away and thus cannot shed any light on the matter. Even worse is that the inquiries with Mr. O'Connell and his associates have not shed any light on who Mr. "MacGowan" may be and why the animus towards yourself and your father.

It also appears that Mr. "MacGowan" may be the man whom the police are looking for in connection with the Longfield estate fire. He was apparently spotted in the area of the house in the day or two prior to the fire, although no one appears to have had any interaction with him that would provide any explanation as to why he should have committed such a heinous act.

In hindsight, I should not have spent a moment listening to the man. That I did so troubles me, even though he seemed at the time to be acting under the trappings of officialdom.

This brings me to the second of my observations, which has to do with poor Phillip Murray. Murray lives still. But he is not the boy he was. We at St. Patrick's were all deeply affected by the tragic accident. Murray was a deeply popular and well-liked boy here at St. Patricks, just as you were. We all felt his loss deeply, as I am sure you did. I have nonetheless come to understand, once again in hindsight, that poor Murray's injury deeply affected me in how I dealt, first with Mr. "MacGowan," and then with you.

*We cannot, as I have heard Father O'Muirhily
tell me time and again, 'unboil the egg.' We must
move on. But I shall do all within my power to
help you, my dear boy. I do hope that I may be of
assistance to you. In the meantime, I have taken it
upon myself, along with the Bishop, to locate Miss
O'Creagh and assure ourselves of her safety and
well-being. I shall keep you apprised of events.*

I am your obd't servant & etc.

The article Headmaster referred to had already started to yellow, as newspaper will often do, and it crackled a little as I opened it with shaking hands:

DEVASTATING FIRE KILLS THREE

*INISHANNON, COUNTY CORK, 10 October, 1844—
ARSON AND MURDER—On this Tuesday past,
during the overnight hours, a house at Longfield
estate burned to the ground. Three were killed,
including Séamas O'Creagh, middleman to
Longfield estate, his housekeeper, Oonagh O'Neill,
and a stableboy, Breandán O'Shea.*

*Mr. O'Creagh's daughter, Eibhlin, was not home
at the time of the fire. Mr. O'Creagh's cousin,
William P. Gogan, who had been living at the
house, is also missing. Inquiries to locate Miss
O'Creagh and Master Gogan are being conducted
by the Royal Irish Constabulary.*

*Inspector Reginald Barry of the Munster constab-
ulary stated that arson was suspected as the scene
was redolent with the odor of coal oil, and a short*

man dressed in funereal black had been seen about the premises. It is not known whether this crime is connected to the late activities of Master Gogan's father, Niall P. Gogan, a noted member of the Loyal National Repeal Association who recently passed away. Mr. Gogan père was for many years a close aide to and confidant of Mr. Daniel O'Connell. He was convicted along with Mr. O'Connell, his son John O'Connell, and several of his close lieutenants, by a jury packed with tried and true members of the Protestant Ascendancy of conspiracy and sentenced to one year in prison and fined £2,000 for his role in planning the Monster Meeting at Clontarf. Mr. Gogan was widely seen as a major architect of the so-called 'Repeal Year' campaign that was ended with the arrest of Messrs. O'Connell, Gogan and several others in October of this past year. Mr. Gogan tragically succumbed to illness some weeks prior to the release this past month of Mr. O'Connell and his remaining lieutenants after their wrongful conviction was overturned in the House of Lords on a writ of error.

The Royal Irish Constabulary is conducting inquiries regarding the fire at Longfield estate, including whether any adherents of the so-called 'Young Irelanders' party are involved. Over the past year, the 'Young Irelanders' party has been accused of calling for violent action in the cause of repeal. Representatives of the Nation, the newspaper founded by members of the 'Young Irelanders' party, have steadfastly denied any connection between the party and the tragedy at Longfield estate.

I ran from the Emigrant Society without so much as a "by your leave" to the man at the enquiries desk, the door slamming loudly behind me. It was time—long past time—to confess all to Mary and to tell her that we were all in terrible danger. As I rounded the corner onto Mulberry Street, a block from Magee's boardinghouse, there was Cian Dineen, as calm and collected as could be. There was something about his manner that stopped me cold, breathing hard from my run. We locked eyes.

Cian broke the silence. "How ya' doing?" he said in a loud voice, reaching his hand out to me.

I took it almost involuntarily.

"Oh, don't be a spoilsport. You'd do the same for me."

"Cian …" I began. "I do want to thank you for getting me back to Magee's place the other night. I do appreciate it. But I have to go."

"Look," he cut in with a note of wistfulness. "Even with everything that's gone on … you 'n' me, we can still be pals."

"I'd like that," I said. "But, sweet Jesus Christ, Cian, I have to go."

"Aww," he said. "You don't gotta give me the cold shoulder, man. We can be pals. An' we was all mighty good pals the other night."

"I don't remember much," I admitted a bit sheepishly. "But I have to go."

I turned to leave and stopped cold in my tracks for a second time. Cian followed my stare, for there was that black-haired Irishman, except he wasn't quite as funereal-looking as when I last saw him. Nor was he a figment of my imagination. Not after reading Headmaster's letter. I could've sworn that the black-haired Irishman was looking directly at me with that same appraising gaze I had seen so long ago in the instant after he murdered Father

O'Muirhily. I thought I saw the ghost of a satisfied smirk as well. My blood ran to ice.

The Irishman vanished into the crowd, leaving me to wonder why he had followed me to Gotham, why, if he meant me harm, he didn't make his move. Cian shook me, grabbed my chin and forced me to look him in the eye. "Don't go to Magee's saloon now. Walk away, and I'll explain everything."

"What?"

"Don't go." He grabbed me by an arm and gave me a pleading look. "For the love of Christ, Billy," he said, switching to Irish. I'd never heard him speak the language before. "Stay away."

"What are you talking about? Is that the man …?"

"I can't … Not now."

"You can't what?"

"I gotta go."

I reached out to grab him. He slipped by me, giving me what to all appearances was another handshake.

With that, he was gone. I whirled about, looking for the Irishman, hoping against hope that he'd reappeared and I could confront him at long last. I became conscious of Blackie staring at me, with an odd look on his face. Where he'd come from was anyone's guess. I shrugged at him, not knowing what to make of Cian, and my head whirling over having clearly seen the Irishman here, in Gotham. Then I remembered Cian's warning about staying away from the boardinghouse. I began running with a burgeoning sense of dread that threatened to overwhelm me.

Blackie caught up to me, grabbing my arm. "Jaysus, what got you going off half cocked?" I ignored him and began to run again. I could hear him behind me, asking slightly peevishly, "An' what did that Judas want wid yers?"

I didn't reply, and I could hear Blackie breathing heavily as he kept pace. As I turned the corner, I once more stopped cold in my tracks. So did Blackie. He swore under his breath.

I yelled, "Sweet fucking Jesus," and began running again. Blackie followed. There were flames shooting out the door of Magee's saloon.

The tocsin was sounded. Slowly at first, and then more insistently. It stopped abruptly, and then the bell rang three strokes, signifying that the fire was in the 'Points (or at least somewhere in the southern part of the city—the Third Fire District). Help was on the way. But it would be many long minutes before my friends at the Phoenix, Hope and Mutual companies arrived. I ran blindly to the boardinghouse. Blackie followed. A dozen people had bolted out the front door, and were standing in the middle of the street looking back at the burning boardinghouse, seemingly enthralled by the wonder of it all. I thought I saw a face on the third story—where our rooms were. The windows looking out from Charlie's rooms were opaque.

I ran to the front door, which was in the center of the porch running the length of the building, and kicked it open. Before I could enter, someone—Blackie, I think—grabbed me by the neck and shoulder, and I landed flat on my back. I looked up to the sight of a giant lick of flame shooting through the open door. I'd have been broiled alive if I'd gone running in.

Blackie hissed at me, "Ye daft bastard. Going in there alone'll be the death o'yers."

"Oh Christ," I cried, ineffectual and impotent. But he was right. We needed water, and quickly, to cover even the most desperate expedition into the burning boardinghouse.

Mrs. Shipley touched me. She had Fíona. *Dia Uas!* She was safe. But what about Mary? Mrs. Shipley didn't know. Sweet Jesus! Mary. I damn near blubbered helplessly. But I caught Mrs. Shipley's eye. Then she was gone.

Where were the Phoenixes?

A swift kick to the ribs rolled me over and I looked up, only to see Lúcás standing above me, his enormous Arkansas toothpick in his hand, the blade glinting in the sunlight. His mouth was grinning madly below his deadened black eyes. Cassidy and his bastard Excelsiors had arrived first.

"A foin' mess ye be havin' here, boys," Lúcás said loftily. "Magee's paying handsomely for his cheekiness, now, ain't he? Brennan's next and Donoho's after that. And you? You fuck. You'll pay the most."

I didn't know whether Lúcás was addressing me or Blackie. But Blackie and I both rumbled to our feet. My fists were clenched in impotent rage.

Lúcás waved his toothpick at Blackie. "I'll spit yers here and now, while yer building's burning, ya *dall* galoot."

"Get on with it, man." Blackie's voice shook with barely controlled ire. "There be *máithreacha* and *wee wains* in there."

Blackie was right. Magee's boardinghouse was sure to be full of mothers and their children. At least Fíona was safe. But what about Mary? Blackie and I were stuck on this porch, the building burning right in front of us, held at bay by this ... *fear buile* ... this godforsaken madman.

"Don't be a hickjop, now, Blackie." Lúcás chuckled dryly. "Be cool, like yer buddy Gogan, here."

I wasn't cool. Not in the least bit. It was just that my feet were rooted to the planking.

"None of us is going anywhere for now. Not you. Not him. Not me," Lúcás observed nonchalantly, gesturing first to Blackie and then to me. "We gotta wait for the hoses."

True enough. We did have to wait for the hoses, even if the Excelsiors were ready to start pumping right now. But they weren't. Their engine was across the street, and no one was attending to it. Instead, the Excelsiors were accompanied by what appeared to be a burgeoning phalanx of Bowery toughs, brickbats, staves and iron pipes in hand, leather coverings and hard hats for their heads, gloves for their hands. They hadn't come to fight the fire. They'd come to rumble. Why? None of this made sense—but then it did. Cian passing me in the street. Lúcás here like a homing pigeon to roost before any firefighter could have arrived.

"It'll be a while," Lúcás observed again, his eyes cruel through their normal deadness. "The wood'll be charring quite nicely in a minute, thank you very much."

"You bastard." I found my voice.

"Fuck you, Gogan. You chose a side. So did I. You lose now. Everything."

I lurched towards him. Blackie gripped me hard, and I went nowhere.

"Steady, boyo." Lúcás grinned madly again.

Shouts and cries arose in the street. The Phoenixes had arrived. The Excelsiors and their Bowery compatriots were no longer milling about the street in anticipation. With a full-throated roar, they flung themselves on the badly out-numbered Phoenixes, who were hardly more than a score, and out of breath from having hauled their engine four blocks. Worse, to a man, they were unarmed. But they fought valiantly until they were almost completely swallowed up by the swirling mob of Bowery toughs. I wondered wildly what would happen if the Bowery thugs and Excelsiors reached the Haywagon, which they were threatening to do at any second as the Phoenixes were steadily subsumed into the ghastly maul. Freshly arriving Phoenixes, who hove into view singly or in pairs, were instantly overwhelmed.

I looked up at the windows. Sweet Jesus, where was Mary?

Lúcás had his barking iron out now as well. As he aimed it first at my gut and then Blackie's, I studied it for the first time. The silver plate was missing from the muzzle of its two-inch barrel and the brass peeked through the cheap silver plate butt piece that was adorned with flowers surrounding a lion's mask. It didn't seem to be the proper sort of weapon to die from.

"Stay here, boyos," Lúcás snapped as he looked around wildly, for what, I didn't know.

We all flinched as super-heated air blasted from the door in front of us and a broken window behind us. I could see the flames behind the open door. I didn't look at the window. No need. Stupidly, the three of us were still standing on the porch, and the porch roof had to be burning by now. But Lúcás was showing no signs of leaving, and even if both Blackie and I attacked him, victory would be pyrrhic. (I thought wildly for a second how valuable a public school education could be, to know what pyrrhic meant, and so fucking useless most of the rest of the time.)

Another cry went up, deepthroated and savage. The Hopes and the Mutuals were here, flying into battle in numbers. The Phoenixes were being given a second life. Magee was leading the charge, a battle-maddened Gaelic chieftain swinging an iron pipe with murderous abandon. I saw him viciously hit one man, who collapsed in a heap, his jaw shattered and blood and teeth all about. The street was now blocked entirely with the struggling maul, which must have comprised above 200 desperate combatants—counting those who had already fallen, insensate, to the cobblestones. I couldn't tell one side from the other. But the tide was now beginning to turn inexorably as bystanders from the 'Points, Roach Guards and Patsy Conroys among them, joined the fray. More bodies fell. There was more blood on the cobblestones. I lost sight of Magee, and I could recognize no one else in the seething mass.

Then I saw real hope for saving the boardinghouse. Not all the Hopes had joined the fray. A precious few had stayed back, and were faking their hoses onto the cobblestones, preparing to attach the first of them to the Haywagon. Other men, the Lord only knew who they were—for all the Phoenixes were battling in front of me or lying insensate in the muck—were clambering aboard the Haywagon. Slowly, at an agonizing pace, the Hopes connected the first hose. Three hosemen, clad in their leather helmets and coats, ran forward to the edge of the fray, dragging their hose with them. The brakemen atop the Haywagon gave a cheer that was faint against the din of the battle in front of me, but likely a roar from their throats, and a giant stream of water shot forth, a burst that went twenty feet as the air blasted from the hose, another spurt went thirty feet, and then there was a steady flow that the nozzleman kept at a hard stream.

Christ in heaven, there was a man who was thinking. The nozzleman directed the water, which was shooting in a hard arc now that the pressure was finally up, directly at the fighting mass, smashing at friend and foe alike. Magically, the Hopes and the Phoenixes and the Mutuals, sensing victory at hand, disengaged, and exposed the by-now battered Excelsiors and their equally battered Plug Uglies and Bowery brethren to the direct fury of the hose.

The three hosemen, hose in hand, charged directly at the Excelsiors. Other men picked up the hose to bring it with the charging hosemen. The Excelsiors and their Bowery brethren wavered, and then broke before the assault, dragging their wounded and fallen comrades with them. Any Bowery b'hoy left behind would not likely see out the remainder of the day. Not after this.

Lúcás, watched the turning tide nonchalantly, as if he expected it. He looked at Blackie and me, and said, "It's been a pleasure, you motherless bastards, but it's time to go."

He raised his pistol and aimed it at my forehead. "By the way," he said, voice tight with anticipation, "thanks for all the help in getting to Charlie. Cian told me you gave him a map to the strong box. And the best of all? Magee knows all about it already. Ye're fucked, Gogan."

What the …? I could feel Blackie's eyes burning into me.

Lúcás shifted his aim to Blackie's forehead. "And good bye to you, you worthless paddy fuck."

I swung hard at Lúcás's arm, but I had been too far away to hit him cleanly. It was just enough. The shot went wide and hit

Blackie in the shoulder, not between the eyes. Blackie went down like a sack of potatoes. Lúcás slashed at me with his toothpick, tearing my shirt and vest, but little else. Then he was gone.

⌒

Now we could fight the fire. Magically, a helmet was placed on my head. The first hose team was streaming water through the open door. A second hose team was right behind them, shooting a fog into the air to protect the lead team. Just like we've always been taught. There was a man beside the door, with a fire axe at the ready. Reflexively, I touched his axe. There must have been something in my look because he gave it to me. Wordlessly. Gladly. I was thankful. I hoped that he knew it.

I crowded near the door.

The nozzleman yelled, "Wait, fer Christ's sake. Yer boiled brains. Ye'll get 'em boiled for real iff'n ye goes in there now."

"My woman," I yelled, conscious that she was not my woman. She was my friend. My family.

He nodded.

"*Imeoidh tú n éineacht le Dé*, paddy." May you go with God.

The nozzleman must have been Irish—and knew that Irish men and women lived here. I nodded to him in thanks, and he and his two compatriots aimed their hose to the side. I passed through the door, skirting the still-streaming water that sizzled and crackled as it hit the smoldering foyer. Every surface was smoking. Water boiling off with the fire's heat blasted steam into my face. I headed for the stairs, which were still ablaze, albeit feebly. The nozzleman must have sensed my need to climb the stairs, for the water cleared a path for me. I prayed that the stairs weren't so badly burned that they couldn't support my weight. Or there'd be no hope for anyone still inside. I thought, Mary, I'm coming. My sweet. My companion.

I could hardly see. There was light from far above the smoke, but it didn't penetrate. I held my breath, counting the precious seconds. How long could I last with the effort of climbing the stairs? My heart pounded. My temples kept time. My eyes stung, and tears were streaming down my face. There was no one behind me. Too dangerous. I was alone.

I crept around the landing and up to the second floor. I felt a rush of cool, clean air from somewhere. A broken window? Were they breaking the windows for me so I could breathe? If so, bad news for me. The fresh oxygen would feed even the most ener-vated fire—and, potentially, broil me alive. Christ Almighty God, but I'd rather run out of air and ruin my lungs with the smoke than die in the flames. No matter. I gulped at the fresh air. My chest convulsed. I could not control it. I needed to get my breathing back so I could continue to move forward—and before I lost the fresh air. Otherwise, I'd die quickly, and painfully, as the smoke and heat seared my lungs. Finally, I made off, and plunged up the stairs.

I was now on the second floor. I considered briefly. Should I look for Charlie? He was right here. No. Mary first. Hard. But necessary. Mary. I ran up the next flight of stairs. The fire hadn't gotten this far. Why? Who knows? Fires are perverse. Wizened old fire laddies'll tell you stories of how fires are worse than the most bewitching of women. A fire'll addle you by luring you into her lair like a succubus, and you'll rush in, drunk with the elixir of desire to conquer her—erotic in its own way, I suppose, and deadly to boot. A fire'll tease you. It'll hide. It'll lie in wait. Just when you least expect it, it'll pounce, and that'll be the death of you. Just like that. If you aren't careful—or lucky (or both).

I threw caution to the wind and sprinted up the final flight of stairs, heart racing. No time to dawdle. I couldn't hold my breath much longer. I was at the third floor landing. To the left. Without thinking. I was an automaton. Three doors. I was there. I pushed on the door to our rooms. Damn it to hell! It was closed. I pushed on the latch, lightly at first, as I couldn't afford to ruin my fingers on the hot metal, and then harder when the metal turned out to be relatively cool. But it was secured from the inside. Christ help her. She must be in there.

I swung the axe, ripping at the hinges. You never swing at the center of the door. That's a fool's effort. You won't get in. All you'll do is tear a hole in the door, which will allow the fire, if there is one inside, to flare out at you—and kill you for your stupidity.

The hinges gave way, and the door hung drunkenly by the latch. I jumped out of the way. Too slowly, of course. If there had been an active fire inside, I would've been singed to a light crisp, at the very least. But there wasn't. Just smoke. I smashed the door away from the latch and it clattered to the floor. From the window, I could hear the shouting commotion outside. The crowd must be moving restlessly. I could hear stomping feet thundering below. Somewhere. Too far away to help me—or to help poor Mary—any time soon. I was still alone. But not as much as before.

I ran through the ruined doorway. Smoke blasted me. My chest was heaving. It must've been nigh on two minutes since I'd last breathed clean air. My lungs were telling me to breathe. But if I did, it'd kill me. I wasted valuable seconds fighting the panic. Jesus Christ! Focus, you fool.

I blindly went to one wall, stumbling over one of our chairs. I stumbled again, this time on my bedding, twisting clumsily and nearly falling. I kicked clear of the blanket and slammed into the wall. Nothing. To the other wall. Still nothing. This was taking too long. I didn't dare smash the window that tempted me just a pace or two away.

To the other room. Stumbling over that chair again. I learn my lessons slowly and painfully sometimes.

At the doorway, the panic rose again in my throat. I was going to lose control and breathe compulsively. I couldn't … and then, there she was, right by the window in her and Fíona's bedroom. Crumpled on the floor, almost in a fetal position. On the other side of their bedding. I stepped around it and knelt at her side. I could feel no breath from her nostrils. There was no time to check her pulse. I picked her up, and held her close, wishing I could whisper something to her. Anything. But I couldn't. My lungs were bursting.

⌒

I don't recall another thing until I was crashing past the first hose team, which was laboriously climbing the first flight of stairs, hose-handlers right behind them. The air was good enough to breathe down here. There was only a little smoke. But I can't remember now whether I ever took a breath. I could only see the front door and the cobblestones beyond. I raced through the door, bounding over the blackened porch, hosemen and other fire ladies jumping out of my way. I'd lost my helmet somewhere. My axe was forgotten as well.

I landed heavily on the cobblestones and lay Mary down. Gently. A crowd gathered around, pushing and shoving, the ignorant fools, and threatened to trample Mary and me.

"Keep clear, yer daft bastards," Magee roared. Blackie was with him, his arm in a bloodied sling. And Tweed. I didn't see them. I just sensed them.

I touched Mary's face. My tears were already flowing. I whispered something or other to her. I touched her hands. Something was clenched in one of them. I blindly took it without thinking, and stuffed it into my pocket. I don't know why. I was still a mere automaton. An uncomprehending automaton.

I knelt there, unfeelingly. Cradling Mary in my arms. I heard someone crooning a lullaby I hadn't heard since my mother tucked me to sleep in those halcyon days before she died.

Magee was kneeling beside me, the thunderous, murderous gleam in his eyes momentarily easing.

"She's dead, lad," he said gently.

I didn't understand. This was Mary.

"She's dead," Magee said, his voice hardening.

I looked at him.

His eyes were opaque as he said to me in a barely controlled fury, "Ye did this, yer daft bastard. Yersel' an' Cassidy. An' now hersel' be dead." He broke off from what he was about to say, rose to his feet and turned away, muttering, "Oh, the waste of it all."

THE END OF BOOK ONE

Acknowledgments

Billy Gogan, American was borne of a quiet moment in May 2009, when my wife, Pat, encouraged me to first put pen to paper and begin to tell Billy Gogan's story. After a few days, I gave her the first few pages. She didn't say much except to say, "make it live." When I "made it live," she smiled and told me to keep writing and has stood beside me every step of the way since. Pat is truly the "indispensable woman."

Larry Habegger has been similarly indispensable. We found each other in a roundabout way, and we worked together for a long time to take a shaggy first draft and slowly produce the book you see today. I cannot sufficiently express my appreciation to Larry for everything that he has done, both in being a brilliant editor and in taking the lead in getting the book published.

In my earliest days of research, when I had at best only the haziest of ideas about Ireland and the United States in the 1840's and knew only a little of what the Mexican-American War was all about, I turned to Theresa A.R. Embrey, MLIS, Chief Librarian at the Pritzker Military Library, and the library's wonderful research staff for help in finding the sources, both primary and secondary, which soon were beyond count.

Eugene O'Driscoll, who is now at Oxford University, rendered me an invaluable service in helping me get the Irish "right." That said, this truly is a point at which I must say that all the credit for this is his, and any mistakes are mine, alone.

I cannot thank Elizabeth Peterson enough, not only for her invaluable research assistance and comments on the book, but also in working with me in our other, "more real" professional lives as lawyers.

To Joe Levine and his wonderful team at CC&G, I can only say thank you for developing such a fantastic website and social media presence. Jen Lipford I must thank for being so very patient with me in filming a piece for the website. They have all taught me so very much about the "brave new world" of book marketing on social media.

To Christie Kennedy, Mary Ryan, Maureen Thomas and all the others upon whom I inflicted early drafts of the book, many, many thanks for your warm words of encouragement along the way.

Finally, I return to Pat, my wife, and my children and their spouses and significant others. Thank you for putting up with me.

About the Author

Roger J. Higgins and his wife reside in Chicago, Illinois, and they are immensely proud of their four children, one of whom is a serving U.S. Marine, and one of whom is Marine turned police officer (happily married to a wonderful high school chemistry and biology teacher). Their daughter is a nurse, and she and her husband (a retired Coast Guard officer) are the proud parents of a baby boy. Their youngest son is an aspiring doctor. As Mrs. Higgins has patiently observed to her husband when he ruminates about the trials and tribulations of raising children, it was together that they went four-for-four with their children, hitting safely at every at-bat. Not a bad day in the batter's box.

Roger was born in England, in the County Cheshire, where he learned early of the orange-striped Cheshire cat, which disappears, leaving only its grin, full of teeth and gums. Roger emigrated with his parents and younger brother to the United States when he was 6¾. When his mother registered him at the local elementary school, he saw fit to wear his English grammar school uniform, which looked a lot like Harry Potter's, except his cap was gray with purple piping and topped by a purple button, and he wore gray short trousers, gray knee socks and a purple clip-on tie with his dark gray blazer. After his mother finished registering him for school, the principal gently asked whether he would like to leave the tie and cap with her for the day and pick them up after school.

Roger demurred. He was fortunate enough to retain both tie and cap (which were never worn again) on the walk home from school.

At the advanced age of ten, Roger taught himself the art of swearing, a skill he found useful in his thirty-odd years of playing rugby, where he was noted for his stone hands, his lack of size for certain positions and lack of speed for all the rest. As a young United States naval officer serving on a guided-missile destroyer many years ago with the lucky number "13" as her hull number (where he met some of the best friends a man can be lucky enough to have), he also learned, as did Captain Horatio Hornblower two centuries earlier, that sometimes having fifty-five oaths at your command can be entirely inadequate to the occasion.

Roger learned the art of leadership from his ship's commanding officer and executive officer, who together led the tired, old ship, which was a bit of a laughing-stock along the waterfront, to win the Arleigh Burke award as the best destroyer in all of the Pacific Fleet. Roger served another fifteen years after that, having had during that time the privilege of being the fire control officer for the U.S.S. *Missouri*'s 16-inch guns, and thus the only naval officer in the world (at that time) under the age of thirty proficient in the ancient—and wonderfully obsolescent—art of major caliber naval gunnery.

Roger became a lawyer after retiring from the Navy with a small pension fit to pay the property taxes. After clerking for a Tax Court judge, who taught him the value of telling your story so as to win your reader to your side, Roger worked for a number of very large law firms, eventually becoming a partner at a firm with the grandest bankruptcy practice of them all. Roger greatly admires the practice group leader's philosophy of practicing law, which is to get the best outcome possible for your client, never re-trade on a deal, and if you must stab someone, don't stab him (her) in the back; look the person in the eye and then stab her. You'll be treated the same way, when the time comes. Oh, and never sell your reputation. Once sold, you can never buy it back again.

Roger continues to practice law at a much smaller and less grand law firm and to write novels to his own taste. He is having a wonderful time doing so.

SNEAK PEAK AT BOOK TWO

Billy Gogan,
Gone Fer Soldier

CHAPTER 1

Nothing but a . . . Bluebelly

WHEN THE WIND DIES, MID-SEPTEMBER NIGHTS in south Texas are hot and humid to the point of suffocation, even a mere 150 yards from the cooling ocean. My shirt and the leather stock binding my neck were sweat-slick and stinking beneath my heavy blue wool serge uniform blouse as I marched post, musket primed, shouldered and bayonet fixed, guarding the bivouac of the Fourth Infantry Regiment against all enemies, foreign and domestic. Forty paces north and forty paces south along the 150-foot-high crest of the soft, sandy dune that formed the backbone of St. Joseph's Island. The dune was a remarkable creation of nature in daylight, sloping steeply down in brilliant yellow-white sand to the ocean on one side and rather more gently on the other down to a pretty and lightly treed plain that stretched to Aransas Bay. On nights such as this, black as sin itself under the low-lying clouds that presaged the heat and humidity, the top of the dune seemed as far removed from the faint, dull glow of the regiment's campfires on the bayside plain as it was from bustle of the Five Points a thousand miles away.

To pass my time without falling asleep on my feet or otherwise tripping in the dark and dirtying my musket—sins which could earn me a dozen lashes and a day bucked and gagged and left to broil in the merciless Texas sun—I concentrated on counting my steps up and down the soft sand, taking care to plant my brogans in the very same footprints I had been making since I began tracing my predecessor's steps. Inevitably, my mind wandered, turning gloomy in darkness as I contemplated for the thousandth time in the past few weeks the unalterable fact that Mary, poor sweet Mary Skiddy, the elder sister I'd never had and my boon companion during the dark days of our passage over the Western Ocean, was dead and buried in Potter's Field up on Ward Island, murdered by Lúcás Dineen and my black-coated Fenian nemesis, MacGowan. In that instant—and in any other instant, for that matter—I would have made a pact with Old Nick himself at any price he asked, just to trade places with her, if only to allow her to reunite with her poor, orphaned daughter, Fíona. Just then I thought that the ache in my heart would kill me as I marched and the guilt of it all would bury me in eternal damnation, if only there were such a thing, for there isn't and without more the long dreamless sleep of death would not have been punishment enough for me.

By and by, though, my mind wandered once more to contemplate the day's doings and this new life of mine as just another bluebelly in C Company of the Fourth Infantry, which I spent keeping my skirts clear of Hoggs, the company First Sergeant, and otherwise doing as little else as possible under the circumstances. The transport ship *Suviah*, which had brought us here from New Orleans, was gone now, presumably back for yet another regiment of doughboys or battalion of redlegs to reinforce Old Zach's (Brevet Brigadier General Zachary Taylor to you) tiny little Army of Observation, which was camped 20 miles south of us, near the little town of Corpus Christi nestled at the conjunction of the mouth of the Nueces River and the head of Aransas Bay. I call Corpus Christi in the fall of 1845 a town, but the "despatch by grapevine telegraph" stoutly maintained that the word was too grand by half, for it was supposedly nothing more than a frontier trading post comprising perhaps 20 or 30 buildings, most of them little more than tumbledown shacks, hardly able to fend off even the most dilatory Comanche raid, were those heathen inclined to foray so far east as the Gulf of Mexico. The army was using the southern tip of St. Joseph's Island as a jumping-off spot to debark supply and transport ships and move men and supplies south across Aransas Bay to Corpus Christi. Ships couldn't sail directly to Corpus Christi on account of the barrier islands blocking the way and protecting the bay—St. Joseph's Island, which stretched north, and Padre Island, which stretched 100 miles south of us to the Rio Grande. Even if the ships could have found a way in between St. Joseph's and Padre Islands (a sand bar blocked the way), the bay was so shallow that boats with a draft of more than a couple of feet couldn't transit from the St. Joseph's depot to the main camp without getting stuck in the mud at least once or twice.

We spent two days unloading men and supplies from the transport ship *Suviah* onto lighters. Once ashore, we dragged or carried everything by hand—there being no mules and no horses other than the officers' mounts—through the dense and thorny vegetation lining the slopes of one side of the dune and down to where the regiment was now sleeping through yet more vegetation that tore at our clothes and shredded our skin. It was backbreaking labor and entirely unnoteworthy except for when, I heard a brief cry and a splash as I was loafing on the fo'csle of the lighter that I had just helped load, and which was tied up alongside *Suviah*. A man surfaced. He seemed to be laboring a bit in the water, weighed down by his boots and clothes.

Without thinking, I kicked off my brogans, shrugged off my blouse and dove into the water. I hadn't been swimming in such a long time that I wondered briefly whether I was now going to drown along with the man who had fallen in. I reached him in a couple of strokes, tapped him on the shoulder as he laboriously trod water and helped him to the lighter, where we were unceremoniously dragged on board.

He was a youngish man. A shoulder strap.

He reached his hand out to shake mine. "Wanted to thank you, soldier. Mighty charitable, getting yourself wet like that on my account. What's your name?

"Private Gogan—Billy Gogan, sir."

"Nice to meet you, Private. I'm Lieutenant Grant, Sam Grant. Maybe I'll see you around sometime."

"Yes sir."

Dripping wet and half-naked, I saluted him, and he made off from the lighter back onboard the *Suviah*, presumably to change his clothes and his rather fine looking boots (far removed in look and quality from my issue brogans)—an opportunity that I would not have, particularly as these were the only clothes and shoes which I still had to my name.

～

But that had been many hours ago, and I had been immediately turned to some task or another. I had not stopped laboring until I began marching post, guarding against ... well, what was I guarding against? An attack by Mexican cavalry? Not likely. We'd heard that there were no Mexican soldiers anywhere near us. But it wouldn't have taken much to destroy Old Zach's little army just then. There were hardly a thousand men in camp, no artillery to speak of and only one regiment of cavalry—the Second Dragoons. So, if the Mexican army did arrive, everybody reckoned that we would be in a very poor way, indeed.

But it didn't matter whether I was here, on top of a deserted sand dune on St. Joseph's Island or back at Governors Island, standing guard along the pier. I was on sentry duty, pacing forty paces north and forty paces south with a 10-lb. flintlock musket on my shoulder—an exercise that will make your arm and neck muscles scream with pain after even a few minutes, if you are not used to it. But I was used to it now after a month or two of soldiering, and I hardly felt the pain anymore. It was the least of my worries.

Right now, stupefaction was the worst, and despite my best efforts, I was in a dreamy state after a couple of hours of pacing, hardly aware of anything. Then a twig broke and one of the low bushes scattered irregularly across the dune rustled just in front of me.

"Halt, who goes there?"

Silence.

"Halt, who goes there?"

There was more rustling. I checked the charge on the flash pan of my musket.

"Corporal of the guard! Corporal of the guard!"

More rustling.

"Halt or I must shoot." I shouldered my musket and squinted down the barrel in the direction of the rustling. "Corporal ..."

I saw a shadow just in front of me, and I began to squeeze the trigger. Then I saw what the shadow was—a little boy, not much above seven years old, barefoot and carrying a line from which several fish dangled.

I did not have trouble staying awake after that. The corporal of the guard, Rónán Finnegan, was a good old sort hailing from County Monaghan, and he complimented me on having been alert. He also told me that, notwithstanding the grapevine, St. Joseph's was apparently not entirely uninhabited, as there were a couple of families living in small wooden huts on the bay about a mile north of us, supporting themselves by fishing and providing transport across the bay to whomever needed it—the boy had come from there and would be returned to his family in the morning. I was relieved as sentry not long afterwards, and I found my blanket for a couple of hours of sleep before reveille.

"Wake up, you filthy bog rat." I heard a scream of agony and realized that it was me. A hobnailed boot had connected with my ribs, and I doubled over in pain. I was then jerked upright. "You insubordinate, filthy, little bog rat."

I snapped to attention. "Sergeant!"

"Corporal Finnegan tells me you insulted Lieutenant Lefort on guard duty last night."

"Sergeant?"

"You filthy, insubordinate …" A fist crashed into the side of my head and I tumbled to the ground. I was pulled back up onto my feet. I snapped to attention, my head swimming.

Then I remembered and cursed my luck. You could spend a year marching post and not ever have to challenge a soul, and I had challenged two different people within an hour of each other. Just after I had damn near killed the little boy, yet another figure had materialized in front of me out of the gloom.

"Halt," I said. "Or I will shoot."

Like the little boy an hour earlier, the figure did not stop moving, nor did he reply with the countersign.

"Corporal of the guard!" I brought my musket to "charge bayonet"—in other words, I was pointing my bayonet at the figure walking towards me. "Halt. Or I will shoot."

Still the figure did not stop moving. Nor did he reply with the countersign. I could hear Finnegan beginning to rustle down at the base of the dune, a hard running climb of a minute or more. I muttered a foul oath under my breath. Then I saw the face of the figure, hardly more than an inch or two away from my bayonet.

"Lieutenant, the countersign." I could not let him proceed without the countersign—on pain of a dozen lashes or worse.

Lefort ignored me and made to walk past me.

"My apologies, sir." I barred his way with my musket. "But unless you give me the countersign, you are my prisoner until the corporal of the guard arrives."

That seemed to snap Lefort out of his reverie. "You impudent bastard. Stand aside or I'll have your guts for garters."

"Sir ..."

Lefort drew his sword and raised it as if to strike me with the flat of it. I should have parried him and disarmed him, but I did not. In those days, many an officer thought nothing of savagely beating a hapless bluebelly with the flat of his sword merely for having displeased him. And I did not want to think of the consequences of striking an officer, even in the line of duty.

"Lieutenant, Lieutenant ..." It was Corporal Finnegan, panting hard from his uphill run.

LeFort said without removing his glare from me, "This man is insubordinate."

"Sir, did you give the countersign?"

Lefort lowered his sword, but he did not reply to Finnegan.

"Sir, Private Gogan was just doing his duty."

Lefort considered Finnegan for a moment, and then acknowledged, "I see."

I breathed sigh of relief, thinking that I had weathered the storm.

But I was wrong. On the strength of my tête-à-tête with Lefort, Hoggs was now kicking me awake. Within the hour, at morning muster, just as the sun peeked over the dune, Hoggs personally paraded me in front of C Company to be bucked and gagged for my insolence to the shoulder strap. Out of the corner of my eye, I could see Lieutenant Lefort standing at attention in front of the company, with a look of stony indifference on his face ... the bastard. I was neither the first man nor the last to be bucked and gagged for seemingly nothing, and so I didn't feel any shame in the punishment, particularly as Sergeant Hoggs, like many native Americans, seemed to take pleasure in punishing the Irish and dutchies who, everyone said, made up half of the army.

That said, I did resent the injustice of it. I had done my duty, and now this. As the drum rolled, I was forced to sit in the sand with my legs bent, my knees crushed against my chest and my arms clasped around my legs. My hands were tied tight, cinching my legs even tighter to my chest. The drum continued to roll, and I was bucked—a splintery pole was shoved over my left elbow, under the crook of my knees and over my right elbow, driving a splinter deep into the flesh above my left elbow. The splinter felt like a dagger probing my arm every time the pole moved even infinitesimally, and my shoulders felt as though the downward pressure of the pole would tear them from their sockets. Within a minute or two, my lower back began to spasm with the effort of staying upright and not falling over onto the end of the pole—which would have earned hard kicks from the corporal of the guard. I was in instant agony. But I could not move a single muscle.

Grinning sadistically, Sergeant Hoggs looked me in the eye as he bent over and dropped a filthy rag into the sand. With a grunt of satisfaction, he picked the rag up and shoved it in my mouth to gag me. The dust and sand from the rag exploded into my nose, my throat and my lungs, and I began coughing uncontrollably, which caused the gag to slip into my throat and made matters that much worse.

Gradually, I was able to calm myself and resign myself to sitting until night fell, hatless and shirtless and motionless in the broiling sun, sand tickling my trachea all the while. As I sat there, not a single soldier in the company, nor in the entire army, for that matter, even deigned to notice my existence. Except for the corporal of the guard (Finnegan, as it happened), who periodically walked around me to check that the ropes binding my wrists were still tight and the rag still firmly in place in my mouth. (But not too firmly. Finnegan was a decent sort, and he didn't want to me to asphyxiate. Not on his watch, anyway.) If any other soldier were to have consoled me (let alone to have given me a sip of water to relieve my suffering) while I was sitting there bucked and gagged, he would have simply undergone the same punishment the very next day.

I'm nothing but a … fucking bluebelly, I thought. Or what the newspapers and the cavalry call a doughboy. The newspapers said that we called ourselves doughboys on account of our using pipeclay to whiten our belts. But the newspapers were wrong. The cavalry called us doughboys on account of the "adobe" soil dust that covers us whenever we march. The cavalry rode, and they felt much the superior for it. But they were nothing more than "bow-legs," on account of all the riding that they do. We called ourselves bluebellies, on account of our blue blouses, and we were proud of it. But what we called ourselves—or each other—or what the scribblers called us did not signify in the least, and it didn't matter whether we were bluebellies, bowlegs or redlegs (artillerymen on account of the red stripe on their pantaloons), we all were naught but mere chattel of the United States Army by virtue of voluntary servitude. How had I gotten to such a sorry place?